Crumbling Talent

Written by:
Qualo Lowery

Cadmus Publishing
www.cadmuspublishing.com

Copyright © 2021 Qualo Lowery

Published by Cadmus Publishing
www.cadmuspublishing.com

ISBN: 978-1-63751-042-1

All rights reserved. Copyright under Berne Copyright Convention, Universal Copyright Convention, and Pan-American Copyright Convention. No part of this book may be reproduced, stored in a retrieval system, or transmitted in any form, or by any means, electronic, mechanical, photocopying, recording or otherwise, without prior permission of the author.

This is a work of fiction; therefore, names, characters, places, and incidents are the products of the author's imagination or are used fictitiously. Any resemblance to actual events, locales, or persons, living or dead, is entirely coincidental.

Acknowledgements

First of all, I would like to thank God! Without Him, none of this would be possible. I got to shout out my wonderful parents, Brenda Blackmon and James Silas, for their love and support. As well as my loving grandmother Betty Brown, aka Big Mama, for the times you stuck by my side during my lonely times. You will always be my rock. Thank you to my beautiful daughters, Shaquala Givens, Jaquala Givens, Z Givens and London, my granddaughter. They were always shooting me ideas and encouraging me to keep going, even when I couldn't see the future. I got to give all my West BLVD and Dalton Village solders a big shout out. Y'all will always be in my heart. Especially, the ones that checked on me when I was incarcerated. A special thanks to Authorhouse and Cadmus Publishing. They helped make my vision possible. Shout out to everyone in Federal prisons and state prisons. Thank y'all for supporting me. Shout out to my cousins, nephews, nieces, and extended family. Lastly, I would like to thank my brother Ron, and my sister Isha, aka Poo. They were my biggest cheerleaders during the process of this book. All of these people hold special places in my heart. A big shout out to my son, Qualo Jr. Love you.

Man, I hope you all enjoy this book, just as much as I enjoyed writing it.

Sincerely,
Qualo Lowery

SPECIAL NOTES FROM THE AUTHOR

This fictional story comes from the author's imagination; and if this story in anyway coincides with real life events, it was purely coincidental. The author spent long days and nights, while serving time in prison for drug charges, writing this book. There were times when he thought he wasn't going to finish his body of work. He would like to say "Thank You" to all the people that helped him on his journey and the supporters that went out and purchased this book. A special thanks to James Morris and Arlena Grier for putting all the right pieces in place for this to publish. Last, but not least, thanks to Iuuiverse and the fans. Without you all, there would be no author Qualo Martez Lowery. Thank You!!!

Contents

PROLOGUE	1
CHAPTER 1	3
CHAPTER 2	5
CHAPTER 3	16
CHAPTER 4	24
CHAPTER 5	31
CHAPTER 6	37
CHAPTER 7	43
CHAPTER 8	49
CHAPTER 9	55
CHAPTER 10	66
CHAPTER 11	77
CHAPTER 12	90
CHAPTER 13	108
CHAPTER 14	113
CHAPTER 15	123
CHAPTER 16	131
CHAPTER 17	136
CHAPTER 18	142
CHAPTER 19	153
CHAPTER 20	158
CHAPTER 21	164
CHAPTER 22	177
CHAPTER 23	183
CHAPTER 24	205
CHAPTER 25	222
CHAPTER 26	239
CHAPTER 27	247
CHAPTER 28	253
CHAPTER 29	258
CHAPTER 30	261
CHAPTER 31	264
CHAPTER 32	270
CHAPTER 33	275
CHAPTER 34	286
CHAPTER 35	295
CHAPTER 36	301
EULOGY	305

PROLOGUE

Year: 1997

I felt like I had lost myself when I went off to college on a basketball scholarship. The reason I say this is because, when I got there, I was reminded that I was a black man living in a white man's world. I tried my best to deal with the new world I was living in but it was too much for me. Especially, when I heard that my kids' mother had had a nervous breakdown. So, I dropped out of college and returned to Charlotte, North Carolina, where I was born and raised to help Denise with the kids. This was after she was discharged from the mental health hospital.

At first, I liked the family life, but it got old quick. Denise and I were starting to grew apart when we were living together. She wanted to be with me but I was having an affair with the streets. Basketball was no longer in my equation, because all I wanted to do was sell drugs and hangout in the streets.

After I broke up with Denise and got my own place, I purchased a little bit of furniture and one of each poster size photos of Martin Luther King and Malcom X. I nailed both photos right beside one another inside my living room and I started having conversations with both photos every time I got depressed. Today was no different.

Most of the time, I fought with both photos about why my

life was so messed up. Usually, Martin would convince me to calm down, but Malcom on the other hand was always telling me to pick up a gun and kill.

Martin spoke, "Your life isn't as bad as you think."

Malcom interrupted, "Don't listen to him Q. He loves the white man too much to see the black man's problem. The gun is the only answer. Go kill you a couple of white men for what they did to your ancestors in the past."

I spoke, "I'm ready to die."

Martin responded, "Don't do it Q. Peace is the only way."

Malcom cut in. "It's the white man's fault that you are in the state you are in. He is the one that brought the drugs to the ghettos. Pick up your weapon and use it for the cause, young man." Today, my gun was in my hand. The .38 special was a gift from my uncle Bear who died from liver cancer. He gave me the gun after someone had broken into my grandmother's apartment when I was 12 years old. I had been keeping the gun cleaned and in a safe place at all times. When I dropped out of college, I started carrying the gun around because of my depression state. My mind kept telling me that someone was trying to kill me.

I raised my gun to my head and pulled the trigger. My life flashed before my eyes. I could hear 2-pac's voice clearly talking to me as I faded out. Was I dead? Or was this just a dream?

CHAPTER 1

Year: 1994…
Qualude

It was six pm. It was almost time for me to be at basketball practice. Olympic High wasn't well known for basketball until I had stepped on the court my sophomore year. I single handedly took the school to new heights. That same year, I met my girlfriend, Denise Mavey after one of my games.

She stood at five-foot-five, had brown eyes, pecan tan skin and long jet-black hair. She had a shy personality in public, but when we were alone, she would open up a little. I had made her a promise when we first met in the summer of 1992. My promise was to marry her if I made it to the NBA. This was why I was on my way to practice in my GMC Jimmy.

When I walked into practice 15 minutes late, my Coach jumped all over me.

"Why are you late, Qualude?" Coach Davis asked in a demanding tone.

"I had to go to my mother's job to meet with my father," I replied.

"You know what time practice starts. You should have went to see him after practice." Coach Davis barked.

"Yes!" was my response.

"You know what time practice starts, so since you decided to do what you wanted to do, I got something I want to do."

Coach Davis was always getting on my case about something. If it wasn't my attending class, it was for my behavior in class. Being that he was the real reason I was on the team, he felt like I owed him something.

"I've went out on a limb for you. That's why I feel like I'm being cheated. Every time I gave you a time to do something or be somewhere, you didn't comply."

Coach Davis had pulled a few strings so I could play on the team. I was behind in my studies due to my earlier years of not doing work and my learning disability. But these two things never got in the way of my ego.

"I hadn't talked to my father since I was a little boy. Coach." I said as I walked over to the baseline, where all my teammates were lined up ready to do baseline touches. This was an exercise that built up the endurance.

"Since you were late, you say your reason is official, then your teammates will pay for what I think."

Coach Davis put the team through a series of exercises while I stood at the baseline and watched. Their mad facial expressions were displayed as they ran up and down the gym floor. Some of them were upset, mad, and angry.

I didn't care about their emotions, because I was the star of the team.

After all the running, Coach Davis shouted, "Hit the showers."

As I was on my way to the shower, he stopped me and said, "You meet me in my office, Qualude."

Once in the office, we had a man to man talk. After the talk I said, "Basketball isn't everything to me." Then I stormed out Coach Davis's Office.

CHAPTER 2

Denise had been waiting on her porch for over two hours before I finally arrived. She was dressed in a pair of blue jeans, Olympic T-shirt and Air Max Mikes. Her long hair was all over her head under a fitted baseball cap that I had bought her for her 16th birthday.

She gave me a serious grin and a distinct facial expression when I grabbed her hand. Then she asked, "What took you so long?"

"My damn stepfather thinks he is in charge of a real Army base. He wouldn't take his short self to sleep, "I responded.

"Do you think we still can make the late show at Queen Park?" Denise inquired.

I looked down at my Time-X watch.

I responded, "It's ten minutes to midnight. We are ten minutes away."

Denise asked "Do you think we can make it before the late show starts up?"

"I know I can make it if you promise me some booty," I said as I opened my jeep door for her.

"You can have it all, if you can make the show."

Denise was a virgin when I first met her. I had popped her little cherry after three weeks of dating her. This had happened after one of my church league basketball games. That night, my cousin Telly and I were right beside each other at a hotel. He was having sex with his girl while I was banging Denise.

When Denise and I pulled up in the parking lot of the theater, I knew we would be cutting it close to get a ticket. The light was already off in the ticket booth. We got out the jeep and walked over to the booth. We managed to get two tickets to the Rated R movie from a guy who recognized me from a newspaper article that I was featured in at the beginning of the high school basketball season. The guy told me that he was a big fan of high school basketball and he would be at my games. Meeting this guy was a perk of being a star.

I handed the tickets to the doorman at movie room three after Denise had grabbed a box of candy from the food stand. Then we sat in the back row. There were couples seated all over the place, and they were kissing and doing freaky stuff like I was planning to do to Denise.

Five minutes into the movie, I dug my index inside Denise's hot pocket. She was enjoying my touch and my lips. Her tongue tasted like the cinnamon candy stick I had bought at the candy stand. Her heart was beating so fast, it felt like it was going to pop out her chest.

I was stimulated from Denise's actions. Her hand was on my penis, and she was stroking it like she was getting ready to put it in her V-Shape.

The security guard interrupted us as he put his flash light in our faces and said, "This is a movie theater, not a hotel."

Then he walked off. We resorted to kissing and holding hands. The movie ended at 1:45 am. After it, Denise didn't want to go home. She mentioned her Aunt Peggy wouldn't mind her being out all night because Peggy was probably drunk.

I asked, "What do you want to do?"

"Let's get a hotel room," She responded.

"To do what?" I asked, as I was playing dumb.

"Sex! Sex! And more sex!" She replied.

We decided to get the room, so we went to West Blvd and picked up a random junkie who had ID. I gave him fifty bucks to get the room and ten for his services. He got it, then I dropped him off and returned back to the room where Denise was waiting in her T-shirt and G-string.

Her hips reminded me of a big stallion's hips, and they were thick and wide. Her butt cheeks looked like two NBA basketballs. When she fell into my arms, I looked in her hazel eyes for a full minute while rubbing her hips. Her whole body was responding to my touch. The lust in her eyes told me this.

We quickly came out of our clothes. Then we wrestled in a wave of passion. It didn't take me long to get to home plate. After a semi hold up, she exploded all over my rod. It was something about this moment that I knew I would always remember. Only time would tell.

Melvin Cheeks, aka MC, walked out of Rob's corner store. I couldn't miss his six-four frame, head full of waves, his brown skin, which was a shade darker than mine as he made his way over to the Golden Wop. I was getting a fresh hot plate of chicken wings when MC entered the building. He asked, "What up, my nigga?"

"Where the hell have you been?" I replied.

He responded, "I got this new hottie."

MC was known for messing around with other guys chicks.

"I heard. What's up with that situation?" I inquired.

"You know that bully kid, Nuke? It's his girl," MC said.

"How is it his girl, but you over her house every night?" I asked.

"That's what I'm saying. But Nuke doesn't get the picture," MC said.

MC couldn't hold back his laugh, and it was like every time we got together; we turned the moment into a laugh fest.

"Stop laughing man," I barked off.

"Stop with your jokes," He responded.

"You know me, I like to live on the edge."

"Man, I don't want to have to come to your funeral."

"Shit man, the girl fell in love with me."

"You must've eaten the pussy!" I said.

"And you know this man," MC said. Then he went back to laughing.

"You better stop sticking your tongue in every hole you come in contact with," I said.

MC was the type of guy who liked to turn females out. He definitely had a fetish for taking sex to the 'Next Level'. Usually, he did it with every woman he came in contact with, but now he wasn't even looking at another woman.

"When are you gonna let me take Denise for a spin?" MC asked.

"When you let me take your gradmama for a spin. You know I love old women. They got that tight wet wet," I responded.

"That's why I got love for you Q. You are a fast thinker," MC said.

"You know I love my grandbaby, too! Especially, you," I said while rubbing MC's head.

We both busted out laughing at my silly comment.

After we calmed down, MC asked me, "Have you saw Telly?" Telly was just as messy as MC when it came to women. He was my cousin on my mother's side of the family.

"No, I haven't seen Telly. Why are you looking for him?" I asked.

"I'm just asking. I heard that girl Peaches got him opened. I also heard she got a man."

"Well, I don't know about her man, but I know Telly has been waxing that ass."

We ended our conversation after I gave MC my cell phone number. I got in my jeep and left the scene.

❖   ❖   ❖

CRUMBLING TALENT

I walked into Olympic High School with the new Jordan's on my feet. My Polo short set matched my shoes. My peers were looking at me as if I was a top-notch celebrity instead of a fellow classmate. The attention didn't bother me, because I was used to it now.

My friend, Big Boo was standing in front of my locker when I arrived.

"What's up superstar?" He asked.

"What do you want?" I asked, as I opened my locker and grabbed my U.S History book out of it.

"Word on these streets is Pop is looking for some ball players to bet money on. It's a big street tournament coming soon! It is called: In Da Hood Tournament."

"Pop the drug Lord?" I asked.

"Yes."

"What are you telling me for?"

"I heard that him and your stepfather got beef."

"For what?"

"Over a young chick," Big Boo said.

"So."

"Your stepfather is running numbers, right?" Big Boo said.

"And?" I said.

"You know he be betting on high school games."

"Man, I don't talk to him."

"Well, Pop is your man. MC is already plugged up with him."

"I'll pass."

"Okay superstar."

The bell rung for first period. My first class of the day was U.S History. A pit stop at the bathroom had taken me seven minutes. I still ended up being late to class. When I walked in class, my short pale-faced teacher rolled her eyes at me. After all, I was late. The class was engrossed in a conversation about the first settlers of America.

"Mr. Jones, what are you doing late again?" The teacher asked.

I didn't have a legitimate excuse to justify my tardiness.

I lied, "I was late because I was using the restroom. I had to take a number two."

The class all busted laughing. Miss Spears didn't like my answer.

She proclaimed, "This is the third time this week you had to do the number two. You might need to see a doctor for that problem you have."

This was only the second week of school, yet I was already wearing out my welcome in her class. I took a seat in the back of the room beside a white girl named Stacey Bishop. She was one of the hottest chicks in the school.

She reminded me of a younger, more voluptuous, Sharon Stone. Her blond hair reached down to her back. Her perfect sexy lips were making my manhood stand at attention as she was licking them. I placed my bookbag over my manhood.

Her scent wasn't anything like the wet dog aroma smell of Brian Deal, that the white guy on the other side of me, possessed. After I had flirted with Stacey for a few minutes, Miss Spears called on me.

"Yes, what is it?" I responded as I looked in her direction.

"Why are you gawking at Ms. Stacey Bishop, as if she was a T.V. screen?"

"Because your lessons are boring," I responded in a bold tone.

The entire class looked at me. I was one of five Africa Americans guys in the class.

"So, you prefer to be the class clown. I would like for you to come in the front of the class with your homework, and discuss or explain the first question of your homework," Miss Spears spoke as she put her hands on her hips.

"My dog ate my homework, Miss Spears," I said as the class erupted in laughter.

"I'm serious Mr. Jones," She said.

"I'm serious," I said with a grin. I didn't even have a dog.

"Ok Mr. Jones, I have something beside the homework," Miss Spears continued, "I want you to start reading out loud from

CRUMBLING TALENT

Chapter One, page ten."

Miss Spears knew I couldn't read. I was embarrassed so I put my head down between my folded arms. My desk felt cold against my skin. There were mumbles from my classmates. This was the first time in Miss Spears' class that I had been put on the spot.

So, I waited until almost time for the bell to ring and said, "I'll read if you bring some real history books with blacks in them, like myself."

This was my way of redeeming myself. My teacher adjusted her purple skirt and then she returned to her desk. The bell sounded before she could save face. All the students walked out of the class except me.

As I made my way to the door, Miss Spears said, "Mr. Jones, I need a minute of your time please." I turned in her direction.

Miss Spears ran her hand through her hair and continued, "Mr. Jones, why did you do that?"

I replied, "You was trying to clown me in front of everybody."

She responded, "I am a teacher, teachers teach students."

"Why did you have to embarrass me?" I asked.

"Look, Mr. Jones, I want you to understand that basketball isn't everything," she replied.

"I know. But my dream is to play in the NBA one day," I replied.

"Have you thought about what comes after the NBA?" She asked.

To be honest, I had never thought about this question until she asked it.

"I really don't mean to bust your bubble, but players get injuries all the time. Career ending injuries," Miss Spears said.

Miss Spears was putting stuff in my head that I had never thought about at all.

"I'mma make it to the NBA. I have to," I said as I turned and hurried out the classroom.

She really had me upset. I was so mad that I released the wrath out on Big Boo for standing in front of my locker.

"Man, get your fat ass out in front of my damn locker," I said, as I pushed him aside.

"What's up star?" He asked while taking his thumb out his mouth.

"I don't feel like talking," I quickly responded.

"Man, it can't be that bad. You're still breathing," he stated.

"Man, get the fuck away from me, fat bastard," I said as I slammed my locker shut after switching books.

I had only about two minutes before my next class. So, I got rid of Big Boo and then headed to Miss Bullock's class. Ms. Bullock was a great teacher, and she had always managed to keep my interest while I was in her class. Math was my favorite subject, so I paid close attention to her lessons.

Miss Bullock had a tannish light skin complexion. She was close to the big 5-0 but she looked much younger. She was dressed in a pink pants suit with flowers in the design. Her brown leather soft bottom shoes made her feet look comfortable in the shoes. Everyone in her class loved her and the way she presented herself.

This class was made up of entirely black students. This was the main reason why I loved it. Not only did we go over mathematical problems and word equations, we also went into weekly discussions on black history. I had learned more about my blackness in two weeks in Miss Bullock's class than I had learned in the last ten years in school.

"Mr. Jones is going to explain the importance of being on time to class," Miss Bullock announced.

Immediately, I thought about something Coach Davis had said. "Time is a valuable asset," I responded.

"That's it!" She said.

It seemed like I was never wrong in Miss Bullock's eyes. She could greatly articulate even the simplest of statements made, while making a simple statement seem much greater.

"I want everyone to brainstorm for a moment," Miss Bullock announced.

While everyone closed their eyes, she called on me to express my vision about my dream.

"If I was rich, I would buy my grandmother a house," I stated.

"Add more details to your vision Mr. Jones," She replied.

"I would invest my money that I will be making in the NBA in my community I grew up in," I responded.

"Have you had this dream before Mr. Jones?" Miss Bullock asked, while trying to make light of the subject. A few classmates were giggling in the background.

I never felt embarrassed by Miss Bullock s comment. I knew they were all in fun. This class seemed to whiz by. I almost forgot I was in school.

The class came to an end right before the bell rung. I rushed to my locker after saying goodbye to Miss Bullock.

My next class was Home Economics. The only reason I had signed up for the class was because of this fine girl named Geneva McInnis. Since I was interested in Geneva, I thought the class would be perfect for me to get to know her. Her sexy brown eyes, big butt and her short cut hair had helped with my decision, too.

When I walked into the Home Economics class, I had received the same attention I received in my first two classes.

"Hey Mr. Jones! Glad you could join us," my teacher said.

"Sorry I'm late," I said as I took a seat in the back of the room right beside Geneva.

The class was made up of five males and fifteen females. It was half and half when it came to the blacks and the whites. Mrs. Parker didn't see skin color either. She wasn't Mrs. Bullock, but she had good traits when it came to teaching students how to cook.

As Mrs. Parker began to teach, I indulged in a discussion with Geneva.

"Let me come over to your crib after school?" I asked her.

"My little sisters are going to be there," was Geneva's response.

"I don't mind if they are there. As long as you and I can get some time alone," I replied.

"I can't do it. My momma might pop-up." She said.

I responded in a joking manner, but I was more serious than a heart attack.

"Well, we can do it outside."

She said, "You are nasty!"

"I know!" I said with a smile on my face. I knew Geneva loved my sense of humor.

That was why every chance I had gotten, I had displayed it to her. Geneva changed the conversation to Denise.

"So, Denise is still your girl?" She asked.

I responded, "We are alright."

"So, I take that as a yes," She replied.

"We are good friends," I said.

"Is y'all fucking?" She asked in a sexy whisper.

"Not like that. You know she goes to Harding High School so I don't get to see her much," I responded.

"That's a lie. I heard she was bragging about how y'all were always spending time together. She told a source I know that your six-foot-three frame belongs to her. She also said your size twelve feet was the size of your penis."

I didn't want to blow my chance with Geneva so I changed the subject to disrupt her focus.

"Yo, I've been trying to get with you for the longest."

"Q, I know you got more girls on your plate besides Denise and me."

Of course, she was right. At the time, I had at least ten girls at school trying to throw their vaginas at me. Most of these young females were future gold diggers. I had tried to let my street smarts pick two out the ten, but this didn't work. I was banging anything that came my way.

After class, Geneva and I disappeared to my jeep. I wanted to do her in the back seat because my windows were tinted, but that would have cheated out first sexual experience together. I didn't want to spoil our new relationship before it got off the ground. I wanted our first time to be an experience that we would always

CRUMBLING TALENT

cherish.

    I talked Geneva into going over to her place. After we got there, we had mind blowing sex. Her head game was on point. I felt like she was trying to suck my soul out my body. Her sex was worth the wait. Like they say, good things come to those who wait. I had waited a whole year, and I was glad I didn't rush the process. I had learned that I was a special person in Geneva's life. She had told me this after she gave me a pair of her red thongs and five hundred dollars. These items were reminders of what we had done.

CHAPTER 3

Telly was standing on his porch when MC and I pulled up in my jeep.

It was 7:30 am according to the clock on the dashboard. We had 30 minutes to kill before we were due at Amy James Recreation Center. Telly strolled his six-foot-four frame out to my jeep, threw his Nike bag in the back seat, and then hopped inside the jeep.

"What's up cuzo?" I asked as I backed the vehicle out the driveway.

"Yo I fucked the shit out of Peaches last night," Telly shouted. He opened his Nike Bag and pulled out the bloody evidence.

"Put them nasty panties back in that bag," I shouted and watched as MC put his hand over his nose.

"You falling in love Telly," MC said.

"Naw man, I got her fiending for the D.I.C.K.," Telly said with a smile.

"I think she got you on the wire like a crackhead on crack. You are the one that's running around with her panties in your bag. That's weird," I said, while smiling in my rearview. MC changed the subject.

"You missed a smashing ass party last night. There were so many women there. I think it was like a ten to one ratio."

"Boy I know y'all got some hoes from that party. Did y'all get one for me?" Telly asked.

"We were too damn drunk," I said.

"I don't believe that. Not Mr. Will Fuck Anything didn't get a woman," Telly said.

My cousin knew me like the back of his hands. We had been close since his grandmother passed from cancer when we were in junior high school. His grandmother was my great grandmother on my mother's side, which made us second cousins.

"You know Mr. Will Fuck Anything got laid. My crime partner was right along with me. Ain't that right MC," I said.

"I can't lie. I got laid last night," MC said with a smile.

"It was a redbone, wasn't it?" Telly asked.

"You know Redbones are Q's favorite. Especially, browed legged ones, with brown eyes," MC said.

"I need to stop hanging around you two. Y'all know too much about me," I stated.

"Come on, Mr. Will Fuck Anything, without you we can't get pussy like that. You the one with the talk game," MC responded.

"Y'all are right. Not to blow my own horn, I can talk a chick out her panties at any time of the month. Even when she's bleeding."

MC and Telly laughed. They loved when I bragged about all the women I had sex with. I guessed it was just our little group thing.

We entered the gym with our gear in our hands. The other team was already warming up. The stands were packed. This church league game was supposed to be leisurely time of fun, but when I noticed Pop was sitting in the stands, I immediately figured a healthy wager had been placed on the game.

MC had been hanging around with Pop for the last two weeks. A lot of people were starting to ask me if MC was selling drugs. I didn't really know what to say. I did notice all the new name brand clothes that he had been wearing recently. I knew for a fact his grandmother definitely couldn't afford to buy them for him.

As we were doing our warm-ups exercises, I noticed MC and

Pop were making eye contact with each other. Big Boo's words came back to mind. 'Pop is looking for some basketball players for the In Da Hood Tournament.' Was Pop at the game to scout the talent? Or did MC invite him?

I dismissed these thoughts and turned my full attention on MC. His whole demeanor was totally different today. He was trying to play the role as the leader of the team, which was my spot. I definitely didn't want my name tied to anything even resembling betting. Especially for throwing a game. So, I approached MC at half time.

I asked him. "What are you doing out there?"

"I'm trying to win. It's the championship," he responded.

"I know, MC, but we have to play as a team. What's up with your showboating?" I asked in a demanding tone. We were the only two in the locker room.

"The game is close. We need to blow these clowns out."

"You haven't never ever been this selfish with the ball."

MC turned his back to me. I knew from the way he was acting that he had a bet on the game. He was doing something he had told me he would never do.

"Now you can't talk?" I asked. He turned and faced me.

"I promised Pop, we would win by at least 15 points," he responded.

I shouted, "You did what?"

"I had to take the deal. Pop said he would throw me two ounces of raw cocaine, which I can turn the two ounces of powder, into three ounces of crack."

"So, it is true? You are fucking with drugs?" I asked in a demanding tone.

"My grandmother can't buy me name brand shoes and clothes like your mother does for you, Q. My grandmother be working all the time and can barely get by. I don't have a mother out here like you. My mother is in federal prison I should remind you. She got 20 years, Q. I got to take care of me and my brother."

I said, "You remember what we said about fucking with

CRUMBLING TALENT

drugs?"

He replied, "I got to get mine."

"So now you're going to throw your future away," I asked.

"I'm just making my future better."

This didn't make any sense to me. MC swore to me that he would never go the route his mother had took in the streets.

"What about your grandmother? What she think about you selling drugs?"

"She doesn't know that I'm selling drugs. I don't have to check in with her. I'm 19 years old now. I can make my own decisions," he responded.

"Money don't make you a man, MC," I stated.

"How you sound? Listen to yourself. You trying to give me advice when you ain't right yourself. You used to break in cars," he said.

"I told you, I didn't break in them cars," I replied.

"Well look, I'm rolling with Pop," He said.

"Let me ask you a question. Did Pop tell you that you could go to prison for a long time for selling crack?" I asked.

"I'm not going to no prison."

"You can't predict the future."

"The future is now and it is looking bright," MC said.

After saying this, MC turned and walked out the locker room.

The buzzer sounded as I walked over to the sink in the room. It was now time for the second half of the game to start. I splashed cold water on my face, and I looked at myself in the mirror. Then I rushed out to my team.

MC and Telly were now engaged in a small conversation. The Coach told me to sit down on the bench. I couldn't believe I wasn't starting the second half. The scoreboard showed that the score was 55 to 52. We were winning but apparently MC and the Coach had a bigger plan to win the bet for Pop. I didn't want to be part of MC's promise he made to Pop, because I knew Pop was a dangerous guy to be dealing with.

I thought about an incident that Pop was involved in a few

months back. A guy was running drugs for Pop until the guy turned up dead. Rumors have it that the guy messed up a package of drugs Pop fronted to him.

When the Coach put me back in the game, it was four minutes left in the 3rd quarter. I took the point guard position. Lil-C, who was the point guard on the other team, took a bad shot. Instantly, I capitalized off his missed shot.

I took the ball to the length of the floor, weaved through several players, leapt from the dotted line, and jammed the ball in the basket. This sparked a ten-point run for us, but we were still losing Pop's bet.

The beginning of the fourth quarter. I threw MC an alley-oop. He slammed the basketball with authority in the basket. The dunk was incredible and the crowd of spectators were on their feet now. Somehow, Telly made a steal, passed the ball to me, and I passed the ball to MC. Then MC shot a three-point shot from the top of the key. It went in without touching the net. The buzzer sounded. The game was over.

I noticed Pop was talking with a fat man who had gold teeth in his mouth. I figured this must have been the guy that had made the bet against Pop. Everyone on the team was happy we had won, but me. I didn't like it a bit.

MC started walking towards me as I made my way through the crowd, back towards the locker room. I hit the shower as soon as I walked in the room. I was more than ready to get away from this situation.

MC waited until I got out the shower and asked, "Do you want your trophy?"

"No!" I said.

I didn't part take in the trophy ceremony. I went straight to my jeep and waited on MC and Telly. When they got in the jeep, they wanted to go celebrate the victory with Pop. This was after MC told Telly about the bet. I dropped them off in front of MC's grandmother's apartment.

MC asked as he got out the jeep, "You sure you don't want to go celebrate?"

I responded with a nonchalant head gesture. I pulled off after Telly got out my jeep.

The sun was still shining bright and the birds were singing when I decided to head over to my grandmother's apartment. It had been about a week since I saw her. When I pulled up in the projects, the place looked alive. There were crackheads and winos running around in the front of the neighborhood.

When I parked and hopped out the jeep, I was approached by a crackhead name Eddie Flame.

He seemingly came from out of nowhere asking, "What's up, Q?"

His eyes were bloodshot red, but he was acting jittery. He looked as if he had been up for days, and he still had on the same clothes that I saw him in two days ago. His hair was ungroomed.

I replied, "Nothing much Eddie."

He followed me all the way to my grandmother's apartment door.

As I stuck my key in the door, Eddie asked, "Do you want a haircut?"

I responded, "Do it look like I need a haircut?"

"What about a shape-up?" He asked.

"Are you high Eddie?" I asked.

"I'm trying to go to the mountain top. Can you help me?" Eddie asked.

"I can't help you Eddie. I don't have any money right now."

I took my key out the front door lock after I had opened it and walked inside the apartment. My grandmother was in the kitchen cooking breakfast when I looked in the room. The mixed smells of eggs and bacon were lingering in the atmosphere.

I walked inside the kitchen and said, "Hey Big mama!"

"What's up, superstar?" She responded.

"I just left my championship game." I replied.

"Did y'all win?"

"Yes, but I didn't accept the trophy, I answered.

"Why?" She asked while flipping the sizzling bacon on to a large plate that was sitting on top of the counter.

"It's a long story." I said as I sat down at the table.

My grandmother was dressed in a light blue house coat, white bedroom shoes and a tropical color scarf around her long hair. Her copper color skin looked like it was glowing this morning. I noticed her freshly done manicured fingernail when she placed a plate of food in front of me.

"Now what's the story?" She asked.

Then she took a seat in front of me. I hesitated for a moment, before I said, "MC is selling drugs."

"Do his grandmother know?" She asked, while picking over her plate of food.

"I don't think so," I responded, as I picked up my fork to dig into my plate.

"When your uncle, LJ started selling drugs, I put his ass out my home," My grandmother replied.

The disappointment in her voice was evident.

"What kind of drugs is he selling?" She asked.

"Weed. I guess." I responded while picking up a slice of bacon and tossing it in my mouth.

"I know that's your friend, but don't you think you are overly concerned. Weed isn't that bad. Hell, I smoke weed to relax my nerves," she answered.

"That's my friend, Big Mama. I'm really concerned about him." I said.

"He has his own life to live," She responded.

"I know, but we have the same dream of playing in the NBA one day."

"Q, just chill. Don't be so alarmed," she responded as we made eye contact.

"Weed is a drug, too, Big Mama," I replied in a commanding

tone.

"Weed ain't like crack cocaine," She stressed her words.

"It's all drugs," I responded, with some bass in my voice.

Then I stormed out the kitchen and went to the living. I didn't want to discuss the issue any longer, so I left out the apartment without even saying goodbye to my grandmother.

CHAPTER 4

I called MC on my bedroom phone at 11:00am. I told him that I needed to talk to him and he agreed to meet me at Revolution Park. This was a park that was a few blocks from MC's grandmother's apartment. When I got there, he was standing on the baseline of the basketball court. He had a basketball in his hand and he was looking up in the sky as if he was listening to God.

After I parked and got out my jeep, I realized there were a lot of weekend warriors at the court. Most of them were strapped up in their basketball gear and they were ready to play ball. Telly pulled up on the scene in his mother's car. It took him ten minutes to join MC and me at the baseline of the court. When he walked up on us, we were at the baseline of the court watching the game that was being played on the court.

Telly asked one of the warriors, "Who got next?"

I started to make a smart comment about the game that we were about to play but decided it wasn't the time for it. I still couldn't get over the fact that MC let Pop talk him into betting on the game.

I didn't want the bet to bite us in our asses so I said, "MC, that was stupid, what you did."

"You still on that. I don't want to talk about that. I just want to shoot some ball." MC responded.

"You should have at least told me and Telly before the game

about the bet.

"Man, I knew you wouldn't have agreed to it," He responded.

"So, you made my decision for me?" I asked.

"What I did was made us some money," He replied.

"Please don't involve me in your bullshit again," I responded, as I grabbed the ball out his hands.

"Yo, I got to get paid Q. I'm not going to be out here in these streets broke. It's not a for sure thing that we are going to make it to college or the NBA," MC replied.

"MC, It ain't all about money. And far as us going to college, we can do that. We just got to start hitting the books," I said.

"Look who's talking. Man, you know you ain't hitting no books. Coach Davis got you," MC responded.

Telly definitely wasn't trying to get in between MC's and my lip boxing match. He just stood in front of us dribbling his leather basketball.

A few of my fans from the neighborhood recognized me and intervened in MC's and my debate. They asked me if I had next game. I told them I did, then MC, Telly, me, and two other guys got on the court.

One of our guys were wearing some tight shorts and some no-name brand shoes. We put him at the center position. The other guy played the strong forward. I took the point guard position, MC played the shooting guard position and Telly played the small forward position.

We ran through the first game as if it was nothing, but the second game our opponents fought back until MC put a full range of jumpers in all five men's faces. Of course, the third game was my time to shine. Really, I had rested up the first two games so I was ready for my shine. I hit ten straight points with a mix of jump shots and dunks. The fourth game was when Telly took over. He put on for the crowd. Then I looked up and saw Pop.

He was standing beside his black convertible 5.0 mustang. Immediately, my mind went back to the championship game. Especially, when I saw Pop take a brown paper bag out of a tall guy's hand after he had walked over to the rim of the parking lot. Pop had done it again. He had bet on the games that we had just gotten through playing.

As MC and Telly walked over to Pop, Pop said, "I got some shoes for you two."

As they walked over to Pop's car, I changed into a clean T-shirt. MC started shouting, "Q! Q! Q! Get over here!"

I walked over to them. Then MC introduced me. "Pop, this is Qualude Jones, aka Q, aka The Nucleus!"

Pop spoke, "I know Q."

I said, "You don't know me on a personal level."

"I've watched you grow as a player over the years. I've also made tons of money off your basketball game," Pop responded.

I asked, "Why are you telling me this?"

"There is a basketball tournament coming up soon. I want you to be on my team," Pop stated.

"I don't think that would be a good idea. You know I play school ball," I replied.

"So do MC and Telly, but they don't have a problem with playing for me," Pop responded.

"I got to run this over with Coach Davis first," I said.

"No need. I already spoke with him," Pop responded.

"Why me?" I asked.

"Why not you? You got talent. You can win some serious money from the tournament. Maybe even five grand towards college," Pop said.

"Let me think about it," I said.

"Maybe the party I'm having tonight at Club Casanova can help you with your decision," Pop stated.

MC knew I had been fantasizing about going inside Club Casanova. I knew he had told Pop this to try to get me to play in the tournament.

"I'll come to the party," I said.

"Bring you some condoms, because there is going to be plenty of pussy inside the building," Pop said. Then he shut the trunk of his car.

We all went to the mall and Pop bought us all sneakers to wear for the tournament. He even purchased us outfits for the party. I didn't feel right about what Pop was doing for us, but I didn't want to disappoint MC and Telly. Pop informed us that we had approximately a week to get ready for the tournament. He also explained that he would be taking all bets against us. Then he gave us the schedule of the six-projects where the games would be played.

After I took in all the rules of the tournament I asked, "What time the party starts?"

"When y'all get there," Pop said.

I hadn't talked with Denise in over a week. She was upset with me because I didn't invite her to the championship game. Her cousin Tasha told me this. Denise was upset with me because of this. Every time I called her at her Aunt Peggy's apartment, she would hang up on me. So, I decided to head over to the projects to talk to her.

The projects were live. Everyone and their mothers seemed to be standing out or sitting on their porches. I waved at a couple people as I made my way over to Denise's building.

In front of the building was Eddie.

He spoke, "Man, what's up Q?"

"What's going on Eddie?" I responded.

"Big Mama just got out the hospital. Why haven't you been to see her?" He asked.

"I just haven't been to see her. I'mma go see her," I said.

My mother had told me that my grandmother was getting out the out the hospital today. It was no big deal, since she had just had gallstones.

Eddie asked, "You still mess with Denise?"

I said, "That's none of your business."

"Well, give me a couple dollars. You know I need me a hit," he said.

"I knew you was going to ask me for some money. I just knew it. I don't have any money," I responded.

"I know you got money. Word in these streets is you are rolling with Pop," Eddie said.

It had only been six hours since I told Pop I would play in the tournament for him. Word of mouth was powerful in the streets of Charlotte.

"I don't have no money Eddie," I said.

"Okay, but don't forget me when you start getting money," He responded.

When I pushed the doorbell to Denise's residence, I could smell the aroma of alcohol on the doorstep. The smell was lingering in the air like someone had poured alcohol on the stairway. I looked around to see if I could find where the smell was coming from. A busted 40 ounce of malt liquor beer bottle was about five feet away from the front door. As I was about to push the doorbell again, Denise's aunt swung opened the door.

She appeared in her white house coat with no underwear or bra. Her eyes were big, wide and glossy. Her short cut hair was all over her head. She had a large cup in her hand. If I had to guess, I would say there was alcohol inside the cup. She gave me a wicked smile before she said, "The little whore ain't here."

Then she turned and headed over to the worn couch that was leaning up against the wall. She swung her hips, and her butt cheeks were bouncing as she stopped in front of the couch.

I wasn't supposed to see Denise's aunt like this. As I was about to walk off, I made the decision to check to see if Denise was in the apartment.

So, I walked inside the residence as Miss Peggy shouted, "You can't just bust up in people's cribs like you are the owner!"

I looked around the living room for Denise. Then I started towards the stairs but Miss Peggy interrupted me.

"You must want me to call the police on you."

CRUMBLING TALENT

I knew Miss Peggy was playing poker with me. She was too drunk to pass a sobriety test. I played along with her little game. Then I asked her could I check upstairs for Denise. She gave me a sinful wicked smile. Then she asked me for money. I told her I wasn't going to give her anything.

"Well you ain't going up my stairs, then," She responded.

My mind was racing and wondering where Denise could be. I was worried about her, and her sister. This was my first time I had ever let my love for Denise leak out into the atmosphere. My forehead had so much perspiration on it that it looked like I had been in a rain storm. My nerves were wrecked.

I made my way up the stairs, while Miss Peggy was protesting at the top of her lungs. I didn't care about all the crazy words she was shouting to me. I was too caught up on finding Denise. Denise's room was neat, clean and smelled like Pine-Sol when I entered it. The bunkbeds were made up like a person from the Army had done them.

The numbers on her little alarm clock said it was six o'clock pm. I had another four hours before the party would begin.

I decided to put Aunt Peggy under interrogation. When I walked back downstairs, she was lying on the couch with the cup to her mouth. I was shocked that she was now bare naked. I had to admit, I did look over her body.

Then I turned my focus back to her face and said, "Miss Peggy, what are you doing?"

"I'm doing what I want to do in my home. If I want to, I can chill out in my crib without my clothes on. It's my prerogative!" She said.

I responded, "Tell Denise I came by."

She shouted, "Fuck that whore!"

I wanted to run and leave her in her insane state, but my conscious wouldn't let me.

I asked, "Why do you drink Miss Peggy?"

"None of your god damn business." She responded.

I moved closer to her to get a glance inside the cup. She didn't move.

She asked, "Do you want to fuck me?"

She had caught me off guard with her question.

I asked, "Excuse me?"

"Do you want some of this good pussy?" She asked.

I asked, "Excuse me?"

"Do you want some of this good pussy?" Miss Peggy asked again.

I couldn't believe Miss Peggy was coming on to me.

Before I could answer her, she stated, "I like to have sex when I am drunk."

I shouted, "I don't want to! I have a relationship with Denise!"

Miss Peggy acted like she hadn't heard my words. She started rubbing herself in between her legs. Her pink flesh from her womanhood was exposed.

I couldn't let this temptation overtake me, so I said, "I'm going to tell Denise."

"Tell the little bitch! She won't believe you anyway," Miss Peggy proclaimed.

The sound of the front door being opened interrupted the insane moment. Denise' sister walked inside the apartment as Miss Peggy quickly wrapped herself in her house coat.

I asked Denise's sister, "Where is Denise?"

She responded, "She's over our grandmother's house."

We spoke some more about Denise and then I left the apartment.

I couldn't get the nasty scene of Miss Peggy out my mind. She had gone overboard. I didn't want to hurt Denise's feelings, so I decided I would keep the incident between Miss Peggy and myself. It was best this way. But I had to ask myself, what if I had crossed that line?

CRUMBLING TALENT

CHAPTER 5

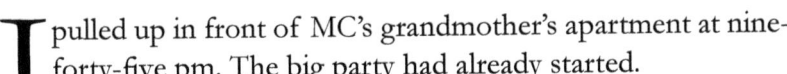

I pulled up in front of MC's grandmother's apartment at nine-forty-five pm. The big party had already started.
Telly was already at the party. My new cellphone wouldn't stop ringing as I was getting out my jeep.
MC strolled out the building with a blunt in his hand and asked, "You want to hit this?"
Usually, drugs weren't my thing but, since this was a special occasion, I took a hit. The blunt helped calm my nerves. It took all my worries away, too. When we pulled up at the club, MC put the blunt out. I wanted another pull of the thing, but I dismissed this thought after I looked at the females in the V.I.P line. There were all shapes and sizes of them.
MC pointed at Pop's cocaine white Volvo sitting in the front of the club. I wheeled my jeep slowly close to it to get a closer look at the machine. This vehicle was a show stopper, and on the front of its tag were the words: 'Money, Power, and Respect'. The letters were solid gold. The seats were creamy white and Pop's name was engraved on both of the headrests in gold. The steering wheel was rose-gold wood. The dashboard had a marble and wooden look to it.
"Damn," I said, as I took notice of the nineteen-inch gold customized rims wrapped in Kumo tires.
"We gonna be large like Pop, one day," MC said.
"I ain't with the copy-cating shit," I responded.

"I know you got your own style, Q," MC said.

"You best believe when I get some real money, I'mma hurt the game," I replied.

"Just don't forget about the little people," MC said.

"Telly was already in the V.I.P with Pop when we walked inside the room. They were sitting at the bar with a crowd of women. There were two light-skinned females on the stage shaking their asses to the beat. A 2pac song was blasting from the speakers. As the song went along, I bobbled my head to the beat. MC rushed over to Pop like a puppy looking for love. I joined them.

Pop asked, "What do y'all want to drink?"

I wasn't drinking age, but I looked like I was twenty-one.

"Give me a Hennessey and coke," I said.

MC ordered the same, and the bartender placed the drinks in front of us and then hurried away. I scooped up my glass and turned to the strippers on stage. I wasn't really feeling the party at the moment. Mainly, because I didn't get to talk with Denise before the party. While my thoughts were solely on her, I noticed her cousin Tasha walking inside the VIP. She walked over to me when we made eye contact.

She asked, "What's up Q?"

"Party Time!" I stated.

"Buy me a drink," she asked.

I knew it was coming, that was why I already had my drink in motion to hand her.

"What's this?" Tasha asked.

"Hen and coke," I replied.

"Hen makes a bitch sin," She said.

I gave her a small, brief, smile before I asked, "Where's Denise?"

"She didn't wanna come," Tasha responded.

"Why?" I asked with concern in my voice.

"She's mad at you for fucking Geneva," Tasha responded before taking a sip of her drink.

"Who told her that?" I asked.

The music changed to a slow jam. The females at the bar were looking at Tasha and me.

Tasha said, "You know how word get around."

"She's mad at me from a rumor," I asked. I was lying.

"Damn right! But I still got love for you," Tasha said.

I didn't think Geneva would have made a big deal out of having sex with me. Being that she was shy, I thought she would keep our little relationship between us. But I forgot about Shadonna. She was always looking for new gossip to spread.

I joined a group of females at the bar when Tasha started talking to MC. I took a seat next to a brown-skinned female who had two glasses of white liquor in front of her. She was sexy and knew who I was. I asked her what was her name after I had made sure Tasha and MC were busy.

My name is Kiki," she said.

"Where are you from?" I asked.

"North Charlotte. I be on Belmont street," She spoke in a sexy ghetto fabulous accent.

I could see a gold crown in the corner of the left side of her mouth. Her body was banging in her black dress.

"What are you doing on this side of town?" I asked.

"The West Side is the best side," Kiki shot back,

"That's the saying!" I responded.

The other females were acting nonchalant, as if they weren't interested in our conversation. I noticed one of them staring at me from the corner of her eye.

"What's her name?" I asked Kiki.

"Nicole Smith," Kiki answered.

Nicole looked like a plain Jane.

"Do she have a boyfriend?" I asked.

"What kind of question is that?" Kiki responded irately.

"A legitimate one," I replied.

"Don't you start using big words on me," she said, with a ghetto attitude.

"Look, I don't mean any type of disrespect, but I got some

important business to handle in the next room," I said.

As I stood up, Kiki said," Are you trying to get rid of me?"

I should have known better than to try to brush her off so quickly. I tossed a twenty-dollar bill on the counter and walked off as Kiki shouted, "You can't just toss money around like I'mma trick."

I responded as I turned back to face her, "You are right, twenty dollars is a little too much for your no manners, sorry ass."

I grabbed the twenty-dollar bill off the counter. She had the courage to push me as if she was a man. I damn near fell over Tasha and MC.

I regained my balance and shouted, "You've done lost your rabbit ass mind."

"Motherfucker, you ain't gone disrespect me. I don't give a fuck if I am on your side of town, bitch," Kiki spoke.

Now her girls were standing behind her, and I could sense by their facial expressions that they were ready for war. This was a publicity stunt, I thought, as Kiki and I were mean mugging each other. The owner came to my rescue.

I said, "She's sweating me. I don't want her in here."

"Young lady, I'm sorry but you're going to have to leave," the owner said.

Kiki and her girls started pulling out their box cutters.

The owner's girlfriend walked up and said, "Y'all got to go. Right now!"

"Well, I'mma call the police if you put me out. And, I'mma tell them he is underaged," Kiki said as she pointed at me.

"Just like a dumb ass, uneducated, hood rat, bitch. Always wanna try to destroy shit when shit doesn't go your way," The owner said.

"Who in da hell you calling a bitch, you fat motherfucker," Kiki shouted back as if she was spitting snake venom.

"Get the hell out of my club before I put my fat hands around your chicken headed ass neck, bitch," The owner spit back.

"If you touch me, I'll send you to hell tonight," Kiki stated.

"I'm already in hell, bitch," The owner shouted as he grabbed her and manhandled her to the exit door. Kiki's girls started swinging their box cutters at the owner. Several large security guards intervened, and I watched as they tossed all the girls out.

Pop hopped on the stage after the owner had slammed the V.I.P door.

He shouted, "The chicken heads are gone y'all. We can party now."

All the strippers hit the stage. It was a total of ten, and they were all from Atlanta, and they all had big butts that looked like you could sit a plate on top of them. Pop was parading around them like he was a bee and they were honey. When they all took off their G-strings, the party went to another level.

A fat guy, by the name of Big Fred, was sitting in the front of the stage. He was making it rain money on all of the strippers. There were so many asses that were popping and clapping to the music, I had to make my way on to the stage. After I got on stage, a fight broke out. When someone hit Big Fred over the head with a beer bottle, he went into a frenzy of throwing his big fist at anyone that got in his space. He even popped a couple of strippers in their mouths.

As the crowd went into a second uproar, I made my way to the V.I.P exit. Telly, Pop and MC were nowhere in sight. When, the first of many gun shots rang out, I rushed over to my jeep. While I opened the drive side door, I could hear bullets hitting the windows and the frames of vehicles. Once in the jeep, I looked around for Telly and MC again. They were nowhere in sight. I decided it was best to speed off. This was after a bullet had hit my jeep.

MC called me the next day and told me about the shooting incident that was flashing on every news station in the city. One of Pop's workers got shot by Big Fred. The guy died from a bullet to the head. MC even described the weapon Big Fred used on the guy.

I asked, "So, are you a witness?"

"I ain't no witness to shit," MC quickly announced.

"Well, if I was you, I would act like I didn't see anything," I said.

MC hesitated and said, "That was fucked up that you left me like you did."

"Bullets were flying all over the place. Hell, I had to save myself," I responded.

I felt a little selfish for leaving my best friend in the heated gun battle, but bullets don't have eyes. I tried to express how sorry I was, but MC wasn't trying to hear it. He still agreed to meet up with me on Monday after I asked him to.

I called Telly after my conversation with MC. He was giving me the cold shoulder, until I apologized for not calling the same night to check up on him. We ended our call after I told him that I was still going to play in the tournament.

CRUMBLING TALENT

CHAPTER 6

The Dalton Village Projects were live when I got out my jeep. Little kids were running around, chasing each other in the hot sun. The atmosphere felt as if it was the middle of summer. The humidity was decent. But all the black people who were standing around the basketball court were making it hotter than hell.

My adrenaline was pumping like I was about to bust a nut. I was so hyped about the tournament; I couldn't sit down. This was an important thing to me. It was just as important to Telly and MC too. We were trying to become city basketball legends.

There were reporters from The Charlotte Observer Newspaper and Channel Nine News on the scene. Both of these media outlets were doing stories on the tournament. The 'In Da Hood Tournament' was similar to the Rutgers Basketball Tournament held in New York City. A few NBA players, like Dell Curry and Bobby Fields, were standing around watching the pre-tournament festivities. They had brought their kids out to the tournament These elements brought on more excitement to me.

I noticed Pop over at the soda stand. He was talking to Butch. The word in the streets was Pop put up ten G's on us. I couldn't believe my stepfather would actually go against the grain.

"Q, I know you're ready to take care of this biz," MC said, as he threw up his hands to get Pop's attention.

"Let's get this money," I said.

"What's Pop going to pay us?" Telly asked.

MC spoke, "He says for every dunk today, he's going to kick out a hundred dollars to each of us. A thousand a piece if we win."

"Cool!" Telly responded.

"I'mma try to dunk the ball every time," I said.

"Who you think Butch put his money on?" Telly asked.

I said, "I think Marco's team. He's a big fan of Marco."

Marco Johnson was a childhood friend of mine, and he was playing college ball for UNCC. The boy was a man among kids. He was six-foot-nine and weighed over two-hundred-thirty pounds. The crowd begun migrating over to Marco as he had entered the opposite end of the court.

The director of the tournament got on a bullhorn and shouted, "The order of the teams has been decided. Each team got a number. Your number is on the chart. The team you will be playing is beside your number. It's a double elimination."

The first team we were going against was from Clanton Park. Clanton Park was a middle-class neighborhood next to Dalton Village Projects. Most of the players from that neighborhood went to Olympic with me, but none of them played on the school's basketball team. We took the court after Marco's team blew out their competition. And we didn't disappoint.

We went on a five to zero run as soon as the game started. MC put out a series of long jump shots from the right corner of the court. Since we were playing make it take it, I knew this game would be quick. All the games went to fifteen. Being that there were only eight teams in the tournament, I didn't get heated up until the semi-finals.

Marco's team destroyed an unbeaten team. He had ended the game with a power slam-dunk, and the crowd went in a frenzy. There was an old woman in the crowd shouting his name as he exited the court. After his game, it was our turn to play.

We eliminated team five. Then, Marco's team beat team two. Now, it was just Marco's team and my team. Everyone in the

CRUMBLING TALENT

crowd was hoping for this matchup. Hell, I wanted the match up, too.

    We started the game shooting flat. Marco was on fire. Telly had been given the task of trying to check Marco. There was no way Telly could stop him. Fortunately, the game ended when I shot a jumper from the right corner. I left my shooting hand in the air after calling all-net. I had to taunt the crowd after we won.

    We had one more game to win before we could be crowned champions. Telly and MC looked like they were totally drained from our hard-fought game. I was hyper than a mother... because I wanted to prove I was a hood basketball legend, too.

    As the second, and final, game began, Marco made a real slick comment. I realized from the comment that he was jealous of me. I hit a jumper in his face after Telly set a pick for me. The ball went back to us.

    Marco said," I'mma take this game like I plan to take Denise from you."

    I responded, "I know you wanna be me, but you can't."

    He replied, "Nigga, I'm already da shit. Why would I want to be you?"

    I said, "Because you can't get no ladies. I heard you be paying crackheads for pussy."

    The crowd started laughing from my comment. I was entertaining them. This was what the hood loved about me.

    Marco responded, "Ask Denise's mother how I paid her, since you wanna go there."

    I couldn't believe Marco would put Denise's mother's business on front street. He had no class. He was trying to get in my head, but I wasn't going to let that happen. Talking trash during a basketball game was my thing, and Marco knew this.

    There was a foul called by the referee on MC. The referee gave the ball to Marco to take it out on the side. Then the game resumed when he threw the ball to his cousin. They went on a five-zero run. Marco was taunting us after every made shot, and he was on fire.

I had to do something to knock him off his square, so I said, "Your girl, Trina, got some slam dunker head."

Marco's eyes nearly popped out his head. He was shocked from my remark.

"Nigga, what are you talking about?" He shouted.

I continued to dribble the ball after I stole it from him.

After I made a basket, I said, "Trina can suck the life out a real man."

"Leave them sucker ass comments out the game," Marco's cousin demanded.

"Then tell Marco to shut the fuck up," Telly yelled.

"I'mma bout to take y'all to school," Marco said after grabbing the ball off the rim.

I looked over at the referee for a rim interference call, but it never came. The referee looked at me like I done something wrong.

"Check that puck ass nigga," I said to Telly.

Marco brought the ugliness out of me.

"You are a punk nigga. Your gay ass uncle Teddy is a real punk," Marco cousin said as he hit a baseline shot.

The crowd went wild. I noticed Denise standing in the crowd, beside her sister.

It had been a whole week since I saw Denise. She was looking good as ever. Her long hair was hanging down to her shoulders and it looked like she had just got it permed. Kesha was my other chick. She was standing about ten feet from Denise. This wasn't good. I called a time out to make sure they weren't going to fight.

Kesha and Denise knew about each other. I lied to Denise about having had sex with Kesha, too. After I made sure Kesha and Denise weren't into it, I turned my focus back on the game.

"Check-up punk!" Marco said as he threw the ball to Telly.

He was now trying to punk Telly, but I intervened," I thought you was something, but you are really a lame ass wanna be."

"Win da game sucker," Marco's cousin shouted.

"But y'all games are garbage," MC spoke.

CRUMBLING TALENT

The score was ten to nine, Marco's team way.

Marco said, "I'mma bout to make love to y'all for the next five points."

Everybody on the court was sweating like it was no tomorrow.

"Play ball!" The referee shouted.

I continued to shout nasty comments about Marco's girlfriend. He wasn't backing down.

"I'm going to grudge fuck your girl after the game," I said to Marco.

The score went back and forward until we tied at 14.

"It's over for y'all clowns," Marco proclaimed as he dribbled the ball by the free throw line. He had his back towards Telly.

I said, "You best make this shot, or y'all are history."

Marco shouted, "Lights out everyone!"

Marco made a quick snappy-head fake and shook Telly almost out his shoes, but as soon as he released the ball, I was waiting by the rim. I plastered the ball to the backboard and I grabbed the rebound. Marco had a stupid face expression on his face now. It was one of those faces like he knew it was over.

"Maybe you can get the ball out the bottom of the net," I said as I dribbled it at the top of the key.

"You better hit the shot Q," Marco said.

As I took a step forward, everything seemed to move in slow motion. Everything seemingly went silent when I crossed Marco's cousin over and came face to face with Marco.

"Ooops," I said, as Marco got caught on a switch again.

This was what I wanted because I knew my first step was exclusive.

"I got you nigga," I continued to say, as I dribbled the ball in front of myself.

"You ain't got shit," Marco shouted back. He was done like a five-minute microwave pizza, but he didn't know.

Telly was posted up under the basket. MC was standing off to the side looking like a spectator.

"Do his ass, Q!" Pop shouted.

The entire crowd was yelling, screaming and cussing at me.

"This is for you Marco," I said, as I started my move towards the basket.

The only thing I remembered about the shot was the swooshing sound of the nets. After the crowd went wild, I saw Pop dancing around like he had just hit the lottery.

I shouted, "I told you, nigga! I was going to make history today."

I looked over the crowd for my stepfather. He was gone. Denise was smiling, right along with her sister. Kesha was smiling too. Pop came in and interrupted my moment.

"Y'all boys did it!" He proudly proclaimed. Then he said, "Let's go celebrate."

We celebrated like the champions we were. But this was only the first of six neighborhoods that we were schedule to play in. I was looking forward to going to all the other neighborhoods. I had something to prove. So did MC and Telly.

CHAPTER 7

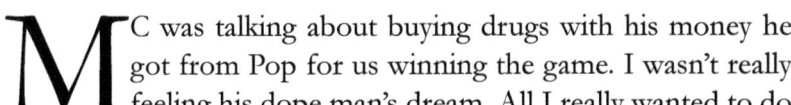

MC was talking about buying drugs with his money he got from Pop for us winning the game. I wasn't really feeling his dope man's dream. All I really wanted to do with my winnings was take Denise out on a shopping spree.

Telly managed to talk me into putting some money in his little proclaimed marijuana business. I gave him three hundred dollars for a quarter pound.

"We can sell weed and crack cocaine," MC announced, while we sat out on his grandmother's porch.

"Man, I ain't trying to go to jail," I proclaimed.

"Come on now, we ain't going to jail," MC shot back.

"If we fuck with crack, we will. Don't you know Bill Clinton just signed a crack cocaine drug bill that's sending black men to prison at a high rate? Most African Americans sell crack. I believe that's why he got the law passed. Do you want to spend twenty years in prison for a little white rock?" I asked.

"Think about all the money we can make. We don't have to get caught," MC said.

"We can get Pop to sell us the work," Telly said.

"I don't know about this," I said.

"Skip all the analyzing, Q. You either in or out," MC spoke.

"I hope this doesn't come back to haunt me," I stated.

The votes were in. I didn't like the idea of selling crack but my boys were on their road to finding glory in the drug game, and they wanted me to be a part of it.

"What about basketball?" I asked, as I handed him some money.

"Don't worry, Pop gonna pay as long as we play for him," MC said.

"We can play ball for Pop and sell drugs for him," Telly said.

My stepfather decided that he wanted to bet against us again. Pop doubled the bet to twenty thousand. I wanted to ask my stepfather why was he going against me, but I dismissed this thought after I received a call from Pop.

"What's up Pop," I said, while looking at MC and Telly.

"I just want you to know, I got a total of 30 G's on the next tournament," He said.

"Cool," I said.

"Tell MC and Telly I want their best when they step on the court," Pop stated.

"Okay, I got you Pop," I said.

I ended the call with Pop.

MC asked, "What's up?"

I said, "Pop put 30 G's on us."

"Damn!" Telly shouted.

"We got to win," I said.

MC's phone interrupted us. It was his brother.

After MC finished the call, he said, "Billy Brown got busted. My brother just told me this."

"Fo-real?" I asked.

Billy Brown was a drug dealer local hero who had all the kilos in the city. He also was a former heavy weight boxer who fought Larry Holmes.

MC continued, "Now, Pop is the biggest cocaine dealer in the streets."

"We got it made now," Telly said.

MC said, "We are about to come up."

I said, "It's almost time for the tournament. Are y'all ready to go?"

"Yeah. Let's go," Telly said.

MC spoke, "We got an hour. I need to stop by my cousin Trisha's apartment."

"Boy, you know I got a crush on her sister Tanya, but I love Trisha," I said.

"Go head, Q, with the bullshit," MC said.

"It ain't no fun if the homies can't have none," I replied.

"Boy, you are a fool," MC said.

"That's what Trisha gonna say when I get in that pussy," I said.

"Go head cuzo," Telly said,

"You can't have them both. You got to give me one."

"I'm selfish!" I said.

We shared a laugh before all of us hopped in my jeep. MC had this thing about his friends trying to have sex with his cousins. He didn't have any sisters so he treated Tanya and Trisha like they were his sisters. And they treated him like the brother they never had.

We pulled up in front of Trisha and Tanya's apartment in Fairview Homes. The neighborhood was live because the sun was shining bright. These projects were similar to Dalton Village Projects. They even had sand out on the side walk for a pathway. As we made our way to the apartment, we noticed a police car riding through. The two officers gave us each a mean-mug, but they didn't stop. MC banged on the apartment door like a policeman. Tanya opened the door dressed in a pair of Daisy Duke shorts, T-shirt and flip-flops.

I said, "Damn you thick!"

She responded, "You better go ahead with them troubles, you know you mess with my sister."

Trisha and I had been off and on all through high school. I asked, "Where is Trisha?"

"She upstairs with my baby," Tanya responded.

Telly and I followed MC into the apartment.

Tanya said, "Y'all can sit down."

We all took seats, except MC. He ran upstairs. Then he returned with Tanya's little girl in his arms. Trisha came down the stairs a couple minutes later. She was dressed in some boy shorts, T-shirt, and bedroom shoes. Her hair was cut in a short, neat, style.

I just stared her until she asked, "Q, why are you staring at me like that?"

Trisha was thick, just like her sister. Their complexions were different. Trisha was a little darker than Tanya.

I said, "You should be happy that I'm looking at you."

"Why is that?" She asked.

"Because it's hard to find a beautiful nigga like me," I said,

"Don't be tricking yourself up in here. You ain't all that," Trisha said.

"Ask your sister, does she agree with you," I responded.

"See, that's why we can't get alone. You got a smart-ass mouth and I can't put up with it," Trisha said.

"You need to take that up with my mother. She is the one that had me," I responded.

Trisha threw a pillow at me. I caught it and threw it back at her.

"MC, why did you bring Q over here? You know I can't stand his ass," Trisha said.

MC said, "Shut up, Trisha. You know you like Q."

"No, the fuck I don't," Trisha responded as she looked at me in a disgusted manner.

I laughed it off.

Telly asked, "Do you got a boyfriend Trisha?"

"Why are you asking me that?" Trisha asked back.

"You know you like my cuzo," Telly said.

"She can't stop fiending for the D.I.C.K," I replied.

Trisha threw the pillow at me again.

Then she said, "You always begging on yourself."

"Because, I'm like that in the bed. You know it," I said.

"Shut up," She shouted.

I was trying to put my bid in for Tanya. She was laughing at me and Trisha.

Tanya asked, "Don't y'all got a game?"

"Yes," MC said, as he handed Tanya the baby.

I said, "Let bygones be bygones Trisha."

Trisha said, "I don't got nothing against Q. Remember, I'm a female, I know how to get revenge."

"You know you my baby," I said.

"No, I'm not your baby. Denise is your baby. Your girl Kesha is your baby, and I can't forget about Geneva," Trisha said.

Trisha had been keeping up on me. Hell, I had lost track of all the women I was having sex with.

"Well, I got to give it to you, you got all the names right, but you left out one," I said.

Trisha jumped off the couch and swung opened the door. Then she shouted, "Get out!"

Then I responded, "I was just playing."

We left the apartment and headed over to Greenville. This community was right across the streets from Trisha's neighborhood. The basketball court by the community center was packed. Everyone and their mothers were out. This chick named Tyra came over to MC like she was the love of his life. MC had had sex with her a few times in the summer. After she gave him a hug, she gave me one. Then we all talked, until Pop pulled up in his Mustang.

Pop got out of the vehicle and then started conversing with this short cocky looking built guy with braids. The guy was a pretty boy type, like Pop. He wasn't an over the flamboyant type, but I could tell he sold drugs. MC, Telly and I walked over to them.

Pop said, "It's game time. Are y'all ready?"

MC said, "Yes."

After our conversation with Pop, we got ready for our first game. I couldn't hit a shot, because I couldn't stop thinking about Denise. She was still upset with me. Telly and MC got on me after I missed two layups. I didn't protest their gestures, because I knew my game was off. We ended up winning the tournament in Greenville. Then we went to North Charlotte and won that tournament too.

CHAPTER 8

The female inside the neighborhood store looked familiar to me. I couldn't place her face until I heard the little girl that was with her say, "Nicole, I want a soda."

I walked over to Nicole with one question.

"Do you remember me?" The little girl walked off.

"How can I forget you, Q," She responded with a smile.

"Where is your crazy friend, Kiki?" I asked.

"She got jail time for selling crack. She's going to be gone for a while," Nicole replied.

"It might do her some good," I said.

"Don't say that," Nicole replied.

"Well, it's the truth," I said.

Nicole came back. "Okay let's change the subject then."

"So, what are you doing in this area?" I asked.

"Is this quiz day?" She responded.

"Just answer my question," I replied.

"Who are you talking to like that, Q?" She asked.

"You, Miss Thang," I replied.

"Since you have to know, I just moved to Dalton Village. I live on death row," She responded.

"Who you live with?" I asked.

"My mother and my niece," She replied.

"Do you got a man?" I asked.

"Yes," She said.

"Well, I don't wanna be your man, I wanna be your nigga," I responded as I touched her hand.

"Boy, stop," she responded, as she pulled her hand away from me.

"Can I have your number?" I asked.

"Do you got a number?" She asked.

"You better not let your boyfriend get it from you," I said.

"He's in jail. He got six months to do," She responded.

"That's good for me," I said.

I followed Nicole through the store like a man on a mission. When she stopped by the milk section, I asked, "You got a baby?"

"Yes. She's six months," Nicole responded.

I touched Nicole on her butt as she grabbed several cans of baby milk from the shelf. I noticed she didn't say anything from my gesture, so I did it again.

She said, "I didn't give you permission to do dat."

"Oh," I said. "I thought you did."

"I told you, I got a man," She said again.

"What do your man got to do with me?" I asked.

Nicole said, "Give me your damn number."

I reached in my pocket and pulled out a small piece of paper with my cellphone number written on it.

"Damn, you stay ready," Nicole said.

"I try to be," I responded^

"What about Kiki?" She asked.

"What about her?" I asked.

"I don't want to be stepping on nobodies' toes," Nicole said.

"I don't know her like that," I said.

"She was talking like y'all already fucked," She said.

"I just met her that night," I responded.

"I ain't trying to let no dick come between her and me," Nicole stated.

"I understand," I replied.

Nicole's niece was coming back from the meat department.

Nicole and I ended our conversation.

Her niece asked, as I walked off, "Did you get his number?"

I smiled to myself as Nicole said, "None of your business."

Denise came walking slowly from behind the house. Right before she reached the recreation center, I blew the horn inside my jeep. She turned her attention in my direction after waving to her cousin, Teddy Bear. He had walked with her to the center.

Denise got inside the jeep on the passenger's side. She quickly closed the door, and said, "Hey."

I responded, "What's up girl?"

"Nothing," she replied.

Denise was acting shy.

"Why do you always wait until it's time for me to drop you off before you want to talk?" I asked.

"I don't know why I always do that," She responded.

"Act like you act when you're on the phone," I said.

After my statement, we rode in silence for about five minutes until I popped in Jodeci's Forever My Lady CD. The hometown boys seemed to live up to the mode. "Baby Want You Just Stay" came floating through the speakers. I looked over at Denise's body as she closed her eyes.

She was dressed in Daisy Dukes and a white T-shirt. Her Air Max Nikes were brand new. I enjoyed admiring her features. Her brown eyes were her best traits. She had bow legs, like her grandmother, and her thick thighs were waiting on me to get in between them.

I knew Denise was feeling the pressure from all the other girls in the hood. They were all chasing me, because they thought of me as their ticket out of the hood. There were so many rumors about me in the hood that Denise thought they were all true. I didn't pay much attention to them because I knew which ones were true and which ones were fiction.

My grandmother asked me about a girl named Shameka who claimed I had unprotected sex with her. Now, Shameka was pregnant and my grandmother thought I could be the father. Shameka told me she found the condom inside her vagina a day after we had sex. I brushed her off due to my relationship with Denise.

Denise opened her eyes and asked, "Q, are you fucking Shameka McDonald?"

I lied, "Hell no!"

Shameka had been trying her best to pin the baby on me, but I convinced her that her boyfriend was the father. I did this by lying about a sperm condition that I didn't have at all. I told her I couldn't have kids because my fake condition.

"Why is everyone saying you fucked her?" Denise asked with seriousness in her voice.

I spit back, "Look, people talked about Jesus."

Denise asked, "Did you stick your dick in her? Just tell me the truth. I'm not going to be mad."

I wasn't going to fall for Denise tactics.

"It's not true."

After the little episode with Geneva, which caused Denise to play dodge ball with me for a week, I wasn't trying to go through that again.

I said, "I'm a one-woman's man. I don't want no one but you."

Denise's vagina was far too good for me to allow her to run off with a clown. Besides, I was the first male she had sex with. She wasn't worn out, like most of the Hood Rats in the hood.

I took Denise over to my mother's house and sexed her so good that she was calling my name the whole time. We had sex for two hours straight until her cousin Nikki called my cell phone and interrupted us, and reminded me that my mother was due in from church. So, I took Denise back to her grandmother's house.

I took a wash-up before I headed to Nicole's apartment. I

CRUMBLING TALENT

purchased a condom from Fast Eddie for a dollar right before I knocked on Nicole's door. She answered the door on the third knock, and she was dressed in some tight boy shorts and a T-shirt. Her hair was pulled back in a ponytail. It was now eight-thirty pm. Nicole's mother was at work.

The apartment wasn't furnished at all.

Boxes of clothes were everywhere in the living room. A large TV was sitting on the floor by the stairs.

Nicole pointed to the stairway, then said, "We can chill up in my bedroom."

I asked her where Lawanda was. She told me that Lawanda was with her mother on the other side of the city. When we entered her room, I noticed her daughter was sleeping in an old crib by the closet. I walked over to the crib and looked in it.

"Her name is Kayla," Nicole said.

"By Willie?" I asked.

"Did Lawanda tell you his name?" She asked.

"Yes. I paid her ten dollars for the info," I said with a smile.

"I'mma get her," Nicole said.

"That little girl is smart. Don't mess with her," I said.

I took a seat on Nicole's queen size bed. Then we made eye contact while.

She asked, "Why are you looking at me like that?"

"You are sexy is hell," I responded.

Nicole had this sex appeal, which was totally different from Denise's. Her slant wise eyes made her sexy, and her butt was wider than Denise.

"I have a question for you. Do you sell drugs?" Nicole asked.

"Yes, I do," I answered.

"You don't got no shame in your game," Nicole responded.

"Why should I?" I asked.

"Because it ain't right," Nicole said.

Nicole was starting to make my blood pressure rise. She wasn't like all the other girls in the hood either. She was the type to ask questions first before she hopped in the bed with someone. She was more of a challenge for me.

"You ain't no saint. You told me Kiki got caught selling drugs. I know you was hanging out with her," I said.

"You got me. Yes, I sell drugs every now and again," Nicole stated.

"Look, I got that work for da low low. Since you gonna be one of my girlfriends..."

Nicole interrupted, "Hold up player. Slow your roll. We can't mix business with pleasure. That's rule number in the official Dope Girls' handbook."

"Okay. I'm cool with that," I responded.

"So, you don't want none of this?" Nicole asked as she pointed at her fat vagina.

"You are very blunt. Now stop playing and get over here," I responded as I tried to pull her by the arm.

She pulled away and said, "I'm not playing player."

"Pussy comes a dime a dozen," I responded.

"Not this fat cat. I got that shit you will run and tell your daddy about," She said as she patted her vagina print.

"I believe you," I replied.

"This is some serious shit right here," She said as she ran her index finger between the lips of her vagina.

I stood up and Nicole met me with a kiss. We tongued for about five minutes. Then we stripped each other's clothes off. When I stuck my penis in her, she let out a loud moan.

Then she shouted, "Damn! You are bigger than I thought. Please, take your time with me."

I laughed to myself. I knew Nicole was trying to run game.

"Wait to you feel this tongue," I said as I dropped down between her legs.

We sexed each other all night. She sucked me dry and I ate her until the sun came up.

I made her tap out, and the crazy thing about our sex episode was, she told me she was in love with me after I told her to get rid of Willie.

CHAPTER 9

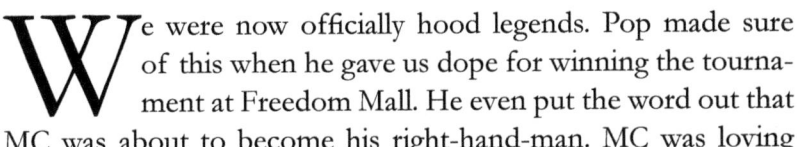

We were now officially hood legends. Pop made sure of this when he gave us dope for winning the tournament at Freedom Mall. He even put the word out that MC was about to become his right-hand-man. MC was loving every moment of it. So were Telly and me.

I couldn't believe how much love we were getting in the streets now. All those whores who used to play hard to get with us were now pouring out their vaginas in our directions. Everywhere we went, women were on us like white on rice. Especially, when we went to parties.

Everything was going perfect until Nicole told me she was pregnant. I accused her of sleeping with other men but she wasn't having that. She went off on me and told me how she left Willie for me. I felt bad about denying the child.

I knew the child was mine. I just didn't want to break Denise's heart.

I turned to my Uncle LJ for help. He didn't have children, but he had knowledge about the world. We talked about women, drugs, the future and then Nicole. He didn't sugar coat anything.

"Unc, I've got myself in big trouble with this chick I just met," I said.

"Who is this chick?" He asked.

"Her name is Nicole. She's from North Charlotte," I said.

"Never heard of her but I can tell you if she's from there, she is a go getter. She's looking for a come up. And you are just that," He said.

"You might be right," I responded.

"Why you say that?" He asked.

"She is pregnant by me," I said.

"Fo-real!" He said.

"Yes. And she doesn't want to get an abortion," I stated.

"If I was her, I wouldn't get one either. You could be her ticket out the hood," Uncle LJ said.

Uncle LJ was right. The young women in the hood were looking for a way out of their circumstances.

I asked, "What you think I should do?"

"Play it by ear. It might not be your kid," Uncle LJ stated.

I was beginning to feel as if Nicole planned to get pregnant by me. Maybe my mind was playing trick on me like the Ghetto Boys said in their song. So many questions were running through my already clouded head, and the main thought at the moment was, is Nicole a gold digger? Her actions hadn't shown she was, but her sassy mouth made me have second thoughts on many occasions.

I changed the subject. Then I told my uncle all about the drugs MC, Telly and me were getting from Pop. He was shocked from this revelation.

He asked, "You sure you doing the right thing?"

I said, "I got to get mine."

The first game of the season was in two hours. Rock Hill High wasn't known for basketball at all. This was why I was perplexed about Coach Davis' decision to put this team on our schedule. There wasn't much media coverage. Just a local guy from the newspaper company down the street from the school. When we arrived in the locker room Coach Davis ordered us to get ready for the game.

CRUMBLING TALENT

Once everyone got dressed, Coach Davis went over his game plan with us, and he included the starting line in his conversation. Brian Woodard, a five-foot-five African American, was our point guard. Mike Sparrow was a six-four forward, T-Davis was our six-five center, C-Reid was our other six-two forward and I was the six-foot-two shooting guard. Everyone on the team could handle the ball, but Brian and me were the primary ball handlers. The offense was going to run through me.

I said a prayer before I entered the circle where all my teammates were standing. T-Davis, who was Coach Davis's older son, lead the team prayer.

He said, "God give us the strength to play at our best. Please watch over us and protect us from injury. Amen."

Coach Davis spoke, "We are going to start in our full court press. I want Qualude and Brian at the top of the zone. I want to fast break this team and press this team all night. I want to run their tongues out their throats."

We broke from the circle as the horn in the gym sounded. It was game time, so we got in a straight line as a team and departed from the locker room like an Army drill team. The blenchers were now packed with over a thousand people sitting in them.

As we started our lay-up line, the home team took the court. The only thing I could say was, "It's going to be a great night for me." This team was very short. They didn't have a rim protector.

The horn sounded again. We exited the court and huddled up on the sideline with Coach Davis in the center of the circle.

He spoke, "It's game time. It's time for everyone to perform. No excuses tonight. Now, like I said in the locker room, we are going to press them all night. If you need a break raise your hand and I will pull you out the game."

We took the court for the jump ball. T-Davis tipped the ball to me. I dribble it straight to the basket and scored. The crowd booed after we set up the press and scored quickly again after a steal.

I was in a zone the first quarter. I scored ten of our fifteen points. At halftime, I had seventeen points and the score was thirty to fifteen. Coach Davis gave a us a prep talk about our defense in the locker room. Then we walked back on the court for lay-up drills. I felt like everyone was watching me.

We remined in control of the game the whole game. The game ended 64 to 54. I scored thirty points. Back in the locker room, Coach Davis told us that we did a great job. Then we packed up and hit the highway.

When the activity bus pulled up in the projects, I could see a crowd of people standing on the neighborhood basketball court. I couldn't make out all the faces in the crowd until I got closer. The first person I spoke to was Marcus Brown. He was a childhood friend of mine, and he was crying like there was no tomorrow.

"What's wrong Marcus?" I asked.

"Travell got murdered," He responded.

Travell was one of Butch's nephews. He had been on the twelve and under team with Marco and me. He was one of the reasons I started playing basketball.

"What happened?" I asked as I dropped my gym bag.

"He was murdered by a dude from Little Rock. Dude shot him," Marcus said.

"When did this happen?" I asked.

"About twenty minutes ago," Marcus responded.

"Where at?" I asked.

"In the middle hole," he said as he wiped his eyes with his hands.

The middle hole was the middle section of the neighborhood. Miss Peggy's apartment was twenty feet from the crime scene. I couldn't believe my eyes when I saw Travell on the ground.

Marcus grabbed my shoulder and said, "That's the dude car right there."

A silver 1975 Cadillac was sitting in the parking lot in front of the guy's girlfriend's building. Marcus told me that the guy had been visiting this girl when Travell and him got into an argument.

CRUMBLING TALENT

The argument spun out of control when Travell made a joke about Rodney King's famous saying 'Can't we all just get along?'

I looked at Marcus and asked, "Why haven't the police got here yet?"

"You know the police don't like to come out here," He responded in a serious tone.

When Travell's mother showed up on the scene, all hell broke loose. Everyone broke down when she broke down. I wanted to console her, but I didn't know what to do.

So, I turned to Marcus and said, "We got to get this dude."

He responded, "Some of the guys that were on the block chased the dude."

I asked, "Do anyone know this dude?"

"No!" Marcus said.

Finally, the police arrived. Then twenty minutes later the Ambulance showed up. Travell was dead. It didn't take a rocket scientist to figure this out.

DENISE

I couldn't believe Travell was dead. It was crazy how everything played out. Qualude was crushed from Travell's death. He showed up at the funeral dressed in all black. He even had pictures of Travell in his hands.

After the funeral I tried to call Qualude and got his voicemail. I tried it again and got it again. Death was something I wasn't used to but Qualude had taught me how to handle it. He told me just to talk about it. He said it's best to get it out of your system.

After staying with my grandmother for three months, I moved back in with my Aunt Peggy so I could keep a closer eye on Qualude. I heard about him selling drugs for Pop. This was shocking news to me, because he had promised me that he would never get involved with drugs. He told me this after he had told me about his father's addiction problem.

It had been a week since I had seen him. When I last saw him, I noticed the aggression in his behavior. He was becoming more and more selfish, and he no longer tried to pleasure me during our sexual encounters. This was a full sign of cheating.

My family was noticing Qualude's new behavior towards me too. Nikki told me Qualude was going through a phase of soul searching. Aunt Peggy told me just to let him be, because he would come back around if he was in love with me. I didn't think this was true.

I was going through a tough time too. My body was transforming right before my eyes at a rapid pace. My breasts were getting big by the day, and my butt was too. My thigs were big as ever, and most of my pants were too tight for me to wear. I had to wear some of my Aunt Peggy's clothes since she was two sizes bigger than me.

1 had missed my period for the third month in a row. There was no doubt in my mind I was pregnant. My emotions were all over the place, and Qualude was running me crazy from all the girls he was messing around with. There were rumors that he had gotten Shameka McGill pregnant. She was days away from dropping her load.

Even though I didn't know exactly what the truth was with Shameka, I knew Qualude was good at keeping secrets. He had told me about a girl name Rhonda he knew who let another man take the blame for her baby and the guy was paying child support and it wasn't the guy's baby. This was why I decided to tell Aunt Peggy about my baby.

She was sitting when I walked in the apartment.

"Hi Aunt Peggy," I said.

"What are you speaking to me for? You don't be speaking to me," She responded.

She was drunk. I could smell the liquor on her breath.

"I need to talk to you about something important," I replied.

"Ain't nothing more important than these bills around here," She said.

"I have a decision to make," I said.

"Why don't you call Betty?" She asked.

"Because I wanted to discuss this with you first," I said, as I took a seat across from my aunt.

"What is it?" Aunt Peggy asked, as she picked up her cup of liquor.

"I'm pregnant." I said.

"Girl, you better get your ass out of here talking crazy. You don't know a damn thing about raising a baby," Aunt Peggy said.

"I know. That's why I'm asking you to help me," I responded.

"Who is this baby by?"

"You know who."

"Do he know?"

"No."

"Why haven't you told him?" Aunt Peggy asked.

"I just haven't," I responded.

"You can't keep it," She replied.

"Why?" I asked.

"You can't even take care of yourself. How are you going to take care of a baby?" she asked.

"I'll get a job."

"A whole baby is a lot," Aunt Peggy said then took a drank from her cup.

"I know how to take care of a baby. I be helping Nikki with her kids," I responded. "You got all the answers," Aunt Peggy responded.

"No, I don't. I'm going to need you to help me."

"I don't know about this Denise."

"All I need you to do is stop drinking. You will be the best aunt and grandmother if you do that," I said.

"I don't know if I can quit drinking. I've been doing it since I was 15 years old."

"We can work on that," I said as I gave Aunt Peggy a hug.

❖ ❖ ❖

QUALUDE

Travell's death was taking a toll on me. No one was asking me if I needed any counseling. My heart was hurting and I was in pain almost every day. The pain wasn't showing on the outside, but on the inside, I was dying. Even though Travell and I weren't blood cousins, we treated each other like we were blood. To cover the pain of his death, I turned to the streets.

Basketball had been put on the back burner, like a bad dish. I was still going to practice, but I wasn't the gym rat I had been in the past. I was missing school, and Coach Davis was becoming concerned with my behavior. He tried to take precautions by setting up an afterschool program for me, so I could get extra credit for my classes. This didn't work.

Hand to hand drug dealing was my future, and West Blvd was becoming my playground. I was selling crack in the late night and still getting up to go to school. The weight Telly, MC and I were getting from Pop was being broke down into twenty rocks. I was bagging up sixteen hundred dollars' worth of rocks off an ounce of crack. The hood was falling in love with me because I was giving out double-ups to the dealers and the fiends. I even created a free day where I gave out free crack to all the people that I was dealing with in the hood. I did this once a month.

I even took my drug dealing to the hallways of my high school. Big Boo was my partner in crime, and he was moving all the product at the school.

When my mother found out I was selling crack cocaine, she summoned me to the living room and asked, "Are you selling drugs?"

"I am doing what I got to do," I responded.

"You don't have to do that," my mother responded.

"Mama, I ain't trying to struggle. I don't like you depending on Butch to take care of you," I replied.

"So that's why you selling drugs. You think I depend on Butch?" My mother asked.

"Yes!" I shouted.

"I tell you what, you get your stuff and get out my house," she shouted, in a demanding tone.

"But Mama," I said in my protest.

"Get out! You can't stay here no more," she said.

We both were in tears. The anger and disappointment in her voice told me that she was serious. The only thing I knew to do was call my uncle LJ.

He answered, "What's up, nephew?"

"So, you heard?" I asked.

"Yes. Your mama called me," he said,

"I need a place to stay," I said.

"You know I got you. But you got to leave Pop alone and mess with me. We need to get a family thing going," he suggested.

Without hesitation I said, "I'm down with whatever."

When I called MC, he answered his phone on the first ring.

"What's up, Q?"

"I got something to tell you," I said.

"What is it?" MC asked.

"My mother put me out," I said.

"Where are you staying?" He asked.

"With my uncle LJ," I said.

MC hesitated and said, "I got some bad news for you, Q."

I asked, "What is it?"

"I overheard Pop talking about black mailing you," MC responded.

"What are you talking about?"

"Your stepfather beat him out of a hundred thousand dollars shooting dice."

"Fo-real?" I asked in a surprise tone.

"Pop is mad as hell about that. He said he is going to report you to the Board of Education for gambling in the In Da Hood

Tournament if your stepfather doesn't give the money back. He's planning to ruin your career," MC said.

"What do I got to do with this? I don't even mess around with my stepfather."

"I know. But you are the only card in the deck that Pop can play."

"I'm dead. My stepfather isn't going to give him the money back," I said.

"Well, kiss your dream good bye."

"You need to talk to Pop for me," I suggested.

"I can't. It's out of my hands," MC responded.

Then MC hung up the phone in my ear. I was wondering what was going to happen to me. I drove my jeep over to Freedom Mall so I could blow off some steam by walking around in the building. Once out the vehicle, I saw Nicole pushing her daughter in a stroller. She was headed towards the mall. As she entered the mall, I blended in with a crowd, so she couldn't see me. I wanted to see what she was up to.

She entered the Foot Locker shoe store on the corner by the food court. There, she was talking to Kayla while she was picking up shoes that were Kayla's sizes. After she chose between Jordan's and Air Maxes Nikes for Kayla, she headed over to the infant section of the store. There, she was trying to pick the right outfit for that baby in her stomach. Finally, she decided on a pair of red PJ s. Then she made her way over to the checkout counter.

I felt like a stalker but this wasn't going to stop me from following Nicole. Once outside, she walked over to her rental car after waving at an African American cop in front of the building. She placed the bags and the stroller in the trunk. Then she put Kayla in the baby car seat in the back seat and jumped in the driver seat.

As I was about to make my way over to Nicole's rental car, a blue Honda drove up alongside of her. A dark-skinned guy with waves in his hair got in the passenger seat. I couldn't tell what they were talking about but, if I had to guess from their face gestures, it was something sexual. When they started kissing, I felt like I had caught Nicole cheating on me. After the kiss, the guy got back in his car and drove away. Then Nicole pulled out of the parking lot.

I followed Nicole to the county jail downtown. She parked in front of the jail and hopped out with Kayla in her arms. She entered the front entrance of the jail. I waited as she went inside to visit Willie. I knew this because her niece had told me that she was doing this every Friday. I had caught her again cheating on me. It was time to confront her about her transgressions.

CHAPTER 10

QUALUDE

I showed up at Nicole's mother's apartment at nine pm sharp. She had given me permission to come over after I told her that we needed to talk about our relationship.

When I walked in, I said, "I saw you the other day at the mall. Who was the dude?"

"What are you talking about?" She answered as she played dumb.

"Who was the dude Nicole?" I asked in a demanding tone.

"You was spying on me?"

"No. I wasn't there to spy on you. Just tell me who the dude was."

"His name is William. He's my ex-boyfriend," she responded.

"Damn! You got me in a love triangle?" I asked.

"You don't love me!" She shouted.

She was trying to turn her wrong around on me.

"I got mad love for you," I responded.

"You just love my sex. You haven't been with a woman experienced like me. It's all lust, Q."

"You are not inside my head. You can't tell me how I feel."

"Trust me. I can see it in your face."

"So, you think you can read me. Well, let me read you for a moment. I know you still seeing Willie," I stated.

"Very funny," she answered.

"I'm serious. I followed you to the county jail."

"So, you were stalking me?" She asked, with a serious face expression on her face.

"You can call it what you want to call it."

"I call it being stupid. I call it being a mother to my child."

"I don't like you going to see Willie."

"Tough luck. You and I ain't married."

"I thought you was finished with him?" I asked.

"I do have a child by him. Therefore, I have to deal with him."

"You should have at least told me you was taking Kayla to see him."

"Kayla isn't your business."

"If you are going to continue to be my woman than she is my business."

"Well, if it makes you happy, I found out he got a girlfriend. He doesn't want me," she said as she crossed her arms across her chest.

"So, you done with him?" I asked.

"Yes I am. You don't have to worry about him."

"Prove it."

"How can I do that?" She asked.

"You can think of something."

"How about this…"

Nicole dropped her pregnant self to the floor, unzipped my pants and went to work on my penis. I almost lost my balance when she made me climax.

"How was that?" She asked as she got off her knees.

"You proved your point. I believe you."

"Now you got something to prove to me."

I didn't see this coming.

"What is that?" I asked as I pulled up my pants.

"I want you to prove that Shameka's baby isn't your child."

"How can I do that?"

"Call her and let me hear you tell her that that baby isn't yours."

"I don't have her number."

"I got it."

Nicole pulled out the number from her jeans pocket and handed it to me.

"No problem, I'll call her."

"I also want you to call Denise."

I was caught off guard by this request.

"Come on, Nicole. I'm not going to call her," I stated.

"Why?" She asked as she stared in my eyes.

"That's a whole another situation. She was before you."

"No, she wasn't," Nicole stated.

"Yes, she was," I said.

"Call Shameka. I'll deal with Denise later."

I called Shameka, and she told Nicole that I wasn't the father of her baby.

"Are you happy now?" I asked, as Nicole hung up the phone.

"No!" She stated.

"What is it now?" I asked.

"I'm not happy because I know you fucking Denise."

"That's none of your business," I said.

"Oh, that how you gonna play it player." She said.

"When you get over Willie, I'll get over Denise."

I left Nicole standing in the middle of the living room, and I went straight to Aunt Peggy's apartment and told Denise to stay clear of Nicole. She didn't even ask why. She was too sick to get mad.

DENISE

I was hurting from finding out that Shameka had had her baby and named her son close to Qualude's name. Tasha went to bed after she disclosed this fact to me. Word in the streets was Qualude was, in fact, Quan's father, but Shameka put the baby on her boyfriend. Just like a nasty Hood Rat.

I didn't know how Qualude persuade her to get her not to go downtown on his ass, but I wasn't going to fall for the same trick. Yes, he was good with his word play, and his sex game was superb, but these two things weren't great to the point that I would deprive my child from knowing who his or her father was. It was time to get some answers.

When Qualude arrived at one am, I was closing in on sleep. He shouted, "Denise, open the door!"

I jumped up off the couch, rushed over to the door and opened it.

"Are you going to let me in?" Qualude asked.

I could tell he had been drinking. The strong smell of cheap liquor was on his breath.

I asked, "Why did you come here like that?"

My mind was all over the place. I feared he was celebrating Quan's birth.

"I feel good. We won by 20 points."

"That's good," I responded.

"Can I come in?" He asked.

"I don't know. Can you?" I asked.

"What's your problem?" He asked.

"You are the problem," I said.

"What's up with you? Why did you say that?" he asked.

"Is Quan your son?" I asked.

"No! I told you, Shameka and I have never had sex."

"Stop lying!" I shouted.

"No need to get upset. Let me come in so we can talk about this in private," He responded.

"No!" I shouted.

The neighborhood was dead. Not a single person was out. Not even a junkie. So, we didn't have to worry about any rumors.

"So, I came all the way over here for nothing?" He asked.

"No, you didn't come over here for nothing. I do have something to tell you," I stated.

"What is it, Denise?" He asked in his slurred voice.

"I know all about what you been up to. I know Shameka's son might be yours and that that new girl Nicole might be pregnant by you."

"All rumors," Qualude answered.

"Well, I got a fact to add to the rumors. I heard you still fucking with Geneva."

"Are you serious?" He asked, in a perplexed tone.

"Yes."

"I don't mess with that girl," he said.

"Yes, you do," I responded.

I thought Qualude was going to keep it real with me, but he didn't.

"I'm going to stop the rumors," he said.

"I hope so," I said.

"Who told you this rumor?" He asked.

"Don't worry about it. Just know I got eyes everywhere," I responded.

"I don't have nothing to hide," he said.

"I hope not," I replied.

QUALUDE

I was sitting in the living room when my cell phone started ringing. I looked at Uncle LJ, and he tossed the phone to me after he grabbed it off the living room table.

"Hello," I answered.

"I had the baby. She is seven pounds, eight ounces. I named her Keosha."

"Who is this?" I asked.

"So, you don't know me now?"

The voice sounded familiar but I couldn't make it out.

"Just tell me who this is," I said.

"This is Nicole, boy. They got me on heavy medication," she stated.

"Damn! I'm sorry Nicole."

"Don't be. I decided to help you out since you are nothing but a liar," she said.

"What are you talking about?" I asked.

"My niece ran into Denise. Denise told her that you ain't claiming my baby."

"Come on, Nicole. Why would I not claim the baby?" I asked.

"Her name is Keosha," she said, as she stressed her words.

"I don't want to fight with you," I said.

"You don't have to. I told Willie it was his baby," she said.

"I thought you said I got you pregnant?"

"I told you that so you could be with me until Willie get out of jail," she said. "I'm in love with him, and I will do anything to keep him."

"So, what if Keosha is really my daughter?" I asked.

"You can see her but she can never know you are her father, "she said.

"I don't know about this Nicole," I said.

I loved Nicole, but I was in love with Denise. I didn't want to lose Denise because of my bad decisions.

"Do you want me to tell Denise everything? I know you love that little red bitch," she spit out. She was upset now.

"I tell you what, let's get a blood test," I said.

"No!" She said.

"Well, I guess you win," I said.

"Damn right, I won. You ain't no fighter," she said.

"This isn't about who won or who could win. It's about Keosha."

"Since you don't want to agree with my terms, I'm going to make sure Keosha never calls you daddy."

Then Nicole hung up the phone on me. She had me in a perplexed state. Why would she lie to me? Why would she lie to Willie? Mental issues, mental issues.

DENISE

I met Tony while Nikki was pumping gas in Aunt Peggy's car. He asked me for my number and Nikki got his number for me.

The only reason I called him was that I was sick and tired of Qualude's transgressions against me. Tony and I decided we would catch a movie.

When I got in his car, I said, "I didn't think you would go on a date with a pregnant woman."

He put the Lexus in drive and said, "You are too beautiful to pass up."

Tony was into basketball, too. He went to the same high school as Qualude.

"I've heard Olympic High got a good basketball team," I said, as I was trying to make small talk.

"We do! Thanks to Qualude Jones," Tony remarked.

"That's my ex-boyfriend," I responded in a dry tone.

"You are kidding me, right?" Tony asked, in an exciting tone.

"No! I am not kidding," I said.

"So, the superstar got a baby on the way?" He asked.

"Yes, we do. I'm four months pregnant."

"I got a question for you. Why are you really going out with me tonight?" He asked with a curious facial expression.

"I like you," I said. "Plus, I'm single. I broke up with Qualude, but he doesn't know yet."

"What did he do?" Tony asked.

"He's fucking every girl he comes in contact with. I hope his dick falls off. Excuse my mouth, but he's been doing me wrong."

"Two wrongs don't make a right." Tony answered back.

"I didn't say I was going to have sex with you," I replied.

"I didn't mean it like that. I mean, you shouldn't go out with me to get back at him." Tony said.

"He got friends. I can have friends," I responded.

"I'm a male."

"He got female friends," I said.

"Like I said, two wrongs don't make a right. Someone has to be the adult. You both are eighteen years old, right?"

"Are you telling me I should be the adult?" I asked.

"You have to answer that for yourself."

"So, you're taking his side?" I asked as I turned towards him.

"It's not about me taking a side," Tony replied.

"Do you think I'm doing this to make Qualude jealous?" I asked.

"Do you love Qualude?"

"I don't love that two timing, cheating no good..."

Tony interrupted me. "You don't have to put on a mask for me."

"I'm not fronting. This is how I'm feeling at the moment."

"You and I both know, if Qualude saw you in the car with me, you'll probably be shitting bricks," Tony said.

Tony was right. I was upset with Qualude. The reason I was upset with him was because I heard he went and saw Nicole's baby at the hospital.

"Look, Tony, I thought we were on a date." I said.

"We are," he replied.

"Well, let's stop talking about Qualude," I said.

Tony replied, "I don't want to get my feelings caught up in you and then you go back to Qualude."

"I'm not thinking about him," I said.

"I hear your mouth, but your heart is saying something different," he responded.

"I'm sorry, Tony," I said.

"Don't be. I know how it is to be in love. I was in love before," he stated.

"What happened?" I asked, in a curious tone. I really wanted to know.

"I caught her cheating," he responded.

"With who?"

"Promise you won't say anything or get mad," he said.

"Why do I have to promise you anything? And why would I get mad about your girl cheating?"

"Because Qualude was the guy she cheated with," he responded.

"I'm sorry. Are you serious?" I said.

"Please don't tell Qualude I told you about this," he replied.

"I'm not. But this is shocking. Is this the reason you looked at me at the gas station?" I asked.

"No. I looked at you because you are a pretty young woman," he said.

"I need some water," I said.

"How about some ice cream?"

"Sure!"

"Now what do you think about me?" He asked.

"You are very attractive. I like dark skinned men," I said.

"Will this be our first and last date?" He asked.

"I don't know. We have to see," I responded.

"One more thang, you need to tell Qualude how you feel. There is no need for you to keep things in," he suggested.

Tony gave me something to think about. The whole time we were at Crown Point Theater, I was thinking about Qualude. After we saw a movie, we played video games and ate ice cream. When Tony dropped me back off at home, Nikki was standing on the porch with the phone in her hand.

"Girl, Q has been over here looking for you," she said.

I responded, "What did you tell him?"

"I told him you caught the bus to the mall," Nikki replied.

"What did he say?" I asked while biting my nails.

"He said someone saw you at Crown Point movie theater playing video games with a guy," Nikki said.

"Was he mad?" I asked.

"You know he was. He didn't stay long."

"Damn! It's all your fault Nikki.

"My fault? You was the one that called Tony," Nikki responded, in her defense.

"You was the one that wrote his number down, "I said in my protest.

"I didn't tell you to call that dark, beautiful, man, "Nikki shot back. "You should have let me have him."

"If you wouldn't have went to that gas station, I wouldn't have

CRUMBLING TALENT

met him," I said.

"Girl get over it. You really need to explore your womanhood and your femininity more," Nikki stated.

"I think I'm still in love with Qualude," I said.

"I thought you broke up with him."

"I did. But I have a change of heart."

"You need to stop playing games."

"He likes to play games. Why can't I play them with him?" I asked.

"You are not a kid anymore. Girl, you are a young lady. You are about to be a mother. It won't be about you anymore. It will be about that child in your stomach," Nikki preached to me.

"So, you think I should tell Qualude how I feel?" I asked.

"Yes," she answered quickly.

"I can't. The boy is already conceited, me boosting his ego won't stop him from cheating," I replied.

"You think expressing yourself to the man you love will boost his ego?"

"You must not know Qualude like you say you do. He got his confidence level so high that he thinks he can do anything."

"So, you don't like that?"

"I hate it."

"Why?"

"He thinks he's the master cheater. He thinks I'm that dumb that I don't know he's doing it."

"Think about the future. If Qualude make it to the NBA, you and your baby will be set."

I asked, "So, you saying just let him cheat on me?"

"What I'm saying is you need to learn how to deal with the rumors and the cheating if you are planning to be with him," Nikki said.

"That's so hard Nikki. I don't know what I would do if I actually catch him red handed cheating on me," I said.

"Look at it like this, if you don't catch him then it ain't cheating. Until then, give him the benefit of the doubt. Stop trying to find something wrong. Enjoy the fun y'all are having, because you're only young once."

"Thank you for the advice, Nikki," I said.

"Anytime girl," she responded.

"Now, how am I going to explain the movie situation to Qualude?" I asked.

"Don't even explain it," Nikki suggested.

"Why not?" I asked.

"Because, he'll be mad at you," Nikki said.

"If I don't explain it, he's going to be mad, "I said.

"Sometime things are best left alone."

"You said tell him how I feel. I'm going to tell him I only went out with Tony to make him mad, "I said.

"That sounds childish. Please don't go there," Nikki said. "You might lose him."

"Okay Nikki. I'm not going to say anything. I'm just going to deny it if he asks me," I said.

"Now you are thinking like a woman," Nikki said. "And you have to remember, a lot of men going to come your way because of Qualude. It's just the way men do."

CHAPTER 11

QUALUDE

When I found out Denise had cheated on me, I couldn't believe it. I could see Nicole cheating on me, but Denise was another story. She was still pure at heart. She wasn't filled with lust like Nicole. On top of all my problems, Pop was still threating to get me banned from going to college. So, I went to Butch's nephews for help.

Tee was Butch's youngest nephew. Travis was in the middle and Big Roger was the oldest. Big Roger was cutting hair for a living, and he was my barber. I stopped in the projects at Butch's mother apartment, and all three of them were chilling out in Big Roger's bedroom when I arrived.

"What's up with y'all?" I asked, as I walked in the room.

Big Roger asked, "Are you here to get your hair cut??"

I responded, "I heard you got your licenses!"

"Yes! Butch helped me get them," he replied.

"Speaking on Butch, he got me in some shit with Pop," I said.

"What are you talking about?" Big Roger asked.

"Pop is threating to ruin my chances of going to college. You know if any college hear that I've been gambling on games, I'm done before I can get started," I responded.

"Why would Pop do that? You was just playing for him in the tournament," Travis replied.

"Butch beat him out some money," I responded.

"Man, that's messed up. But, speaking of money, we heard you was making all the money in the hood," Tee said.

"You heard right, but I don't have enough to pay Pop. Butch beat him out of a hundred G's," I said.

"Don't worry about that, you got bigger things to be worried about. I heard you got Denise pregnant. You know that's my girlfriend," Tee said.

This little twelve-year-old was serious. This little brat reminded me of my little brother.

I said, "If you wasn't my cousin by marriage, I would have been fucked your mama. I love me some tall, black, African looking women."

"Go head with that," Tee responded, as he tried to punch me in the arm.

I said, "Don't joke if you can't take one."

Travis and Big Roger busted out laughing at my remark. They knew I was only kidding.

Big Roger said, "Sit down in my chair, Qualude."

His chair was an old office chair that he had found at a dumpster outside the neighborhood. One of the legs on the chair was broke which made it lean to one side.

I sat down in it, and Big Roger began to cut my hair.

Travis asked, "What are you going to do in the Basketball game, Friday night?"

"You know I'mma show my ass. I might show my ass to the point, I might get you some pussy."

"Go head, Q. You always like to brag."

"Don't go there. You know I got you your first piece of pussy. And your second piece of pussy," I said.

"You always got to show out," Travis responded.

"Hey, I wouldn't be myself if I didn't show up and show out," I replied.

Tee said, "You think you all that. I am going to tell Denise about all the women you got."

"I know I'm all that. You can tell her, she ain't gonna believe

CRUMBLING TALENT

you," I said.

"That ain't cool to say, Tee. You can't snitch on Q," Big Roger said.

I responded, "Big Roger, what are y'all teaching this brat?"

Tee said, "I ain't no brat."

I said, "You are a Mama's Boy and don't you forget that. You are going to live with your mother until she passes away."

Tee said, "You don't know the future."

I said, "Look, Tee, maybe one day you will be like me. Then you can get Denise. That will be well after you are in your 30's, but I know you still are going to be living with your mother. By then, Denise won't mean nothing to me."

Big Roger said, "Don't be so cold, Q. Tee is just a little boy."

"Well, he needs to stay in a little boy's place."

"Boy you are a fool, Q, "Travis said.

I turned the subject to Travis.

"Travis, you know I had a crush on your sister back when we were kids. It's just something about big girls that do something to me," I said, while laughing.

"Butch whipped your ass for messing with my sister. I remember that," Travis said.

"Big Roger and Travell was the ones that dared me to get on top of her when she was asleep," I responded.

Big Roger broke out laughing.

Travis said, "I miss Travell."

I responded, "I miss him, too. You know what I miss most about him?"

Tee asked, "What you miss most about him?"

"I miss him beating them drums at church. Boy, he would beat them drums like he was a professional," I said.

We all got quiet for a full minute.

Then Travis said, "Q, you got to hook me up on Friday. I know after the game you gonna have some girls."

"Your mama will kill me if she knew I was out here getting you pussy," I said.

"Go head man, why do you always have to try to get a laugh," Travis said.

Big Roger said, "I thought you was going to be gay when you was little, Travis."

Travis asked, "Why you say that?"

"Because you hung around your mother and sisters so much," Big Roger stated.

I said, "I thought the same. That's why I let you hit you-know-who, while I was going with her."

Big Roger, "Damn Cuzo, you ain't never let me hit a girl you was going with. You only let me hit Pig."

Pig was one of the neighborhood bust it crack-heads babies.

"Hell, I gave you the game too. You know how to get women now," I responded.

Then I pulled out a crack rock.

"You see this rock here, it can get you money, pussy, TV's and cars," I said.

Travis said, "Put that up. We don't need Tee seeing that."

Tee said, "I don't like crack rocks. You need to get that stuff out of my grandmother's apartment."

Big Roger shouted, "Shut your scary ass up Tee. As a matter of fact, get out my room."

I said, "Don't put the little nigga out. Let him see the real."

Travis said, "He talks too much."

"Are you going to say something about what you saw in here Tee?" I asked.

"No," Tee responded.

"This is street education. You gonna need this Tee."

"I'm not going to say nothing, "Tee said.

After Big Roger finished cutting my hair, I brought up Butch's name.

"Look Big Roger, I don't have nothing against Butch. Hell, I don't care if he cheated on my mother, but when he started treating me wrong because I saw him, now that was messed up."

Travis said, "You need to let that go."

CRUMBLING TALENT

I said, "I can't let that go. Butch gave me one of the worse ass whips of my life. The nigga traumatize me when he whipped me when my teacher lied on me about stealing her fishing rods back when I was in eighth grade."

Travis responded, "I remember that."

"Don't y'all know the teacher called two weeks later and told my mother that her husband had taken the fishing rods out her car and cleaned them and she had made a mistake by thinking I stole them. Butch took that white woman's word over mine. I was through with him that day."

"Come on, superstar, let it go," Big Roger said.

"Maybe one day I will, but right now, no," I said.

I ended my conversation about Butch and then got into a conversation about how to treat a woman.

"Look y'all, I'm going to give y'all game that I learned from my father when he was around," I said. "He told me to always make love to a woman's mind. See, a woman don't just climax by you sticking your dick in her. You got to fuck her mind. You do that by teasing her," I stated.

"What are you talking about?" Tee asked.

"This might be too much for you, Tee. This is for Big Roger and Travis," I said.

Big Roger said, "So, you saying just tease her by acting like she's the only woman."

"Yes. Make her feel special. Touch her all over her body when she gives you permission. I don't want one of y'all to get a rape charge," I said.

"I will never get a rape charge," Tee said.

"Never say never, Tee," I said.

Big Roger said, "Get up out my chair."

"It is time for me to go," I said.

I gave Big Roger ten dollars for cutting my hair. Then I gave all of my cousins slaps on their hands and left out the apartment. It was time to go sell some dope. I hit the block in the front hole of the projects, and I stood out on the block for about an hour before I went home.

When I finally caught up with Nicole after had she gotten out the hospital, she was holding a grudge.

She asked, "How da fuck did you find out where I stay?"

"Your brother, Sam," I answered.

Sam gave me his baby momma's address and told me that Nicole was staying with her in Piedmont Court Projects.

"I don't want you around," She said.

"Why, Willie outta jail?"

Nicole looked good. Her hair was done up in a nice style with her bangs hanging over her forehead. She was wearing red lipstick and some eyeshadow. The light green, ultra-tight, fitting dress was showing off her curves, cuts and corners. She definitely didn't look like she had just given birth to a child. She looked better than she did the night I had met her at the club.

"Willie is on his way to pick me up," she said.

"Where is the baby?" I asked.

"It's not your baby," she stated, in a hatful tone.

"I didn't come here to fuss and fight."

Nicole interrupted, "You don't have a baby here. We already discussed that when I was in the hospital. Willie is her father."

"You are tripping," I said.

"You got too much stuff going on in your life, Qualude. Let me do you a favor. This is my child, so I should have the right to decide who the father is," Nicole uttered.

"You really sound childish, Nicole," I said.

"I carried this child for nine months, you didn't."

"I brought you the food to feed that child," I responded.

I was sounding petty like her.

"But Keosha came from me," she said.

"She came from me first. I planted that seed," I replied.

"You're just a seed donor, just like your father," she said.

CRUMBLING TALENT

Nicole was trying to get under my skin.

"That's why I'm here, so I won't be like my father," I said.

"Q, this ain't no come when you want to be a daddy game. Being a father takes being in a child's life twenty-four-seven. Keosha don't need a part time father," Nicole said.

"Just listen to me, Nicole. You know my past with my father. You know I don't want to be nothing like him. So why you keep trying to make me feel like I'm trying to be like him?" I said.

"You shouldn't have disowned her," she responded.

"You are tripping," I said.

Nicole was trying to show out for the bystanders on the block in front of the building. I was sick of her game, so I waved her off and went got in my jeep. I didn't have time to fight with her. I looked at her as she walked in the apartment and got our baby girl and returned to the porch. I turned the key and the engine came alive. I pulled off thinking, Nicole is going to be trouble.

I went straight to my basketball game. We were playing West Charlotte, a historical black school, and this was the same school Geneve's brother had won a high school basketball championship at when he was in the tenth grade. Coach Davis was waiting on me when I pulled up in the parking lot. He was mad at me because I didn't take the bus with the team.

He asked, "Where have you been?"

I spoke, "I had some business to take care of."

He said, "We have to talk."

We entered the Gym and we walked to the locker room. I got dressed for the game. Then we hit the court. We went on a ten on run when the game started. At halftime, we were up by five.

Coach Davis waited until the team took the court before he pulled me back in the locker room and said, "I heard you been gambling on the games. I'm very disappointed in you."

I responded, "No, I haven't, Coach. I would never do that. It's all a rumor. I wouldn't put my future in jeopardy.'"

He said, "Pop came to me. He said you gambled on games with him."

I thought Coach Davis knew about the tournament I had played in for Pop.

He continued, "I want this to be the first and the last time I hear you are or had gambled on games. If I hear it again, or if you breathe wrong, you will be through here."

I knew Coach Davis was serious because he benched me the second half. We still won.

❖   ❖   ❖

QUALUDE

Denise called me at my uncle LJ's apartment. I was getting ready to go to sleep when I looked at the caller ID.

"Hello," I said.

"We need to talk," she said.

"About what?" I asked.

"I'm pregnant!" She said.

"What?" I asked.

"Yes. I am pregnant," she said, as she stressed her words.

This new revelation was going to change my life. I was no longer going to just be defending myself, but I would have to defend for Denise and the baby.

"How far along are you?" I asked.

"I am four months," she responded.

"What? Why did you wait so long to tell me?" I asked.

"I thought you would notice."

"Boy, I don't know what to say."

"Say you want it," she responded.

"I do want it. But I don't know anything about taking care a baby."

"Me either. But we can learn as we go."

Nicole had taught me a lesson about jumping the gun when it came to claiming kids. I didn't want to claim Denise's child until I knew for sure it was mine.

"Did you tell Tony Kit?" I asked.

CRUMBLING TALENT

Denise had denied the fact that she went on a date with Tony when I had asked her.

"There you go again. Why do you have to bring up his name? I didn't have sex with him."

"But you went out with him."

"We just talked about you the whole time. I didn't get pregnant by talking to him."

"I think you two done more than talked," I said.

She interrupted, "Please Qualude, you got to believe me. I would never cheat on you."

"You cheated when you went out with Tony."

"I promised you, I didn't have sex with him."

"But you went out with him."

"Can you forgive me? I forgave you for all the stuff you done."

"I don't know."

"Now you are being selfish."

"No, I'm not. I just don't want to make a fool out myself."

"How are you going to make a fool out yourself?"

"If the baby in your stomach ain't mine, I will be the laughing stock of the hood."

"It is yours. There is no doubt about it in my mind."

"Well it's doubt in mine, because I don't know how long you been messing with Tony."

"You are crazy. I only went out with him one time."

"I don't know that."

I ended the call with Denise when I told her I needed to get some rest for school. Then I sat up thinking about if the baby wasn't mine. I came to the conclusion that Denise hadn't been cheating on me. As a matter of fact, I was still the only person she had had sex with.

DENSIE

I was sitting in the living room waiting on a cab so I could go to my doctor's appointment. Aunt Peggy was going with me, but we couldn't take her car because it wasn't working. It needed a new timing belt. Qualude had promised me that he would go to the doctor with me. He had lied.

When the cab finally arrived, I was upset with Aunt Peggy because she had been in the kitchen drinking liquor. She was now drunk. We got in the cab and she got into a lip boxing match with the driver. He wanted to call the police on her but I convinced him not to.

Once in the doctor's office, I was called to the back by Doctor Clark.

He did a quick physical on me. Then he took my blood pressure and then did a ultra sound. Aunt Peggy watched the whole process.

After he went to get the images of my baby, Aunt Peggy said, "I'm taking you to Taps. You need to go to school."

Taps was a school for pregnant teenagers. Nikki had been a student at the school. She had attended for a month before she quit.

"I'm only going if you take me every day," I said.

"I can do that," Aunt Peggy responded.

Doctor Clark returned to the room, then he said, "Your little girl needs you to be active."

Aunt Peggy said, "I knew it! We need some girls. We got all boys."

I said, while sticking out my lips, "I wanted a boy."

Doctor Clark responded, "Maybe next time."

Aunt Peggy replied, "It ain't gonna be a next time."

I said, "Qualude wants a boy. He gonna be mad."

"You get what God gives you," Aunt Peggy said.

Doctor Clark gave me the picture of my baby. Then I got dressed and Aunt Peggy and I headed out to the lobby. Once in the lobby, I called Nikki.

She asked, "What are you having?"

"A girl." I responded.

"That's good! We need some girls in the family," Nikki responded.

"Qualude wants a boy," I stated.

CRUMBLING TALENT

"Why it always have to be about Qualude?" Nikki asked.
"Because I love him, and he wants a boy," I said
"Girl, you sound childish right now," Nikki responded.
"I know he wants a boy because he told me," I said.
"Well, you got a girl. Be happy."
"Have he called?"
"Who?"
"Qualude."
"No, you know that boy is probably on the block somewhere."
"He told me he was going to come with me today. He lied Nikki," I said, as tears flooded my eye lids.
"Are you crying?" Nikki asked.
"Yes."
"Where is Peggy?"
"She over by the door waiting on the cab."
"Look, Qualude probably got a good excuse why he didn't show up."
"Stop taking up for him, Nikki."
"I ain't taking up for him. I am just saying he's a good person.
"I just feel like I'm doing this all alone," I said.
"You ain't alone. Peggy and I got your back," Nikki responded.
"Aunt Peggy said I got to go to Taps. I don't need no school in my life right now," I said.
"Don't be like me, Denise. Education is the key to a better life. We got to break the curse," Nikki replied.
"I don't know, Nikki. I just don't know, Nikki." I said.
"Do you still think Shameka's son is Qualude's son?" Nikki asked.
This question came out of nowhere.
I asked, "Why you ask?"
She said, "Because it like you are emotional. I believe you want a boy because you think Shameka's son is Qualude's."
"That not it," I responded.
"Then why are you stressing?"

"Nicole got a girl, and I believe that's Qualude's baby," I said.

"What?"

"Yes. She had a girl. Everyone in the hood is saying it's his baby."

"How you find out?"

"Qualude told me when she had it. He said she called him while she was at the hospital," I said.

"So, he told you he's been with her?"

"No. He is denying it. I don't believe him though."

"Did he say anything about taking a blood test to clear up this situation with Nicole?" Nikki asked.

"When I brought up the subject about the test, he brought up Tony Kit's name. He told me if he gets a test for Nicole's daughter, he's going to get one for my baby," I said.

"What did you say?"

"I told him we can do it," I said.

"What did he say then?"

"He got mad and left me on the porch," I responded.

"Y'all be tripping."

"No, it's all him Nikki."

"If he brings Tony's name up again, tell him to just get a test."

"I am."

"I'mma talk to you when you get here," Nikki said.

"Okay," I responded and hung up Aunt Peggy's cell phone.

❖   ❖   ❖

QUALUDE

Just when I thought things couldn't get no worse, Uncle LJ got robbed. A guy name Tim Mosely had hit him in the head with a pistol and took nine ounces of crack from him. When I walked inside the apartment, Uncle LJ was sitting on the couch holding his head.

"What up? I got here quick as I could," I said.

"I'm in a messed-up situation. I owe Pop money," he said.

CRUMBLING TALENT

"What are you talking about?" I responded.

"I got Pop to front me some crack. I didn't tell you because I was planning to break away from him," Uncle LJ said.

"What do this have to do with you getting robbed?" I asked.

"I don't have the money to pay Pop," he responded.

"I got money," I said.

"How much?" He asked, excitement in his eyes.

"I got seven thousand," I replied.

"That's not enough to pay him," he said.

"How much you owe him?" I asked.

"Twenty thousand dollars," he responded.

"When do you have to pay him?" I asked.

"In two days."

"I can get all the money," I said.

"From where?" He asked.

"Butch! I know where he keeps his money for his number business," I responded.

"For real?" He asked.

"Yes. I got you." I said.

"Thanks Nephew."

"I got one question. Why would you go mess with Pop after I told you he was trying to blackmail me?" I asked. I had told my Uncle about the blackmail plot when I moved in.

"I don't know Nephew," Uncle LJ said.

I went over to my mother house the next day. I still had my key to the house. I went straight to Butch's closet, where he had the cash stashed. I took thirteen thousand. Then I returned to Uncle LJ's apartment. He was waiting in the living room on me.

I said, "I got the money." Then I tossed the bag on the table. I watched as Uncle LJ opened the bag with the money in it.

He said, "You did it, Nephew."

"Yes, I did," I answered.

"I promise you; I will return it when I flip it a few times," Uncle LJ stated.

"I believe you unc," I said.

CHAPTER 12

QUALUDE

After Uncle LJ paid Pop, we got busted with small amounts of crack on West Blvd. I was sick when Officer Funderburk took Butch's money from me. When we got to the police station, Officer Funderburk took us to different rooms. Uncle LJ and the driver, Donnie, was put in one room. I was put in a room across the hall from them.

Officer Funderburk walked in the room and asked, "Do you play ball for Olympic High?"

I responded, "Yes. The playoffs are next week!"

He replied, "You might not see the playoffs."

"Why?"

"You got caught with three grams of crack. That's a year in prison for you."

"What?"

"Yes. It's your dope, right?"

"Come on, Officer Funderburke."

"Do you have any information for me?" He asked.

"No! I don't have information for you. I'm not a snitch."

"Well, I'm going to get your bond set at a high price. See how you like that."

"Look, I'm not a drug dealer."

"I know you're not, but your uncle is. I know your uncle handed you the three grams when I got behind y'all. He's trying to let you take the fall because his record is bad."

Uncle LJ had told me to take the three grams charge for him because his record was, in fact, bad.

Officer Funderburk continued, "I'm telling you Qualude, you are making a big mistake."

"I really don't want to take you to jail. It would be hard for me to look at my son if I take you to jail."

I had been friends with Officer Fanderbuck's son all through junior high school.

"I know it's part of the job. Trust me, your son won't lose any sleep because I'm in jail," I responded.

"My son might stop talking to me if you get some time in prison."

"You don't have to play mind games with me. I'm claiming the three grams. They are mine."

"So, your loyalty is with your uncle?" Officer Funderburk asked.

"Yes. Family is always first when it comes to loyalty."

"I don't think he'll be that loyal to you. I believe he'll send you to prison quicker than God can get the news," Officer Funderburk responded.

"Why do you say that?" I asked.

Officer Funderburk walked around the table and got in my face.

Then he smiled and said, "He knows you got a lot to lose. If he really had your best interest, he would take the charge."

Officer Funderburk was right. Uncle LJ wasn't thinking about my future. He was only thinking about himself.

I said, "I did the crime, so I must do the time."

"You sure about this?" He asked.

"Yes, I am sure. I got people in my corner that will go to bat for me."

"I'm going to ask you one more time. Do you want me to take you to jail?"

"Yes."

"I have a question. Who do you have that will go to bat for you?"

"Coach Davis will get me out of this," I said.

"I know Coach Davis on a personal level. When I get through talking to him, he won't like you."

"So, you going to mess me up with Coach Davis?" I asked.

"Coach Davis doesn't like drug dealers," he said.

"I'm not a drug dealer."

"Your uncle is. That's why I need you to help me take him down."

"Why do you want my uncle so bad?"

"He's messing up the neighborhood. Dalton Village projects need me to protect it."

"People have the reason of choice."

"Not when they are addicts."

"I have addicts in my family. My uncle Teddy and my aunt Jackie are addicts. I haven't seen you in the hood helping them."

"If I get your uncle off the street, that will help your Uncle Teddy and your Aunt Jackie."

"I can't help you."

"Well, you are about to get another number."

"What are you talking about?"

"You are going to prison. You are already on probation for breaking in cars when you was sixteen."

"Do what you got to do."

"Are you sure?"

"I'm sure."

Officer Funderburk charged Uncle LJ, Donnie and I with selling cocaine. He also charged Uncle LJ with trafficking crack cocaine. This charge carried a ten-year sentence in state prison. We all were looking at prison time..

Uncle LJ got Donnie and me out after he got himself out. We started selling crack together again. It didn't take us long to build up to a kilo.

CRUMBLING TALENT

❖   ❖   ❖

QUALUDE

Officer Funderburk caught me slipping again. I was on my way to school when he pulled me over.

When he walked up on the driver side of my jeep, he said, "I know you are dirty, Mr. Jones. Give me the drugs."

I responded, "What are you talking about?"

"Please don't make me use force on you, Mr. Jones," he said.

"I don't have anything illegal," I responded.

He pulled me out the car like I was a common criminal. Then he placed the handcuffs on me and put me in his patrol car. I knew it was over with when he called in backup. His backup brought a drug dog. The dog went straight to my gas tank. Ten grams of crack was there.

Officer Funderburk said, "I'll take him in, Jim. Thanks for the dog."

I was processed and the judge at the jail gave me a ten-thousand-dollar bond. I called Big Mama. She answered on the first ring.

"What are you doing in jail again?"

"I got busted on my way to school," I said.

"I didn't think it was true you was selling drugs like everyone was telling me but I should have knew better. Your grandfather, Ben, was real slick. I should have known the apple didn't fall far from the tree."

Big mama was talking in riddles.

I said, "Call Uncle LJ and tell him to get a bondsman to get me out. My bond is ten-thousand dollars," I said.

"So, your uncle got you selling drugs?"

"I don't have time to fight with you Big Mama. The phone is about to go out," I said.

"Ain't nobody tell you to be grown and get yourself locked up. As a matter of fact, I don't want you to come to my home anymore. As long as you selling that stuff don't come here."

Big Mama hung up the phone on me. I was sick. I didn't know what to do. Two hours later, Uncle LJ paid my bond. They called my name at the intake for me to leave. Uncle LJ was waiting in front of the jail in a rental car.

He opened the door and asked, "What was you thinking nephew?"

I said, "I've been selling drugs in school. I thought Big Boo told you."

He responded, "Big Boo didn't tell me shit. Look man, you are crazy. Why would you sell drugs in school?"

I replied, "Because it's young crackheads in school and young drug dealers that need crack."

He said, "You know, you might have messed up your career."

I said, "I don't have the credits to graduate anyway. So, it doesn't matter."

He said, "What do you mean?"

I said, "Coach Davis has been getting my teachers to change my grades so I could play ball."

"Fo-real," he responded, like he was surprised.

"Yes. I have been faking it to make it. Big mama and my mama think I'm graduating. I lie to them. I feel bad about it," I said.

"So, Coach Davis has been using you?" He asked.

"Yes. Fuck him and that school," I said.

"No nephew. You can't take that type of attitude towards your situation. You got to find a way to finish school. What about summer school?" Uncle LJ said.

"My ego won't let me do it," I responded.

"You got to drop the ego," he said.

"I'm in the drug game now. Look what we been through."

"You got the wrong attitude. I'm sorry to tell you, you can't sell drugs your whole life," Uncle LJ replied.

I said, "Unc, I don't want to talk about this right now. Man, drop me off at the city bus station."

He asked, "For what?"

I responded, "I need some time to myself."

CRUMBLING TALENT

Uncle LJ dropped me off at the bus station. I took the number ten bus to Big Roger's neighborhood.

I went straight to Big Roger's new apartment. When I arrived, he was sitting in the living room with his roommate. Big Roger introduced me to Jazz and then Big Roger and I went to his bedroom.

He spoke, "You want a haircut?"

"Boy, I need one. Go head and cut me," I said.

"Sit down in this chair," he responded.

Big Roger had a kitchen chair in the corner of his bedroom. I sat in it and asked, "Where is Travis?"

"He's on his way over here," he responded.

"How is he getting over here?" I asked.

"The city bus, "Big Roger responded.

"What are y'all doing tonight?" I asked.

"We are going to Sugar Shack tonight! Do you want to go with us?" He asked.

"Naw, I don't have no money. You know I just got out of jail."

"Look, I'mma pay your way, "Big Roger responded.

"Okay. But I got to be home before two am," I replied.

"Don t worry I got you," he responded.

Travis showed up 30 minutes later. Big Roger, Travis and I climbed in Big Roger's car. His reverse gear didn't work, so when we pulled up at Club Sugar Shack, we pushed the car in a back parking space close to the exit. Once in the club, Big Roger brought us drinks. Then we hit the dance floor.

It had been a while since I had been on a dance floor. Since I grew up doing the Michael Jackson dance, it came back natural to me. Several girls surrounded us. Travis wasn't a dancer, so he sat back watching us. Out of nowhere came J-Bone. He was from Dalton Village Projects and he was a great dancer.

He asked, "What's up, Qualude?"

I said, "Nothing. I just got out."

He responded, "I heard. You know, all the niggas in the hood was hoping you didn't get out."

"Why?" I asked.

"They were putting their bids in for Denise," J-Bone stated.

"Fo-real?" I asked.

"Naw. I was just joking," J-bone said.

J-Bone walked off and started dancing with this thick, big butt, girl. He was freaking her. The music changed to Biggie Smalls "One More Chance" song. J-Bone was all on this girl's butt until a guy knocked him out cold. Big Roger punched the guy that hit J-Bone. Then a shot rang out. I looked back at a guy in a wheelchair five feet away from us. He and I made eye contact. Travis saw him too. He had shot Big Roger, but the bullet wasn't affecting him.

Big Roger shouted, "Let's go."

We picked J-Bone up to his feet. Then, we all turned and rushed out into the long hallway that led to the front of the club.

As we got to the lobby, Big Roger looked at me and said, "I think I got stabbed in the stomach."

He was holding his stomach with both of his hands. A blood spot of blood was on his shirt. When he removed his hands, I saw a hole.

"Sit down," I suggested, as we got to the lobby. He sat down against the wall. I shouted, "Call an Ambulance!"

The crowd was running out of the club, and people were falling all over each other.

Big Roger said, "Don't leave me, Qualude."

I responded, "I'm not going to leave until the Ambulance get here."

Travis was standing over Big Roger.

As I was looking towards front entrance for the Ambulance, Big Roger said, "Go head and go. I don't want you to get in trouble with your probation officer."

I didn't want to leave his side, but I knew if I didn't, and my probation officer found out, I would be put back in prison.

The next day, I went to see Big Roger. He was sitting up in his hospital bed with his girlfriend, Angie, on his side.

When I entered the room, he spoke, "I can't believe you are out."

I asked, "Why you say that?"

He said, "I just thought you was never going to get out because most young black men that are going to jail for drugs are getting ten to twenty years."

I said, "God got me, Big Cuz."

He quickly changed the subject.

"Do you know that dude that shot me?"

I responded, "No!"

He said, "Well, we use to go to West Mecklenburg High School together. His name is Peewee. We fell out over a girl back in the day. The girl had a baby. He thought I was the father."

"So, you believe that's why he shot you?" I asked.

"Yes!"

Big Roger didn't look bad. He looked like he was just getting some rest.

Angie interrupted, "You need your rest. You don't need to be talking about nothing."

Angie looked high. I had heard she was using drugs but I couldn't judge her, because I was selling them.

I asked, "How are you, Big Roger?"

He responded, "I don't feel too good. This hospital is going to kill me. They can't get the bullet out. They say the bullet keeps moving and they can't find it. They also said it's messing up my insides."

"Man, that sounds bad," I answered.

"It is bad. I don't think I'mma make it, cuzo. If they operate on me one more time. I believe it will be over for me," Big Roger responded.

Charlotte Memorial Hospital was known for killing people. Especially black people. This hospital did just that to Big Roger. When I found out he was dead, I was sitting out on the block.

I was shocked because a detective walked up on me and said, "Big Roger is dead. Are you going to let his death be in vain?"

I said, "I can't help you. Please get away from me. You are trying to get me murdered."

I felt bad when Detective Macfadden walked back to his car. I called Travis.

He answered, "Hello."

I said, "The cops are asking about who killed Big Roger. Have they been to your place?"

He said, "Yes. I told them I didn't know nothing."

I asked, "Why did you do that?"

He said, "I can't put my mama in danger."

Travis was thinking like me.

I said, "If I hear anything, I'll call you."

He asked, "Are you okay?"

I said, "No. I don't know what to do."

A week later, I pulled up at Big Roger's funeral in my jeep. I didn't get a warm welcome. It was clear to me that his mother thought it was all my fault that he had gotten murdered. Her demeanor was cold as ice towards me. She didn't even give me a hug. It was like she didn't understand I was hurting just as much as she was. I had spent a lot of years with Big Roger. We were close, like brothers.

His mother watched me the whole time I was in front of the casket. Big Roger looked good. The people at the funeral home had dressed him in a nice suit. His hair was cut neat. As I walked away from the casket, I noticed my mother on the second row, behind Big Roger's mother. She just stared at me. She didn't even smile.

Once outside, I got back in the jeep and broke down. I couldn't believe Big Roger was dead. There wouldn't be no more haircuts by Big Roger, fun times and life lessons together. He was gone. A piece of me dead the day he died.

❖   ❖   ❖

DENISE

Qualude called me and asked, "Can you meet up with me?"
I said, "Yes."
"Where do you want me to meet you at?"
He replied, "Come to the Front Hole close to West Blvd."
I met him at the stop sign close to West Blvd. I got in his jeep and he pulled into traffic. It was late, so my Aunt Peggy was asleep and Nikki was watching TV. I didn't have to worry about them worrying about me.
Qualude asked, "How are you doing, pregnant girl?"
I answered, "I'm doing okay, Hot Boy. Your name is ringing like a phone in the hood."
He said, "That's why I haven't been to see you. Everyone want to know he murdered Big Roger."
"Word is you let the wrong man get locked up for the murder," I answered.
"People can be so cruel," He said.
He was upset. I could tell Big Roger's death was bothering him.
I asked, "Do you know who murdered him?"
He said, "Yes. Big Roger told me right before he passed away. I don't know why he didn't tell the police himself."
I said, "Because he didn't know he was going to die."
Qualude looked at me and said, "He knew he was going to die. He told me before he had his last operation."
"Why is everyone saying it's your fault that he's dead??" I asked.
"Because I won't talk to the police about death," he replied.
"You know everyone want closure for his death," I said.
"But I don't want to put no one in harm's way for talking to the cops," he responded.
"I understand what you are saying, but what about his mother?" I asked.
"Please don't do this right now." He said.
"I'm just saying. What if it was your kid?" I said.
He shouted, "Travis was there, too. He knows what hap-

pened."

"He's not as brave as you, Qualude. You are a leader." I said.

"I can't do. I just can't."

"Are you worried about the street code?"

"No!"

"Well, why?"

"Like I told you, I don't want to put no one in harm's way. I couldn't live with myself if something was to happen to you," he answered.

"It's okay if you don't do it, but you got to live with it."

"I know. Why you got to keep on talking about this?" He said.

"I have one question. Are you still upset with Butch about cheating on your mother?" I asked.

"No! Why are you asking me that?" He asked.

"I was just thinking, you didn't tell the police about the murder because you was mad at Butch," I responded.

"I don't know why you would think that about me."

"You know how you like to get revenge. Don't act like you wasn't mad about Butch whipping you because he thought you stole those fishing rods from your teacher."

"I would never not help my family because I'm mad."

"Well, you was mad at Big Roger's mother, because she laughed in your face when Butch was whipping you," I said.

"Please stop Denise."

Qualude had told me the story about the fish rods when I first met her.

Qualude turned the jeep on the freeway. We were heading towards Carolwinds Amusement Park.

He said, "I don't hate Butch that much, or his sister, to not help them."

I said, "Don't dwell on it no more."

He responded, "How can I not?"

I knew Qualude was going through a lot, but there was nothing I could do to help him.

He continued, "You know I might be going to prison for a

CRUMBLING TALENT

year."

I asked, "For what?"

He said, "For those two drug charges."

I said, "So you leaving us."

He said, "Just for a year. Can you wait on me?"

I said, "Yes."

"Are you mad at me?"

"No! I'm mad at your uncle. You know he should have took his own case. Why would he ask you? And why would you take it?"

He answered, "He has a bad record. His record would have sent him away for about ten years.

"What about you? You got a baby on the way. You might not even get to see the baby born."

"I know."

"Your cousin, Ladricak, told me Uncle LJ don't care about no one but himself."

"She talks too much," he responded.

"I'm family. She gonna tell me everything now."

"I forgot you was family. But we aren't married."

"We can get married if you want."

"I'm not ready. Maybe one day."

I kissed Qualude on his cheek. He took me over to Uncle LJ's apartment and we had sex for three hours straight. He took out all his stress on me. He didn't hurt the baby, but it felt like he was trying to. He dropped me off back home in the projects. I learned a lot about Qualude in that little bit of time with him. I now knew he was a struggling black boy trying to make something out his life in this White Man's World.

QUALUDE

When I walked in Coach Davis' office, I knew he knew I had been arrested and charged with selling cocaine again. The look on his face told me he wasn't going to let this go.

He said, "Didn't I tell you that you couldn't afford to get into any more trouble?"

I responded, "Let me explain Coach."

"There is no need to explain, Qualude. I got to let you go. You have brought too much negative attention to the basketball program here and me."

"So, it's about the program and you only?" I asked.

"Yes, it is. You must understand something, son. I went out on a limb for you. I put my job in harm's way for you."

"I understand everything you did for me Coach Davis, and I appreciate but I brought this school back from the dead. Olympic High hadn't been to the playoffs in twenty years."

"I agree."

"So, why you can't help me this time?"

"I tried Qualude. Trust me, if I could I would, but the judge I know at the courthouse said there is too much media attention. He also said your second charge warrants a prison sentence.

"He is the judge. He makes the rules in the courtroom. He can overlook the charge if he wants to."

"Too many eyes are watching your case. If the media hadn't got ahold to it, then he could have easily gave you some more probation. But the media has it now. He just can't do it."

"So, now I'm going to prison?"

"Yes."

"I don't know anything about prison,"! said.

"I'm sorry, son, but I suggest you get familiar with it."

"You suggest I get familiar with it. What kind of Coach is you? You already done gave up on me."

"You gave up on yourself when you decided to sell drugs."

"All the stuff I done for this school and you just going to give up. I made this school money off the sports here. Before I stepped on the court, this school couldn't get no one to come to the games."

"I understand your point, and I know you are upset about this situation."

I interrupted, "Yes, I am upset, because I know it's something you can do."

"It's nothing I can do. For God sake Qualude, you are not looking at the big picture. All you had to do was stay out of trouble, but no, you couldn't do that. You done this to yourself. You can't blame no one but yourself."

Coach Davis was right. I had made a lot of bad choices and decisions.

"So, this is my end here at Olympic?"

"Yes, it is. It's not personal son. Look at it as a learning experience."

"I looked at you like a father. You are supposed to fight for me and protect me."

"I don't have anything to fight with. You got caught red-handed. I really done all I could," Coach Davis said as he poured himself a cup of coffee.

I felt like crying but the tears wouldn't come.

"Please, Coach Davis, give me one more chance," I begged.

I knew if I didn't beg him that my life would be changing for the worse. Without school, I would be just a nobody. A bum. Without basketball, I wouldn't be able to live.

"I can't. You have been in too much stuff. Your cousin is dead because of you."

"So, you are believing the rumors, too?"

"Detective MacFadden said you knew who murdered your cousin, but you let the police lock up the wrong person. He also told me you was the reason the guy shot your cousin."

I interrupted, "All lies."

"I thought you was a team player. I thought I taught you that."

I said, "I'm not a policeman. It's not my job to solve their case."

"You are sounding selfish right now."

"Maybe I am, but you know I'm not selfish. If I was I would have put my family in harm's way."

"How is that?"

"I don't want to talk about it."

"Two of your cousins are dead. Don't you think it's time to make a change?"

"That's what I was trying to do with the basketball, but it's over now."

"One day you will get the message, because right now, your mind is closed."

"I closed my mind to bull crap, Coach. And what you are feeding me is just that. I'm from the projects, where no one cares about who killed who, because no one is going to protect a snitch. It's like slavery, you are a house nigga and I'm a field nigga. You will never understand how hard it is in the field."

"Please don't look at life like that. Just because I made something out my life doesn't make me a house nigga. You have the wrong mind frame about life."

"I got to look at the reality. I'm just A Crumbling Talent. You was trying to make me into a house nigga, but I failed the test. I understand clearly now."

"You are going to be okay. Don't beat yourself up so much. And please, work on your way of thinking, because the field nigga and the house nigga thing is really crazy."

"I know it sounds crazy to you, Coach, but remember the truth is crazy. Just look at history."

"We can sit here all day and talk about this, but I can't. But I want you to know life is a journey, and you are going to learn lessons along the way. You just have to take heed to the lessons."

"So, prison is part of my life journey?" I asked.

"For now."

I left Coach Davis' office and went to the bathroom by the gym. Denise's cousin was standing by the doorway. She was a twin.

She asked, "What are you up to? Are you skipping class?"

I responded, "Today is my last day here. I just quit."

She responded, "I did too. How about we go to the locker

room and have some fun before we leave?"

I said, "We can leave our mark."

Denise was far from my mind. I didn't have a second thought about having sex with her cousin twin. I needed the time with her to release the stress that I had built up in me. Yes, I pounded her out and her vagina was making so many different kinds of weird sounds that I climaxed in her.

I dropped her off in the projects and went straight to MC's grandmother's apartment. Telly and MC were sitting on the porch.

I stepped out my jeep and said, "What's up with y'all?"

MC said, "I quit school last week."

I responded, "Well I quit today."

Telly asked, "Why?"

I said, "Coach Davis kicked me off the basketball team."

MC asked, "For what?"

"I know y'all heard I got busted again. Well, he told me not to get in anymore trouble, and I did."

"What happened? How did you get busted?" Telly asked.

"Officer Funderburk caught me while I was on my way to school. I had ten grams on me," I responded.

"What are you going to do now?" Telly asked.

"He can get out on the block with me now. We can take over the Westside," MC said.

"I can't get out on the block with you, MC, because I got to do a year in prison," I replied.

"How you know you got to do a year?" Telly asked.

"Coach Davis told me that the drug charge warrants a year," I responded.

"You are going to need a good mouth piece, and I got just the right one," MC said.

"I am going to need a lawyer. Do you have a lawyer number?" I asked.

"Yes. His name is Norman Butler," MC stated.

"Give me his number," I requested in a demanding tone.

"I got it in the crib, let me go get it," MC said

After MC walked in the apartment, Telly said, "I think I'mma going to try college out. I'mma try North Carolina Central out. I think I can get my parents to pay my way."

I said, "That's an all-black college. I thought you wanted to go to North Carolina for basketball."

"You know football is my first love. I believe once I get there, I can get the Coach to get me in a work student program so my parents won't have to pay for the whole thing."

"So, you ain't messing around with the basketball?"

"No. Basketball is your thang, Qualude."

"Basketball isn't my thang anymore. I'm just a Crumbling Talent. My basketball career is over before it started. I'm glad I don't have to worry about Pop exposing me about gambling for him."

"So, what are you going to do with yourself?"

"I don't know."

"Do like Mom-Bo taught us."

Mom-Bo was my great-grandmother. She was big on Jesus and prayer.

"What is that?"

"Pray about your situation."

"Come on, cuzo. You gonna talk about God right now. I'm at a crossroad here."

"Just try it and see if it works. It might work for you."

MC returned from the apartment with the number in his hand. He gave me the piece of paper and I called Norman Butler.

After the call, I said, "I got to take Norman fifteen hundred dollars by Friday. He said he's gonna make sure I don't get more than a year. He said he might be able to get me more probation."

MC said, "I told you, he is a great mouth piece. He got connections."

I said, "I appreciate your help, MC. And no, I'm not hanging on the block with you."

He responded "You don't know what you are missing."

I took the fifteen hundred dollars to Mr. Butler. Then I headed to Uncle LJ's apartment. I walked in the door and I found him asleep on the couch. I wanted to confront him about what Officer Funderburk said about him asking me to take the first drug charges, but I dismissed the thought and went to bed. I was good for the moment.

CHAPTER 13

DENISE

I was in pain. I had been in pain all night. Aunt Peggy told me that I was going to have the baby in a couple of hours. After her statement, my water broke. Then she took me to the hospital. Once there, they put me in a room and my baby girl started to come out of me. I was hoping Qualude could be at the hospital, but he was due in court.

Qualude didn't even get to sign our daughter's birth certificate. I was upset with him because of this. He told me he would be at the hospital for her birth, but he lied. He also lied about all the girls he had been messing around with. Shameka and Nicole told people in the hood that their kids were, in fact, Qualude's. They both did this while I was in the hospital

When I arrived home, Nikki was waiting in the living room.

She said, "Look at the new mom. She looks like she just had the baby."

I responded, "I still look good, girl."

Nikki was trying to be funny. Her jokes were always out of line and off beat.

She responded, "Let me hold the baby!"

I handed Nikki the baby. Then I took a seat. Aunt Peggy rushed to the kitchen and came back with a cup of liquor. I could smell it as she took a drink.

Aunt Peggy said, "You know I ain't taking you to see Qua-

CRUMBLING TALENT

lude."

Nikki interrupted, "His mother said she wants Qualude to see the baby."

"When did she say that?" I asked.

"She called yesterday. I guess she heard you had the baby."

"So Qualude told his mother he is the daddy?" Aunt Peggy asked.

"I guess he did," I replied.

Qualude told me that he wasn't going to tell his mother he was the father of my baby until he got a blood test. I guess he had a change of heart.

"Have he called, today?"

"No!"

Aunt Peggy interrupted, "He called from jail before I came over to the hospital. I cussed his ass out and I told him not to call here no more."

I asked, "Why did you do that?"

"He don't want to claim your baby, then he ain't talking to you."

"You shouldn't have done that Aunt Peggy. I don't need you in my personal business."

"I was the one at your side when you was having the baby."

"I know, but you still shouldn't have done that."

"Don't tell me what I shouldn't have done. I am the one that's going to be taking care of this baby."

"Why do you always got to be so cruel to Qualude?"

"That boy got too much stuff going on in his life. They say he got his cousin Big Roger murdered. Why do you even want to be with someone like that?"

I interrupted, "No, he didn't. He didn't have anything to do with it. He was just there."

"Well, why he didn't tell the police who did it?"

"Because he was afraid to. He didn't want to put me or the baby in danger."

"So, that's what he told you?"

"Yes. He doesn't know the guy who murdered Big Roger on a personal level," I said.

Aunt Peggy responded, "You are so stupid and you believe everything that boy tell you."

I responded, "I believe him because he has never lied to me."

"You are so dumb. I thought you had a little sense. I can see you are dumb like your retarded mother. That boy got you dick whipped, and you are acting like he has gold in between his legs."

"Why you always think it's just about sex, Aunt Peggy? Why you think someone can't just love me for who I am? Are you mad that you can't get a man that care about you like Qualude cares about me?"

"Well, if he cares so much, why isn't he here?" Aunt Peggy asked with a strong tone.

"Why you always have to be so hateful?"

"I'm not hateful. I'm just keeping it real, like y'all be saying."

"I don't want to fuss and fight with you Aunt Peggy. I wish we could just get along, "I stated.

She responded, "Well, you need to go to your room if you don't want to have this conversation."

"I am a grown woman now. I don't have to take your nonsense."

She quickly responded, "If you are going to stay under my roof, you going to take anything I dish out. So, you better get used to it. Don't get brand new up in here because you got a baby. I will put my hands on you."

"I'm not going to entertain your nonsense."

"So, you think what I'm saying is nonsense? So, was it nonsense when I took you and your sister in when y'all mother got on crack cocaine? Was it nonsense when I went out and sold my body to take care of y'all?" Aunt Peggy asked.

This was all new to me. Aunt Peggy had managed to keep all her secrets to herself over the years. She had never said anything about my mother's crack addiction.

Nikki interrupted, "Come on Peggy, you don't have to go

there with Denise."

She responded, "The little bitch doesn't appreciate nothing, and she doesn't know what it takes to take care of someone. She doesn't know that I'm the only person that cared about her when they were going to throw her and her sister into the hands of the Social Services. I fought for her selfish ass and she haven't told me once that she appreciated what I done for her. She has never said thank you in no kind of way. Now her sister has but she hasn't. Now her sister knows how to say thank you. She understands me."

I said, "I hate when you drink liquor. That stuff brings out the hate in you."

Aunt Peggy responded, "You hate that I drink liquor because it gives me the courage to say what I'm thinking about your selfish ass. You don't think about no one but yourself. You think it's all about you."

Nikki said, "Come on, Peggy, leave her alone."

"She needs to hear this," Aunt Peggy responded.

I said, "Give me my baby, Nikki. I don't want to hear nothing else from her drunk self."

I grabbed my baby from Nikki and went straight to my bedroom. Once in my room, I broke down crying. Aunt Peggy was right about me. I was selfish. I didn't care about no one but myself. This was my reality.

I called Qualude's mother. She answered on the first ring.

"Hello."

"How are you doing, Mrs. Jones?"

"Who is this?"

I responded, "This is Denise. I called because I want you to know I got the baby at home and if you want to see her you can."

She responded, "So, the baby is my son's?"

"Yes."

"Y'all made me a young grandmother."

Qualude's mother had had him at the age of 15. She looked more like his sister than his mother.

I said, "What are they going to do with Qualude?"

"He has to go to court next week. They revoked his bond because he got that other drug charge, and as you know he was already on probation for breaking in the cars when he was sixteen," Mrs. Jones responded.

I asked, "When are you going to see him again?"

She replied, "Next week."

"Can the baby and I go?" I asked.

"Sure."

"How much time you think he's going to do?"

She said, "The lawyer he got said a year, but these things can be tricky. We just have to wait and see."

I said, "Mrs. Jones, I don't know what to do. I'm afraid."

"It's okay to be afraid."

"I know you don't know me that well, but your son has told me a lot about you."

"I'm sure he has. I hope what he said was good."

"It was"

"I heard you had a little girl."

"Yes, I did."

"I'm going to tell Qualude you had the baby when he calls."

"Okay."

"What is the baby's name?"

"Shaquala."

"That's odd."

"I named her after your son."

"Can I talk to you later? I have to get ready to go to church."

"Sure."

Qualude called right after his mother hung up. He didn't get to talk long, because it was close to count time in the county jail where he was being held at. I told him about the baby before the phone went dead.

CHAPTER 14

QUALUDE

When I showed up for court, the room was packed with convicted felons waiting to be sentenced. My lawyer told me that my sentencing would be swift and fast. He was right. The redneck judge entered the court right after I took a seat. Then my name was called by the clerk in the room.

I walked slowly up to the front of the court room where my attorney Norman Butler was waiting on me.

"How does your client plea today?"

"Guilty your honor."

"Well, I can see that the state has agreed to give your client three years in state prison. Is this correct?"

Three years! Mr. Butler told me that I wouldn't even do a year. I had to say something. I raised my hand. The judge recognized me.

"Would you like to speak, Mr. Jones?" The judge asked.

"Yes! I was told I would get a year in prison. Now you are saying I'm going to have to do three years," I responded.

"So, you don't agree with the plea?" The judge asked.

Mr. Butler touched my shoulder and said, "Your honor, my client doesn't understand how the system works. I will explain it to him after the process."

"We don't want to violate his rights," the judge said.

My attorney said, "He agrees to the three years."

"Does he have any family in the court room?" The judge asked.

"No, your honor. His mother was supposed to be here but she had to work. His father is in rehab. And, he has a child now with his girlfriend, Denise. She couldn't make it because she had a doctor's appointment," my attorney said.

"Okay. The plea is granted. Take the defendant into custody."

I spoke as Mr. Butler walked next to me as we headed towards the cell area. "Do I have to do three years?"

"No! As long as you don't get into any trouble, you'll be out within nine months."

"Where am I going?" I asked.

"Polk Youth Center. It's not that bad." Mr. Butler responded.

"Call my mother and let her know where I'm going," I requested.

"Okay," he responded.

I spent two weeks in the county jail fighting for my life. It was like everyone in the cell block was trying to prove something. There were fights over the phone, TV, and the extra trays of food. I felt like an animal the whole time I was there. When I got to prison, things changed for the better.

Polk Youth Center was located in Raleigh, North Carolina. It was down the street from Central Prison, also known as The Wall. My age prevented me from going there. I was happy about that because men were getting murdered there at a high rate.

When I walked through the gates at Polk Youth Center, I was met by a guard who acted like he was an Army drill sergeant. He was issuing commands.

"Stand straight up in line. Keep your head up. No talking." He continued, "You are now the property of the state of North Carolina. You will only get to make two calls a month, so get used to it. I'm your parents now, guys."

This was all new to me. I wasn't used to someone commanding me what to do every minute of the day. When I got to my dorm, I met a guy name Finest, The God. He was from North

CRUMBLING TALENT

Charlotte. He knew Nicole's brothers. He introduced me to all the guys that were from Charlotte. Then he introduced me to all his God Body buddies.

The God Body stuff was new to me. I grew up in the church, and I believed that Jesus died for my sins. The God Bodies didn't believe this. They believed the white man was the devil and the white man was created by a scientist named Yahcuf.

Two months in prison, Finest tried to get me to convert.

I said, "I came to prison to pay my debt, not lose myself."

Finest was a great debater. He could turn the simplest conversation into a debate.

"The white man got your mind. You're a slave to his lifestyle."

"What are you talking about, Finest?" I asked.

"Did you know this is mass incarceration we are a part of?" Finest asked.

"No. And I don't care."

"You don't care because you was out there in the free world killing your own people with drugs," Finest said.

"And?" I responded.

"You are lost. You are a slave to the system," Finest answered.

"Look, Finest, I don't want to be a five percenter."

"Because you are an eighty-five percenter. You are deaf, dumb and blind."

"I don't mean no disrespect, but I didn't come to prison to make friends or change my faith," I responded.

"You know what, Qualude, I respect your decision but it's my duty to enlighten you to my culture. See, the white man is a savage. All he does is steal, kill and rob. Go back and do your history on him. You will see that he stole our culture from us," Finest stated.

Finest was starting to get on my nerves, even though he was spitting facts.

"Okay, I agreed with that part of history. But what about us as black men? We are killing each other at a high rate," I replied.

"Everything falls on the white man, because he brought us

here to America."

"So, you saying he's the cause for us killing each other?"

"Yes. He robbed our communities of their leaders by placing them in prisons and jails around the country. Without the leaders, who's going to lead?" He asked.

"The white man doesn't tell us to go out and do crime."

"But he limits our resources, so we have to go out and do crime. He gives our women welfare checks and food stamps and tell them we ain't fit as men to care for them and the kids," Finest said.

This stuff Finest was stressing to me was deep. I saw these things taking place in my community.

"So, what are we supposed to do?" I asked.

"Turn from the white man's ways. We got to bring our communities back."

"Look, I had a great chance to be something in life, but I blew it," I said.

"It's not your fault, God," Finest responded.

Finest was still trying to convert me. I wasn't having it. I knew a culture, or anything that man created, could be corrupted. The bible had told me this.

"Don't call me God. I'm just a man," I requested.

"The bible says we are Gods," Finest shot back.

"Well, fly over that fence." I said, as I was trying to bring some humor to the conversation.

"Now you are trying to be funny."

"No. I'm being real," I responded.

"Maybe if you came to one of the Gods meetings, you would get a better understand of yourself."

"I know myself. I fucked up my life. But I'm going to get back on track."

"How you going do that?"

"I'm going to get my GED. Then I'm going to try to go to college."

"I heard that before," Finest said. Then he walked off.

CRUMBLING TALENT

The next day I received a letter from Denise's cousin, Nikki. I read over the letter twice before I made out what she was trying to say. Denise's grandmother wanted to admit Denise into mental health faculty for choking my daughter. I had already made my two calls for the months, so I couldn't call.

I sat up all night thinking of the right words to write Nikki. I wrote a few lines and I informed her with these lines to tell Denise's grandmother that I appreciated her help. I also informed her that I would call Denise's grandmother at the beginning of the month. The next day, I dropped the letter in the mailbox and went to see the Chaplin.

I asked the Chaplain to pray with me for Denise. After my time with the Chaplain, I went to school. It was time for me to take my GED. I didn't feel good about taking the test because of the letter from Nikki. But I took the test anyway and passed by a point.

My case manager placed me in the clothes house after I received my GED. This job was easy from the start, and all I had to do was fold blankets after they came out the dryer. I folded over two-hundred blankets before the new inmates showed up at noon. I had to take fifty blankets to the intake area every time a bus came in. After two weeks on the job, MC was brought in.

I hadn't talked with MC the whole time I had been locked up. I wrote him a letter when I was in the county jail, but he never wrote back. I was upset with him for not being there for me in a time of need. Even though I was upset with MC, I was happy to see him.

Before I could speak with MC, I had to wait until he was assigned a housing dorm. I got lucky. He was assigned to the same housing dorm as I. His bed was two bunks over from mine, which made it easy for us to talk after the lights were off.

He spoke, "I know you mad at me."

I said, "No. I got myself in this situation."

"I should have been there for you," he responded.

"I'm right. This time has taught me some valuable lessons about life."

"I wish I can say the same, but I damn near went crazy while I was in the county jail."

"The county jail is crazy."

MC looked me in the eyes and said, "You don't belong here. You have too much talent to be in prison."

"Look who's talking. You supposed to be in college, too."

"College ain't for me."

"You never even gave it a try. So how do you know it ain't you?"

"I just know."

"Did Pop tell you this?"

"You know Pop wanted me to go to college."

"At one time, I think he did, but I feel like he didn't help us by giving us drugs to sell."

"Why do you have to always judge me?"

"I'm not judging Pop. I'm stating the facts."

"That's what I hate about you. You think you know everything."

"I may not know everything, but I do know that Pop wasn't a friend."

"Pop is a friend."

"I can't tell. I heard he let you take a fall for a stolen car his nephew stole."

"His nephew doesn't have a record."

I knew MC was going to take Pop's side.

I responded, "You didn't have a record."

"His nephew has a chance to be something in life."

"You think Pop's nephew's life is more important than yours?"

"You don't understand."

"I understand. I just don't want you to end up like your mother."

"Leave my mother out of this."

"I can't MC. And you know why."

"I know I made promises to my mother that I wouldn't sell drugs or come to prison, but I had to do what I had to do to eat."

"That's not good enough for me."

"Look who's talking, you are the one that had it made. You had your mother."

I could hear the seriousness in MC's voice.

I said, "You made the choice to deal with Pop."

"You did, too. Pop told me that your uncle owed him money, and he also told me that you stole from your mother's house to buy drugs."

"I only did it to help my uncle LJ. That what family do."

"I know blood is thicker than water, but you stole from your mother's house."

"It wasn't my mother's money. It was Butch's money."

"That don't make it right."

MC knew how much I didn't like Butch. He also knew about Butch's cheating ways.

I said, "I feel like I done the right thang. I saved my uncle's life."

"You caused more troubles to your mother's relationship with Butch. He is still cheating on your mother."

"I know what I did was wrong. You don't have to remind me. I know I owe my mother for what I did. That's why I'm trying to better myself while I'm here."

"Okay new dad."

MC and I talked the rest of the night about our futures. We decided we were going to use our time in prison wisely. I helped MC get enrolled in school. He wasn't dumb, as he put out to the world. He was actually smart. I knew his IQ was high when it came to basketball, from being a teammate of his over the years, and it was the same in the classroom. MC was just lazy.

Trouble came knocking a month before MC was supposed to get released. We were playing in a basketball tournament that the prison was hosting, and I got into a fight with a guy named Jimmy from Winton Salem. The fight started because MC was talking junk to him. Jimmy was a big, six-foot-four, dark skinned guy that didn't take no stuff. He didn't like the fact that MC was trash talking to every team we went up against, so when we got to Jimmy's team, he told MC not to say a word to him.

The first part of the game, MC didn't say a word, but when Jimmy's team took a ten-point lead, MC started mouthing off at Jimmy. This took Jimmy out his game. We came back and won the game by three points. Jimmy was mad about the loss. He wanted to fight MC. I stepped in and he swung on me and hit me in the face. I hit him back. A fight broke out between Jimmy's team and our team.

After my shower, I put on fresh clothes and went and laid on my bunk. The mail lady had left letters from Geneve, Nicole and Rhonda on my bunk. I opened Geneve's letter first. I was shocked to learn how much she cared about me. In the letter she said she missed me and wanted to be with me. I thought it was just lust, but her words cut through my soul. I didn't know that she really loved me. I thought it was just my talent that she loved.

Next, I opened up Nicole's letter. She was talking crazy, like always. She wanted child support, because she heard that Denise had taken out child support on me.

It was a drama stunt. I put a letter together, and in it I told Nicole that I would tell Willie the truth about our relationship. Then I moved on to Rhonda's letter.

Rhonda was this girl I was creeping around with while I called myself being Denise's man. I stopped creeping around with Rhonda after she had told me that she was pregnant. She was living with her boyfriend and his sister when she told me I got her pregnant. I didn't think the child was mine, because I was using rubbers with her whenever we had sex.

CRUMBLING TALENT

I dropped Rhonda a few lines right before walked over to MC's bunk. He and his bunk partner were sitting on his bunk. They were listening to late night slow jams. His bunk partner walked off when I took a seat.

MC said, "R-Kelly is Da man."

I said, "Yes, he is."

"I'mma buy his CD when I get out."

"I'mma buy it, too."

"I only got two weeks left," MC stated.

"I'm right behind you," I stated.

MC took a plea for three months for the car conviction. He was lucky that he didn't get more than three months, because he was on probation for disorderly conduct when he pled guilty for the stolen car charge.

MC asked, "What are you going to do when you get out?"

His question caught me off guard. I hadn't really thought about what I was going to do when I stepped out of prison. One thing I knew, for sure was that I wasn't going to sell drugs, but I knew I couldn't close the door on that option, because I knew it was going to be hard for me to get a job because of my record.

I responded, "I don't want to sell drugs."

"I'mma keep it real. I'm going back to da block."

"Why?"

"Because there isn't nothing for me but the block."

"You smart."

"I don't even have my GED."

"A GED is just a General Education. It don't tell who you are."

"The school stuff ain't for me. I'm not you."

"You shouldn't give up so easy."

"I'm not giving up. I'mma be big in the drug game."

"You just don't get it MC."

"Get what, Q?"

"That the drug game ends with death or prison."

"My mother told me that once."

QUALO LOWERY

"Well, I think it's time you take heed."
"You have your life to live. And I have mine."

CRUMBLING TALENT

CHAPTER 15

DENISE

I turned the small radio down that was sitting in the window seal in the living room of my Aunt Peggy's apartment. This was after I took a seat on Aunt Peggy's front porch. I lit a Newport, and then turned my attention to a group of kids who were playing in the dirt field in front of the building. My mind flashed to my daughter. I didn't want her to grow up in the projects like I did. Qualude promised me that he was going to take me out the projects when he made it to the NBA. What a liar. I knew he was full of crap. He lied to me about Keosha. He lied to me about selling drugs and he lied about not being a playboy. I found out that he had had sex with over half of my so-called friends and my cousins. If he hadn't gone to prison, I wouldn't have found out how nasty he was. My heart was hurting, but I couldn't turn my back on the love of my life. My mother told me it wasn't love that I was feeling for him. It was lust.

My cousin, Nikki, interrupted my thoughts about Qualude when she walked out the front door of apartment.

She spoke, "Girl, you don't need to be smoking that cigarette. You just had a baby."

I responded, "My baby is almost five months."

"Still, that isn't good for you."

I blew smoke in Nikki's face after she sat on the porch next to me. I had picked up my nasty smoking habit after my visit with Qualude. Seeing him locked up almost caused me to have an emotional breakdown. Plus, I found out that he had other girls on his visiting list, and this caused drama between us. When I asked him about these girls, he denied them. I cared that these girls were on his visitors list, because I saw them as threats.

Nikki waved the smoke out of her face, before she said, "I'm not your maid. I'm not going to keep cleaning up after you."

I asked, "What are you talking about?" Nikki was always trying to get on my nerves. Her and her three kids had moved back in after she lost her apartment. My relationship with my cousin was good, until I heard she had tried to have sex with Qualude. Her attitude had changed towards him and I. She was no longer praising him. After he quit high school, she stopped doing it.

She responded, "You left your clothes and your baby clothes all over the living room. You know how Peggy is."

I said, "I clean up after your kids and you. So, go head on with da drama."

"It's not drama. I'm just saying that you need to get up on yourself. Qualude isn't the only boy in the world."

"He's a man. Not a boy."

"Excuse me, Miss Thang. But I want you to know that he's a boy to me. Men don't go to prison."

"Look who's talking. Your two baby daddies are in prison."

"For yo infor, Tony is the only baby daddy I got."

"Well, why do you keep telling Peggy that you don't know if Tony is the father of your three kids?"

"Because I was cheating on Tony."

"Whore."

"Your Mama."

Big Boo came walking up the sidewalk.

He shouted, "Denise, when is Qualude getting out?"

I shouted, "When he finish serving his time."

Big Boo's fat ass was always coming around asking about Qualude, but wasn't sending him money or helping me with my baby. Qualude had made sure Big Boo was alright before he went to prison. He told Big Boo to look out for me, but Big Boo's fat ass was tricking off with all the junkies in the hood.

When Big Boo walked up on the porch I said, "Don t bring your fat ass around here unless you bringing some money."

He asked, "What are you talking about?"

"Qualude told me he left you some dope."

"He did. But I fell off."

"How da fuck you fall off?" I asked with an attitude."

Big Boo said, "The police chased me, and I had to throw the package."

Big Boo was lying. I knew he was lying, because I had witnessed him chasing crackheads around the neighborhood.

I said, "You are a lying fat fucker."

"Why you think I'm lying?"

"Because I saw you tricking off with Pig."

Pig was this junkie that lived two doors down from me.

Big boo responded, "You ain't see me with Pig."

"Yes, I did."

"No, you didn't."

"Yes, I did."

Big Boo got mad, and walked off. I resumed my conversation with Nikki.

She said, "Candy is on her way over here."

"What are y'all hoes up to, now?"

"Nothing."

"Y'all up to something. I know y'all whores."

"It takes a whore to know one."

Candy was my favorite cousin. She was good at doing hair and dancing. These things were what we had in common. My cousin, Nikki, was jealous of our relationship. She even told me.

I spoke, "I'm waiting on the mailman. He needs to bring his ass on."

"I don't know why. Qualude ain't writing your ass."

"Why do you always have to spoil the moment?"

"I'm just being real."

The only problem Nikki had with Qualude was that he was in prison. She didn't like men that were in prison. That's why she was so mad at her baby daddies.

I spoke, "Qualude is coming home to me. That's all that matter."

"I don't think so. I heard he's been writing his other baby mama, and they are planning to be together."

"He told me that was a rumor."

"That's what's wrong with you. You believe everything Qualude tell you. Even his lies."

"He lies to be because he doesn't want to hurt me," I said, in his defense.

Nikki shot back, "He lying to you about the baby he has by Nicole. I saw that little girl. She looks like him."

I wanted to hit Nikki in her big mouth, because she was talking too much about Qualude, but I would have been wrong, because I had seen the little girl and she did looked like him.

I responded, "He said it ain't his baby. Therefore, it ain't his baby."

"What are you going to do when Nicole demands to take a blood test?"

"She can't make him take a test."

"A judge can."

I didn't know too much about the court system, but I knew a judge had the power to do anything in his courtroom.

I said, "Just drop the subject."

"Why do you always want me to drop the subject when thangs don't go your way?"

"I don't want to discuss this anymore."

My tone of voice let Nikki know that I was serious. We sat in silence until Candy pulled up in her mother's car. She stepped out of the car wearing some two-inch heels and a yellow and black short-cut dress that made her butt look like a nest of bumblebees had stung it. In her right hand, she had a brown paper bag, and in the other hand, she had her pocketbook. I started smiling as

CRUMBLING TALENT

Candy was walking up the sidewalk towards us. She was working that dress. The guys standing on the block couldn't take their eyes off her. Candy was loving the attention, too, and she put a little exact sassiness in her step before she reached us.

Nicole asked, "Why you always have to make a scene?"

Candy responded, "Because I'mma star."

I said, "Them niggas were on you like you was a piece of steak."

"I am," Candy said.

Nikki said, "It ain't all about you."

"Yes, it is," Candy responded, with some sassiness in her voice.

Candy's body was better than mine, because I had just dropped Shaquala. On a scale of one to ten, she was a seven. Her face took away two points, and her short hair took away the other point. She was always wearing her hair pulled back into a ponytail. This didn't matter to the men that were always drooling over her, because all they ever look at was her body.

I asked, "What took you so long?"

"Girl, I met this fine ass dude at the store. He wanted to take me out to lunch."

"Did you get baby wipes?" Nikki asked.

"Yes. And Rich Boy's number," Candy responded.

"What kind of name is that?" Nikki asked.

"It's his nickname," Candy replied.

Candy handed me the bag with the baby wipes in it. I stood up to go in the apartment, and I felt a sharp pain in my stomach. I grabbed at my stomach.

Nikki asked, "What's wrong?"

I responded, "I got a sharp pain in my stomach."

"You ain't coming on your cycle, are you?"

"No."

"What is it, then?"

"I don't know."

Candy and Nikki helped me into the apartment. I took a seat on the couch. The pain was still there. Nikki and Candy could see that I was in pain. They both offered to get me something for my suffering. Nikki offered aspirin, while Candy offered me some weed. I took the weed. It helped with my suffering a little bit. After smoking a blunt with Candy, I walked upstairs and checked on Shaquala. She was still asleep. I joined Candy and Nikki back on the porch. They were talking about me when I walked out the front door.

I asked, "Why are y'all tricks discussing me?"

"Because, you are dick whipped," Candy said.

"I'm not dick whipped," I responded.

"Yes, you are," Nikki said.

"No, I'm not," I said, then gave them my overbite smile.

Nikki cut in. "I don't know how you can stand there and keep lying. You know Qualude got your ass whipped."

I wanted to blast Nikki's ass, because she knew I knew that she knew Qualude fucked the twins. I didn't blast her because I didn't know if Candy knew.

I said, "Some people can be so phony. They know more about my man than I do."

Nikki responded, "I know you ain't talking about me. If your man would keep his dick in his pants, then there wouldn't be nothing to talk about."

I wanted to slap Nikki's ass, but I knew I would have had a fight on my hands.

So, I said, "People need to stop trying to chase my dick."

"I don't chase dick," Nikki said. "And I wouldn't never chase a dick you had."

Candy cut in. "What did I miss? Where is all this beef stuff coming from?"

"I don't have beef. Denise just need to wake up and smell the coffee, because Qualude is passing out dick like a school teacher passes out lessons."

"Are you serious, right now?" I asked.

Nikki said, "Damn right, I'm serious!"

Candy said, "Y'all need to chill out."

CRUMBLING TALENT

Candy started laughing. I didn't see anything funny.
So, I said, "Y'all bitches want my man."
Candy said, "I don't want no jailbird. They can't fly."
I said, "I saw you checking him out, Nikki. I don't like that shit, and you know it."
"You are tripping. I have never looked at Qualude in anyway but a brother, and you know this."
"What about the time I caught you staring at him at Betty's house, and you told me that you wasn't?"
"I told you I wasn't staring at him. He had something in his hair, and I told him about it."
I caught Nikki staring at Qualude at my grandmother's cookout. She made up this crazy lie about him having something in his hair. I confronted her after he left. She told me it was nothing, but I saw the lust in her eyes. The kind of lust a whore can't hide.
I spoke, "Let's drop the subject before I blank out my mind."
"If you blank out your mind, you better made sure you blank back, because you know I don't care about getting my hands dirty," Nikki stated.
I didn't want to fall out with Nikki over Qualude, but she was trying me like I was still a little girl.
Times were changing, and I wanted her to know, so I said, "We ain't little girls no more."
Nikki could see that I was serious. Candy got in between us.
Nikki spoke, "Girl, you know I will whip your ass. Just because you got a baby don't mean you can beat me."
The sound of the front door caught my attention. It was Aunt Peggy. She was dressed in a pair of tight shorts, t-shirt and slippers. Her hair was in a ponytail. She looked upset.
Peggy said, "Y'all know better. Y'all know I don't have nowhere to live if I get put out."
I said, "Nikki talk too much."
She responded, "No, you talk too much."
I could see that this lip boxing match wasn't going anywhere, so I said, "I'm tired of your shit, Nikki. I just can't stay under the

same room with you any longer."

Aunt Peggy said, "If you going to live here, you going to have to get along with Nikki."

"I don't see that happening," I responded.

"Well, get out!" Nikki shouted.

My grandmother told me if I had any trouble, I could live with her. This was why I cussed Aunt Peggy out, packed up my clothes and baby, and left. It was time for me to move on. I was sick of being ghetto.

CHAPTER 16

QUALUDE

I had two months left before I would be released. MC was a week away from going home, and he still hadn't gotten his GED. I tried to get him to promise me he wouldn't sell drugs, but he wouldn't. I felt like I could make something out of my life after I had received my GED. He felt like it was just a piece of paper, with no purpose.

When MC left, I did some soul searching. I still didn't know what I wanted out of life. Here I was, eighteen years old with two kids, by two different girls, and not a pot to piss in or a window to throw it out of. My mother didn't want me at her house, because I had stolen the money from Butch. When I called her to ask her if could I do my parole there, I could hear in her voice that she didn't want me there. The phone went dead before she could answer my question.

When it was time for me to be released, my mother had told the parole officer that I could stay there, but when I got there, my little sister spilled the beans about Butch not wanting me there. I knew Butch wasn't going to forgive me, even though my mother did.

I thought my jeep would be parked at their house when I got there. To my surprise, Butch had sold my jeep to one of his friends. This set of an argument between Butch and me. After the argument with him, I called his mother and told her what he did. She told me that I deserved it, because I stole his money. I was hurt from her comment. I thought she would take my side since she knew how much I cared about my jeep. She knew this because I had given her rides to work and told her stories about how much I cared about it.

Losing my jeep had taught me a valuable lesson. I learned that family and friends could hurt you, too. This was what made me stop messing around with Big Boo. I was upset with him, too, because he didn't write me a single letter or send me any money while I was paying my debt to society. I considered him family and I loved him like a brother, but he had disappointed me.

Denise told me that he came by while I was locked up. She told me this after I moved in with her and her grandmother.

After several weeks living with Denise and her grandmother I learned a lot of things about her that I didn't know. Denise was a spoiled brat and, when she didn't get her way, she made the people around her feel her wrath. Denise and I were getting into fights about me staying out late. Her grandmother would take my side, because she liked the fact that I was trying to be a father to my kids.

The father routine played out fast. I was getting bored of sitting around Denise and her grandmother all day. That's why I turned back to selling drugs. I hooked back up with my uncle, but I didn't move in with him. Then I hooked up with Melvin. He was selling drugs for Pop again. He wanted me to get down with Pop, but I told him no. He was still messing around with ZZ. ZZ was still messing around with Nuke.

Telly called me a day after his birthday and told me that he had gotten into a fight with Peaches' new boyfriend. He found out that Peaches' boyfriend was Nuke's cousin.

I asked Telly if Peaches was worth fighting over and he said, "Yes. Because she is now pregnant by me."

I asked, "How do you know?"

He responded, "Because she told me."

I didn't want to disappoint my cousin because we had always

had each other's back whenever a problem arose. Telly wanted me to go with him to find Peaches' new boyfriend, because the guy had got the best of him in a fight in front of Peaches.

I agreed to go after he said, "You know I would go with you if you had beef with someone over Denise."

Telly and I rode over to Pine Valley, a middle-class neighborhood, where this guy lived. After riding past the guy's house several times, Telly let off several shots from the hand gun I got from, my Uncle Bear. Telly didn't point the gun at the guy's house because he didn't want to kill an innocent bystander. He just wanted to put fear in the guy.

Two weeks later MC's brother got killed. This shocked me, because Me-Month didn't bother no one. He was shot and killed by the guy Peaches was messing around with. Telly felt like it was his fault, because Me-Month was riding with him when the guy shot up his car. MC took Me-Month's death bad. He felt like the bullet was for Telly. I felt the same, but I didn't say it.

Me-Month's funeral was packed. I rode to the funeral by myself, because I didn't want people see me crying like a baby. Me-Month was my friend too that's why I felt like I had to do something about his death.

After the funeral, I called up MC. He didn't want to talk to me. Two weeks later, the guy that murdered Me-Month was gunned down at a nightclub. Case closed.

After the guy that killed Me-Month was murdered, MC and I started back hanging out together. We were drinking and hitting every club in the city. Nitro's, this strip bar off Betties Ford Road, was our favorite spot. We would go there to pick up chicks and take them to a motel and have sex. This became our weekend routine.

Denise didn't like the fact that I was hanging out with MC. She thought I should be home with her and the baby. I loved my daughter, but I wasn't ready to be a family man. The streets were calling my name, and there were too many women in the street for me to be with Denise. She and I were getting into fights about me staying out late. Most of the time, I would pick a fight with her because I didn't want to be there.

Her grandmother would take my side. This would make Denise mad and she would call her grandmother all kinds of names.

I still wasn't dealing with Big Boo, because he didn't send me any money while I was in prison. He took it hard, because he started hanging out with Lonnie. He thought he was making me mad by doing this. I told him that I hoped he didn't get hooked on drugs. Big Boo told Lonnie what I said, and this caused Lonnie and me to fall out.

QUALUDE

My daddy came back in the picture after he found out I was getting money. He came over to Denise's grandmother's house in the middle of the night. Denise had never met my father before this night. She was caught off guard when he asked me for some crack cocaine. I gave my dad what he came for and then I told Denise not to tell anyone what she had seen. She was upset with me because I had done this transaction in front of her.

Then she asked, "Have you ever sold my mother crack?"

I said, "No."

I didn't think Denise believed me, because she had witnessed me give my own daddy crack. This made her hate me. She started saying things like: "You need to find a place to stay and get a job." I had the money to move out, I just didn't have credit to get my own place. Denise and I still were having sex, but it wasn't every day. This is what made me think she was cheating on me.

One afternoon, I came home to find Denise talking to a guy that we both knew from Dalton Village Projects. I was shocked that this guy knew where we were living. I had been serving this guy crack to sell for about six months. When I pulled up in my car, they both looked surprised. I hopped out my rental car and walked over to them.

CRUMBLING TALENT

Denise said, "J-Rock is looking for you."

I asked, "What da fuck you doing over here J-Rock?"

He responded, "Someone broke in my crib."

I asked, "What do that have to do with me?"

"I thought you might know."

I wanted to f J-Bone up, but I didn't want the police to come because I had crack inside the house.

So, I said, "I don't know. Now, get in your car and get out of here."

CHAPTER 17

DENISE

I almost had a heart attack when I saw Qualude pull up in his rental car. I was trying to be cute, but J-Rock wasn't paying me any attention, because he was mad about the drugs that had been taken from his house. When I made eye-contact with Qualude, I could see that he wanted to kill me. We had been having our fights about him coming in late, and on several occasions, I had found girls numbers in his pockets.

I knew Qualude was jealous, but not to the point that he would embarrass me in public like he did. He grabbed me by my hair and dragged me into the house. Everyone in the neighborhood was watching. My grandmother didn't say a word. After J-Rock left, Qualude beat me up. He didn't beat me bad, but I thought I was going to lose my baby. He didn't know I was pregnant. I decided to tell him when he started beating me again.

He stopped beating me and sat on the bed and asked, "Who's baby is it?"

I was in tears. I spoke, "It's yours."

"How is it mine and we haven't been having sex?"

"It only takes one time."

"It's not mine."

"Yes, it is."

"No, it ain't."

"Who's is it then?"

"J-Rock's."

"No. I didn't do nothing with him. Never have."

"You lying whore."

Qualude had never called me a whore before. I knew this was a new chapter of our lives. He treated me like I wasn't worth the air I was breathing. This caused me to start abusing my daughter.

❖ ❖ ❖

QUALUDE

After I caught Denise with J-Rock I didn't trust her anymore. Even when she told me that she was pregnant, I didn't believe it could be mine. I was only having sex with her once a week. I didn't think I could get her pregnant because we were using rubbers. One time the rubber popped in the course of us having sex, and we kept going. But I didn't think she had gotten pregnant.

It was time for me to do something with my life. I wanted to make a change, and I was sick of selling drugs and messing around with all the different women. I decided I was going back to school. But I didn't know what I would take up. I always wanted my own business, but I didn't know what type of business I wanted to go into.

When I told Telly about my plan, he said, "College might be good for you. It wasn't for me."

Telly had gotten himself thrown out of college after a big fight. This happened while MC and I were doing time at Polk Youth Prison. His parents were still mad at him about getting thrown out because they had paid for him to go. I didn't know if college was for me, but I wanted to find out. I ran the idea by MC. He thought I was crazy. I didn't think it was crazy, because I still could play ball, and I now knew how to read and write now.

I ran into Marco, who was now playing for UNCC. He told me it was never too late to go to school. He was on his way to the NBA, after having a great game against North Carolina Tarheels. Telly and I watched that game and I reminded Telly that Marco and I had won the 12 and under city basketball championship when we were young. This sparked a debate about who was the best out of my hood.

I said, "You know I'm the best."

Telly said, "In your mind, you are the best. But Marco is the best, because he is on his way to the NBA."

I responded, "I taught that boy. He use to have two left feet."

"But them two left feet landed him on the pro scout list. He's projected to go in the high second round. He's going to get pay to play."

"I'm not a hater, but he's not the best. He haven't played where I played. I played in prison."

"That don't make you the best, Q."

"You don't know about prison ball."

"I know there are a lot of thugs that don't know the game in prison."

"That's where you are wrong at. You need to stop watching TV."

"I didn't learn that from TV. I hear people talking about the joint."

"I've been there and done that. There are some of the best basketball players in prison. As a matter of fact, there is a lot of talent in prison that people don't know about because they are afraid to go there."

"Who wants to go to a prison?"

"I didn't want to go, but while I was there, I learned that there are some good people there. Everyone in prison isn't bad."

Telly didn't respond. This subject was out his reach. He didn't know anything about prison and he didn't want to know. He had expressed this on many occasions. I ended the conversation and asked Telly, "Would you like to go to college?"

He responded, "My parents don't have the money."

I said, "I'mma find a way for both of us to go to the same college."

He asked, "How are you going to do that?"

CRUMBLING TALENT

"I'mma find a way."

Telly knew I was good at convincing people to give me what I wanted. He had seen me do this with females through the years. There were times when I got him sex when it didn't look good for the home team. My ability to talk people into doing what I wanted them to do came from Big Mama. She had told me, if I could get people to listen to me that I could get them to do whatever I wanted them to do.

I started working out at the YMCA on Morehead Street. To my surprise, Marco and his cousin were working out at this gym, too. There were other CBA players working out at this gym. These guys were not as good as me. They just took the right road, meaning they finished high school on time and went on to college. My road was different. I finished school in prison, after going all the way to the 12th grade and then quitting high school.

These workouts were not easy. These guys put me through several hard tests, but I passed them all with flying colors. My jump shot was something they hadn't seen at all. It was a mix between Michael Jordan and Dell Curry. My quick release was like Dell Curry's and my swag was like Jordan's. I was labled the biggest trash talker in the gym. I enjoyed just being me.

After several weeks in the gym, I felt like it was time to put my talent to the test. I called up Rod Seaford. He was one of the top AAU Coaches in the city, and he knew about me when I was in high school and he tried to reach out to me after I was kicked off my high school team. I didn't get to talk to Rod after I was put off the team, but I did call him after Marco told me he wanted to help me.

Rod was still Rod. He told me that he had a college that needed a player like me, but I had to be willing to give up the streets. I told him I was done with that lifestyle. He believed me, because he set up a tryout at this Junior College in Winston Salem, North Carolina. He even told me to take Telly along with me. Two weeks before we were supposed to go, I was hanging out with MC, and I decided to break the news to him.

I said, "I'm going to college."

He responded, "Quit playing."

I said, "I'm not playing. It's a junior college in Winston Salem."

He said, "That's good. What are you going to do in college? You are a drug dealer."

"Play ball."

"For real?"

"Yes. Rod Seaford got me a shot."

"That's great."

"You remember when we were in prison, and I told you to get your GED?"

"Why do you have to bring that up?"

"Because you suppose to be going with me."

"College isn't for me."

"You know you want to play ball."

"I can play out here in the streets. Everybody know how good I am."

"The world don't know."

"I don't care if the world know."

"You know the dream."

"That's your dream, not mine."

"All you got to do is want it, too."

"Them people ain't going to let me play for their school. I don't have my GED."

MC didn't know that I always thought he was better than me, and I knew he didn't think so himself.

"I'll take your GED test for you," I said.

He responded, "You crazy."

I said, "I love you like a brother. I'll do anything for you."

"You know I cannot let you take that test for me," he responded.

"So, you going to take it?"

"Yes."

"When?"

CRUMBLING TALENT

"Whenever."
"I'mma get Rod to set you up."
"Do that."
"Don't let me down."
"I got you, Q."

CHAPTER 18

QUALUDE

I dropped MC off at ZZ's house after we left the strip club. She was dressed in some tight shorts that showed off her round butt. She smiled at me as she helped MC into her house. He was drunk from all the shots we had taken at the club. He didn't even tell me good bye.

I stopped by the Waffle House and picked up a Patty Melt and two Waffles for Denise after getting off the phone with her. After getting Denise's order, I headed over to the gas station right beside the Waffle House. After I pumped my gas and purchased Denise the apple juice she was craving for, I turned to find Nuke staring at me. I didn't have beef with Nuke, but I didn't trust him because of his beef with MC.

I got back into my rental and grabbed my .38 special. I made sure that Nuke couldn't see the gun. As he drove past, he smiled at me. I knew what he was doing. He was testing me. He knew that MC and I were close, but he didn't know how close we really were. The next day, MC called me and told me that Nuke had showed up at ZZ's house while he was there. MC said he had to jump out the back window when Nuke started kicking on the front door. I thought this was just some, drama but I was wrong.

The next day, Nuke came to SandHurst looking for MC. I didn't like this, so I said something to MC about it.

He said, "Don't worry about Nuke. He's just mad that I'm still having sex with ZZ."

I responded, "I think you need to leave her alone. She is trouble."

He said, "She isn't trouble. The girl don't want Nuke."

I responded, "She might not want him, but he still think they are a couple."

He said, "You don't know what you talking about."

"Look. I've been on both ends. I know how you feel and I know how he feels. ZZ is just playing both of y'all."

"But I'm not giving her nothing."

"You giving her the attention. That's what this is all about."

"She don't even like attention."

"Yes, she do."

How do you know? You don't know her."

"You blind."

"No, I'm not."

I left MC's crib thinking about how he was going soft for ZZ. I couldn't believe my partner was pussy whipped. How could he let a chick like ZZ get him whipped? This question floated through my mind all day. I couldn't stop thinking about MC's situation, because I felt like Nuke was going to do something to him.

I turned my attention to Denise after I arrived home. She had all my stuff packed up.

She said, "You have to go."

I asked, "What's going on?"

"I don't want you no more."

"You tripping."

"I'm tired of you. You been playing me."

"What are you talking about?"

"You been having sex with everyone in Dalton Village Projects."

"Who told you this?"

"Don't worry about it. Get out!" She shouted. This made her grandmother show up at our bedroom door. My daughter was in her arms.

She asked, "What's going on?"

Denise said, "He's been cheating on me."

I said, "No I have not."

"He's lying. He know he's been cheating."

"No, I have not."

Denise's grandmother said, "He don't have to go nowhere. He can stay here as long as he want. He can sleep downstairs on the couch."

"I want him out of here!" Denise shouted.

Her grandmother responded, "This is my house. You don't pay no bills up in here. So, therefore, you don't tell who can stay or go."

I knew why Denise's grandmother was taking up for me. She really liked me and she didn't want to lose the hundred dollars I was giving her every month. Plus, all the pizza she could eat through the month. I hadn't broken the news about college to her or Denise. I decided it was time.

After I told Denise and her grandmother that I was going to college, all hell broke loose. Denise threw my clothes out of the apartment into the street. I moved out and got my own place. The two-bedroom apartment costed three hundred dollars a month. It didn't take me long to turn the apartment into a drug spot. I was back at my old behavior.

In the first month, I made so much money that I put down payments on two cars. An Acura Legend Coup and a light blue 929 Mazda. Both of these cars were updated models. I put twenty-inch rims and costly sound systems in both cars. Denise didn't like this. It was like she was jealous.

When she found out where I was staying, she showed up at my doorstep with her cousin Tasha on her side. It looked like her belly was about to pop at any moment. Her hair was pulled back in a ponytail and she had on old sandals.

As she banged on the door, she shouted, "I know you are in there!"

CRUMBLING TALENT

I was laying on the couch with a girl name Sherie in between my legs. I had met her the night before. I got Sherie to hide in my bedroom closet while I talked to Denise and Tasha. I told Denise I was still going to college.

She said through the crack of the front door, "You are a lying motherfucker. You are not going to college. You love these streets too much."

Denise was right about I was in love with the streets. But college was still one of my goals.

I said, "I'm going to school. Just watch and see."

"You are lying like you always do. You are too lazy to go back to school."

Denise didn't understand that I wasn't lazy at all. Selling drugs was more than a job. I had to watch myself twenty-four hours day.

I said, "Look who's talking. You didn't even finish high school."

"You wouldn't have your GED if you hadn't gone to prison," she responded back.

"It doesn't matter where I finished at, I got my GED."

"It's your fault that I didn't get to finish. If you wouldn't have gotten me pregnant, I could have finished school."

"You was going to Taps."

Taps was a school for pregnant teenage girls. Denise was going to the school and quit after a week. I learned about this from her sister.

She spoke, "You and your dreams. It's time you come back to the real world."

"This is real."

"Like you told me you was going to the NBA. Look what happen. You lied. My Aunt Peggy was right."

"F you and your Aunt Peggy. Now, get out from in front of my apartment."

I opened the door after my statement.

Denise looked at me and said, "You don't want me to go

downtown. Trust me. I will."

"If you put those white folks in my business, you better not ever say nothing to me."

"When this second one come, you better be here. If you don't, I will put them white folks in your business."

Denise walked out the door behind Tasha. I slammed the door after she left. I went to the closet and opened the door for my one-night stand. She looked afraid.

She asked, "Is it safe now?"

I said, "Yes. You can come out."

YEAR 1996 SUMMER.

Forsyth Technical Junior College looked like a high school to me. There was a student body of five thousand people. This was four thousand more than what Olympic High had enrolled in it. I didn't know if college was really for me, but I planned to see. My plan was going exactly like it was put together, and it was now time for Telly, MC and me to meet Coach David Soloman.

We made our way to the large white and blue building on the westside of the campus where his office was located. The whole campus was made up of the school's blue and white colors. The blue and white colors were far from my high school red and light-blue colors. But I liked the colors.

We were met by a guy name Ramon, who was also from Charlotte when we arrived at Coach Soloman's office. I knew him from playing high school ball against him. He played with Marco at North Mecklenburg before Marco went on to play at UNCC. Ramon was a shooting guard in high school and he was a high IQ player that didn't have the grade to go to a D-1 school. I had met Ramon at Rod Seaford's AAU try outs back when we were in high school.

Ramon welcomed us with open arms, when he said, "Welcome to Forsyth Tech. Y'all going to love it here."

CRUMBLING TALENT

Then he walked us to Coach David Soloman's office. We walked through the lobby area of the building, where there were pool tables and a sitting area where students were sitting out reading and doing work. I fell in love with this atmosphere.

Coach Soloman was a built, Jewish, nerdy looking guy that loved basketball. He wasn't nothing like the slim pretty boy type that Rod Seaford was.

Coach Soloman was waiting inside his office with six of the team players. All the guys had on Forsyth's t-shirts. I knew they were on the basketball team because the t-shirts had the -school name beside the words, basketball team.

Coach Soloman spoke, "I like to welcome y'all to Forsyth Tech. We are a family here. We want y'all to be a part of our family. Rod has told me about each of you. I think y'all can help the team, but most important, I want y'all to know that this is an opportunity that everyone don't get. And I want y'all to enjoy this experience, because it don't last long. Two years is not a long time."

After Coach Soloman's little speech, he introduced us to each player. There was Nate who was 6'6 from New York. Toot was from Winston Salem, who was 6'5 along, with his cousin Jermaine who was 6'7. OJ and John were from High Point and they had played ball in high school together. They both were 6'3 guards.

This white guy, named Mark, introduced himself as the team Run boy. He had no problem with this name. In fact, he encouraged me that it was okay to call him Mark: The Running Man because he was always running around for one of the players.

Mark was a likeable guy, and he was very smart but he didn't look like he was. His appearance threw people off because he dressed like he was a homeless person. His clothes looked dirty. This didn't stop me from becoming his friend. Ramon and Mark gave us a tour after Coach Soloman had us sign a couple papers.

After our tour, we returned to Coach's office. This time Coach shook each of our hands and then took us into another office behind the big office.

After we walked in, he said, "This is my main office. I like to call it the man-cave. This is where I do my X's and O's for the games."

I could tell from the pictures that Coach was a big basketball fan. Rod Seaford had told me that Coach played when he was in the army, but wasn't that good.

Coach continued, "Do y'all like what y'all see?"

I said, "Yes. I'm a big Michael Jordan fan. I was wondering if you could let me have that picture of him on your wall."

The picture had MJ's signature on it.

He spoke, "That's against the Junior College rules. A Coach cannot buy players things. I don't know what code of conduct that is under, but I know it's in the code of conduct book."

Telly said, "He's playing around Coach."

MC said, "Yes, he is."

I said, "No, I'm not."

Coach changed the subject when I looked at him.

Coach Soloman said, "Are y'all ready for some basketball?"

We all said yes. After Coach Soloman asked us a couple of questions, we headed over to the program building. This was where all the money for tuition was paid. It was also where we had to apply for pell-grants. Since we were good at basketball, and the school needed players, we were moved to the front of the line. While we waited for our pell-grant paper work to be processed, we went over to the education center. This was where pre-testing was taking place. Coach got us in with the snap of a finger.

MC looked at me for help when the pre-test lady asked us if we all had finished school. Telly answered first. Then I said, "Yes." The lady looked at MC. He said, "No." The lady took MC to another room. Telly and I sat down at different computers after the lady left. Our names were punched in the system by another blond-haired, middle age, woman. She told us to take our times with the test. Then she left. Two hour later, the lady returned and told us time was up. Telly and I walked out into the

CRUMBLING TALENT

hallway where MC was waiting. He looked confused. I asked him how did everything go. He told me that he was told by the aid that he was on a 9th grade level. I wasn't surprised. I knew MC wasn't book smart. Coach Soloman insured MC that he would be on the team if his skill matched what he was looking for. After Coach told MC this, he told and me that we would be taking college transfer classes. These were classes that most basketball players took to get by. Coach insured us that the classes wouldn't be hard, and as long as we produced on the court we wouldn't have to worry. I thought to myself, here I go again.

We returned back to Charlotte after a long day in Winston Salem. We decided to celebrate our step towards going to college. I took everyone to the strip club. I paid for lap dances and the drinks.

MC asked me if I was really ready for college.

I said, "Yes."

"What about the drug game? Who's going to run your drug house?"

"I'm thinking about give it up."

"You sure?"

"I really want to change. I don't want to be 30 years old, still selling drugs."

"Doctors do it all the time," MC remarked.

"I'm not a doctor," I replied.

"But you love the streets," he said.

"That may be true, but I was thinking that I could make something out my life since Denise is about to have another baby."

"I thought it wasn't yours?" MC asked.

I told Telly and MC that Denise wasn't pregnant by me. I only did this because I caught her talking to J-Rock.

I responded, "I was upset at the time when I told y'all that she wasn't pregnant by me."

"So, it is your kid?"

"Yes. I guess," I said.

"I wish I had a baby. You lucky you going to have two," MC

stated.

"It's not luck. I'm a stud," I retorted.

"You have a big ego," MC said.

"You should know, my son," I said.

Telly interrupted, "Y'all know Peaches pregnant again. She is the same amount of months as Denise."

"That mean we are the fathers?" I asked.

"You know you was dropping me off at Peaches' house before you would go to Denise's crib," Telly said.

"What do that mean? There could have been a guy going out the back door," I said.

Telly said, "It's yours. Let s drink to our kids."

We took down a few more drinks before we picked out a couple strippers to leave with us. MC told me that he didn't want one. I was cool with that because that meant more for me. I dropped Telly off at Peaches' house.

Then the craziest thing happened. MC threw up on one of the strippers. I was so embarrassed that I gave the strippers three hundred dollars apiece and dropped them off at their hotel room. MC was still ready to hang out. I was ready to go in, but I didn't want to take my friend home drunk. So, I stopped by the liquor spot off West Boulevard and purchased a six pack of beer. I knew we didn't need no more alcohol, but I purchased it hoping that it would help with the way MC was feeling.

MC convinced me to take him over to ZZ's house after we drank the six pack of beer. She was standing on the porch when we pulled up. I didn't know she was drug dealer. She was making a sell as I pulled in her driveway.

He said, "ZZ is getting money out here."

I asked, "You got her selling?"

"No. She got her own package," MC said.

"Your girl don't need to be selling drugs."

"Look who's talking. You sell drugs. How you going to judge her?"

"She's a girl. She's an easy target."

"She got a gun."

"She can have a gun, but will she kill?"

"Have you ever asked yourself that question?"

MC had me at the moment. I had never thought about taking someone's life.

I responded, "This isn't about me. This is about your girl selling drugs on a dead-end street."

"Why do you always have to ask me about my girl? Do you want her?"

"No."

"Well stop talking about her."

MC hopped out the car before I could respond.

I rolled down the window and said, "Don't forget, we going to the gym in the morning."

ZZ shouted, "Hi, Q."

The way she said my name had me thinking she was flirting.

MC said, "Don't be doing that ZZ."

She didn't pay him any attention. She said it again. He grabbed her by her neck and pulled her into the house. I looked down at my watch and noticed it was close to three am. My mind went to Denise. She was now staying with Peggy again. I thought about calling her, but I knew she wouldn't get up and come out, so I called my next-door neighbor.

Shelby was a thick, light skin, girl that caught my eye when I had first moved into my apartment. She had let me know she wanted me from the start. I knew my cars, money and clothes helped with her decision. I knew she was a gold digger, but I didn't care. I just needed someone I could call and get off some stress. This was what Denise didn't understand about me.

Shelby and I had spent some time together before, but didn't have sex, because I was fighting off a STD that I had caught from a one-night stand from a girl that lived in South Side Projects. She didn't know I was recovering from the STD, but I told her that Denise had in fact given me a STD, and this was the reason why we were not together. My lie sounded good to her, because she still wanted to have sex with me.

The real reason Denise and I had broken up was because she caught me putting one of the horse pills I had received from the doctor at the health department in her plate of mac-n-cheese. When she caught me, I still didn't tell her the truth. I blamed her and she believed that she had given me a yeast infection since this STD had the same symptoms. When she found out from the same doctor that she couldn't have given me a yeast infection, she went crazy on me. The bad part about the whole situation was Denise was three months pregnant. This had happened right after I caught her with J-Rock.

Shelby was waiting in front of my apartment when I pulled up. She was dressed in some tight short, t-shirt and slippers. As soon as we got inside my apartment, we went at it. This was some of the best sex I had ever had. R-Kelly played in the background while we got it on. The whole twelve play CD played all way through before we came up for air.

CHAPTER 19

QUALUDE

The next morning, I woke up to find that Shelby was gone, but she had cooked me breakfast before she left. I had eggs, grits, bacon, pancakes and a note thanking me for the twelve play I gave her. My throat was dry from all the sex. This was why I headed to the kitchen when I stepped out of bed. The smell of the food took over my nose.

After eating me a plate of food, my phone interrupted me. I thought it would be Shelby, but to my surprise, it was Trisha. I hadn't talked to Trisha in months.

I asked, "What's up?"

She said, "Why haven't you been answering the phone?"

"Because I've been asleep."

"You haven't been asleep all morning."

"How are you going to tell me what I've been doing?"

"You still a damn liar."

"You have nerves to be calling my phone, talking shit."

"I didn't call to make this about you, Q."

I interrupted, "Then what do you want? Some dick?"

"Hell no. I don't want your nasty ass dick. I called because your friend is in the hospital."

Trisha was a master at playing games. This was why I wasn't take her serious.

I said, "Don't be calling over here playing. I don't have time for you. I got some new pussy I need to be taking care of."

"I'm not playing, Q."

I could hear the serious in Trisha voice now.

I asked, "What friend?"

"MC."

"What happen?"

"Nuke jumped on him while he was asleep at ZZ's house."

My heart dropped. I couldn't believe that MC had been asleep at ZZ's house. Usually she would take him home.

I asked, "What hospital he's at?"

"Carolina Medical Center."

"Is he alright?"

"He's in a coma."

"Stop playing Trisha."

"I'm not playing."

I rushed over to the hospital after I got off the phone with Trisha. When I walked inside the hospital, I almost lost my mind. ZZ was standing in the lobby area, talking to the police. I walked past her and headed over to MC's father. He was still recovering from the loss of Me-Month.

I asked, "Is Melvin alright?"

He responded, "He's in a coma."

MC was a mirror image of his father. They both were long and slim. MC's father looked like he was on his way to church. His suit was fresh and his shoes looked new.

I asked, "What happened?"

"That girl let that nigga, Nuke, in her house while my son was asleep. He beat Melvin with his hands. He beat him so bad that it caused him to shut down. The medical people had to bring him back."

I couldn't believe what I was hearing. I didn't think that MC would get caught slipping. He was always on point.

I said, "Is he going to be alright?"

"The doctor said he could come out the coma today or ten years from now. It's all up to him now."

"Did they get Nuke for this?"

"No."

"Don't worry. He going to get his."

"Don't do nothing stupid, son. Let the police do their job."

"Why is ZZ here?"

"She came here with Melvin in the medical van."

"Can I see Melvin?"

"They are only taking family, right now."

"He's like my brother."

After my statement, we were interrupted by Telly. MC's father hadn't forgiven Telly. His facial expression told me this.

I spoke, "Telly, let me talk to you."

I pulled him to the side, and told him it wasn't a good time to be at the hospital. He understood, because he could read MC's father's facial expression. We left and headed over to West Boulevard.

The block was live. There were people everywhere due to the fact that there was a car wash at Mr. Rob's corner store. I pulled in to the store parking lot to get my 929 washed. Telly hopped out of my car and went in the store and grabbed a six pack of beer. We sat there watching the crackheads as they were washing my car.

Telly started a conversation about what had happened to MC.

Half way through the conversation I said, "I'mma get Nuke for this."

Telly responded, "Man let the police do their jobs. We trying to get out the hood."

"Fuck that. He tried to kill MC. We don't know if MC is going to be the same."

"It's not your beef."

"It is my beef. That's my best friend."

"I'm your cousin, and I'm telling you to let this go. We got too much to lose."

"I don't care."

"What about your daughter? Do you want her to grow up

without her father?"

"No. But I have to do something. The streetz is going to be talking."

"Fuck da streetz. You have a future playing ball. You got what it takes to get out the hood."

"These streetz raised me. When my mother gave me up, I turned to these streetz to keep me sane."

"The streetz didn't raise you, Qualude. Big Mama did."

Telly had a point. The streets didn't raise me. Big Mama was the person that had taken me in when my mother me couldn't raise me. She taught me right and wrong. She was my mother and father when she had to be. In a sense, Telly was right but the streets were in me. I had learned things in the streets that Big Mama didn't teach me. I learned that loyalty went a long way in the streets. Being raised in an era when people were killed for a little white rock, made me realize, that life was too short to be playing around.

I spoke, "I don't know what I'mma do when I see Nuke."

"I hope you don't do nothing."

"I cannot promise I will not do nothing."

The craziest thing happened next. I noticed Nuke walking down the block. He looked like he didn't have a worry in the world. I couldn't control myself. I thought I would be able to control my anger, but I was wrong. Telly could see that I had murder in my eyes.

He spoke, "Cuzo. He isn't worth it."

"I cannot let this nigga get away with hurting MC."

I walked slowly over to my car. The crackheads were wiping it down. I opened the door to my car and reached under my seat. As soon as I came up with the gun, Telly was standing in my pathway.

He spoke, "I cannot let you do it."

"Get out my way."

He shouted, "No!"

"Man get the fuck out the way."

"You got to shoot me first."

Telly knew how much I loved him. He knew I would never harm him in any way. This is why he blocked me from getting to Nuke. When I turned my attention back to Nuke, I felt Telly's hand around mine. We struggled over the gun until he gained control of it.

I shouted, "Fuck that gun!"

Then I took off over to Nuke. He met me with a strong right hand. I had took the punch and rushed him with a series of blows. I connected to his jaw. He grabbed me and wrestled me to the ground. Once on the ground, Nuke got on top off me. He hit me in the face two times before I flipped him over and punched him in the face twice. We locked up again before Telly came over. I thought he was going to help me, but he didn't. The crackheads that washed my car broke Nuke and me apart.

When we got up, Nuke shouted, "You don't have anything to do with MC and my beef."

I said, "That's my best friend. I'mma get you for the shit you did to him."

"Fuck that sucker."

I tried to get at Nuke again and two of the three crackheads grabbed me. I took off towards my car. To my surprise, Telly hadn't put the gun back in the car. I slammed my door shut.

Nuke smiled and walked off after saying, "You should have taught your boy how to fight."

CHAPTER 20

QUALUDE

A week had gone by since the fight with Nuke. Trisha came by my apartment the day after the fight. She told me that MC wasn't getting any better. She told me that I needed to go see him. I let her know that I would go over to the hospital and see him if she went with me. She agreed to go with me after we had sex.

It had been almost been two years since we had hooked up. The reason we broke up was because she had sex with my play brother. After she had sex with him, she told me she only did it to get back at me because she heard I was having sex with a girl name Denise. I hadn't had sex with Denise yet, but I had been talking to her about it. I didn't think this was cheating at the time, but boy I was wrong.

Trisha and I arrived at the hospital to find ZZ standing in the lobby. This time the police wasn't in her presence.

Trisha said, "I got to check this bitch."

I responded, "No."

Before I could get the word all the way out of my mouth, Trisha walked over to ZZ.

She asked, "What da fuck you doing here?"

ZZ responded, "I came to see my man."

Trisha said, "You got nerves to be here. I think you should leave."

CRUMBLING TALENT

"I don't have to go nowhere. This is a public hospital."

I stepped in between the two girls and said, "This is not a good time for this."

Trisha said, "I want to beat your ass, ZZ."

ZZ responded, "You can't beat me bitch. I will walk the dog with your ass."

ZZ looked a little bigger than Trisha, but Trisha was taller. Both girls had on blue jeans, t-shirt and Nikes. ZZ's hair was under one of MC's fitted caps, and Trisha had her hair in a ponytail. They both looked like they were ready for war.

MC's father showed up out of nowhere. I was glad, because I didn't want to have to break of a fight.

He spoke, "I hope y'all are here to pray for my son."

Trisha said, "Hello, Uncle Melvin."

I watched as Trisha gave her uncle a hug, but not taking her eyes off ZZ.

Mr. Melvin spoke, "We don't need no drama over here today, because MC's mother will be here any minute now."

Trisha asked, "They let Aunt Joy out of prison?"

Mr. Melvin said, "Just to see if she could help Melvin come out his coma. They think his mother's voice could help if he hears her."

I wasn't a doctor, but I knew that MC was tough, and he would pull through. There was no doubt in my mind that he would come out the coma, but I still had my doubts about how much brain power he would have. Mr. Melvin told us that the doctors said there is a chance that MC wouldn't be the same.

I asked, "What do you mean?"

Mr. Melvin responded, "There is a chance that his speech could be damaged. The blows he took to his head caused him to have bleeding on his brain."

I wanted to break down crying. It was going to be difficult to accept the fact that MC wasn't going to be the same.

Trisha shouted, "It's all your fault ZZ. If you wouldn't have been trying to be a player, my cousin wouldn't be in there fighting for his life."

ZZ responded, "If MC would have fought back like he said he was going to do, then he wouldn't be in a coma. He the one said he was going to whip Nuke ass, not me."

This was new information to me. MC had never told me he challenged Nuke to a fight. This just wasn't in his character. MC wasn't a fighter like myself. He was more of the funny guy and the lover boy.

I spoke, "You know MC isn't a fighter, ZZ. Why did you let Nuke in the house while he was asleep?"

"That's my point. He wasn't asleep. He was sitting in the living room when Nuke climbed through the back window."

The streets had the story all wrong. Here was ZZ telling what she saw firsthand. I didn't want to believe her, but when she started crying, I knew she was telling the truth. I could tell she was feeling guilty about the situation. A white doctor popped out the room's door.

He said, "You all may come in."

Mr. Melvin walked in first. Then Trisha and me. ZZ turned and left. I was surprised but I knew how it felt to be somewhere that people didn't want you. It was best she left because the scene turned serious when MC's mother entered the room a couple minutes later.

When she had walked in, she broke out in tears. She was handcuffed and dressed in a blue jumpsuit. Her hair had been done for the occasion. She looked the same as she did in the picture that MC had hanging up in his bedroom. It had been over ten years since his mother had seen him in person. I knew the reasons he never went to see his mother. These were issues he was still dealing with.

The sound of the vitals machine beeping took over the atmosphere when his mother touched her son and spoke.

"Hi baby. It's mama."

The doctor entered and said, "Keep talking to him."

I watched as his mother talked to him like he was a baby. This moment made me think about my mother. She was still upset about me disrespecting Butch when I got out of prison.

I watched as MC laid in the bed like he was asleep. He looked like he was at peace. His head was wrapped up in white wrap, but I could still see his eyes. The wraps on his arms reached from the top of his arm to the bottom of his arms. This made me try to picture what had happened that night at ZZ's house. I pictured that he was laying in ZZ's bed and Nuke came in, but I dismissed this theory after ZZ had told us real story. Now I was thinking that he just let Nuke beat him.

I was now feeling guilty about dropping him off at ZZ's house. The fight with Nuke didn't help with my guilt. It made me realize that I needed to get out of the city of Charlotte before I was shot and killed or laying up in the hospital like MC.

It was hard for me to watch someone suffer. Especially a friend. Seeing MC in this state made me think back about my uncle Teddy who died from Aids. I didn't get to tell him how much I loved him. Even though he was on drugs, and doing God knows what, I still loved him. He had taught me so much. Now that MC was fighting for his life, I didn't want him to die without telling him how much I loved him and appreciated him as my friend.

Watching his parents exchange greetings gave me the sense that they were not on good terms. I didn't like the fact that they had to see their son in the hospital. This made me want to get revenge. The hate I had for Nuke now, was showing on my face. I couldn't hide it after seeing my friend looking like a mummy with tubes hooked to him like he was a science project.

His mother asked the officers could they take off the handcuffs. One of the officers took off the handcuffs while the other blocked the door. I didn't think Melvin's mother was a threat, because she was humble and obedient. This made me reflect back to when I was at Polk Youth Prison. The way these officers were treating her in a time of crisis made me feel like all officers were the same. The officers at Polk had scarred me with their treatment and made me look at life differently.

I watched as MC's mother looked over his body. Her face expression gave me the sense that she was upset. She was close to tears. I thought she was going to break down like she did when she learned Me-Month was dead, but she didn't.

She spoke, "Why god? Why God?"

I wanted to say something, but I kept my mouth closed. Trisha looked at me like she wanted me to say something.

I spoke, "Talk to him. Touch him."

MC came to life when his mother touched him. His brown eyes opened like the doors of a church during a wedding. My heartrate increased. I thought I was going to pass out.

I watched, as his mother said, "It's me baby. It's really me."

I could tell from MC's face expression that he didn't believe that the woman that was standing in front of him was his mother.

MC asked in a low voice, "Is this a dream?"

"No baby. It's really me."

This mother and son exchange went on for ten minutes. Then it came time for me to speak.

I said, "I'm glad you aright."

He started laughing. I didn't understand why he was laughing.

The doctor said, "Laughing is good for him, but I think something is wrong."

He wouldn't stop laughing. It was like I missed the joke. The doctor asked everyone to clear the room.

On my way out, MC shouted, "Q!"

The tubes in his nose made it hard for him to talk. I understood him, but I didn't respond. He shouted again.

His mother said, "Talk to my son."

I turned and said, "Are you alright?"

"Where am I?" he asked.

The doctor said, "I think it's best you all go. Melvin Junior needs his rest." His mother wanted to stay, but once the doctor ordered us to leave, the correctional officers pulled her towards the door.

Once outside of the room, his mother said, "He isn't himself."

I could see that he wasn't himself from all the tubes that were in his nose and the IV's in his arm. This made me feel more guilty than I was already feeling.

His mother asked, "Can you tell me what happened to my son?"

I said, "I don't really know, but I'mma find out. And I'mma do something about it."

MC's mother shook her head in approval of what I said.

Mr. Melvin said, "Betty I hope you ain't up to your old tricks. Don't be putting things in the boy's head."

Miss Betty said, "Don't judge me Melvin. Just because I was busted with drugs, don't make me a bad mother. I was just trying to provide for my boys."

"You was being selfish, and you know it."

"Maybe I was, but I provided for my boys when you couldn't."

"That's the past Betty."

"The past brings on the future."

"We don't need you."

"From the looks of things, you didn't do a good job with the boys. Me-Month is dead and Melvin is laying up in that room out his mind."

"How can you judge me?"

"I'm not judging you. Only god can do that. But I want you to know that you could have been a better father to my boys."

"I was here for them when you were not."

"You were free, but you didn't make sure they had a relationship with me."

"You made a choice Betty."

"I made a choice to take care of them boys. I don't regret that choice."

"Well, you have to live with it."

Trisha interrupted, "Y'all don't need to be fighting, MC is fighting for his life and he need y'all."

I was proud of Trisha. This was the first time I had seen her go against drama. Usually she was causing the drama.

CHAPTER 21

QUALUDE

When I left the hospital, I called Telly. He told me that Nuke wanted to kill the beef. Then he had told me that he didn't come over to the hospital because he didn't want to run into Mr Melvin. I knew Mr. Melvin was still upset with Telly about Me-Month's death. MC had told me that his father didn't forgive easily, even though he went to church every Sunday.

I told Telly to go see MC, then I called Denise. She asked me about MC's situation. I told her that I didn't know the whole story. Then she told me what she had heard. It was the same story ZZ had told me at the hospital. I ended my conversation with Denise and called my uncle LB. He gave me the same story that ZZ and Denise had told me.

Then he asked, "Are you still going to college?"

I told him I was still going to college, and I advised him that he needed to be looking for a way out the drug game.

He brushed me off by saying, "College isn't for everyone nephew. I wish you the best, and I hope you do good there. But remember, when it's all said and done, you have to be true to yourself. You have to ask yourself if you are happy with your life."

My uncle was right in a sense. I was only going to college because I thought it was the right thing to do, but I really didn't

CRUMBLING TALENT

like school. Even when I was in high school, I only liked gym and the girls. The stuff I had learned in high school hadn't prepared me for the real world. There was no class about how to deal with death. Or how to take care of a kid without money.

It had been almost a year since I had left Polk Youth Prison. My life had changed for the better, because I was making two-thousand dollars a week selling drugs. I could have almost any girl I went after in the street. So why college? College was another challenge for me. By going to college, I was going to prove to everyone that knew me that I was smart and that selling drugs and playing ball wasn't all I could do. But first, I had to get revenge for what happened to Melvin.

Telly called me and told me that our friend Greedy had been picked up for the murder of the guy that killed Me-Month. It shocked me, because Greedy wasn't the type you would think would kill someone. Greedy was the guy that liked chasing girls all day. His mind was never on hurting anyone. But Me-Month and him were close.

I turned on the news to see Greedy being put in a police car. I didn't understand what made a guy like him kill. I was the guy with the bad attitude and the bad history. He had never been to jail or been stopped by the police. Nuke and Greedy were close, too, and they were hanging out the night of the murder. I was told this by Telly.

Nuke was still on my hit list. I didn't care that MC was doing better, all I cared about was getting Nuke back for what he did to MC. My uncle told me that I didn't have to do anything, because Nuke would pay for what he did to MC. I didn't know how Pop felt about the situation, but I knew that I was going to get Nuke for what he did to my friend.

I visited MC every day for two weeks straight. Most of the time, his father and Trisha were there. This was why Telly never went with me. I always told Telly about MC's progress when I had goten up with him. He would tell me to tell MC that he was praying for him. This said a lot about Telly.

I still had about two weeks before I had to report to school. I purchased new clothes and all the necessities for the apartment that Telly and I would be sharing. I was looking forward to starting over, but my unfinished business with Nuke was still on my mind. The two weeks went by two days.

Telly and I headed to Winston Salem for our meeting with Coach David Soloman. It was time for us to move into our apartment. To my surprise, Coach Soloman had us a roommate wait-

CRUMBLING TALENT

ing on us. Cory Dawkins was from High Point, North Carolina. He was an only child that had never lived without his mother. His skills on the court was great. He was six foot seven, and quick as a rabbit. We clicked as soon as we met.

Telly and Cory didn't click the first day they met. The second day was a different story. Telly had found out that Cory liked to play video games like him. This was the connecting fact between the two. After we got settled in, we got ready for practice. I thought college was going to be like high school. It was very different.

Coach Soloman gave us two of a days. This was difficult for me, because I was use to practicing one time a day in high school, not two times a day. This took time to getting used to. After the first week, I wanted to quit.

I called Big Mama and told her that I was thinking about quitting. She told me to keep my butt in school. After I talked with Big Mama, I called my mother. We were still not getting along, because of Butch. But I put that to the side and still asked her for advice.

My mother told me to stay in school. I told her I was running out of money, because I wasn't selling drugs like I was when I was in Charlotte.

She said, "You need to stop selling drugs. And keep your mind on your school work."

I still had a week before school would begin. This was enough time for me to get all my issues in Charlotte taken care of. I told my mother I was finished selling drugs and I was going to let my cars go back to the dealers because I could no longer pay the payments. This was hard for me, because my ego. But I did it.

Denise didn't like this news, because she thought I was going to leave her a car for her and my daughter. When she found out I was not going to be supporting her any more, she was upset. Her attitude towards me changed. Her Aunt Peggy planted the seed in her head that I was going to leave her if I made something out my life. This wasn't the case. I was hoping to make something out my life so Denise wouldn't have to never work.

My life changed quick. I went from living in a nice apartment with all the money I could spend, to living with three roommates, and sharing everything from a bathroom to food. This wasn't new to me, because at Polk Youth Prison, I had learned how to share and appreciate a good friendships. I had started having second thought about college the first week of school. This was because I wasn't used to getting up early, and for the first two days I was late to class.

Telly promised me that he would make sure I was up before he left for his first class after I had told him how I was feeling. He lived up to his promise.

The second week of school, Cory's mother purchased him a 929 Mazda. It was the same model I had before I took mine back to the dealer. We used his car to get around in. I told Cory about my past and so did Telly. He told us about his life of being an only child. This brought us closer, and we formed a brotherhood.

College was going good for the first month until I got a call from my mother. She told me during this call that LJ had gotten locked up for drugs and that he was going away for about a year or two. I was upset because LJ promised me, he was going to help me while I was in college. He had broken that promise.

My mother also told me that my father was out of rehab again and wanted to see me. I was excited because I wanted a relationship with my father. I had heard that my father wasn't really clean the first time he said he went to drug rehab. My father was now a strong believer in God. His rehab stunt had helped him find himself and God. I was happy to hear all this from my mother and I had promised my mother I would meet with him when I came back home for the weekend.

The weekend came and I met up with my father at his wife's apartment. I didn't even know my father was married. To my surprise, my father had two other kids I had never met by his wife, who was also an ex-drug addict. His wife was pretty, and her demeanor towards me was friendly. My brother and sister were tots. Both of them were walking.

My father introduced me to his wife and my siblings, and then we took a ride in his new Cadillac. I was proud to see that my father had gotten clean and got his life on track. When my father told me that he went to truck driving school for six months and received his CDL, I was shocked. After we dropped his wife and my siblings back off at her apartment, we had a father and son moment

My father asked me to get out the car when we got up town by the shelter for the homeless. I stepped out the car into the cold. My father had parked up on the curve about a hundred feet from the building. He was walking towards the building when I called his name.

"Pops."

He turned around and looked at me before he said, "Come on son."

After my father turned and walked towards the building again, I had took notice of his new look. His hair was trimmed neatly, displaying a head full of thick waves. His black slacks looked like they had just been pressed at the cleaners. The white cotton shirt he was wearing looked pressed, too, and his snake skin loafers looked like they had a coat of black polish on them. Standing at six-foot even, my dad looked good after getting clean. I was still shocked that he was clean.

My mother and grandmother had always called my father the seed donor, but this wasn't true. My father wanted to be a father to me. His days of being strung out on crack were still deep down in my memory, but the nightmares I had as a kid about my dad were now gone. All the stuff my mother and grandmother had told me about my dad were not true. I found this after my father opened up a conversation about his past when we walked in the shelter.

He spoke, "There are some things I need to tell you. All the stuff your mother and grandmother told you about me are not true."

I said, "Pops, I don't want to talk about that."

"Let me finish."

"I really don't want to talk about that."

The visions of my father sticking that needle in his arm when I was a kid flashed to my mind. I had witnessed my father shoot dope on several occasions when I was just ten years old. The stains on my memory were hard to wipe away. Especially, the ones when he made me hold his arm so he could find a vein.

My father continued, "I brung you here because I wanted you to see how blessed you are."

I responded, "Pops, I know about homeless people."

He said, "It's just not about these people being homeless. It's about their stories. All these people have a story."

I looked over the room. There were over fifty people in the room. Most were men. The place looked clean and it smelled like pine-sol. There were microwaves sitting on a table in the corner of the room. There were several TV's playing different programs. This was my first time inside this building. But I had bypassed it on many occasions.

A woman sitting at the front desk asked, "Will you two being staying tonight?"

My father answered, "No. We just here visiting."

"This is not the time for visitors," the huge white woman said.

She was dressed in a pair of jeans, t-shirt and Nikes. Her hair was pulled back in a ponytail.

My father responded, "I just brought my son here so he could see how this place works. So, when he makes it to the NBA, he can come back here and help."

The woman stared at my father. Then she asked, "Don't I know you?"

My father said, "I don't know. Do you?"

"Have you stayed here before?"

CRUMBLING TALENT

It seemed like it took my father forever to answer but he said, "Yes. When I was using."

I didn't think my father ever stayed at the Shelter. I always thought that he had lived with my grandmother.

The lady said, "I remember you now. Your name is Johnny."

My father said, "Yes."

"I'm Miss Sue. I'm the person that called 911 the night you OD'd here."

I could tell that my father didn't want Miss Sue to bring up this episode of his life.

He said, "Everyone has a story."

Miss Sue responded, "We thought you was going to die. When they found you in the restroom with the needle in your arm that night, we made a new rule about having needles inside this building."

My father said, "That part of my life is over. I turned my life over to God."

"That's great. Maybe you can attend one of our NA meetings and tell the group how God changed your life."

"I would like that."

"How about right now?"

"Right now?"

"Yes. There is a meeting going on in the back room right now."

"I don't think right now is a good time. I have my son with me."

"Your son can go in with you. You know the rules. You can tell him the rules before you go in."

"I don't think this is a good idea."

I said, "Maybe next Miss Sue. There is somewhere I have to be."

I could tell that my father was relieved that I came to his rescue.

He said, "Maybe when my son makes it to the NBA, he could come back and do something for this place."

Miss Sue said, "That would be nice."

Before Miss Sue could get another word out of her mouth, my father said, "We have to be going. I don't want my son to be late."

I watched as my father rushed out the door. Then I told Miss Sue that if I made it to the NBA, I would make it my duty to come back and reward the place for saving my father. She told me that I didn't owe the place a penny, because God would take care of the place and what she did for my father was part of God's plan. I thanked her before I walked out and joined my father in the parking lot. He was smoking a cigarette.

When I walked over to him, I asked, "Are you alright?"

He blew the smoke out his mouth and said, "I thought I was ready for this."

I asked, "Ready for what?"

"Coming back here. This was the place where I almost left this world."

"Don't feel bad Pops. God wasn't ready for you to leave, because if he was you wouldn't be here."

"Thank God I'm here."

"I'm glad you here Pops."

"I thought I would never here you say that."

"Why would you say that?"

"Because of my past."

My father hadn't been in my life when I was a kid. And when I did see him at my grandmother's house, he was always high. There were so many times that my father had promised to come see me, but didn't. This caused me to hate him, but the real reason I had never stopped loving him was because I had faith that one day he would stop using and I would see the real him.

I spoke, "I only know what my mother and Big mama told me about your past."

He said, "You know, sometimes people can make a story up and make it seem real."

I said, "I remember how you use to promise me stuff Pops, and you didn't hold to your promise."

CRUMBLING TALENT

"It was the drugs son. I wasn't myself."

"Why did you start using the drugs?"

"That's something I'm not ready to talk to you about."

"Why?"

"I'm just not ready," My father said and then threw the cigarette on the ground and smashed it with his shoe.

I responded, "We both are men. Men should be able to talk like men. I'm not here to judge you, Pops. I just want to know you better."

"I love you son. I have always loved you."

After my father shared his inner feelings, I barked off a smart remark.

"If you love me, why wasn't you there for me as a kid. You didn't love me. You loved the drugs more than me."

My father didn't blank from the comment. It was like he knew this moment was due.

He spoke, "The drugs had me. I thought I could handle them. In the end, the drugs showed me."

The flashback of me holding my father arms while he was preparing to stick the needle in his arm came back to my mind. This time, the red light that was in his bedroom was in the equation. Plus, the funky bed that he had laid in after he pulled the blood-filled needle from his arm. Bleach to the brain couldn't remove this memory. This was why I had never tried hard drugs.

My father's statement made me mad. My hands started sweating, and I wanted to explode on him and let all the balled-up anger that I had for him come out. I wanted him to know about all the times I was mentally and physically abused by my mother's boyfriends. The times I cried myself to sleep because I just want a relationship with him.

After gathering my thoughts and keeping my composure, I said, "In order for you to continue to be in my life, I want the truth."

My father turned away from me like he was about to walk away. Then he turned around and said, "I killed someone when I was around your age."

"You what?"

"They say I killed a man at a club."

"They who?"

"The police."

"Was you ever charged?"

"Yes."

"What happened?"

"The charges were dismissed."

"So, you didn't do it?"

"They didn't have enough evidence to convict, so they threw out the case."

"Who was the guy?"

"That's not important."

"So, that's why you started using drugs?"

My father turned away from me and pulled out his pack of cigarettes. He lit up one after pulling it from the pack. I watched as he blew the smoke out his mouth once again.

He spoke, "The drugs help."

"Are you still using?"

"No."

"How do you deal with the guilt now?"

"I just smoke me a cigarette."

"Did you kill the guy?"

"I don't know. I was drunk."

"You should know if you murdered someone or not."

"Rob Slim say I did. But he will never tell because he say I did it for him."

"Who is Rob Slim?"

"The guy you met in the county jail. He taught you the rules about prison."

"That's why he was so friendly. You killed a man for him?"

"Like I say, I don't know what happened. I was too drunk."

This new information about my father was mind-blowing. I would have never guessed that my father had killed someone.

CRUMBLING TALENT

He never displayed a mean side in front of me, but other people had told me that he had one. I didn't know if I should believe my father, or take his story as a lie, because in the past he had lied about little things.

My father continued, "Listen son. You have a talent that people wish they had. Don't waste it. Don't be a Crumbling Talent like me. Yes, I could play ball before the drugs."

No one had never told me that my father could play ball. I thought I received my talent from Big Mama, because she had been a ball player back when she was younger.

I asked, "Why did you ever tell me this?"

"I don't know. I didn't think it was important."

"I want to say I'm sorry, Pops."

"For what son?"

"Because I thought you didn't care about me."

"I want you to know that I always cared about you. And if someone told you different than they were probably trying to protect you."

I could tell my father was sincere about what he was saying. This was our first real father and son conversation. In the past, he was too high to talk to me. Now that he wasn't high, he was a different person and this was what I had always been craving to see.

My father and I were interrupted by two men walking towards the shelter.

The one with an old Braves baseball cap, jeans and torn t-shirt spoke.

"Do y'all have a light?"

I noticed that the other guy was dressed in dirty clothes, too. His face was ashy and his finger nails were black. He looked like a mix breed. The coat that he was wearing was missing some buttons but I could tell that the cold wasn't getting to him.

My father spoke, "I got a light."

I watched as my father handed the dark-skinned guy his lighter. My father told the guy to keep the lighter. I didn't understand this.

When the two guys walked off, I asked, "Why you let the guy keep your lighter?"

"I know them faces. They need the lighter so they can light up their crack pipes."

"How you know that Pops?"

"You sell drugs. You know."

"I have been wanting to talk to you about that. I stop selling drugs."

"You needed to."

"One more thing. I want to say sorry for selling you drugs."

"I want to say I'm sorry for even asking you for drugs."

CRUMBLING TALENT

CHAPTER 22

THREE MONTHS LATER.
DENISE

When Qualude told me that had to stop selling drugs, I was shocked. In the past I would have encouraged him to stop, but now I needed the money he had been giving me. When he told me that I had to go to the welfare office and sign up for food-stamps and a monthly welfare check, I was devastated. I didn't want to go to social services and stand in line and beg for a handout. But I did. This was so embarrassing, because I had been bragging to my family about how I would never get on welfare.

When I started getting on welfare that changed the way I looked at Qualude. I was now blaming him for everything that went wrong in my life. My frustration got the best of me when I found out that Qualude had been giving Nikki money for Keosha. This sent me rushing over to Qualude's mother's house.

I got Tasha to take me over there after she got her boyfriend to let her borrow his car. When we pulled up in front Qualude's mother's house, she was sitting on the porch talking on the phone.

She didn't recognize me at first, but when I got out with my big belly, she asked. "What are you doing over here?"

"I need to talk to you," I said, as I walked up on the porch where she was sitting in a chair.

She didn't even offer me a chair.

She spoke, "Talk to me about what?"

"Your son," I responded with attitude.

"My son isn't here."

"I know that."

"Well, as you know, my son and me are not on good terms, because he don't like Butch."

"I didn't come here to discuss that. I came here because I need you to tell me if that's Qualude's baby by Nikki."

"I don't know anything about no baby by Nikki. I don't even know Nikki."

I said, "Don't lie to me."

I told Tasha to stay in the car, because I didn't want her to hear what I had to say to Qualude's mother. But she got out the car when she had heard the tone of my voice change.

Qualude's mother spoke, "First of all, I don't have to lie to you, and secondly, I don't appreciate you coming to my house and asking me about someone, my son is dealing with. Thirdly, you need some manners, because you didn't say hello or how are you doing when you got out the car."

"You already think I'm not good enough for your son, so why should I have to respect you? You don't respect me, because you could have told me that your son was F-ing Nikki."

Tasha asked, "Is everything alright Denise?"

"Yes."

"I don't keep up with who my son is having sex with. You know I'm a church going woman, and I try to stay out my son's affairs," Qualude's mom said.

"That isn't what he said," I responded.

"What are you talking about?"

"He told me that you didn't like me."

"I never said I didn't like you. I just think you too young for my son."

"Age ain't nothing but a number."

"I used to say the same thing when I got pregnant with Qualude. His father slick talked me into have sex. I wasn't nothing

CRUMBLING TALENT

about fifteen."

Qualude's mother looked young. If I didn't know, I would have thought she was his sister. Her light skin was the same color as mine.

I spoke, "I love Qualude, and he love me."

"Girlfriend, you know love cannot pay bills."

"That's the other reason I'm here. Your son said he isn't going to be able to help me out with our daughter."

"You know the boy is in school. He don't have the money."

"Can you help me?"

"I have bills myself. I'mma tell you like my mother told me when I had Qualude, she told me that I had that baby, so therefore, I have to take care of it."

"So that's what you telling me?"

"Yes."

"This is your granddaughter we talking about."

"So?"

I wanted to go ghetto on Qualude's mother, but I didn't because Tasha was with me. Plus, I didn't want his mother to call the police on me for disrespecting her house.

I tried my best to keep my composure, but when she said, "Don't come to my house without calling me," I looked at Tasha and said, "Let's go before I blink out my mind, because she don't know me."

I knew the story about Qualude's mother leaving him with Big Mama. He had told me when he moved in with me and my grandmother. I also knew why he called his mother by her first name. This was something Big Mama implanted in him to get his mother back for leaving him with her. I didn't like these games that were being played by Qualude and his mother. Tasha and I left Qualude's mother's house and headed over to West Blvd. Since I had moved back in with my grandmother, after I had a fight with Aunt Peggy over Nikki wearing my clothes, I hadn't talked to Aunt Peggy. I decided it was time to go talk to her.

Aunt Peggy was sitting in the living room drinking a beer

when I arrived. She wasn't drunk, but she was on her way there. I wobbled inside the living and sat down.

She asked, "What da hell you doing over here?"

"I came to say I'm sorry."

"You sorry!"

"Yes."

"I don't believe you. The way you cussed me out and then took Shaquala away from here without telling me where you was going had me worried. I was trying to stop drinking, but when we had the fight I started back."

"That's why I'm saying I'm sorry. "

I knew Aunt Peggy was trying to stop drinking. The way she started chain smoking told me this.

She asked, "Where is my baby?"

I responded, "With Betty."

"When are you going to stop running and get back in school?"

"I don't need school."

"Yes, you do."

"You didn't finish school."

"Because I had to take care of Nicole."

"I never liked school."

"What are you going to do with your life? You think Qualude is going to come back here and get you after he finishes college or make it playing ball? Girlfriend, you need to wake up. He is going to leave your butt right here in Charlotte."

"Why do you have to spoil a good moment?"

"I'm just telling you the real. You need to wake up. This is the real world."

"Can you please not talk about Qualude anymore?"

Aunt Peggy took a drink and then started laughing. I wanted to punch her in her face because I knew she was laughing at me.

I said, "That's why I moved out. You don't do nothing but wish bad on people."

"I don't wish bad on people. I tell the truth. The truth will set you free."

CRUMBLING TALENT

I knew this was the alcohol talking, so I said, "You need to stop drinking and maybe you can get a man."

She responded, "I had your man."

I couldn't believe my ears. My heart almost went through my chest. I looked at Aunt Peggy to see if she was playing, but she was serious.

I said, "You need to quit drinking, because it got you saying the wrong things."

"Don't tell me what I need to stop doing, because I'm grown. And yes, I had your man." After Peggy said this, she stood up.

I said, "Don't get in my face.

"She said, "I will beat your ass like you stole something if you keep talking."

"Fuck you," I shouted.

Before I could get another word out of my mouth, Aunt Peggy hit me in it. I grabbed my mouth and noticed that one of my braces had been knocked loose. I broke out in tears.

Tasha came to my rescue. She shouted, "Leave her alone, Aunt Peggy. You know she's pregnant."

Tasha was 20 pounds bigger than Aunt Peggy. I had seen them get in to it before and Tasha let Aunt Peggy beat her up. This was right after Tasha had turned 16.

Aunt Peggy shouted, "Get out my face bitch.'

Tasha stood her ground. She said, "No. Leave Denise alone."

"Bitch, if you don't get out my face, I'mma slap the shit out of you."

Aunt Peggy had always been very verbally abusive towards Tasha, my sister and me. We had gotten used to it over the years. But now that I didn't need her, I didn't have to stand for her abuse.

I spoke, "I'm not afraid of you any more Aunt Peggy."

I watched as Aunt Peggy stared Tasha down. I thought she was going to hit Tasha. That's why I spoke up.

Aunt Peggy turned to me and said, "I don't care if you are pregnant. I will beat your ass."

I said, "No, you want."

Aunt Peggy slapped my face again. Tasha grabbed her, and they struggled in each other's grip until they hit the glass table inside the room. Tasha landed on top of her. I watched as they wrestled like they were part of the NWA wrestlers team. Nikki came down the stairs and broke up the fight. Someone in the neighborhood had called the police. When they knocked on the door, we were cleaning up the room like nothing happened. They made a report and left.

Nikki had told the police that we were all in the living room horse-playing. The cops brought the story. The reason I think they brought the story was because Tasha's hair was messed up and Nikki was smiling the whole time. Aunt Peggy was upstairs, hiding in her bedroom looking out the window the whole time the police were there. I was told this by a neighbor. I left Aunt Peggy's apartment in pain after I had told her how stupid she had acted. She didn't say a word because I had threatened to call the police back and take charges out on her for slapping me twice if she tried that again. She knew I wasn't playing, because I had told her I was still thinking about telling her rent lady about her drinking problem.

Tasha and I left. We went over to my grandmother's house, and I told Tasha that I was sorry for bringing her into my and Aunt Peggy's mess. She accepted my apology and told me that she was happy that I stood up to Aunt Peggy. I told my grandmother about what happened, and she told me that I needed to stay from over Aunt Peggy's apartment. I agreed to stay away from there. Then I went and called Qualude at school. I told him everything about what happened between Aunt Peggy, Tasha and me. I thought he was going to come home and quit that school and be with me, but he didn't. He told me that I was wrong from the beginning, because I had disrespected Aunt Peggy's apartment by going over there after I was told not to.

I wasn't looking for this from Qualude. I got mad and hung up the phone. He called me back but I didn't answer.

CRUMBLING TALENT

CHAPTER 23

QUALUDE

When Denise had called me at school, I was doing my homework inside Coach's office. Coach Soloman gave me the phone and left out of the room. I had given Denise Coach's number and told her only to use it if she had an emergency. The situation was not an emergency. After she told me the whole story about the situation she had with her mother, I told her that she was wrong and then hung up.

When Coach returned to the room, he asked, "Is everything alright?"

I responded, "My daughter's mother is having a family problem."

"Is everything okay?"

"Yes and no."

"What's the problem?"

"I really don't want to talk about it, Coach."

"We all need someone to talk to about our problems."

"I always been able to handle my problems myself."

"Like I told when you first came here, we are a family here. When you hurt, I hurt. Now tell me what the problem so I can help."

"I'm having second thoughts about being here."

"Why?"

"My daughter's mother is always having problems. These

problems didn't start until I got here."

"Maybe she's just missing you.'

"I don't think that's it, because I been going home weekends since I've been here."

"Do you love this girl?"

"Yes."

"Do you love her enough to leave her?"

"What are you asking me Coach?"

"I'm talking about your future. You need to focus on it. Right now, you are worried about the wrong thing."

"Coach... I love this girl. I don't want her to leave me and I'm not planning on leaving her."

"How long have you known this girl?

"About three years."

"How old is your daughter?"

"Seven months."

"Do you plan on being with this girl all your life."

"Yes."

"Do you plan on having more kids by her?"

"She's pregnant now."

"Wow."

"Please don't judge me Coach."

"I'm not judging you, Qualude. I'm just surprised that you have another kid on the way and I don't have one."

Coach Soloman hadn't told me much about himself. He was outgoing, but he never talked about his family. The team was his only family that he had.

I found this out when he said, "You are a lucky guy to have a family. I wish I had my own blood family."

"Why you say that, Coach?"

"Because I don't have no one. My mother and father was killed when I was 20 years old. I was very close to my parents when they were killed in a car accident."

This made me look at Coach Soloman different. This was why he treated everyone at the school like family.

CRUMBLING TALENT

I spoke, "I'm sorry to hear that Coach."

"Don't be sorry. I have grown from the incident. I now know that life goes on, and that death is a part of life."

"You make it sound so weird."

"Life can be weird. So can death. I didn't understand why God had taken my parents from me until I realize that it was for my own good. I was an only child growing up. My parents were older when they had me. This made it hard for me, because I wanted siblings. I remember when I was a kid and wanted a big brother to help me with the neighborhood bully. My parents looked at me like I was crazy. But I didn't know that I was their blessing. What I'm trying to say to you is, you are your daughter's mother blessing. From what you told me about y'all relationship, she doesn't appreciate you. But she love you."

I interrupted, "I feel like she don't appreciate me."

"Why do you feel like that?"

"Because she don't respect what I'm trying to do."

"Why you say this?"

"Because she told me. She rather I sell drugs."

"This is a new revelation."

Coach was an understanding person, but I didn't think he would understand my situation. To my surprise, he gave me insight that I needed.

When he told me that he could arrange for Denise to move into an apartment with me and get the funds to pay the bills I asked, "What do I have to do?"

"Just win on the court."

I didn't know if it was a good idea to move Denise and our daughter to Winston Salem with me. I was enjoying my freedom but I did miss her and my daughter. Especially my daughter.

Before I left Coach's office I said, "Give me some time to think about this Coach."

"Take as much as you like."

I left Coach Soloman's office thinking about the offer. I really wanted to be able to raise my daughter while I was attending college. The reason I wanted this was because my parents didn't raise me together. I wanted to break the long cycle that my grandfather started. He ran out on my grandmother. My father ran out on my mother.

When I arrived home after class, I walked in to find Telly and Cory with an apartment full of white females. Both of them had started going out chasing white females after the first week of school. They used their basketball fame to get these females. To my surprise they had bring me one.

She introduced herself as Kelly. Her hair was black with brown ends on the tips. Her face was smooth with dimples. I liked her body. It was thick and in shape.

Kelly spoke, "I'm a big fan."

I said, "You don't know me."

She responded, "I watch you at your basketball practice all the time."

"You do?"

"Yes. I can see that you are going to help the team this year."

"You go to Forsyth?"

"Yes. I'm trying to be a nurse.'

"That's good."

"Don't get off the subject of you."

This female had my full attention. She was far from Denise. She wasn't selfish like Denise, and she didn't make everything about her like Denise did.

I said, "I'm a little shy when I meet people."

"Well you don't have to be shy in front of my crew and me. We are not special like y'all."

"What do you mean?"

"We don't have talent."

"You think basketball is a talent?"

"I know it's a talent. Everyone can't play it."

I had never thought that playing basketball was a talent until my twelve and under youth Coach took my cousin Travell and me to the local newspaper place after we had won the twelve and under city basketball championship. After our pictures were printed in the paper, I was famous around the neighborhood and my junior school.

Kelly responded, "I can't play. Maybe you can teach me how to play ball."

Kelly was flirting.

I said, "If I teach you, what are you going to teach me?"

She responded in a sexy manner, "We will think of something."

"You got a deal."

Kelly handed me a beer after she introduced me to Lin and Gin. They were sisters, and most of the guys on the team had had sex with them. I was told this by Kelly when she pulled me into the bathroom to talk to me in private. She also told me that she had a relationship with Nate. Nate and I didn't see eye to eye after the first practice. He wanted me to follow his every command. I bucked his leadership and told him I was my own leader. He told Coach Soloman and he pulled me to the side and told me that every great man was once a follower. I told Coach it was going to be hard for me to fall in line, because I was used to being my own man, but I would try. Now that Nate's ex-girl had come to me, I couldn't pass up the chance to pay him back for going to the Coach on me.

Kelly spoke, "I have to let you know that I had a relationship with Nate."

I said, "I don't care."

"Well, he might make it hard for you if he finds out about us."

"I liked you from the moment I laid eyes on you, but I have to tell you that I never been with a white girl."

"Have you ever been with a woman? Because I'm not a girl."

"Yes."

"Color don't mean anything. Women all have the same thing."

"Where I'm from, we just don't go after white woman."

"Like I said, color doesn't exist with me. I see your heart and your heart is telling me you want me."

Kelly had me hard as a rock. I had never had a woman be so sexual with me. I had girls that talked nasty to me, but never live out their fantasy. Kelly had me under her spell. When she kissed me on the mouth, she sucked on my tongue like it was a piece of hard candy. This went on for about five minutes.

When we came up for breath she said, "That was great."

I responded, "It was."

She asked, "Is it the same as kissing a black woman?"

"Yes."

The kiss with Kelly felt the same as kissing a black woman. There wasn't much difference.

She asked, "I always wanted to have sex with a guy inside a shower."

I asked, "You didn't have sex with Nate inside a shower?"

"No. He don't like water."

I wanted to laugh when Kelly told me that Nate was afraid of water, because he almost lost his life when he slipped and fell into the deep end of his parents' pool when he was a little boy. But I didn't.

I said, "Everyone has a fear."

"Not me. I'm not afraid of anything. I'm willing to try anything." Then Kelly kissed me again.

I responded by getting lost in the moment. The thought of Denise came to my mind when Kelly reached for my zipper on jeans. I didn't want to cheat on Denise, but I was caught in the moment. I had always wanted to have sex with a white woman. Even when I was in high school, I would sit in class thinking about how it would feel to have sex with one.

I spoke, "I don't have a rubber."

"You don't need one. I'm clean."

"I have a girlfriend."

It doesn't matter.

Even though Denise and I wasn't on good term, I still looked at her as my girlfriend.

I watched as Kelly turned on the shower. Then she took off

CRUMBLING TALENT

her jeans and t-shirt. She didn't have on underwear or a bra. Her center was clean shaved and her breasts were smaller than Denise's by three cups.

She asked, "What are you waiting on?"

I said, "I don't think this is a good idea."

"It's a wonderful idea. All you have to do is enjoy the moment."

"What about everyone in the next room?"

"I won't make any noise if you don't."

Kelly had me trapped in a corner. I wasn't use to a woman being in control.

I said, "I have to get a condom."

"Do what you have to do. I will be here waiting."

I watched Kelly get in the shower and grab the soap and lather herself up. She was making these faces that were turning me on. I really didn't want to cheat on Denise, but I was weak to my flesh.

I let my little head get in the way of my big head. I walked out the bathroom door and made sure it was secured before I walked back into the living room where Telly and Cory were entertaining Kelly's friends. I called a team meeting in the kitchen. Cory and Telly rushed in.

I spoke, "I need y'all help."

Telly asked, "What is it, Q?"

I responded, "I need condoms. I ran out."

Telly replied, "I don't have any."

Cory said, "I don't either."

I said, "I need one of y'all to make a store run."

Telly said, "I can't. I'm wasted."

Cory said, "I'm too messed up, big bro."

I said, "You two are not good for anything."

Cory said, "We got you the girl."

Telly cut in, "I'm going back to the party. I'm trying to get me some."

I asked, "What about condoms?"

Telly said, "I don't need condoms. I have plastic bags."

"Plastic bags?" I asked.
Telly said, "Yes. They work."
I had never tried to put a plastic bag on my penis.
I asked, "Do it really work?"
"You might need two, Q. You know you hung like King Kong."
I asked, "Where are the bags?"
Telly responded, "In my room drawer. It's better to be safe than sorry."
Telly's comment made me think about the girl that gave me the STD. She was pretty and clean. Her demeanor was like Kelly's. She wanted to have sex.

DENISE
I tried Qualude's apartment number. No answer. I didn't understand why he hadn't called me. He told me when he got out of school that he was going to call me. He lied. This wasn't the first time he had lied and it wasn't going to be the last. I decided to call his mother and apologize.
I had called Ladricka first and got Qualude's mother's number from her. Then I called Mrs. Brenda.
When she came over the line I said, "This is Denise. I'm calling to apologize to you."
Brenda asked, "Do you really mean it? Did my son tell you to call me and apologize?"
"No. I was sitting here and decided to call because I was wrong."
"Yes, you were."
"I didn't call for you to rub it in my face. I called because I want to have a good relationship with you because of Shaquala."
"I love my granddaughter to death but if I have to put up with the stuff you and Qualude got going on, I will remove myself from her life."
"I was upset. I'm sorry."

"I accept your apology."

"Do you want to see Shaquala?"

"Yes."

"How about I bring her over there?"

"That would be nice, but I have to go pick up Qualude and Telly from college in about an hour."

"Qualude didn't tell me he was coming home for the weekend."

"He didn't?"

"No, he didn't."

"Well I'm supposed to leave to go pick him up in the next hour. He hasn't called and told me not to come."

My relationship with Mrs. Brenda wasn't bad, but it wasn't good either. I didn't trust her because she was always trying to cover up for her son.

I asked, "Can I ride to Winston Salem with you?"

"I don't have a problem with it. But I think it would be a good idea to call my son first."

"Let's surprise him."

"What if you get a surprise?"

"It's time I know the truth. I need to know what your son want in life. I need to know if he wants me and my kids or the streets."

"I know he love you."

"How do you know?"

"Because my son don't introduce me to no girls. But he didn't deal with you."

"He didn't introduce us. You saw me at Big Mama's apartment and you asked me was I pregnant by him."

"Maybe it happened that way, but I know he love you."

This was Mrs. Brenda's first time holding a conversation with me. When I went with her to see Qualude in prison, she didn't say much to me.

"Well, if he loves me, he will not mind if I ride with you to pick him and up."

I could tell that Mrs. Brenda had stuck her foot in her mouth. She really didn't want me to ride to Winston Salem with her, because she knew how much of a dog her son was. She knew that it was a possibility that her son could have a female at his apartment. This didn't stop me from putting her to the test. I had to see if she was telling me the truth about her son.

QUALUDE

After I got the sandwich bags from Telly's bedroom, I walked slowly back to the bathroom where Kelly was waiting.

I knocked on the door before she said, "Come in, Q."

It was like she knew I was coming back. When I walked in I could see that Kelly was still in the shower. Her hair was wet and her nipples were hard.

She asked, "You got the condom?"

I responded, "Yes."

"Well come on in."

The bags in my hand were small. I didn't see how I was going to put both bags on my penis.

After I took off my clothes, Kelly commanded, "Turn off the light."

I did as she commanded. I couldn't see her after the lights went out. I had to feel my way over to the shower. Kelly reached out to me once I got close to her.

I asked, "Are you on the pill?"

"Why do you ask?"

"I'm just asking."

"No."

I didn't want another kid. Plus, I didn't want to catch another STD. The embarrassment I went through when I had the STD was enough to kill a man.

I said, "You know Nate is going to find out."

She responded, "Forget Nate. I'm here with you. Now be quiet and have sex with me."

Kelly grabbed my penis and stoked it several times and then asked, "Can I suck it?"

I responded, "Sure."

I had heard all the talk about white women having the best oral sex. Kelly proved to me that the saying was, in fact, true. She took me in her mouth so fast that I thought she was going to eat me. I could feel every inch of her lips and tongue. This girl was a professional. The way she used her hands and her tongue gave me this disposition.

Denise was far from my mind now. All I could think about was the way Kelly was trying to swallow me. Her throat was warm and wet. All the stress that was in my body seemed like it was sucked out of me when I exploded. She had done me up in two minutes.

She said, "You were a little excited."

I said, "Yes. I guess I was."

"How about I let you taste me?"

"I don't do that."

"There is a first time for everything."

"Not that."

"You acting like I wasn't great."

"You were great. I just don't eat stuff that can get up and walk away from me."

"Why didn't you tell me that before you let me do you."

"You took charge before I could do anything."

"Well at lease give me some sex."

"I'm finished."

"You finished?"

"Yes."

"You didn't do anything."

Kelly didn't understand me. She didn't know I didn't go for women that were easy, and she didn't know sex didn't control me like most guys I knew. Sex was just sex to me. I didn't get nothing out of sex with a woman I didn't love. This moment made me realize that I loved Denise. Because I didn't feel like I could Love a woman like Kelly.

I spoke, "I enjoyed you. I hope we can do this again."

She responded, "You just going to leave me like this?"

I was out the shower now. I turned on the light and started putting on my clothes when Kelly asked me this.

I said, "I didn't really want to have sex with you because you used to have a relationship with Nate."

"You think this a game?"

"Yes."

"It's not. I really like you."

"I have to be truthful. I can never take you serious because you had a relationship with Nate and you sucked my dick the first time we ever met."

"I was taught if you love someone that you give them your all."

"I can see your point. But I don't love you. You don't even know me."

"I know enough about you."

"You nice and all, but I don't see myself being with you."

"Now that you got what you want, you don't want nothing to do with me?"

"You seduced me."

"That will not be the story when the newspaper get it."

"What are you talking about?"

I watched as Kelly stepped out the shower and picked up her blue jeans. She didn't even grab a towel.

She spoke, "I will scream and say you rape me if you don't do what I say."

I said, "I didn't rape you."

"Who you think the police will believe?"

"You wouldn't."

"Yes, I would."

"What do you want?"

"I want you to make love to me."

CRUMBLING TALENT

"You crazy."
"I will scream if you don't make love to me."
"Go head."
Kelly shouted, "Rape!"
The music in the living was blasting. No one could hear Kelly. I grabbed Kelly and covered her mouth. She tried to bite me.
I said, "Stop."
She said, "I will not, unless you have sex with me."
Then she grabbed at my soft penis.
I said, "No. I'm not going to have sex with you."
"Fuck me. I need it. Please."
No."
We struggled inside the bathroom for about a minute before I gained control of her. She started screaming. I put my hand over her mouth again.
Then I asked, "Why are you doing this?" Then I removed my hand.
She said, "Because, I want to get Nate back."
"What did he do to you for you to try to hurt me?"
"He left me for a black woman. He told me he didn't like black women because his mother left him when he was little. He said his mother dropped him off at his grandmother's house and never returned."
"What do I have to do with you and Nate's situation?"
"Well ever since you arrived here, he has treated me like shit. He blames you for trying to take his leadership role on the team."
"I still don't understand."
"You are a threat to what he's doing here. He feels like you can take his spot as the leader and mess up his chances of getting in a D-1 school."
"That's crazy!"
"Not in his mind. Nate is very insecure about everything."
"Why do you want to be with a guy like him?"
"Because I know the real Nate. He just needs someone to love him."

Kelly had me wondering if Nate put her up to this. I asked, "Did Nate tell you to do this?"

"No!"

DENISE

I was upset with Qualude after Telly told me that I couldn't ride with his mother to the college. I told her that he said I could ride with her. As we were riding on the freeway, I told her I lied.

She asked, "Why did you lie?"

"Because I knew you wouldn't let me ride with you if I told you the truth," I responded, as I gave my daughter her bottle.

"I should turn this car around and take you back. If my grandbaby wasn't in here, and I wasn't so far out of the city, I would."

"I'm sorry, but I need to see Qualude."

I could tell that Mrs. Brenda was upset but I didn't care. I needed to see if Qualude was cheating on me. He had been dodging me ever since he enrolled in school. After our fight at his apartment, he stopped coming around me. And when he did come around, he didn't say anything to me unless it was about our daughter.

Mrs. Brenda spoke, "I understand. I know you love my son."

"But I don't think he love me anymore."

"What makes you think that?"

"Ever since Shaquala was born he's being acting different."

"What do you mean?"

"He doesn't tell me he love me no more. He don't treat me with respect like he use to."

"Why do you think he's acting the way he's acting?"

"I really don't know."

I knew Mrs. Brenda wasn't stupid. She had been around the block before I even had thought about stepping off the front porch. She knew it was something I did to make her son not trust me.

CRUMBLING TALENT

She asked, "What did you do?"
I said, "Nothing."
She said, "There is something."
I didn't know if I should open up to Mrs. Brenda, but I did.
I said, "Your son caught me talking to this guy named J-Rock."
"What happened?"
"I wasn't trying to get with J-Rock. I was just talking when your son pulled up in the parking lot when we were living with my grandmother."
"What did my son say?"
"He grabbed me by my hair. That's when I told him that I was pregnant with this baby. He told me that he didn't think he was the father because we hadn't been having sex like we normally did."
"What did you say?"
"I told him that it only takes one time."
"I have to ask you this. I don't want you to get upset. Did you have sex with someone other than my son before you got pregnant?"
"I have to be truthful. Your son is the only person I ever had sex with," I lied.

QUALUDE

I managed to get Kelly to agree that our situation never happened. This was after she had told me all about her and Nate's situation.

I gave her insight about her relationship with Nate after she told me that her father disowned her because she was in love with Nate. This was my first time that I had been put in a situation where a woman was trying to use me to get back at her ex.

After I helped Kelly get dressed, I walked her to my room and let her rest in my bed. She was still crying when I closed the door to my room. I walked inside the living where Telly and Cory were still entertaining Kelly's friends. I pulled Telly and Cory back in the kitchen and told them what had transpired between Kelly and me. They both were shocked from the revelation.

Telly said, "I'm sorry man. I didn't know she was still messing around with Nate."

I said, "She isn't fooling around with Nate. He dropped her like a bad hate. She still wants him but he doesn't want her."

Cory responded, "It's time to get these girls out of here."

I said," Not so fast. We don't want Kelly to leave here upset."

Telly said, "You didn't do nothing to her, did you?"

I said, "No."

Telly said, "Well, I'm about to throw these chicks out of here."

"No."

"Why?"

I said, "Just give Kelly some time alone. She will be alright once she finishes crying."

Cory said, "You sure you didn't do anything to her?"

I said, "Yes."

I wanted to tell Telly and Cory that I let Kelly perform oral sex on me, but I didn't. I didn't think it was important since it didn't mean nothing to me. I grabbed a beer out of the cooler that was sitting in the middle of the floor.

Then I said, "Y'all go have fun. I will take care of Kelly."

I watched as Telly and Cory walked back in the living room and joined the girls. I grabbed another beer and walked to my bedroom. While walking to my room I thought about the day I told Denise that I had given her the STD. Her words echoed through my ears as I opened my bedroom door.

Denise had said, "Your dick is going to get you in trouble."

Kelly was laying in my bed with her back turned to me when I walked in the room. She didn't have a single piece of clothing on.

I asked, "What are you doing?"

She responded, "I'm just relaxing."

"Without your clothes on?"

"I feel better naked."

"Well this isn't a good look."
"You wasn't saying that when you had your dick in my mouth."
"I think it's time for you to go."
"You are just like all men. Once y'all get what y'all want, y'all want to get rid of me."

I didn't know how many men that Kelly had been with, but from listening to her talk, it was a lot. She was constantly using the words "y'all" and "all men" during our conversation. This was disturbing.

I said, "I sorry for not being the man you thought I was."
"Don't be sorry. I don't need you or any man."

I knew Kelly was hurting in the inside because every man that had been in her life had hurt her.

I said, "I wish we hadn't met like this," I said.
"Like I said, you are like all the others," she responded.

Kelly was up out my bed now. I watched as she put on her clothes. While watching her, I noticed a pill on the floor. I walked over and picked it up.

She said, "That's my pain pill."
"What is it?"
"Nothing of your business."

Kelly snatched the pill out my hand. I watched as she put it in her mouth. She smiled after she swallowed the pill.

She spoke, "You will never understand me. I'm too much woman for you and Nate. Both of you are dreamers. I like dreamers. But you two will never get to live out y'all dreams."

I asked, "What are you talking about?"
"You will see."

When Kelly started towards my bedroom door, I noticed a plastic bag in her hand.

I asked, "What is that?"
"This is what going to get me all the money I need. These are your seeds. See, I spit them in this bag after you forced me to suck your dick."

"Are you crazy? I didn't force you to do nothing."

"That's my story."

"You better change your story."

"My friends will back me up. Once the news get it who will you think they will believe? I'm a white, young, woman. You are another black rapist."

"Please don't do this Kelly."

"It's too late."

I tried to grab the bag out of Kelly's hand. She pulled away and dotted out my bedroom. I chased her down the hallway to the living room. Once in the living room, we wrestled over the bag in front of our friends. Kelly started screaming. This didn't stop me from taking the bag out her hand.

Once I got hold of the bag, Kelly shouted, "He raped me."

I said, "She's lying."

Everyone looked at me like I was guilty.

She spoke, "The bag has his semen in it."

I shouted, "She tricked me. She told me that she liked me and she wanted to have sex with me. I didn't force myself on her."

"I didn't trick him. He forced himself on me and then made me suck his dick."

"That a flat out lie."

"The evidence is in that bag that he took from me."

DENISE

When we pulled up in front of Qualude's apartment I could tell something was wrong. The front door to his apartment was wide open. Telly was standing on the front stairway with two white girls. Another white girl was crying and shouting from a red Honda that was parked in front of the building.

Mrs. Brenda told me to stay in the car when she got out. I didn't want to stay in the car, but Shaquala was asleep in the backseat. Plus, my stomach was hurting from the baby kicking. I watched as Mrs. Brenda walked up on the stairway of Qualude's

CRUMBLING TALENT

apartment. Telly met her. I couldn't read their lips, but from his hand movements, something had taken place inside the apartment that had something to do with Qualude.

The girl in the Honda pulled off and the other two girls waved at Telly and got inside a black Lexus and pulled off. I decided it was time for me to get out and see what was going on. I grabbed Shaquala up out of her car seat and walked slowly up to Qualude's apartment.

Telly smiled at me and said, "He's in the bathroom."

Mrs. Brenda was coming out of the bathroom when I walked out through the door.

As I laid Shaquala on the couch, she said, "Qualude is in the shower."

I noticed Cory inside the kitchen cleaning the floor with a rag. Qualude had told me about Cory, but I had never seen him or talked to him. This was my first time visiting their apartment and seeing Cory. From the description Qualude gave me of him, it was on point. I walked in the kitchen after Mrs. Brenda took a seat on the couch beside Shaquala.

Cory looked up at me when I asked, "Do y'all have some clean glasses?"

He responded, "Who are you?"

I said, "Denise."

He said, "It's nice to finally meet you."

I responded, "I need something to eat and drink.'

"There is some chicken and mac and cheese that Qualude cooked for us last night. You can have my grape soda I have in the cooler."

"Thank you."

I fixed a plate and grabbed a soda out of the cooler. Then I returned to the living room. Telly turned on the TV, and I sat there watching the news while I ate the food. Something in the air wasn't right. I could feel the tense inside the room, and when Qualude walked inside the room, I started thinking about the three girls that I had seen when Mrs. Brenda and I pulled up.

I didn't do the math right then, because I was focusing on my daughter. Now that my stomach was full, I could think.

I asked, "Who was those girls?"

Qualude responded, "Who told you to make yourself at home?"

I said, "I told myself to make myself at home."

Mrs. Brenda cut in, "Do not start, Qualude. You should be happy to see your kids' mother."

"I don't know if that's baby in her stomach is mine."

I responded, "This is your baby. You need to stop acting stupid."

"I don't know if it's mine. I caught you with J-Rock."

"We were not having sex."

"But I did catch y'all talking out front of your grandmother's house."

"That's not sex. You cannot get pregnant from talking to someone."

Qualude had never put me on the spot in front of his mother. This was the first time that he had even talked about us in front of Telly, too.

He spoke, "I have to be real with you, Denise. I don't think that's my baby."

I wanted to break down crying right then, but I kept my composure.

I said, "You can get a blood test."

"You don't have to worry about that. I was already thinking about the blood test."

"If you want one, I want child support, because you ain't doing nothing for my daughter right now."

I had to put him on blast in front of his friend and family. This was a hit to his ego, and I knew this would make him mad because he had promised me that he would always take care of Shaquala and me.

Mrs. Brenda spoke, "Y'all don't need to be fighting in front of my grandbaby. Wait till y'all get alone and then handle y'all

CRUMBLING TALENT

business."

Mrs. Brenda grabbed Shaquala off the couch after Shaquala opened her eyes.

I wanted to blast Qualude some more about how he had been treating me, but I kept this to myself and said, "I didn't come here to fight with you. I asked your mother could I ride with her because I wanted to see you."

Qualude said, "I told you I wasn't ready to deal with you."

I responded, "You cannot turn me on and off when you want to. Either you going to be with me or not."

He responded, "Right now, I'm trying to focus on school."

"That's the problem. You are too focused on school to know that I'm thinking about moving on."

Mrs. Brenda cut in, "Didn't I tell y'all to stop?"

Qualude said, "I didn't tell you to bring her here."

Qualude was talking to his mother like I wasn't even there. This pissed me off.

I said, "I lied to her."

Mrs. Brenda said, "This girl wanted to see you. That's why she lied to me, so she could come see you."

I thought Qualude was going to be happy to see me, but he wasn't.

When he said, "All y'all girls want one thing. That is to hurt me. Y'all want to kill my soul."

Mrs. Brenda said, "That's enough, Qualude."

He said, "No. I'm sick of all these girls trying to bring me down."

I asked, "Bring you down? You always make trouble for yourself. I didn't tell you to sell drugs. You chose to sell drugs because you wanted to."

"No. I sold drugs so I could take care of you and the baby."

I said, "You was selling drugs long before Shaquala was born."

"When I found out you was pregnant, I dedicated my life to selling drugs."

"It was still your choice. I didn't put no gun to your head," I responded.

He said, "You don't get it."

I watched as Qualude walked down the hallway to his bedroom. He slammed the door to his room after he walked in. I continued to eat my food. I wasn't going to let him wreck my nerves. I knew he was going through something, but I couldn't put my finger on it.

CHAPTER 24

QUALUDE
TWO WEEKS LATER

The incident with Kelly had me on edge. I didn't mean to lash out on Denise, but Kelly had me thinking about my future. Before she left, she told us that she was going to report me to the police. I didn't think they had a case until Coach Soloman called me at Big Mama's apartment.

He spoke, "I have some bad news."

I could hear the seriousness in his voice.

I asked, "What is it?"

He hesitated before he said, "You might have a warrant for your arrest."

"For what?"

"Rape."

When I heard the word, rape, it was like the wind was knocked out my lungs. I thought I was about to have a heart attack. The first person that came to mind was Kelly. How could she?

I said, "Coach, this is all a lie. I didn't rape no one."

"I have some friends in the DA office. You don't have to worry about nothing. I will have you in and out the jail before the media gets wind of what's going on."

"I didn't do it, Coach."

"I know you didn't. I believe you son."

"What do I have to do?"

"Come back to Winston Salem and turn yourself in."

"I didn't do anything, Coach."

"We will get through this son. Just come back here."

I didn't want to turn myself in, because I hadn't raped Kelly. She made up a story that the DA believed. She told the DA that I got her drunk and put something in her drink that made her fall asleep, and this was when I raped her. The only hole in her story was that there was no physical evidence. This was a plus for my side, because it was hard to prove rape without physical evidence.

I didn't know if I should tell my mother or Big Mama, because there wasn't really anything they could do. I told Telly after I arrived back at school. He couldn't believe it.

He asked, "You think Coach can help?"

"He told me not to worry."

"When do you have to turn yourself in?"

"Tonight. Coach is coming by to take me to the jail."

"You think he will let me go too?"

"I don't know."

DENISE

My trip to Qualude's apartment didn't go well. He didn't like the fact that I had lied to his mother. I thought he was going to be happy to see me but he wasn't. I could tell that something was wrong with him, because he wasn't acting like he usually acted when he saw Shaquala and me.

After I had returned home, I called Tasha and told her about my trip. I gave her all the details about how Qualude's apartment looked and I even told her about the three white girls I saw at his apartment.

She asked, "You didn't blink out your mind and go ghetto?"

"No," I said.

She asked, "Do you think he was messing with one of those white girls?"

"I didn't even ask him. I was too upset."

"What was you upset about?"

"Those white girls and the fact that he treated me like I wasn't shit. He even said that this baby in my stomach isn't his baby."

"Why did he do you like that?"

I hadn't told Tasha about the time Qualude caught me with J-Rock. I didn't think it was a good idea to tell her, because she would have spread it around the projects that I was messing with J-Rock. I didn't need this rumor on me, being that Qualude already thought I was messing around on him.

I spoke, "Because he caught me with J-Bone."

"He caught you cheating?"

"No. I was just talking."

"Why didn't you tell me when this had happened?"

"Because I know how you are. You would have told the whole hood."

"So, that baby in your stomach could be J-Rock?"

"No. This isn't J-Rock baby. I told you I didn't cheat on Qualude."

Tasha wasn't trying to hear me. She was already judging me after I had told her that I was caught with J-Rock.

She said, "I knew you were getting dick on the side."

"No, I wasn't. I love Qualude."

"That don't mean you wasn't cheating. "

"I love him."

"But do he love you?"

Qualude had told me on many occasions that he loved me. Now that I was pregnant with this baby, he hadn't said the word love for the last seven months.

I said, "I think he still love me."

Tasha said, "Don't be no fool. You should know if someone love you or not."

"He love me."

"Well, why did he have them white girls in his apartment?"

"He told me that Telly and Cory invited the girls over."

"And you believed him?"

"Why not?"

"Because he caught you cheating. He has a pass to cheat."

"I wasn't cheating. I was just talking."

"He doesn't see it like that. He see it as you were cheating."

"I didn't look at it like that."

You need to wake up. Qualude is in the process of moving on."

When Coach pulled up in his car, I was sitting on the front stairway of my building. Telly asked Coach Soloman could he ride along. Coach told him that there was no need, because I would be right back out. Then we got in Coach's BMW and left.

On our way, Coach spoke, "I want you to know I believe you."

I said, "Coach, I want you to know I appreciate you helping me. Whatever happens, I want to thank you for taking a chance on me when no one else would."

Coach smiled and said, "It's not over. You are going to make it out of this."

I responded, "I hope I do. Rape is a serious crime."

Coach Soloman asked, "Do you believe in God?"

I said, "Yes."

"Well, God is going to get you out this situation."

When we arrived at the jail, a short white man with black hair was waiting with an officer at the front door of the intake area. He Introduced himself as Mr. Black. He was the head DA of Forsyth County. He walked Coach Soloman and me inside the jail and took us to a room where we were told to stay until he returned. While he was gone, Coach Soloman and I talked about our first game at Bluefield College in Virginia. I was excited about playing my first college game, but when Coach Soloman told me that I might not get to play if the DA decided to charge me, I was devastated.

CRUMBLING TALENT

When Mr. Black returned, he had a stack of papers in his hand. The uniformed cop was no longer with him.

He spoke, "I need you to be truthful with me. I'm going to asks you some questions and I want you to answer them best you can."

I asked, "Do I need a lawyer?"

Mr. Black asked, "Do you want a lawyer? Because it is your right."

I responded, "Do I need one?"

"If I find that you committed a crime, you will need one."

I knew the process of being charged with a crime. I was playing dumb, hoping this would help with Mr. Black's decision of not charging me with a crime.

I spoke, "I didn't do anything."

He responded, "That's what I'm about to see. I have some questions. I need to ask you about the day Kelly Rose came to your apartment."

I said, "I didn't rape that girl."

"Let me finish."

"I promise you I did not break the law."

"What happened that day?"

I gave Mr. Black a short version of what had happened between Kelly and me. I left out the part about the oral sex.

He asked, "Did she perform oral sex on you?"

I didn't know if I should lie or tell the truth about the oral sex, because I didn't know what Kelly had told Mr. Black.

I asked, "What did she say?"

He responded, "She said you made her have oral sex with you."

"That's a lie," I responded.

Coach Soloman looked at me like he was trying to read me. I wanted to say something to him, but I didn't. I didn't want to say the wrong thing and turn Coach Soloman against again me. I had earned Coach Soloman's respect by being truthful with him. I didn't want to ruin our relationship by telling a lie about what really happened that day at my apartment.

I said, "I never been charged with something like this."

Mr. Black pulled a piece of paper from the stack and said, "This is a copy of your record. You have been to prison for selling drugs and breaking and entering."

"Yes, I have, but I have never been charged with raping anyone."

Mr. Black gave me this look like I had said the keyword to a word puzzle.

He said, "I never said anything about rape."

I looked at Coach for help.

He spoke, "I told him that a girl was trying to get him charged with rape."

Mr. Black said, "I told you not to say anything to him, David."

Coach said, "He's like a son to me."

Mr. Black said, "You messed up my investigation."

Coach asked, "How?"

"Because you gave him notice about this meeting. I told you to tell him that I just want to ask him some question about a girl."

Mr. Black was hoping that I said something that would give him probable cause to lock me up. He didn't get his wish, because I hadn't broken the law. Kelly had lied. I knew she lied, but Mr. Black didn't think so. After our meeting, he got a judge to issue him a search warrant for my apartment. The police took away my bed linen and the clothes that I had on the day Kelly was at my apartment. There still was not enough evidence to get me charged, because there was no DNA on any of the evidence.

WINTER 1996
DENISE

I was starting to feel depressed, because Qualude wasn't paying any attention to me. He was more focused on College and he wasn't coming home on the weekends. Every time I called him;

he would say he was too busy to talk. Tasha was right. Qualude was moving on.

I decided it was time to confront Qualude about his neglect towards me. I told his mother to tell him that I needed to talk to him and to call me at the hospital. This was after I went into labor. Qualude called me at the hospital after I had Jaquala.

He was upset that he didn't get to be there for her birth, but I reminded him that he was the one that wasn't answering my phone calls.

I tried to call him right before I was driven to the hospital by Nicole's boyfriend. Like I said, he didn't answer, so he missed out on Jaquala's birth.

When he came to the hospital the next day, he was so happy that he told me that he wanted to marry me. Aunt Peggy rolled her eyes at him like she didn't believe him. Her and I had made up again after she saw the baby. Qualude didn't like Aunt Peggy, and the reason was me.

The spark in his eyes towards me was no longer there. This hurt me, because I had given him two beautiful daughters and dedicated my life to him. He didn't appreciate this and it showed in his demeanor.

My daughter had come out weighing six pounds. Her head was full of hair and she looked like Shaquala. She had Qualude's eyes and his nose. There was no way he could deny her, because she looked too much like him. When Tasha and Candy came over to the hospital after Qualude left to go back to school, I told them that Qualude wanted to marry me. Tasha was happy for me, but Candy wasn't.

She said, "You going to marry a dog."

I responded, "He's not a dog."

"Girl, he done had every girl in the hood. I have a list of names I can give you."

Tasha cut in, "Why do you always have to hate? Why you just can't be happy for Denise?"

Candy said, "Because Denise can do better. There are other

men out there that would love to be with her."

Tasha asked, "How do you know Qualude don't want to be with her?"

Candy responded, "Because he's a dog. And dogs need more than one partner."

I watched as Candy and Tasha went at it about my relationship with Qualude. They both made good and bad points.

I cut in, "Both of y'all are right, but all relationships are not perfect. I like what I have with him."

Candy said, "You deserve better."

"This is what I want, Candy. I love Qualude."

Candy said, "But do he love you like you love him?"

This was a question I had never asked myself. If Candy wouldn't have brought this to my attention, I wouldn't have even considered if he now loved me or not. My relationship with Qualude was now just going through the motions. To me, this was all happening because of the kids, I thought, as I started to cry.

❖   ❖   ❖

QUALUDE

I left the jail feeling good about the situation with Kelly. There was not enough evidence for Mr. Black to charge me with a crime. Plus, there were no witnesses. Kelly had told Mr. Black that her friends were in the living room when the rape took place. They confirmed that they were in the living room, but they didn't hear anything. They helped Mr. Black with his decision whether to charge me or not.

I found out that Kelly had a mental problem. This was brought out when Coach Soloman threatened Mr. Black with a lawsuit. Coach Soloman had the school's lawyers look up Kelly's medical history. They found out that Kelly had once been treated for a mental illness, and she was still taking medication for it. This gave Coach Soloman the power to get Mr. Black to stop pursuing me and focus on Kelly.

CRUMBLING TALENT

I thanked Coach for going to bat for me. Then I decided I should have a conversation with Nate about the situation. He didn't have any hard feelings towards me and agreed to meet with me. We met at Coach's office and talked about what had happened between Kelly and I. I thought Nate was this spoiled kid from upstate, but he was alright.

Nate spoke, "I heard what happened to you. It's all over the school. Take this as a lesson."

I responded. "I learned a lesson. Trust me, I will never put myself in a situation like that again."

"I wanted you to know I'm not upset with you. Kelly and I were cool, but I knew something was wrong with her."

"I didn't go after her."

"That don't matter. What matter now is, you didn't get charged with a crime. You have another chance."

"I really didn't rape her. She lied."

"Like I said, it don't matter now. What matters the most is you still get to play ball. I want you to know that I was praying that you wasn't charged with a crime."

"Thanks man."

"That's what teammates are for. We are family."

Nate made me feel good. After we had our conversation, we left Coach's office and went over to my apartment. The whole team came over and we had a semi-party. We drank beer and took down shots. Nate even called a few women over. The night went smooth. The next morning Nate invited me to his work place.

I was shocked that Nate was a baker. He was great at making muffins. The muffin shop was all his until 9:00 am. We had gotten there at 6:00am. For three hours, Nate schooled me about all the different kinds of muffins he had to make. He did this while making them. I caught on quickly, and I even thought about asking Nate to help get me a job at the place, but that came to an end when Nate told me that he was only making minimum wage.

We became close and led our team to ten straight victories. Nate even shared his dream with me. His dream was like mine.

He wanted to go to a D-1 school, and then play in the NBA. Life was good now.

QUALUDE

My life was going well until I got a call from Denise's grandmother. She told me that Denise was pregnant again. I didn't want to believe her, because I hadn't been having sex with Denise that much. We were only having sex on the weekends. This was something I wasn't ready for. I didn't understand how Denise could let herself get pregnant.

When I arrived at her grandmother's house for the weekend, Denise wasn't there. She was at the mall doing some shopping for our daughters. I made myself at home and called Big Boo. It had been a while since I had talked with him. When he had answered the phone, I could tell he was shocked to hear from me.

I asked, "What's been going on?"

He responded, "Nothing."

I asked, "I just called to say I was thinking about you."

"I thought you didn't want anything to do with me."

"I was upset."

"Creep told me that you was going to call."

It had been a while since I had seen Creep. He had got back on drugs. I had stopped speaking to him and asking about him when I heard this.

"How is he?"

"He talks about you all the time. He say you going to the NBA."

"I hope so."

"When you do, don't forget about the little people."

"I will never forget about the hood."

"Word is that you have already forgot about the hood."

I had stopped going to the projects after I got into school, because I didn't want to get into any trouble. I had learned my

CRUMBLING TALENT

lessons from giving a so-called friend a ride and the drug charge.

"I still got love for the hood."

"Well, you need to show it by coming through sometimes."

"I'm in town. Maybe I can come through there."

"That will be great. When?"

"How about tonight?"

"I'mma tell Creep."

I hung up the phone after talking to Big Boo. Then, I went to the living room where Denise's grandmother was watching TV.

I asked, "Did Denise tell you what time she was coming back?"

Miss Betty answered, "No."

"Who did she go to the mall with?"

"Tasha drove her."

"Well, I have somewhere to go. Can you tell her I will be back later?"

Miss Betty hesitated before she said, "I need to talk to you about Denise before you leave."

I asked, "What is it?"

"I think Denise need help."

"What are you talking about?"

"I caught Denise talking to herself."

"We all talk to ourselves sometimes."

"Well, Denise has been answering herself after asking herself questions."

"So, you tell me that she's asking herself questions and then answering them?"

"Yes."

"How long has this been going on?"

"Ever since she had the baby."

"Jaquala or Shaquala."

"Jaquala."

"Why didn't you tell me when it first started?"

"I didn't think nothing of it. I just thought it was stress."

"Have she done anything strange other than talking to herself?"

"That's what I wanted to get to next."

Miss Betty looked worried. I could tell that she was concerned about Denise.

She continued, "I caught Denise choking Shaquala."

"You what?"

"I caught Denise choking Shaquala about a week ago."

"What did you do?"

"I took Shaquala and I threatened Denise. I told her that if I ever caught her choking Shaquala again, I would have her locked up."

I couldn't believe what I was hearing. Denise had never displayed this type behavior towards our kids while I was around. She was always gentle and motherly with them.

I said, "There has to be something going on with her in order for her to be doing this."

"I heard her say that it's your fault that your daddy don't want me anymore."

"What was that supposed to mean?"

"I was hoping you could tell me."

Miss Betty had me confused. I had never told Denise I didn't want her anymore. There were some times that I had gotten mad at her, but never said I didn't love her.

I said, "I have to speak with Denise about this."

Miss Betty said, "No."

"What do you mean?"

"You cannot say a word to her about this."

"Why?"

"She will make my life hard."

"What are you saying?"

"Ever since you went off to college, Denise had been another person. She is very disrespectful."

"How?"

"She cuss me out and call me all kinds of names."

"Why didn't you tell me this long ago?"

"I didn't want you to get into any trouble. I know you have an attitude and she has one."

"I have to say something to her."

"Please, don't."

After Miss Betty asked me not to say anything to Denise, Denise came walking through the front door. Tasha had Jaquala in her hands.

Denise asked, "Please don't, what? What are you begging him for?"

I said, "She is not begging me for nothing. We were just talking."

"I hope y'all wasn't talking about me."

I said, "I need to speak to you alone."

"What do you have to talk to me about?"

"When we get alone, I will tell you."

I excused myself and Denise followed me to her bedroom.

On my way down the hall I thought about how I was going to bring up the subject about her behavior. The best way was to convince her that it was my fault that she was changing.

When we stepped in the room, Denise asked, "What do you want to talk about?"

"About you and the kids."

"What about me and the kids?"

"Is everything okay?"

"Why wouldn't it be?"

"I know this college thang is new to you."

She interrupted, "You are the one that left us here. You waited to the last minute to tell me you was going off to college."

I could hear the disappointment in Denise's voice.

I said, "It's all my fault. I should have told you first. But we were upset with one another."

"You don't understand what I have to do here with these kids."

"Trust me. I understand."

"No, you don't," Denise shouted.

I said, "You don't have to shout. I hear you."

"No! I will shout if I want to. You left me here with these kids.

I thought you loved me."

I interrupted, "I do. That's why I'm going to college. I want to make a better life for us."

"I know you have moved on. I'm not stupid. Peaches told me that Telly was fucking a white girl. She found the white girl's number in Telly's pants pocket."

"What do that have to do with me?"

"I remember when I came with your mother to pick you up. There were three white girls at your apartment. I believe those are the white girls Peaches is talking about. One of the girls told Peaches you raped her."

I couldn't believe what I was hearing. I thought that Telly was more careful than me. He had proved to me that he was slipping.

I said, "The girl lied."

"You raping bitches and shit. What's wrong with you?"

I shouted, "I didn't rape no one."

"I don't believe you. I think you did it."

Denise hurt my heart when she said she believed that I had raped Kelly.

I responded, "This isn't the reason I asked you to come to your room."

"Well, this is the reason I've been acting crazy."

"You could have talked to me about it."

"You never answered the phone when I called."

"But that wasn't a good reason to harm my kids."

"What are you talking about?"

Denise made this face that proved that she was guilty. She responded, "I didn't do anything to my kids."

"You don't have to lie to me."

"I'm not lying."

"I know the truth. I'm not mad. I just need it to stop."

"Who told you I was abusing my kids?"

"It don't matter. It needs to stop."

"My grandmother told you. If she did, she's lying. Since she wants to tell you a lie, I'mma get her in trouble by reporting that

CRUMBLING TALENT

she's committing welfare fraud."

"Your grandmother didn't tell me nothing."

"I know she told you. She trying to get my kids took from me."

"She not trying to get our kids took. She love you. She will never do that."

Denise broke out crying.

I didn't understand why she was crying until she said, "You don't love me anymore. You going to leave me."

I grabbed her and pulled to me.

I said, "No. I'm not going to leave you."

"Peggy told me you was going to leave me. She also told me you tried to have sex with her."

I knew I should have told Denise about the day Peggy tried to seduce me.

I said, "Peggy lied to you."

She said, "Please don't leave me. Please."

I responded, "I'm not going to leave you."

After I got Denise to calm down, I drove over to Dalton Village Projects. Big Boo was standing out on the block serving a crackhead when I pulled up. Creep was standing a few feet away from him.

I hopped out the rental car and asked, "What's up with y'all?"

Big Boo responded, "I just out here grinding."

Creep cut in, "I can't believe it. It's the superstar."

I said, "I'm not a superstar yet."

Creep said, "You big time. You in college."

"That don't mean nothing."

"It means a lot. You ain't out here like me and Big Boo."

I didn't look at life like Creep thought I should look at it. I knew at any minute I could be back on the block risking my life for some money. It was a blessing from God for me to even get to go to college. Creep was dressed in all black like Big Boo. They were working as a team catching selling. Being back in the hood made me realize that it was in me. I was never going to be an

Uncle Tom like most blacks I knew in college.

I spoke, "The hood will always be in me. I will never change."

Big Boo said, "That's what I like to hear."

I said, "I know you didn't think I was going to change."

"I'm not going to lie. I thought them crackers was going to change you."

"Never. I'm hood for life."

"Told you, Creep. My nigga is never going to change."

Creep said, "I thought Melvin was Qualude's nigga."

"Melvin is his friend. I'm his nigga."

Creep asked, "What's up with Melvin?"

I hadn't been over to the hospital in about two weeks. I didn't know how Melvin was doing.

Big Boo spoke, "The word on the street is Melvin is getting out the hospital soon. He's in recovery."

Creep asked, "I know you going to do something to that dude Nuke for hurting your best friend."

I knew what Creep was doing. He was trying to get under Big Boo's skin and see if I was down with the hood.

I spoke, "I'mma go see Melvin tomorrow."

"Tell him I said get better."

After an hour of talking to Big Boo and Creep, Big Boo brought up Geneva's name. He told me that Geneva had come through the hood looking for me in a green Navigator Jeep. Her brother had just got a six-million-dollar contract with the New Jersey Nets. I knew this from watching ESPN.

I asked, "Did she leave a number?"

"No. But she did tell me to tell you that her brother is having a party this Sunday at CJ's nightclub downtown."

I hadn't been to a club since the night Pop got shot. I hadn't seen Geneva since I went off to prison. When I got out of prison, I didn't think to look for her because I heard while I was in prison that she had moved out of the city.

I asked, "You want to go with me Big Boo?"

"I don't have nothing to wear."

CRUMBLING TALENT

"All that money you making out here. You should have something to wear."

"It's a hard shoe event. I don't wear hard bottom shoes."

"There is a first time for everything."

Big Boo responded, "I got to pass."

I left the hood with my mind on Geneva. I had to hit this party, because I knew everyone in the city with a name was going to be there. Even though Geneva's brother didn't think I was good enough for her, I knew the real reason he didn't want me with her. He thought I was just trying to play her for money. I didn't care what he thought I was going to the party to see her.

CHAPTER 25

DENISE

After Tasha and Qualude left, I approached my grandmother in the living room about what she had told Qualude.

I asked, "Why da hell you tell Qualude that I be abusing my kids?"

My grandmother said, "You know you do."

"They are my kids. I can do what I want to do to them."

"It's not right, Denise. You know better."

"Stay out my business."

"As long as you in my house, I'mma be in your business."

"You need to get you some business and stay out of mine."

"If it wasn't for the kids, I would have been put you out."

"You think I like staying here? I'm only staying here until I get approved for my apartment."

My grandmother didn't know that I had signed up to get a section-eight apartment when I had signed up for food stamps and a welfare check.

She spoke, "You can get out now and leave the kids."

"You will never get my kids."

"You need help. Something is wrong with you."

"Ain't shit wrong with me," I shouted.

"Why are you raising your voice?"

"Because I can. I'm grown."

CRUMBLING TALENT

"You got to respect my house."

"I pay you to stay here."

"You don't pay me nothing."

"All the food I put in here with my food stamps, and I pay the cable bill."

"You don't understand. I don't need you to do nothing here. Before you got here, I was doing just fine."

"Don't worry. I will be out of here when they call me for my apartment."

"I don't think I can wait that long."

My grandmother had never had an attitude with me. She always treated me like I was her favorite grandchild.

I spoke, "Well I don't have nowhere to go."

"I already talked with Peggy."

"I don't want to go back over there."

"I want you out."

"I'm not going nowhere," I shouted.

"Don't make me call the police."

"Call the police."

I thought my grandmother was just blowing smoke. When the police showed up at her house, I was shocked. My grandmother told the police that she wanted me out of her house. They came to my bedroom and told me that I had to go because my name wasn't on the lease. I was devastated. I couldn't believe my grandmother was going through with this. The police gave me a ride to Peggy's apartment. She was waiting on the porch with Qualude's mother. I was so embarrassed that I walked right passed both of them and entered the apartment. I could overhear them talking about me after I put Jaquala in Aunt Peggy's bed beside Shaquala.

Aunt Peggy told Qualude's mother about me abusing my kids. I wanted to go out there and cuss Aunt Peggy out, but I didn't want to ruin another place to live. After about an hour of listening to them, I found out that Betty had called the Mental Health Department on me. I was hurt and confused. Was I really abusing my kids? I didn't think so.

QUALUDE

Big Boo and I arrived at the party after hitting the mall. We both were dressed casually. The party was filled with the city bailers. It had been a while since I had been out on the town. The town didn't seem like it had changed. Big Boo and I hit the bar after entering the VIP. Geneva had kept her word. My name was on the guest list.

I mingled around in the crowd before I finally came in contact with Geneva. She was dressed in knee high, snake skin, red and black boots. Her outfit looked like she had it tailored made and it matched her red and black wrap that was around her hair. She had on a lot of makeup, in which I had never seen her wear. I was liking this new person I was looking at.

She asked, "What took you so long?"

I asked, "How you know I was coming?"

"I got word you was in town. I knew you was going to come just to see how this party had turned out."

Geneva knew that I didn't have anything against her brother, but when she and I were in a relationship, he was running around town telling people that he didn't like the way was doing I her. I didn't know what Geneva was telling him about our relationship at the time, but it had to be bad, because every time her brother ran into me in the street, he always gave me a disapproving look.

I responded, "I only came to see how you was doing."

"Stop lying. You know you wanted to get up in this VIP. This is the hottest spot in the city."

Club CJ's was the hottest spot in the city. It had a disco ball that was the size of thirty basketballs. There were two large bars that served the best mixed drinks in the city, and there was a picture booth with different backgrounds. The atmosphere was out of this world. This was the life.

After about an hour in the club, and five shots of white gin, I asked Geneva to leave with me.

She asked, "Where are we going?"

"To a hotel room."

After I got rid of Big Boo, and had another shot, she asked "Don't you have a girlfriend?"

Denise was far from my mind. After hearing that she was abusing my kids, I was now thinking about leaving her. My heart was with Denise, but I didn't want a girl that was going to be insecure and abusive.

I spoke, "No I don't have a girlfriend."

The alcohol was talking. Before I could finish my sentence, Geneva grabbed me and kissed me. I had never been the one to tongue kiss, but the alcohol was doing all the work. After our kiss, Geneva said goodbye to her roommate, Shawn, whom I had never met, and then we were on our way.

When we arrived at the Embassy Suites on Woodlawn Road, Geneva pulled out her credit card.

She spoke, "We have moved on up like the Jefferson's. We balling now."

I knew Geneva was only trying to be funny, but I didn't think her comment was funny.

I said, "You don't have to rub it in my face that your brother is in the NBA."

"Maybe one day you can be in the NBA."

"If I make it, I make it."

"We can live like this every day if you make it."

I felt out of placing being with Geneva. Even though sex was on my mind, I didn't have any desire to make Geneva my woman. She just wasn't my type. Most of the women that I went for had a trait that my mother had, but Geneva didn't. She reminded me of my Aunt Jackie, who was always doing stuff without thinking it through.

Once inside the suite, there was no talking. We went at each other like we were two porn stars. Geneva wasn't the same old young inexperienced girl back in high school. She had learned a few tricks, and she knew all the sensitive spots on my body. Especially my penis. She was really gentle with it while she worked her magic. After I climaxed, she kept me hard. Then she brought me around again. My toes were curling in towards the ceiling after another strong orgasm.

I spoke, "Hold on."

Geneva was trying to catch her breath. I was out of breath from trying to keep her from sucking my insides out of my body.

She spoke, "You don't like?"

"Yes. I'm just tired."

"You remember when we were in high school? You talked like you was all this and that after we had sex. You knew I didn't have much experience. Now that I'm ready, you cannot handle me."

Usually I didn't kiss and tell, but a couple my teammates were talking about all the girls they had had sex with over the summer, so I told them about my chapter with Geneva. They teased her after I told them.

I spoke, "Just give me a minute."

"Get your rest. I got some more for you in a minute."

The alcohol was still controlling my thinking, and I was no longer thinking about how Denise would feel if she found out I was at a hotel with Geneva. This thought only came to my mind because Geneva kept bringing up Denise's name. After Geneva returned from the shower, I was rock hard again. This came from the help of her soft lips wrapped around the head of my penis.

I spoke, "Please, let me get some rest."

"It seems to me that you are ready," Geneva said, as she took her mouth off my sword.

"Not really."

Geneva was a classic woman in the street, but a freak in the sheets.

She spoke, "I want you inside of me."

I watched as she got on the edge of the bed and opened her legs so I could see inside her V-Shape. The lights in the room was dim, but I could see her clearly. Her cleaned shaved volcano

CRUMBLING TALENT

looked like it was ready to erupt at any moment. I watched as she warmed herself up with her fresh manicured fingers. Her juices engulfed her fingers after she went in deep. She bit on her bottom lip as I continued to watch. She made some moaning sounds that I had never heard her make before. This turned me on.

I walked over and put the head of my meat stick on the mouth of her V-shape. Then her moaning got louder. I grabbed one her breasts while I entered her. Her walls were so wet, I almost lost control, but I managed to hold myself together. Her moaning wasn't helping.

When she pulled at my butt cheeks and whispered, "F-me," in my ear, this was the last straw. I exploded. I was like a microwave. I was on one minute, and off the next.

Geneva gripped and grabbed me with her walls until I was back hard. It didn't take more than a minute.

She asked, "You enjoying yourself?"

I said, "Yes."

The radio was playing R-Kelly's 'Your Body Calling Me.'

The song made me remember the time when I caught the STD from the girl out of South Side Homes Projects. Here I was having sex without a rubber, and knowing that Geneva was the type to have one-night stands with anyone that she felt like could please her.

DENISE

The next day after my grandmother threw me out, she had the nerve to call me. I didn't want to talk to her because I was still upset with her. I told Aunt Peggy to tell her that I was no longer her granddaughter. Aunt Peggy didn't do that. She just told my grandmother that I didn't want to talk. After Aunt Peggy hung up the phone, I received a call from Tasha.

She spoke, "Girl. I got something to tell you."

I asked, "What is it?"

"I saw Qualude at the Big Party at CJ's last night."

Tasha had tried to get me to go out to the party but I just didn't have any interest.

She continued, "He was dancing all up on Geneva."

"Are you sure?"

"Yes."

"Did you say something to him?"

"No"

"Why?"

"Because I just didn't."

"You know he's going to say he wasn't with her."

"But he was."

"If you would have said something to him, then he couldn't say he wasn't there."

Tasha knew that Qualude had cheated on me. I told her how he tried to feed me some pills he had received at the health department for the STD that he had caught from the girl out of South Side Projects.

She asked, "Are you going to say something to him?"

"Yes."

Qualude had promised me that he was going to spend the weekend with me and the kids. He had lied, because he didn't even come to Aunt Peggy's apartment after the party. When I called him, he claimed he spent the night at Big Mama's apartment. This was after I had told him that Tasha saw him at Club CJ's.

After I hung up on Qualude, I went to my bedroom and put on me some clothes.

While I was putting on my clothes, Peggy walked in and said, "You look pregnant."

"I'm not pregnant."

"You are. Your nipples are big and your ass is spreading. You having all these different mood swings."

I shouted, "I'm not pregnant."

"I don't care what you say. I know you pregnant. I watched

you through your last two pregnancies."

My Aunt knew me like a book. She knew I was pregnant. I didn't want her to know I was pregnant, because I didn't want her to judge me. I watched as Aunt Peggy left out of my room with Shaquala in her arms.

She shouted, "I'm going to the store. I'll be back."

I finished getting dressed, then looked at myself in the large mirror in my room. My stomach looked big. After playing around with my belly button, I turned on my radio. Power 98 was having a contest for pregnant women. This sent me thinking about Qualude. Here I was, pregnant again by him, and he wasn't trying to be with me. I could tell he loved me, but I didn't feel like he was in love with me. He had taught me there was two different types of love.

My Aunt Peggy hadn't taught me anything about love. It was always hate with her. She had taught me how to hate people and myself. This was why I was ready to get away from her. She had only took me in because she wanted me to help her buy food with my food stamps and pay half her rent with the welfare check. I played along with her little game because I didn't want to be at my grandmother's house any longer. My grandmother had really made me mad when she told Qualude that I was abusing my kids. In her mind she thought that I should get some help, but I didn't need help. I wasn't like the white people that kill their kids and then try to put it on a black man.

I grabbed Jaquala, walked down stairs, placed her on the couch and turned on the TV. A woman on a commercial was pregnant. This sent my thought back to my Aunt. Was she trying to pick me? Or did she know I was pregnant? What if I got rid of the baby? Would she be mad? Would Qualude leave me? My Aunt knew how bad I wanted a boy. I had told her that I wanted a boy because this would make Qualude want to stay with me forever. She had told me that I was crazy and stupid and that a man will not be with you just because you having his kids. In a sense, she was right. But I didn't want her to be.

❖ ❖ ❖

DENISE
The thought of another baby was driving me crazy. This was the third month I had missed my monthly cycle. I didn't want my Aunt Peggy to be right. She had told me that I looked pregnant the second time I missed my period. We had gotten into a heated argument and almost came to blows, because she was telling the truth.

Qualude had told me to get my tubes tied after I had Jaquala, but I had refused because I wanted to have a son for him. I didn't know if I should tell him, because he had told me that he didn't want any more kids, and if I got pregnant, he would leave me. This was why I didn't tell him when he asked me about my stomach after we had sex. Now that I knew the truth, I had to get rid of the baby.

I picked up my kitchen phone and dialed up the number Tasha gave me. The number was busy again, and the busy signal was getting on my nerves. This was the tenth time I had dialed this number. The reason I was calling this number was because I was thinking about having an abortion.

The sound of my daughter brought me back to reality. I rushed to the living room where Jaquala was laying on the floor. She had fallen off the couch. She was in tears when I picked her up.

I shouted, "Shut up."

Jaquala continued to cry.

I shouted again, "Shut your mouth, you little bitch!"

I watched as my daughter continued to cry. I didn't care that she was crying. Crying was good for her. She didn't care when I was crying over her daddy. She didn't even know that she was the reason why her daddy didn't pay any attention to me anymore. He was too busy with college, and when he came home on the weekends, he gave her and her sister all his attention. This was why I was going to make her pay for how her father was treating

CRUMBLING TALENT

me.

I grabbed Jaquala up and tossed her in the air. Then I tossed her on the couch. She was still crying. I could see the terror in her eyes. This sent pleasure through my body. I wanted her to feel my pain that her daddy was putting me through by not paying any attention to me. She was feeling it and I was going to make her feel more, until the knock at the front door interrupted me.

I walked over to the door and looked out the peephole. It was Candy. I hadn't seen her in months. I decided not to answer the door. I took Jaquala upstairs and tossed her on my Aunt's bed. She was still crying. I knew Candy could hear her. I didn't care, because I was going to finished what I started.

I lit up a blunt and took a few pulls before I said, "You look just like your damn daddy."

I blew the smoke in her face. I could hear Candy still at the front door knocking.

I shouted, "Y'all want to call me crazy. I'mma show y'all crazy."

I picked up Jaquala and took her over to the window.

I opened the window and yelled out, "Y'all think I'm crazy. I'mma show y'all crazy."

I hung Jaquala upside down by her legs. I could see the blood rushing to my daughter head.

Candy shouted, "Denise! What are you doing?"

QUALUDE

I woke up the next morning to find Geneva gone. I couldn't remember the last thing she said to me before she walked out of the suite. I felt used and confused. The reason I felt used was because I had never had a woman leave me at a hotel. Especially in a bed alone.

I stepped out the huge bed to find my boxers shorts on the floor with a note on top of them. Geneva knew how to play mind games.

The note said: "I better not be pregnant. You know my brother will cut me off. See you next time."

The note was all I had to go on in order to find Geneva. I didn't even take time out to get her phone number. I was too busy trying to please myself with her body. While thinking on this note, I was interrupted by a knock on the door. I walked over and pulled the curtain back. The cleaning lady was standing at the door with the cleaning cart. I slipped on my clothes and let the lady in. Then I headed downstairs to the buffet.

After I enjoyed a wonderful breakfast that was pre-paid by Geneva, I called my mother. She was cooking breakfast when I called.

She asked, "Where did you stay last night?"

"Why?"

"Because Denise has been calling over Big Mama s looking for you all night."

"What did you tell her?"

"I didn't tell her anything. I didn't answer when she called me. This was after Big Mama told me that she was looking for you."

"Where is she now?"

"She's back over at Peggy's place."

"What is she doing over there?"

"Miss Betty put her out last night."

"Why?"

"That's why I called you. I thought maybe you would know."

The only reason I could come up with why Miss Betty would put Denise out was the abuse against my kids.

"I have to tell you something," I said.

"What?" My mother asked.

"Denise has been abusing the kids."

"What! Why?"

"I don't know. But when her grandmother told me, I pulled Denise in her bedroom and asked her about it."

"How long has she been doing this?"

"I don't know."
"I'm going to call Social Services."
"No."
"Why?"
"They might take the kids."
"You can get the kids."

I wasn't ready to take on the responsibility of taking care of two kids. My mind was on finishing college and going off to a D-1 school. Then off to the NBA.

I spoke, "I'm not ready to take on the responsibility of taking care of Shaquala and Jaquala."

"Sometimes life brings you things you not ready for, but you have to be willing to adjust in order to make it work."

I didn't have any problem with adjusting to a situation. I had been doing this all my life.

I said, "I just don't think I can do it."

"I will help you."

My mother had a guilty conscience about leaving me with Big Mama when I was a kid. This is what made her want to be a mother to my kids.

I said, "Let me think about it."

After I finished my conversation with my mother, I called Denise. She answered on the second ring.

I spoke, "Good morning."

"Don't good morning me," she answered.

I could hear the unhappiness in Denise's voice.

I asked, "What's with the attitude?"

"You."

"What did I do?"

"Tasha told me she saw you at club CJ's last night."

I didn't know if I should lie or tell Denise the truth, so I asked, "Where are the kids?"

"Don't change the subject."

"I didn't call to fight with you."

"You are nothing but a liar and a cheater."

I wanted to tell Denise that she was nothing but a child abuser, but I said, "I just need to talk to the kids."

"They are asleep."

"It's after noon."

"They need their rest."

"Well I'mma come over later."

"For what?"

"To see the kids."

"You don't want to see me?"

"Yes, but I want to see the kids more."

"What do that supposed to mean?"

"I miss my girls."

"You don't miss me?"

"Yes, but I miss them more."

"Ever since I had Shaquala and Jaquala you have been treating me like you don't want me anymore."

"That's not case."

"What is the case?"

"I just been busy with school and basketball."

"I feel like you don't want me no more. Is it because that white girl?"

"It has nothing to do with no white girl."

I hadn't heard from Mr. Black after he decided not to charge me. Coach Soloman told me not to worry about being charged in the matter. I hadn't told my mother about the matter, because I didn't get charged. Denise was using the situation to keep me in check. I didn't want her to say anything about the matter to any one, because I didn't want to ruin my new good boy image.

She spoke, "I need you to come over here."

"I thought you said the kids were asleep."

"They are."

"I told you, I was coming over later."

"I want you to come now."

"I can't."

"Why? Because you at the hotel with Geneva."

I didn't think to wait until I left the hotel to call. I knew Denise was probably looking at the caller ID.

I said, "Let me explain."

"There is nothing to explain."

Denise hung the phone up on me before I could finish what I had to say. I tried to call Denise back after she hung up on me. She didn't answer. I left the suite after I went back to it and searched it for Geneva's number. While driving to Big Mama's apartment, I decided to stop by Rob's Store on Remount Road.

There were people everywhere. I noticed the police standing on the corner looking over a man lying in the street bleeding. Then I noticed Telly standing with a guy we grew up with, named Showtime. Showtime was known for robbing people. I didn't have nothing against his MO, because I knew that all black men couldn't go to college or work a job.

I pulled in the parking lot where Nuke and I had the fight. I stepped out of my car and joined Telly and Showtime. The sun was shining and the air was cold. I could smell gas in the atmosphere. After looking over the scene, I noticed several pieces of car parts in the middle of the street.

Telly spoke, "It's been a wreck."

I asked, "What is that dude doing in the middle of the street?"

"Nuke beat him with a baseball bat."

Fo-real, I asked.

"Yes."

"Where is Nuke?"

"Nuke ran off before the police got here. I think he's hiding out at his grandmother's house."

The guy that was laying on the ground was a crackhead.

I asked, "Why did he do it?"

"The word is they say the guy owe Nuke money."

I knew the rules to the streets. This was why I didn't feel bad for the guy, but I was upset with Nuke. The police didn't charge Nuke for beating MC up. MC told the police that he didn't want to file charges. I understood his position, but I knew his father didn't like it.

Showtime spoke, "I heard you in college playing ball."

"Yes."

"So, you left the dope game alone?"

"Yes."

"I heard y'all two was clean, but I didn't want to believe it."

Showtime had just gotten out of prison for robbing a bank. He had done two and half years in state prison. While in prison, he had learned how to read and write, but he was still looking for a big lick.

When he told that he was friends with Nuke, I said, "I don't fool with him."

"I heard what happened to MC and I heard about y'all fight."

"I want to kill Nuke."

"Them are some strong words."

"Fuck Nuke."

"I don't suppose to tell you this, but I got love for you Qualude. Nuke and I been hitting licks together. We robbed two houses on the North side last week. Nuke shot a dude in the chest during one of the robberies. I heard the dude live and he's looking for Nuke."

"What that got to do with me?"

"Dude put money on Nuke's head."

"What about you?"

"He don't know I was with Nuke."

"What this got to do with me?"

"I know how mad you are with Nuke. I know you want him dead."

Showtime was right about me being mad at Nuke, but I didn't want him dead.

I said, "Nuke is going to get himself in some trouble he cannot get out of."

"The guy that got the money on his head is a Jamaican."

"What?"

"Yes. Dude want him bad. I don't want Nuke to tell the dude

about me if they catch him."

"They who?"

"The dude got goons looking for Nuke. They been riding around the hood."

Telly cut in. "They rode up on me. They pulled out guns the size of telephone poles. Then they shouted in their deep crazy sounding accent."

"Where is Nuke?" Telly said.

Showtime said, "I saw the BMW they were in. They riding four deep."

Telly said, "They came in a van too."

I knew Telly and Showtime were not lying. I had seen the BMW the night before, on my way to Geneva's brother's party.

I asked, "Have they been over here today?"

"No, "Showtime responded."

Telly said, "I saw them about an hour ago."

"Y'all think Nuke know?"

Showtime responded, "No."

Showtime had always been cool with me. We had never had any type beef. Even when he found out I busted out his aunt's car window because I caught her cheating with Butch, he didn't get mad.

I asked, "So, you think Nuke will tell them you was with him?"

"If I had to bet money on it, I would say he would. Especially if they were making him suffer."

"So, what you going to do?"

"I don't know."

Showtime and Nuke were the same size in height, but two different people. Showtime was outgoing and a people person, like myself. On the other hand, Nuke was quiet and antisocial. They both were brown skin with slim bodies. I guess this was why ZZ liked them both. I heard ZZ was having sex with Showtime. This was why I was confused when Showtime told me that he was going on another lick with Nuke on Sunday night.

I asked, "Are you messing around with ZZ too?"

Showtime smiled and said, "It ain't no fun if the homies can't have none."

I asked, "Are you going on the lick with Nuke?"

"Yes."

"Who is the vic?"

"Your baby mama's brother."

"Denise's brother is 12 years old and he live with Denise's aunt."

"Not that baby mama. I'm talking about Nikki's next to oldest brother."

I didn't even know that Showtime knew about my daughter by Nikki. Then it hit. Butch could have told him.

I asked, "Why him?"

Showtime ran his hand over his bald head and smiled.

"The word on the streetz is, he's the man. He got a connect out of Oakland. They say the dude who is his connection is a Blood gang member."

"I don't know."

"Well, we going to kick that door in."

I knew Nikki was living with her brother's told girlfriend in Piemont Courts Projects. When Showtime told me that Nikki's brother was keeping the bricks there, I felt like I was about to have a heart attack. Even though I didn't have a relationship with Nikki, I didn't want anything to happen to her.

I said, "Don't do it."

"The move is already in the making. We going to wait until they go to sleep and then kick it in."

Showtime didn't know that Nikki and my daughter were staying in the apartment.

I said, "My daughter lives there."

"You know the game."

Showtime walked off after he made his statement.

Telly asked, "What are you going to do?"

"I don't know."

CHAPTER 26

DENISE

Candy called my grandmother and told her that I had hung Jaquala out a two-story window. Betty got on the phone and called Qualude's mother and told her what I done. Qualude called me and told me that he was going to have the kids taken from me. I told him I would kill them and then kill myself if he tried to take the kids.

When Peggy returned, Candy told-Peggy what I had done.

She spoke, "I knew there was something wrong with you. I think you have a post-stress problem."

I didn't know what Peggy was talking about.

I said, "I don't have anything wrong with me. Candy just trying to make something bigger than what it is."

"Why did you hang that child out the window?"

"I was just playing."

"That's is no way to play."

I was upset with Candy, because she told Peggy and then left. Yes, I was wrong for hanging my daughter out the window, but I knew this would get Qualude's attention. Michael Jackson had hung one of his kids out the window. He didn't get in trouble for doing it.

I said, "She isn't hurt."

"That ain't the point."

Peggy had a point.

I said, "I was just trying to get Qualude's attention. He has been so business with college and all."

"You did that for that stupid boy."

I cut Peggy off.

"He's not stupid. He's smarter than you. You didn't finish school."

"This is why I didn't want to take you back in my home. You are so disrespectful. I asked you a question and you go and say something that don't have nothing to do with what I asked you."

"You called Qualude stupid. You know how much I love that boy."

"I don't think I can handle you staying here anymore. You going to end up getting me put out. Now, how many people were outside when you hung that baby out the window?"

"I don't know. I wasn't counting or looking to see who was watching."

"You have to find you somewhere to go. I can't take you staying here no more."

"What about my kids?"

"They can stay, but you have to go."

"If I go, they going with me."

"You don't have nowhere to go. Betty don't want you at her house, and you know you can't go stay with Qualude in Winston Salem."

"Qualude will think of something. You ain't getting my kids."

"Like I said, I want you out my home."

I could see in Peggy's eyes she was for real. Her demeanor was different from the last time we had our fight. Her words were firm and she didn't take her eyes off me the whole time she was talking to me.

I spoke, "I'mma get out. Just give me a couple days."

"That's all I'mma give you."

❖   ❖   ❖

CRUMBLING TALENT

QUALUDE

I told my mother that Denise had hung Jaquala out of Peggy's apartment window. My mother didn't even tell me that she was going to call the city Mental Health Department on Denise. It shocked me when I learned that my mother had reported Denise. I learned this from Denise.

As I read over the report, I thought about when my mother left me with Big Mama when I was just five years old. This made me hate my mother. Here she was trying to get my kids took from me. She wasn't thinking about there was a chance that my kids could be placed in a foster home.

I took a trip to my mother's house to confront her. My mother was standing on her front porch when I arrived at her house. I knew she didn't want me there, because it was almost time for Butch to come in from work. I didn't care. I needed some answers. I walked up on the porch and joined my mother.

Then asked, "Why?"

"I knew you was going to find out. Yes, I reported Denise. She's been hurting those kids for a long time."

"What are you talking about?"

My mother took a deep breath than said, "The reason I've been going to get Shaquala every weekend from Denise is I found marks on Shaquala's body where Denise has been abusing her."

"What are you talking about?"

"You know."

"No, I don't. "

I didn't know about any marks on my daughter. I just knew that Betty had told me that Denise was beating my kids.

I spoke, "I only know what Betty told me."

"Well, Denise has been beating Shaquala. Shaquala has marks all over her body."

"Why didn't you tell me this when it happen?"

"I thought you knew."

No."

"Well, it's been going on since you been in college. Shaquala has trouble going to sleep by herself and she will not stop crying when I drop her back off with Denise."

"What you think we should do?"

"Take the kids from her."

"How are you going to do that?"

"Go to court."

"No."

"This is the only way. You know Denise will not give the kids up unless the law is involved."

I could see in my mother's eyes that she was serious. I didn't know what she was going to do but I didn't want my mother to do something that was going to cost me to lose my kids.

So, I asked, "What if we lose in court?"

"We will not lose. Denise is unstable mentally. This is a good reason for the court to grant you custody."

I knew about Social Services, because Big Mama used to threaten my mother by saying she was going to report her to Social Services. My mother and Big Mama used to get into it over the check that the Welfare Office use to send. Whenever Big Mama didn't do right by me with the money my mother would threaten her by say she was going to report her. This became a game of vice or verse. In my case, Denise was mentally unstable because no woman in her right mind would have hung her baby out of a two-story window.

I felt a little better about the situation when I left my mother's house. Even though my mother and Betty didn't think Denise was fit to care for the kids, I still felt like she could. This was why I went over to Miss Betty's house and told Denise that she better shape up before Social Services take our kids. We got into a fight over the report.

She said, "I know you mother reported me. I know she don't like me."

"She never said she didn't like you."

"I could see it in her face when she drop Shaquala off."

"Well, she thinks you beating on her granddaughter."

CRUMBLING TALENT

"If I am, it's my child."

I was shocked to hear this out of Denise's mouth.

I said, "Shaquala is just a baby."

"She's my child and I can do what I want to do to her."

"So, you did put them marks on her body?"

"Yes."

Before Denise could get the word out of her mouth, I hit her in it. Blood came pouring out her mouth.

She shouted, "You hit me."

I hit her again. Then again. She didn't even put up a fight. A knock at Denise's bedroom door brought me back to reality.

Miss Betty shouted, "What's going on in there?"

Denise was crying now. I gave her a look like I would kill her if she said anything.

I said, "Everything is okay." Then I whispered to Denise, "I should kill you for putting your hands on my kids."

Denise knew I was serious. I had told her about the abuse that I had suffered at the hands of Butch. This was why I didn't understand why she would put her hands on my kids. After Miss Betty walked away from the door, I grabbed Denise by her neck. This was the first time I had ever put my hands on a woman. Big Mama had taught me not to put my hands on a woman.

I said, "You lucky."

Denise said, "You love them kids more than me. You don't love me no more."

I took my grip off Denise's neck. Then I looked her in her eyes and asked, "So, this is why you been abusing the kids?"

"Yes. I hate I had them. I only had them because you wanted them."

"You crazy."

"I'm crazy in love with you. You make me crazy."

"But why the kids? Why make them suffer?"

"Because I knew it would make you pay me some attention."

My mother's words came to mind. Denise was really unstable.

I said, "If you lose the kids, you deserve it."

I watched as Denise broke down crying. She knew that if she lost the kids that she would lose me.

She said, "Please, don't leave me."

I said, "Fuck you."

I left Denise's grandmother house upset. I now knew the truth. Denise had been abusing my kids because she wanted to get my attention. I didn't understand this, because I had never been in a serious relationship, and I had never been taught this side of life by Big Mama. After I left Denise's grandmother house, I went over to Nicole's brother's girlfriend apartment in Piemont Court Projects. While riding over to the projects, I thought about everything Denise had said. She knew about me cheating on her and she was willing to put up with it. I felt bad, but I couldn't be with her because of her behavior towards our kids.

When I pulled up to Piemont Court Projects, I noticed several crackheads standing out on the block. Being from the hood gave me a sixth sense of knowing when trouble was around. In this case, there was no trouble, but I still had my guard up. I wasn't worried about anything happening to me, because most of the people in the projects knew my father, and they knew about how my father killed a man when he was just sixteen years old.

I noticed that my father's Cadillac was gone from the parking lot as I rode passed his building. He lived two buildings over from Nicole's brother's girlfriend's building. I didn't know if he knew her, but I had told him about her and Keosha. He didn't judge me. He told me not to be like him. I knew exactly what he was saying to me when he told me this. I decided it was best just to show up at Nicole's brother's girlfriend's apartment, since this was an emergency. I knew she wouldn't mind. I stepped out of the car and walked slowly to apartment 2324. The door was wide open, and there were kids playing out front of the building. I looked at the kids to see if Keosha was in the crowd. She wasn't.

I could hear music playing inside the apartment when I arrived at the door. This was after I had passed the ten little boys and girls. I knocked on the screen door loud enough so the knock could be heard over the music. 2-Pac's 'All Eyes On Me' was blasting from the radio inside the living room.

There was a girl around Nicole's age dancing inside the room. She turned towards me when the song went off.

She asked, "Who is you?"

This girl was ghetto as hell. Her pants were so tight, that I could see her pussy lips through the pink pants she was wearing. Her hair was in a short cut style. She had makeup on and her earrings reminded me off a chick in the 80's.

I said, "I'm looking for Nicole."

The girl responded, "You still haven't answered my question. Who is you?"

I said, "I'm Qualude. A friend of Nicole."

The girl s face expression went from not knowing to being excited.

She said, "I have heard a lot about you."

"You have?"

"Yes. Nicole talks about you all the time."

I was surprised to hear this. I thought Nicole was so much in love with Willie that I thought she hated me.

I asked, "Where is she?"

"She's upstairs."

Before I could get another word out my mouth, the girl shouted Nicole's name. Nicole came downstairs looking good as ever. She had her hair done like I liked it. It was pressed out and hanging long. Her blue jeans were hugging her thick hips and the shirt she was wearing matched her Nike Air Maxes.

She asked, "What are you doing over here?"

"I need to talk to you about something."

"Didn't I tell you that Willie be selling drugs in the hood?"

Nicole had in fact, told me that Willie was selling drugs, and that he was hanging out in Piemont Courts.

I said, "This is important."

The girl spoke, "I'mma leave you two alone."

"You don't have to go nowhere Cresha."

Nicole had told me about Cresha on several occasions

Cresha said, "I feel the tension. I'mma go outside for a while."

I watched as Cresha went out the door before I asked, "Where is Keosha?"

Nicole responded, "You don't need to be asking about her. I told you we don't need you."

I knew Nicole was still mad at me, because I quit selling drugs. I was no longer giving her money for Keosha.

I said, "I didn't come her to fight with you. I came here to tell you that some dudes from the westside is watching your brother."

"Watching my brother for what?"

"The word is he's the man out here."

I could tell from the large screen TV and the leather white furniture inside the room that her brother was getting money. I knew a Welfare Check couldn't buy these things.

Nicole responded, "They don't know what they talking about." She turned towards the kitchen.

I said, "I just came to give you and your brother the heads up."

"Well ain't nobody selling drugs out this apartment."

She was lying. I knew Nicole's brother had her watching the drugs. This was why she wasn't worried about money.

I said, "Just take heed. These boys are serious."

I turned to leave.

She spoke, "I'mma tell Sam."

Sam was Nicole's next to oldest brother. I had met him once. I left Nicole standing in the living room. I hopped back in the rental car and headed over to Telly's mother's house. It was time to go back to school. Life in Charlotte was too complicated. I needed to get back to where things were simple. School was the answer.

CHAPTER 27

DENISE

After Qualude had told me it was over, I went into a deep depression state. I wanted to kill myself. I started cutting myself with a razor to relieve some of my pain. I cut myself mostly where people couldn't see the cuts. One afternoon, my grandmother had caught me. She walked in the room while I was cutting myself on the leg.

She had asked, "What are you doin?"

I tried to hide the cuts by letting my pant leg fall over the cut. But my grandmother had already seen it.

I said, "Nothing."

She said, "You cutting yourself."

"No, I wasn't," I shouted.

She asked, "How long have you been doing this?"

I said, "None of your business."

"It is my business, because you are in my house."

"I can get out your house."

"You need help."

"No, I don't."

"Yes, you do."

"It's all your fault."

"What are you talking about?"

My grandmother really didn't think it was her fault that I started cutting myself. She was the reason Qualude had left me.

I said, "You are the reason Qualude left me."

"You need some help. I'mma call the Mental Health people. They can help."

"No."

I had raised the razor where my grandmother could see it.

She said, "Your Uncle Junior needed help. They helped him."

I knew the mental history of my family. My Uncle Junior had been mentally unstable around my age. He was shipped off to a mental ward after his eighteenth birthday. My grandmother took him back in after he had spent a year in the ward of the state. She started getting a check for him when he had moved in with her, but after a month she had put him out but continued to get his check. After Junior went to jail, the check stopped coming.

My grandmother had continued, "They will pay you to get help."

I had heard this when my Uncle Junior was placed in the Mental Health ward.

I said, "I don't want no check."

"You need the check and money. It will help you with the kids."

"I don't need no crazy check. If you want that check you need to act crazy."

I had seen how the medication had changed Junior from a nice young man into a slow drug nuisance. This was how my grandmother was taking care of herself. She was getting checks from the state and the government. By her being overweight, she was receiving a check for being disabled. Now, she was trying to get a check for me and control of the food stamps and the welfare check I was receiving for my kids. She was the one that was insane. Especially if she thought I was going to let her talk me into thinking I was crazy.

She spoke, "All you have to do is talk to a case worker."

I shouted, "No!"

I didn't know my grandmother had already filed a report to the Mental Health Department about me. When two men, dressed in

CRUMBLING TALENT

white suits, showed up with a lady that looked like a patient herself, I knew they were for me. I watched as my grandmother went out and spoke with them before they entered the house. Earlier, I had agreed to let Qualude's mother keep my kids. This was only because I thought this would keep Qualude's mother from going forward with trying to get my kids.

When the men grabbed my arms, I started screaming at the top of my lungs.

The white lady with the big brown glasses said, "We are going to give you something so you can calm down."

I could see in this lady's eyes that she was serious about her job. The smell of urine hit the air. I was so afraid that I pissed on myself. The lady still hit me in the arm with the large needle that she pulled from her black bag. I could feel the liquid flowing through my veins. It was warm. Then it went cold. My vision got blurred and then I felt like everything was moving slow. I could hear my grandmother asking the doctor if I was going to be okay. Then I went out.

DENISE

When I woke up, I was dressed in a white gown with no shoes in a padded room. There was a window in front of me. There was no clock inside the room, so I didn't know the time. I felt like I had been asleep for days. I walked around the room for a full minute before I was interrupted by the doctor who had hit me with the needle. She was escorted in the room with two white males on her side. They were not the same two men that grabbed me up at my grandmother's house.

She spoke, "I hope you had enough rest. You been asleep for two days."

I asked, "What did you shoot in my arm?"

"Something that made you rest."

"I'm not crazy. I don't belong here."

"We know you are not crazy. You just need help dealing with your illness."

"I don't have an illness."

"Yes, you do. We did some tests and we looked into your family history."

"I'm not ill. If I am ill, I caught it from my boyfriend."

"It's not that kind of illness."

"What are you talking about?"

"You have a condition that's call Bipolar."

"What is that?"

"It has to do with mood swings."

"It's because I'm pregnant I'm having different mood swings."

"We know you are pregnant. We found that out while we did some blood work on you. But we also found out that the chemicals in your body are not balanced. This is coming from the condition you got from your mother."

"My mother?"

"Yes. We used to treat her, before she stopped coming."

I hadn't seen my real mother since Peggy had taken us in after my real mother left me and my siblings in a burning apartment. The state gave Peggy custody of me and my siblings after my mother didn't show up in court. After we left court, Peggy ordered us to call her mother. This was something I didn't like, but I did it after several butt whippings. That had been over ten years ago. My mother had been addicted to crack and used her body to support her habit. I hadn't seen her in years. I didn't know she was using crack when she got pregnant by my father. The doctor said the crack cocaine usage could have helped trigger the condition in my mother, since the gene ran in her family.

I asked, "Can I give this to my boyfriend?"

The doctor started laughing. I didn't like her response, so I asked, "What's so funny?"

"I'm just laughing at your humor."

"What is humor?"

The doctor looked at me like I was crazy. I didn't know the

meaning of the word humor. I had heard Qualude use the word, but I had asked him what it meant.

So, I said, "You have to speak words I understand."

The doctor said, "First, let me introduce myself. My name is Doctor Gates. I'm your doctor. Like I said earlier, I used to treat your mother. I helped her get a disability check for her disease. Using crack is a disease."

I shouted, "I don't want no check. There isn't nothing wrong with me."

"Why were you cutting yourself?"

I looked down at the cut markings on my leg. There was no time to hide them. The doctor had already seen them.

I said, "I just did it for attention. I wanted to get my boyfriend's attention."

"Did you get his attention?"

"No. He don't know I cut myself."

"I want you to be truthful with me. How long have you been cutting yourself?"

"Not long."

"How long?"

"About a month. I started after Qualude left me."

"Why did he leave you?"

"He went to college," I lied.

"Now you have to be truthful."

I didn't know how Doctor Gates knew I was lying.

I said, "He found out I was hitting my kids. It's all my grandmother's fault. If she wouldn't have told Qualude, we would still be together."

After I got through venting, the Doctor said, "Denise, there was more to your breakdown than your grandmother."

This shocked me. I had had a nervous breakdown and didn't know.

"We are going to run more tests on you."

"I'm not crazy."

"I don't think you're crazy either. I just want to make sure that we don t miss anything.

    This Doctor needed to be choked by her neck. But I didn't do it, because I didn't want her to put it in her report that I was crazy.

    I asked, "Can I use the restroom?"

    "Yes."

CHAPTER 28

QUALUDE

I was surprised when I received a call from my mother right before I was about to go out the door for school.
She asked, "Did you hear about Denise."
"What wrong?"
"She's in a mental health hospital."
"How did she get there?"
"Miss Betty called them on her."
I knew Miss Betty thought that Denise was on the verge of going insane, but I didn't think she would call the mental health department on Denise.
I asked, "Where is my kids?"
"Miss Betty have them."
"How long has Denise been in there?"
"For about two days."
Denise hadn't called me in two days. I should have known something was wrong.
I asked, "When is she getting out?"
"Miss Betty said they have to make sure Denise is not crazy."
"That's still not telling me when she's getting out."
"They don't know. What Miss Betty did tell me was that they think she's Bipolar, and he had had a nervous breakdown."
"What do that mean?"
"Denise has an emotional disorder."

"Can I go see her?"

"No. Miss Betty say they will not let anyone see her until they finish running tests on her."

When I ended my call with my mother, I called Miss Betty. She came over the line after three rings.

I spoke, "I hope you doing okay."

She said, "I'm fine."

I said, "You know why I called."

"Yes."

"What happened?"

"Denise needs help. She's been mistreating the kids again."

"Why didn't you tell me first before you decided to call mental health on her?"

I'm sorry, Qualude, but I was still upset about her hanging Jaquala out the window."

"Where are my kids?"

"They are downstairs playing."

"Do you know when Denise is getting out of that place?"

"They don't know. It could be days, months or even years."

"What have you done?"

"She needed help."

I interrupted, "Denise isn't sick. She just wants attention. My attention."

"How do you know? You are not a doctor."

"Doctors can't solve all problems Miss Betty."

Miss Betty was a lady that had grown up counting on the system. Her mother had been the same way. Denise's mother had joined the club right before Denise and her siblings were taken from her. Miss Betty's way of thinking had been passed down from her mother. She didn't know how to survive without the welfare system.

I continued, "I can come get the kids later. I'm coming home tonight."

"You don't have to come to Charlotte tonight. Stay there and get your education."

CRUMBLING TALENT

"It's okay. I can take some time off."

"Don't do that. I can handle the kids."

"I will call you when I get out of school. Kiss my kids for me."

"Don't worry, Qualude. I will not let the social services people take your girls."

"Excuse me? What did you say?"

"I said, I will not let the social service people take your girls."

"What do you mean?"

"I forgot to tell you that, if they find Denise is unfit, they are going to take the girls. I didn't mean for this to happen."

Miss Betty started crying over the phone. I didn't know if she was putting on an act or not. The truth of the matter was that someone was lying, and I was going to get to the bottom of it.

Miss Betty asked, "Did you know Denise was cutting herself with a razor?"

"No."

"Well, she had been doing it for a while. I caught her one day when I heard the girls crying. They were both laying on the floor watching her as she cut herself. That day, I didn't say nothing to her, because I didn't know if she would hurt the kids."

All this new information that Miss Betty was giving me was making me hate Denise. I was still in love with her, but I didn't know if I wanted to be with her if they found out that something was wrong with her mentally. This whole situation was wrecking my mind. I didn't know why I didn't see it in her. She was always fine to me.

I talked to my kids before I said goodbye to Miss Betty. Then I walked to school thinking about how I didn't recognize that Denise was mentally losing it. I went through the day like a zombie. I couldn't stop thinking about Denise and the kids. I didn't know what type of treatment she was going through. I didn't know if she really wanted to kill herself like Miss Betty was trying to put it. On the other hand, I didn't know if I could handle two kids. I was still a kid myself.

When the day ended, I rushed to my apartment and told Telly

and Cory about Denise's situation. They both had a lot to say.

Telly spoke first. "I think you should stay here. You have worked too hard just to get in college."

Cory cut in, "I don't have kids, but you going to need college to get a job if you don't play ball anyway."

Playing ball was the last thing on my mind. I was too focused on my kids to even be thinking about something else. I didn't want my kids to end up in the hands of Social Services.

I spoke, "I might have to leave school for a while."

Telly responded, "You can't do that."

Cory cut in, "We been having too much fun. You can't leave."

I said, "My kids need me. If I don't go back and get them, they will end up in the system. I don't want that to happen."

Telly asked, "Can you get your mother to take care of them?"

I responded, "My mother got her own life to live. I can't ask her to do that for me."

Cory cut in, "What about Big Mama?"

I had told Cory how Big Mama had helped to raise me.

I responded, "She will not do it."

Telly spoke, "Whatever you decide to do, I'm with you."

My mother arrived around 7:00pm. She was dressed in a sweat suit and tennis shoes. Her hair was done in a nice style. Her demeanor was friendlier than usual.

When I got in the passenger seat, after Telly and I put our bags in the trunk of the car, I said, "I'm thinking about dropping out of college."

She asked, "Why?"

"My kids need me, I'm not going to let them get trapped up in the state system," I responded.

She answered, "They are not going to the system. I will take them in myself before I let that happen."

I didn't know if I should trust my mother. She was the same woman that left me when I was five years old. Her statement didn't put my mind to rest. I was happy just to know that she would take them.

CRUMBLING TALENT

I relaxed the whole ride to Charlotte. While relaxing I thought about my future. College was okay, but the drug game was always better.

CHAPTER 29

DENISE

After spending a whole week in the mental health hospital, I was released into my grandmother's care. Shaquala and Jaquala were waiting on me in the living room when I arrived. I thought they were going to be happy when they saw me, but they were not. They both ran and jumped into my grandmother's arms. She had to tell them that everything was okay.

I wasn't hurt by their actions. I was glad they didn't come to me, because I was still mad at them and my grandmother. They were the reasons I was taken away from Qualude. They didn't understand how I was feeling about the whole situation. My heart was hurting from not being able to see and touch Qualude. The whole week I was away, I thought about him.

I rushed to the phone after I went to my bedroom. I dialed Qualude's number at his school. I got an answering machine. It was Friday, and it was after school hours when I called again. No answer. I called Qualude's home. No answer. So, I decided to call every fifteen minutes throughout the night. I filled his answering machine up with over fifty messages. At midnight, I broke down. I cried until the early morning.

Around 7:00pm I called Qualude's mother at her job. I needed to know how she felt about me going off to mental health. Plus, I knew she could get in contact with Qualude if I pushed her enough.

When she came over the line, I spoke, "I know you are wondering why I'm calling you at your job. I'm calling because I want you to know I'm fit enough to take care of my kids and I don't want any beef with you anymore."

She responded, "I didn't know you were home. We need to talk, but I'm busy at the moment. Can I call you later?"

"Yes."

Before she hung up, I asked, "Where is Qualude?"

"In school."

I walked in the living room after I went to the kitchen. My grandmother was watching TV. My kids were asleep in the couch.

I spoke, "It was messed up what you did to me."

My grandmother gave me this puzzled face expression. Then she looked towards the cordless phone that was laying on the floor next to her fat legs.

She spoke, "I didn't do nothing to you."

"Yes, you did. For one, you took me from Qualude. Number two, you got people thinking I'm crazy."

My grandmother said, "I never said you was crazy. I said you need some help."

"You calling Mental Health on me didn't help. That only added to my problem."

"I swear. I didn't mean for you to get hurt if you did."

My grandmother had fear in her eyes. Especially since I had a butcher knife in my hand. I took the knife from the dish rack right before I entered the living room.

I spoke, "How could you do that to me?

"I swear. I didn't mean to hurt you."

My mind was telling me to stab her, but my body wouldn't move. My grandmother made me realize that I wasn't crazy.

I said, "If I was crazy, I would have already stabbed you with this knife."

"Please, Denise. Put the knife down."

I put the knife down and said, "You are a curse. I have to get away from you. You are the reason my Uncle Junior thinks he's crazy. You are the reason my mother thinks she's crazy too," I said.

After disclosing how I felt about her, my grandmother walked back to her bedroom. I sat in the living and cried myself to sleep. Four hours later, I received a phone call from Qualude's mother.

She asked, "What do you want to talk to me about?"

I said, "I want you to know I'm not crazy. I can handle my kids."

"Well, I believe in second chances, but if I hear anything about you putting your hands on my grandkids again, I'm going to report you."

"You don't have to worry about that."

"Okay now."

I asked, "Now where is your son?"

She responded, "He's still in school. He's coming home this weekend."

"Tell him I need to talk to him," I said.

After I hung up with Qualude's mother, I left about fifty more threatening messages on his apartment phone's mailbox. I wanted him to know it was going to be my way or no way.

CHAPTER 30

QUALUDE

I couldn't believe Denise was out of the Mental Health hospital. In my eyes, she was still crazy. I really didn't have a clue that she had been abusing my daughters. I had seen her yell at them, but I didn't take it as abuse. I just thought she was being a mother, but when I was told by her grandmother that she had hung my daughter out a two-story window, I almost lost my mind. On top of all this, Denise was pregnant again.

Denise had the nerve to call me and threaten me. She had said, if I didn't come see her, that I would never see my kids again. I didn't know if she was planning on killing my kids or killing me, so I told my mother. My mother had reported her to Social Services the next day. A lady from Social Services had showed up at Denise's grandmother house the next day and made a report. A week later, the lady called my mother and told my mother that they would be investigating Denise again.

I returned to school after I visited my kids at Denise's grandmother's house. She wasn't there when I had my visit with my kids. Miss Betty and I had a long talk about what the lady from the Social Services had said. Miss Betty told me that I was going to have to get the kids if the lady from Social Services found that Denise was an unfit mother. I felt guilty about having my mother call Social Services, but I knew it was for the best.

Once I got back at school, I focused on my grades. My grades were slowly dropping, and Coach Soloman told me that if I didn't make a 2.5 grade point average, that he would have to release me from the team. After Coach gave me this information, I found out that Telly wasn't going to come close to having a 2.5 grade average. I felt like it was my fault that both of us were failing. Being the oldest out of us, I should have been more responsible.

Cory, on the other hand, was an honor student. First semester, he helped us with our work. Second semester, he told us that we had to stop partying and start doing our work. I didn't listen. I continued to party and skip classes. When report cards came out, I passed all my classes with C's. I had a 2.5 and I got to continue to play on the team.

The next week I went home for the weekend and found out that MC had been discharged from the hospital. I received the news from a junkie name Foots, who hung out around Rob's corner store on Remount Road. I saw Foots at the store because I was there to meet with Ty.

Ty was a local drug dealer who I knew from West Blvd. When he pulled up in a brand-new Lexus with twenty-inch rims on it, I smiled at him. His gold teeth were sparkling as he stepped out into the sunlight. I waved him over to my rental car.

After he took a seat, he said, "Boy, I'm happy to see you."

I responded, "I feel the same."

"Did you hear what happened to Nuke?"

I hadn't heard anything about Nuke. When I went off to college, I took my focus off of him.

I asked, "What happened to him?"

"He got killed last night."

"Damn! I don't want to sound like a cop, but who did it?"

"The word is he was trying to rob someone over in North Charlotte when he was shot in the chest. I heard your boy, Showtime, took him to the hospital and dropped him off. But it was already too late."

"Fo-real!"

"Yes."

CRUMBLING TALENT

I thought about the day that I told Nicole that her brother was a target.

I asked, "What do the cops know?"

"Nothing. They are calling it a drug deal gone bad."

After I arranged to meet with Ty later, I drove to Telly's house. He was sitting on the porch playing with his pit bull. I exited the car and walked slowly up the driveway.

Telly asked, "Who got killed?"

I said, "It's that obvious?"

"Yes. You was looking like that when I told you Me-Mount was dead."

I spoke, "Karama is a bitch."

I hadn't wish death on Nuke, but I wanted him to pay for what he did to MC. The crazy part about the whole situation is that everyone lost. Nuke lost his life and MC lost apart of himself that he couldn't get back. His basketball career was gone.

He could no longer play ball like he once did. There was no more quick, witty, trash-talking that he was known for, or the exploding to the rim and finishing with a beautiful dunk. This was the trade in for him messing around with ZZ.

After I gave Telly the 411 on Nuke's death, I received a call from MC.

His words were slurred. He sounded like he was drunk.

He asked, "Can you come get me?"

I asked, "Where are you?"

"I'm at my grandmother's apartment out here by South Mecklenburg High School."

After MC gave me the address, Telly and I drove out to it. I still had two-thousand dollars of my finance check that I received from school. I was planning to purchase some cocaine with it from Ty and flip the money so I wouldn't have to keep on asking my mother for money.

MC interrupted my plan, because Ty called me when I was in route to MC's grandmother's apartment. I told Ty that I would get with him on a later date. He agreed to get with me before I returned to school. Then I ended the call.

CHAPTER 31

QUALUDE

MC's grandmother's new place was a step up from her Sand Hurst apartment. The complex parking lot looked like a new car lot, and there were dogwood trees that circled the whole complex. There were also bushes that were neatly trimmed like small snow cones that were stationed in front of every building. MC's grandmother's apartment was on the second floor. Telly and I walked up the pine wooden steps that looked like they were wet from a coat of gloss. A big burgundy big wheel was sitting in the middle of the hallway when we reached MC's grandmother floor. I pushed it out of the way with my right foot and then knocked on MC's grandmother's door.

MC opened the door. He looked a few pounds lighter, but he still had that glow in his eyes. The Tarheels shirt and jeans shorts looked two sizes too big, but his Jordan's looked like they were fresh out the box. MC still had his head full of waves. His grandmother was sitting on the couch when he opened the front door. She said hello, then she walked towards one of the two bedrooms. Her body looked frail in her light blue housecoat. MC's new girlfriend, Maria, was sitting on the love seat. She looked like she was mixed with Mexican and Black, and there was even a little white in her features.

I asked, "You ready to go?"

MC responded, "My girl tripping. She don't want me to go

anywhere."

MC seemed fine to me. But I knew something was wrong when I took notice of his speak. It was still slurred. It sounded like he had been drinking.

His grandmother shouted from her room. "Take him out. He needs some air."

I looked down the hallway in search of MC's grandmother. I didn't see her.

Maria made a face that showed that she didn't agree with MC's grandmother.

I didn't want to be in a beef with MC's new girl so I said, "It's up to you, MC."

Telly was watching the scene. Maria was trying to play the insensible role. She was nothing like ZZ. There was no big butt, but she did have nice eyes and hair. Her complexion was the same color as Halle Berry.

MC spoke, "I do need some air." After his statement, he looked at Maria and said, "Please don't get mad."

It was more like he was begging her. MC wasn't himself. I had never heard him beg a woman. In all the years I had known him, he had controlled all the women he was in a relationship with. This was the guy that taught me a little bit about women.

Maria said, "Just bring me something to eat back."

MC responded, "I got a hot dog for you."

Maria said, "See, Q? He's not fit to be out."

MC didn't even formally introduce me to Maria. This was another red flag that told me that his head injury was serious. I convinced Maria that MC would be okay in my care. Then Telly, MC and me headed out the door.

Once inside the rental car, I turned on MC's favorite song.

At least, I thought it was his favorite song. AZ's 'Sugar Hill' came blasting from the speakers.

MC spoke, "I don't want to hear no music."

I turned the music off, and we rode in silence for about five minutes, until I asked, "How about some 2pac?"

I pushed the 2Pac CD in. It was one of the Double CD's. 'Check Out Time' came on.

MC said, "That's my song."

The red light at MC's grandmother's intersection caught me. There were two girls around our ages that pulled up next to us in a Black BMW. The driver was the same complexion of Maria. MC noticed her. I watched as my friend rolled down the window.

Telly and MC had been nonexistent to each other, until MC said, "Telly, move on the other side so I can let my chair back."

Telly did as MC asked. The girl on the passenger side of the BMW let her window down. I could see that they both were dressed in the same color sun dresses. They looked like they were on their way to the club.

I asked, "What's up?"

"Hello there," the passenger responded.

She was dark skinned, with long hair. Their demeanors told me that they were looking for some fun, because they both were smiling.

I asked, "Where are y'all headed?"

"Right up the street," the driver responded."

"Where is right up the street?" I asked.

"TGIF's," the passenger responded.

These two girls had game.

I asked, "Can we join y'all?"

"Only if y'all are paying," the driver shouted over her music.

It sounded like she was playing a song off 2Pac's Double CD.

These two girls didn't seem like gold diggers so I said, "Money ain't a thang."

I still had the two-thousand dollars that I got from my school inside my pocket. This was more than enough to foot the bill. I was back on my B-O-B. Back On Bitches. I didn't plan on adding a new girl to my list of girls, but these girls were fine. The driver's hair was shoulder length and her skin was flawless. When we arrived at the restaurant, I noticed her butt cheeks as she got out of her car. They looked like two volleyballs bouncing together as she

CRUMBLING TALENT

made her way to the front of the restaurant, where another girl was standing. The girl that was standing at the front entrance was dark and big boned with a long ponytail wrapped in a gold scarf that matched her gold outfit. I could see her open toes sandals that revealed her freshly done pedicure.

Telly spoke, "She's my type."

I thought this girl was by herself, but another girl walked out of TGIF. She was heavy set and was wrapped in a tight dress that looked like a piece of a curtain. She had a scarf on her head that matched her purple dress. I was having a change of heart about buying dinner. Here I was, fighting with the thought of pulling off and leaving, because I didn't know there were two more women. I didn't even know these women names, but I was about to buy them dinner. The thought of Denise came to mind. What would she think? What would she do if she caught me here?

I dismissed this thought after the driver walked over and introduced herself.

"I'm sorry. I 'm so rude. My name is Indonesia. My friends call me Indoo."

I asked, "Is that a name of a country?"

I was trying to make small talk.

She responded, "Yes. It's South East Asia."

Her friends were looking like they were getting a little worried. Telly and MC were just watching us.

I asked, "Those your friends, too?"

Indoo smiled and said, "They already have us a table. You ready to meet them?"

MC started laughing. I started thinking that something was really wrong with him.

Indoo asked, "What's wrong with him?"

"Car accident," I responded.

MC said, "No, it wasn't a car accident. I was in a fight with Nuke."

Telly hit the back of the seat. I turned around and looked at him.

He said, "I don't think this is a good idea."

I tried to ease the situation by saying, "That's the weed talking."

Inside the restaurant, things were no different. MC was talking crazy. He was making the girls paranoid. Indo gave me a look like they were all uncomfortable. This was after they had all introduced themselves. Sandy was the passenger, Carol and Caroline were the two girls that were at the front of the restaurant when we arrived. They were sisters.

Sandy made a circle around her head indicating to her friends that she thought MC was crazy. The girls put MC on trial after we ordered our food. They were like some policemen in an interrogation room.

Sandy asked, "So, MC. Who beat you up?"

"This guy name Nuke," this insane jerk responded.

I couldn't believe it. I had to intervene.

I said, "Have y'all heard that new 2pac?"

MC said, "I have." His voice was still slurred.

When MC busted out this response, I put my head down. There were people looking around from other tables because he was loud enough for them to hear him.

I said, "It's the weed."

Telly said, "That's that fire."

Carolina and Carol said, "We smoke."

Sandy said, "It's not weed. MC is crazy. Something is wrong with this guy."

MC was acting like the Rainman.

Indoo said, "Y'all girls chill out. It might be the weed."

I couldn't continue to watch these girls make fun of my friend. I looked at my watch and said, "Man, time is flying."

Indoo asked, "You have some where you have to be?"

I responded, "I almost forgot that my mother is having her birthday dinner tonight. I have to be there."

"You just got here," Indoo responded.

"I know. Maybe we can do this another time."

Sandy asked, "Are you still going to pay for our food?"

MC said, "Yes. He got money."

I wanted to slap MC in his mouth, but I knew this wouldn't solve the big bill that was due at the end of the meal.

I said, "Here is a hundred and fifty. This should do."

Carol asked, "What about drinks?"

I pulled out another fifty-dollar bill, placed it on the table and then pulled MC to the exit of the building. Telly followed behind us. I didn't even get to say goodbye to all the girls, but Indoo stormed out the door after us.

She said, "I'm sorry for what happened in there."

"You don't have to be," I responded.

We watched as Telly helped MC in the car.

Indoo said, "I know there something wrong with MC."

I asked, "It's that obvious?"

"Yes."

"I guess I was trying to fool myself that he was okay."

"You was just being a true friend."

"I guess I was."

I watched as Indoo pulled out a card from her pocket.

She spoke, "Here is my card. Call me."

I took the card and watched as Indo walked back into the restaurant.

CHAPTER 32

DENISE

I thought Qualude would be happy that I was out of the hospital. To my surprise, he wasn't. He didn't want to see me. I was told this by my grandmother. I blamed her for all my problems. She was the reason that our family was in the state it was in. My Uncle Junior was running the streets, chasing after the drug man, and my real mother was also doing the same. Everything was out of order. That's why I decided it was time to get my own place.

My nineteenth birthday was coming, and I was told by my social worker that I would be eligible for an apartment. I was also told that I could be put on the fast track for this apartment. I told my social worker that I wanted to move to a place that was close to the uptown area of the city. When it came time for me to move, I was told that Piemont Court Projects was the only place that had an opening. I took the apartment because I was eager to get away from my grandmother. Right before I moved in, I was told by my social worker that she had used my mother's name to get the apartment since my mother's name was already on the waiting list. I was mad, because I knew I would have to deal with my mother. But this didn't stop me from moving in.

After I moved in to my three-bedroom apartment, I had my son a couple days later. Qualude was at school when I had Qualude junior. I named the baby after Qualude, even though we were not married. He wasn't mad. I thought he was going to be mad, because he had told me that he didn't want his son to have the same name as his. His reason was that he didn't want his son to be teased like he was when he was a kid. I overlooked Qualude's logic. I didn't care if he disagreed with me, because I felt like we should have been married long time ago and that our kids should have had his name. But sometime things don't always go like they are planned.

My apartment gave me a sense of independence. I no longer counted on my grandmother to do everything for me. My social worker came by once a week to make sure I was okay, and she even got me more food stamps and helped me get my kids into a good daycare. This gave me more time to think about my future. Here I was, no education, three kids, and staying in a drug infested area. Things didn't look to bright.

I started feeling like life was eating me alive after Qualude told me he didn't want me anymore. I didn't know if he was seeing that white girl at his school or messing around with someone other than the white girl. I didn't have the means to travel to his school that's why I continued to call him at his coach's office. Most of the time, I would leave messages to the secretary to give to Qualude. Most of the messages would be false alarms about the kids, and he would call back. This would set off a lip-boxing match between us and I would tell him that I just wanted to hear his voice.

After months of fighting with Qualude over my behavior, I decided it was time to end my life. I no longer wanted to live. My kids were getting on my nerves to the point that I didn't care if they went in to the care of social services. My social worker was no longer coming by, so I didn't have to act like I cared about my kids anymore. They were the reason that Qualude and I weren't getting along.

I decided I was going to take my life quick. A gun would do the trick, I thought, while sitting in my living room watching the soaps. But I didn't have access to one. I didn't want to ask Qualude for one, because this would put him on alert. So, I decided I would set my apartment on fire with me and the kids inside it. But first I had to write a note. While writing the note, Aunt Peggy showed up. She was dressed in some Daisy Duke shorts and a t-shirt. Her hair was in a small ponytail. Her sandals were brand new. I let her in the front door after I sat the note down on my wooden table in the middle of the room. I didn't think to hide the note since I was in my own apartment.

Aunt Peggy spoke, "I was in the hood, so I decided to drop by. Where is your kids?"

"They are in daycare," I responded.

"What time they get out?" Aunt Peggy asked.

I said, "Around four."

The clock on the wall read 3:20pm.

Aunt Peggy asked, "What were you doing before I arrived?"

I looked over at the note on the table. Peggy noticed.

I responded, "Nothing."

Aunt Peggy said, "I need to use the bathroom. I've been drinking beer."

I pointed to the stairs where my only bathroom was located. Then I watched as Aunt Peggy walked up my stairs. I went to the kitchen and started dinner. While preparing dinner, I thought about Qualude.

When Aunt Peggy walked in the kitchen, after her bathroom break, and I noticed the note in her hand. I didn't take Peggy as a reader, because she never opened a book in front of me or even took a look at the newspaper.

She asked, "Who wrote this?"

It shocked me that Aunt Peggy was giving me the benefit of the doubt. Usually, she was jumping to conclusions when it came to me or my sister.

I asked, "What is it?"

"It's a crazy note. Someone is talking about killing."

I interrupted Aunt Peggy. "I think my mother had that."

My mother hadn't even been to my apartment. Even though

the apartment was in her name, she hadn't come to it, because I told her after I saw her on the street close to my apartment that I didn't want her to visit.

Peggy responded, "I didn't know your mother wanted to kill herself."

I replied, "I didn't know either."

"Them drugs got her gone. Maybe we need to get her some help again."

My mother had been to rehab over a dozen times.

"Maybe you can talk to her. She be down the street on 18th."

"I think I should do that before we find her somewhere dead."

I placed a piece of the chicken in the hot grease that was on the stove.

Peggy spoke, "One thing you can do is fry some chicken."

I responded, "I guess I can. But Qualude think different."

"You still worrying about that boy. There are too many more boys out in the world to be worrying about him. You act like he got gold in between his legs."

Aunt Peggy didn't understand that it wasn't just about sex with Qualude and I.

I said, "I know Peggy. I have been with other guys."

In fact, I had been with two other guys. The two weeks Qualude and I was apart, I had sex with two different guys that Candy had hooked me up with. I only did it because Candy had dared me to.

"I didn't think so. You be acting so crazy over him that I thought he was the only one."

"No. And if you don't believe me, ask Candy."

"That's my girl. Maybe you need to call the guy up and let him know you are single."

"I don't think he wants me now."

"Why?"

"I have three kids."

"Kids shouldn't stop you from having a life."

"But I don't want anymore."

"Make him put on a rubber."

I couldn't believe I was having this conversation with Aunt Peggy. In the past, she was too drunk to talk to me. Now that she was trying to change, she didn't drink during the week.

"I guess I have to get over Qualude."

"Maybe you can go out with me now. You are over eighteen. You are grown."

"I don't know Aunt Peggy. You know how you get when you get drunk."

"Think about it. I can come and get you this weekend and Nicole can watch the kids."

"Let me think about it."

I made Aunt Peggy a plate of Rice, gravy, corn and fried chicken. Then, I grabbed a glass out the dish rack and poured her some grape Cool Aid. My mind went back to Qualude.

CRUMBLING TALENT

CHAPTER 33

QUALUDE

Coach Soloman's office became Telly and my hang out. There was a pool table and other table games to play in the lobby of the building. Telly and I knew the building like the back of our hands. There was even an area that we called the quiet space where we could do our homework. Most of the time, we got the team manager to do our work. She would do the work for us and we would copy it in our handwritings. I felt guilty about her doing my work, but I needed a 2.5 grade average so I could continue to play ball.

Coach Soloman gave us a week off after going on a five-game winning streak. This was after we had beaten St. Paul; an all-black college out of VA. The game was one of the best games I ever played in in my life. There was so many beautiful black women at the game that I thought I was in a black man's heaven. I was enjoying the college life. This was what I thought it would be like.

The craziest thing happened when we arrived back in Winston Salem. We met three white girls at the Food Lion, across from our school. Cory was the one that spotted the girls by the beer cooler in the right corner of the store. They were trying to decide if they wanted to buy Budweiser or Budweiser light. After they picked up two cases of Budweiser light, Cory approached them.

He asked, "Are y'all about to have a party?"

The ring leader spoke, "You didn't even ask us our names?

Cory responded, "I'm sorry. How rude of me. Now what is y'all names?"

The ring leader said, "I'm Chis."

Then she pointed at Sydney, who was slim and had on a two-piece oriental designer garment that looked more like a cooking outfit than pajamas. Her physique was average. Her firm breasts were pointed out underneath her top. She was around Denise's height.

Chis continued, "This is Jill."

She pointed at Jill, who was cute in her own way. She was also dressed in pajamas like Chis and Sydney. Her hair was pulled back in a long ponytail with a Blue and White Tarheels rubber band wrapped around it. She was a little taller than Chis, who was two inches taller than Sydney. Her PJ's were loose fitted and Tar Heel color.

Cory spoke, "These are my roommates. Telly and Qualude."

Chis asked, "Are you named after a drug?"

Both of her friends started laughing. Sydney had this weird quacking sound laugh that resembled a duck.

I responded, "Yes. My grandmother named me."

I didn't want to lie about how my grandmother came up with my name, so I changed the subject.

"Enough about me. Where are y'all on y'all way to?"

Jill spoke, "We are on our way to a rave."

I asked, "What is a rave?"

Everyone looked at me like I was crazy.

I asked again, "What is a rave?"

Telly said, "It's a party. Where there is different kinds of lights glowing all over the place while weird music is playing. Plus, there is drugs and alcohol."

Telly had attended several raves back in high school. I didn't go, because I didn't like to hang around white people. His high school was mainly made up of middle- and high-class whites.

Chis spoke, "Y'all can join us if y'all like."

Cory said, "We will love too."

CRUMBLING TALENT

Even though I had started believing that all whites were not bad, I still felt like something could go wrong by hanging out with these girls.

I pulled Telly and Cory to the side and said, "I don't know about this."

Tell spoke, "It will be fun."

Cory said, "You got to go."

I really wanted to pass up the party, but I didn't want Telly and Cory to come back to the apartment talking about all the fun they had. So, I went along. First, we had to stop by our apartment and get our PJ's. I put on my Polo PJ's and my blue and white Polo slippers. Telly put on his Tommy Hilfiger house coat and matching slippers. Cory dressed himself in a no-name brand pair of PJs that his mother had purchased for him right before he had moved in with us. We all put on light green shower caps to add character to our outfits. Then, we all hopped in Sydney's Range Rover.

I couldn't believe how hip these girls were. Sydney had the latest rap CD's in her CD changer. There was Outcast and 2pac. I let the girls know I was a big 2pac fan. They turned on 'All Eyes On Me' by 2pac. While listening to the song, I came to the conclusion that these girls were just looking for a good time. They were all college students who were attending North Carolina in Chappal Hill. They all had checkbooks and came from money.

We pulled up in front of this big warehouse on a service road that I had never see before. I could see all kinds of sport cars and high price trucks in the gravel parking lot. The music inside the warehouse could be heard outside.

Jill was the first to speak.

"I need a pill."

Her green eyes lit up. I noticed Chis messing around in her pocketbook. She came out with a greenish-blue pill. It wasn't that big, but it was big enough for all three of them to share it.

After they shared the pill, Chis asked, "Do y'all want one?"

I said, "No."

Telly and Cory said, "Yes."

They took a piece of the pill that Chis had taken out of her Prada pocketbook. Chis ate the remainder of the pill when I rejected her again.

She gave me this nonchalant look and said, "More for me."

Telly and Cory tried to convince me that the pill would make the experience in the party better. I didn't believe this, because I had seen what crack could do. I didn't want to seem like a party buster so I took the blunt of weed that Chis passed me after she lit it up. The weed didn't smell like the weed that Cory, Telly and I smoked. It had a sour smell.

After about five minutes, I was tripping. It was like I was seeing things.

We all entered the club after Sydney handed each of us a bottle of water that she had pulled out of the cooler that was in the back of the truck. The weed had me on cloud nine, now and my throat was dry and I wanted more water after I took down that bottle. When we got in the club, Chis paid for everyone a drink. I ordered water, because I was too high to drink alcohol. The club had all kinds of races inside it, and everyone was mingling like color didn't matter. Looking from my eyes, everything was moving in slow motion. I noticed a side show with a white girl and a black girl. They were kissing like there was no tomorrow. They both were nearly nude in a large steel cage, and all the different colored lights were making it hard for me to keep up with them. The music and the weed had me thinking like I was in a time zone, and my life wasn't moving. Everything seemed so vivid. The freshness in this new experience had me wondering what had Chis put in the weed. I decided to ask her.

I spoke, "We need to talk Chis."

Telly was on the dance floor with Sydney and Cory was at the bar with Jill.

Chis asked, "You like that PCP?"

"What?"

"PCP is mixed inside the weed."

"Why didn't you tell me?"

"I didn't think it matter."

"I don't do hard drugs."

"Well you done it tonight!"

Chis seemed like she was talking in slow-motion.

I said, "I'm ready to go."

"We just got here."

"I don't appreciate what you did to me."

"What did I do?"

"You give me PCP."

"I just wanted to give you a good time."

"I could have a good time without drugs."

Chis turned away from me. Everything was still moving like it was in slow-motion, the music even sounded like it was dragging, and the lights were affecting my vision.

I put my hand over my eyes as I asked, "Chis, how long this stuff last?"

"You have about another hour."

I looked at Chis' watch on her wrist. The clock read: 12:00. I had been high for two hours.

I said, "I need more water."

Around 2am, I headed for the door. Chis joined me after she grabbed another drink from the bar. As we were walking out of the door, foam was flying everywhere.

Chis spoke, "This is part of the show."

Once outside, I felt a sense of newness. I was back to myself after being high for almost for four hours. Chis opened the back door for me after she climbed in the driver side of the back of the truck. She turned on the radio and then climbed in the back of the back seat with me.

2pac's 'Keep Ya Head Up' came blasting from the speakers. Chis turned the song down just enough so we could hear each other.

She asked, "Do you have a girlfriend?"

I said, "No."

"Well that mean I can do this."

Chis kissed me in the mouth. I could feel her thick tongue as she pushed it against my tongue. We fell in to the wave of passion, and before I knew what was going on, I was inside of Chis' mouth. This was my second time getting oral sex from a white girl. It wasn't any different. I had heard all these stories about how white women were better than black women when it came to oral sex. This wasn't true.

Before we could finish, we were interrupted by a security guard. He flashed the light on us, chis had been choking herself, and I was near my point, when the light had hit both of us in the face. Chis grabbed her PJ's. There was no need for us to rush. We had been caught. The security guard didn't call the police. Thank God. He just asked us to leave. Chis called Jill on her cell phone and told her what had happened. A few minutes later, Telly, Cory, Jill and Sydney came walking out the club. They were all in happy spirits.

Things went to a whole different level when we arrived back at the apartment. You would have thought that I would have learned my lesson from dealing with Kelly, but I didn't. I was still curious about intercourse with a white girl. Oral sex was the same with a white girl as it was with a black. I came to the conclusion that it depended on the person on how great the sex was, and this came after Cory had disappeared to his bedroom with Sydney and Telly went to his room with Jill.

Once I reached my room with Chis, I sped up the process. This was after Chis had returned from the bathroom from freshen up. I stuck my tongue down her throat and kissed her hard.

We got lost in the lust until she broke off the kiss and asked, "Are you ready for me?"

I said, "Yes."

"Are you sure?"

"Yes."

"Have you ever tried anal before?"

"Is that something new?"

"Maybe for you."

I asked, "Are you on the pill?"

"Yes, you don't have to use a rubber."

I didn't want to ruin the moment, so I grabbed Chis by her head and stuck my tongue down her throat again. She broke off the kiss again.

She asked, "Do you know a girl name Kelly?

Chis question caught me off guard.

I responded, "No."

It had been over six months since the incident with Kelly. I hadn't seen her or heard anything from her.

Chis spoke, "Good."

There was something about that made me feel uneasy after she asked me about Kelly. I still went along and had sex with her. After several hours of sex and doing more PCP, I felt like my head was about to bust. Somehow, I managed to fall asleep as the sun was coming up. The next afternoon, I woke up with a hangover. I couldn't remember a single detail about what Chis said before she left. I didn't even know what time she had left.

I put on my shorts and t-shirt once I had stepped out of bed. Then I made my way to the bathroom inside my room. The light had been turned off the night before, and it was still off. I hit the light switch, and the first thing I noticed, written in red lipstick, was a message on the mirror.

It said: 'You Have Been Infected With The Aids Virus.'

This message almost sent me into a state of shock. I started breathing hard until I thought this was one of Telly's or Cory's joke. But when I saw Kelly's name signed at the bottom of the mirror, I knew this wasn't a joke.

I rushed to Telly's and Cory's rooms to see if they had received the same message. They both told me that they hadn't had sex. I showed them the lip stick message after they told me that they didn't have any of the girl's phone numbers.

I sat in my room all night thinking about my Uncle Teddy, who died from Aids. His death had been slow, and had suffered a lot, because most hospitals didn't want to deal with him, because of his sickness. At the time, there was not much that could be done about the Aids virus after it reached a certain stage.

When I came out of my room the next morning, Telly and Cory were waiting on me. I told them that I planned to get a test and that they shouldn't worry about me. They both agreed to keep the matter between us. This was all I could ask from them.

I went through the day like I was a zombie in a movie. When I arrived back at my apartment, I received a call from Denise. She told me that someone had reported her again to Social Services, and she believed it was my mother or Peggy. After Denise gave me all the factors of why she thought it was my mother or Peggy that reported her, I told her that I would be coming home. She didn't protest. I knew she wouldn't.

After I got off the phone with Denise, I called Peggy. She answered on the second ring.

I asked, "Why are you trying to get my kids took from me?"

"I'm not trying to get the kids took from you. I rather you come home and get the kids, because Denise is crazy."

"No, she's not."

"I have proof."

"What is it?"

"I have a note she wrote. She was going to kill herself and then kill the kids."

"You lying, Peggy. I don't believe you."

"I know I've done some things that you don't like, but I'm telling the truth. I still got the note."

"What it say?"

"I rather not say. I just want you to know that you need to come home and get your kids."

Before I could respond, Peggy hung up the phone. I tried to call her back, but she wouldn't answer. I now knew who called Social Services. There was no need to call my mother.

❖   ❖   ❖

A week went by before I could have a meeting with Coach Soloman.

When I walked into his office, I already had my mind made up that I was going back to Charlotte and get my kids. I hadn't discussed my future with any one, because there wasn't anyone, I knew that would understand my decision. This was why I waited until the last minute to tell Telly and Cory.

Coach Soloman was sitting behind his desk going over some plays he had made up when I had walked inside his office.

He looked up at me and said, "What's up, Q?"

I responded, "I have a few things on my mind that I need to discuss with you."

"Is this about the apartment that I'm supposed to help you get for you and your kids' mother?"

"No. It's about me."

Coach was dressed in sweatpants, t-shirt, and black Nikes. His black glasses looked too small on his face.

Coach spoke, "I have been meaning to inform you that I pulled a few strings for you this quarter, too."

"Coach. I know you had my grades changed."

"Who told you?"

"I don't have to be smart to know that you did that for me."

"I want you to know that I only done it for your own good."

"Well, there is something I have to tell you."

"Shoot."

"I have family problems. I think I need time away from school to clear things up."

"Is it Denise and the kids?"

"Yes."

"I told you, I can help you with them."

"This is something I have to do as a man, coach."

"What's the problem now?"

"The Social Service people in Charlotte are going to take my kids. I can go there and fight for them, or let them go into the state system."

"What do you need me to do?"

"Nothing. I'm a man. It's time I stand up like one and handle the situation myself."

"Look, Q. You have talent. Talent that most people dream about. But it's no good if you let people continue to get in your way."

"What do you mean, 'people?' Denise is my kids' mother. She means the world to me."

I didn't mean it like that. What I'm trying to say is, you have to think about your future. You are averaging twenty points, two steals, five rebounds and five assists a game. These numbers can get you in a D-1 school, and maybe to the NBA."

"What about my family?"

"I told you, I can help you with that, but you have to want to help me to keep winning here."

"That's all you want, Coach. You just want to win. Well, I have morals and values, and I love my family more than winning. This is why I'm going back to Charlotte and fight for my kids."

"What did I say wrong?"

"You didn't tell me to go fight for my family. The word win is all you know."

I stood up and put my school hat on and turned to leave. I knew Coach wasn't going to let me go without a fight.

He spoke, "If you quit, you will be making the biggest mistake of your life. I'm not saying this because I need you to play ball for this school. I'm saying this because I know it's hard to a black man in white America.

Right now, you are at a crossroad. It's your decision to take the right road. Everyone comes to a crossroad in life, and we must decide what road to take. I took the road to being a Coach, and right now it's my job to get you to understand that everything isn't going to be smooth in life. As your Coach, I ask you to do what you think is right for you and your family."

"Thanks, Coach."

"Remember, I'm here if you need me."

I thought Coach was going to ask me to sell my soul, but he didn't.

"Okay."

I left Coach's office feeling like I made the right decision. It was time to let Telly and Cory know about my decision.

CHAPTER 34

DENISE

When I picked up the phone inside my bedroom, I looked at the clock on the wall. It was two minutes after three in the evening.

Qualude spoke, "School isn't for me."

I asked, "What's wrong?"

"I'm sorry Denise. I feel like it's my fault that you are going through what you are going through."

"I don't understand."

"I know about Peggy calling Social Services on you."

"How do you know?"

"She told me."

I didn't know that Aunt Peggy had called Social Services on me. I thought Qualude's mother did.

I asked, "Who are you going to stay with?"

"That's why I called. Can I stay with you?"

I didn't even hesitate. I said, "Yes."

Before Qualude ended his call with me, he told me how much he loved me and that he was never going to ever leave me again. I told him I loved him and then told him about my court day. He agreed that he would go with me, but first he had to tell his roommates that he was leaving school.

I agreed that he could stay as long as he didn't bring up stuff in the past that I had done. He agreed.

CRUMBLING TALENT

Two days later, I was in court facing child endangerment charges. Qualude couldn't make it, because he was still trying to discharge from school. I met with my court appointed attorney right before we walked into the courtroom downtown. To my surprise, the charges were dismissed. This was after I saw Qualude's mother standing off to the side, talking to a black woman that looked like a lawyer.

She walked over to me and said, "You get to keep your kids."

I hugged her tight, and told her how much I appreciated her.

Then I asked, "Did you tell Qualude about this?"

She responded, "No. You need to tell him."

QUALUDE

It was hard to tell my cousin and my friend Cory, that I decided that school wasn't for me. When they both walked in after a long day of classes, I was standing in the living room waiting. They both were dressed like they were ready to go to basketball practice.

I said, "I'm leaving school."

"Why?" Telly asked.

He had this look on his face like he wasn't ready for this.

I responded, "Denise is about to lose the kids to the State."

"What happened this time?" Telly asked.

He knew me like a book. He knew I wasn't going to let my kids go into the hand of Social Services.

I said, "Denise has to go to court for my kids. I have to be there just in case they want to give them to me."

Cory looked puzzled. He wasn't use to all my drama, he had grown up in a middle-class neighborhood where he had never had to worry about the things I was going through.

Cory asked, "What about the team?"

"Y'all are good without me."

Telly asked, "Is this about the situation you had with Kelly?"

"No," I responded.

They both gave me a look like they didn't believe me.

"Maybe I should talk to coach," Cory said.

"I already have."

"You sure this isn't about Kelly?" Cory asked again.

"No."

"You know we got your back. We can protest this." Cory looked serious.

"No. There is no need for a protest," I replied. "I know you have heard things in school."

"I didn't believe anything that I heard," Cory said.

There was talk in school about my situation with Kelly. Telly had told me that people were saying that I had raped Kelly.

Telly spoke, "Ever since Chis left that message on your bathroom mirror, you have been acting strange."

I interrupted, "This isn't about the message. It's about my kids."

Cory cut back in, "Your mother can get the kids."

"No, she can't. Denise's family would never let her get the kids. Plus, my mother don't think all the kids are mine."

I had never told anyone this.

Telly spoke, "What are you going to do if you don't get the kids?"

I responded, "I don't know."

Telly and I were taught to believe in God. His mother and Big Mama had instilled this in us. I said a prayer after I called my mother on her cellphone to make sure she was on her way. After I had gotten off the phone with her, I watched Telly pack up his bags. He decided that he was going to quit, too. After he told me that he would go to hell with me and back, I knew that my cousin was one of the most loyal people in my life. I felt bad that he was following in my footsteps, but I had to do what was best for my kids. I didn't want them to be running house to house like I did as a kid. I wanted to raise them like my father hadn't done for me.

CRUMBLING TALENT

❖   ❖   ❖

QUALUDE

Six months passed like six days. I purchased a new apartment and moved out of Denise's apartment. This was after we had a big fight about the kids. I went back to West Blvd, were I started selling drugs again. I picked up like I had never stopped. My Uncle got out of prison and joined me in my life of crime.

It didn't take long before there were rumors in the city about me having Aids. This was after a girl had died that I had a short relationship with after I had broke it off with Denise. I didn't even know that Tiffany was sick. I used a condom with Tiffany, but it had popped. I had stopped when it popped and got another.

That night came back to my mind when I heard that Tiffany was rushed to the hospital and later died. The whole west side of the city knew she had Aids, except me. This was crazy, because I had never thought I would be fighting for my life for something so serious.

When I got sick and couldn't shake the cough, I decided to go get a check. This was after the Health Department people came around looking for all the people that had had sex with Tiffany.

Big Mama was at her apartment the day the health department people came to the door for me. Tiffany's ex-boyfriend had told them I had sex with Tiffany. I thought it was crazy at the time, but actually he was helping me.

I arrived at the health department at 9:00 am. The parking lot looked like a used car lot, and the building looked like it was an old hospital. This was my second time at this place. The first time was when I gave Denise the STD. That had been almost two years ago.

I looked at myself inside the mirror in the rental car before I had stepped into the sun. I fixed my sweat suit, ran my hand through my waves and then made my way to the front door of the building. I walked through the door and took a turn towards the STD department. I walked up to the counter where a black, young lady was sitting in a chair reading a newspaper.

I spoke, "I'm here to get a checkup."

The lady asked, "Do you have an appointment?"

"Yes."

"You have to speak up louder, sir."

I knew what this lady was trying to do.

I said, "Yes."

"What is it for?"

There was a crowd of about thirty people sitting in the lobby waiting.

I looked back at them and said, "For a checkup."

The lady ran her fat fingers over a list and then said, "I only have two 9:00am appointments. What is your name?"

I let out a cough before I said, "Qualude Jones."

"I have your name. Take a seat."

I took a seat in the lobby beside a girl that looked like she was in her early teens. She had a baby on her lap, and the baby was asleep. She reminded me of Denise, in a way.

Sitting in the lobby of the health department made me realize that I was at a crossroad of my life. If I had Aids, I didn't know what I was going to do. But if I didn't, I was going to change my life for the better for my kids' sake.

When my name was called, I stood up and made my way over to the entrance of the treatment area. The whole lobby of people turned their attention towards me.

This was after the nurse asked, "Are you here for an Aids test?"

The nurse caught me off guard.

I responded, "Can we talk in the back?"

This pale face, fiftyish something, nurse took my chart out the first nurse's hand and escorted me to an examination room. This was the same nurse that had taken me to the back room when I had had the gonorrhea. She remembered me, because of the way I had cried about getting the shot in my rump. Once in the room, she gave me a gown to put on. Then she took my blood pressure and my temperature. Everything was normal.

Then she said, "Here are some brochures about different venereal diseases."

After I took the brochures, she asked, "Did we treat you once before?"

I responded, "Yes."

She smiled and left the room. I looked over the brochures. Especially, the one about Aids. The signs were there. I had a dry cough, sweats and upset stomach all the time. I thought about all the information that I was taking in. Then I compared it to my Uncle Teddy's signs when he had died from Aids. Tears came to my eyes. Was this the end? Was I going to die like my Uncle? What would the world think?

My deep thinking came to an end when this white doctor with a long, pointed, nose entered the room. He was tall with a smooth face, and his smile looked sincere.

He took off his black glasses before he asked, "Are you okay?"

"No," I answered, like I was dying.

"You sound like something is very wrong."

"I think it is."

"What's the problem?"

"That's what I need you to tell me."

"You have to tell me what hurts."

"Everything."

"Open your mouth."

The doctor pulled out a wooden stick that was small enough to move around in my mouth.

He spoke, "I see a little inflammation."

After the doctor took the wooden stick out my mouth, I said, "I had this cough for almost three weeks."

"Did you go to the hospital?"

"Yes. The pills the doctor gave me didn't work."

"Do you know the name of the pills?"

"I'm not sure. But I can call my girl and she can tell you."

"Do you smoke?"

"No. Not really."

"What do you mean?"

"I smoke weed every now and then."

"I'm going to take a blood sample and we will try to find out what the problem is. I'd like to get you to sign some papers."

"Sure."

"I would like to know all the women that you have had sex with in the last three years."

There was a long list. The first name that came to my mind was Chis.

I spoke, "I think this girl name Chis might have gave me the Aids virus."

"How do you know it's her?"

"Well, she left a message on my bedroom mirror after we had sex."

"How long ago was this?"

"About six months."

The doctor wrote a couple of sentences on his chart. I couldn't make out what he wrote, because he turned in the opposite direction when he had done this.

He spoke, "You know, you have to get HIV virus before you can get the stage of having full blown Aids."

I knew a little bit about Aids, because my Uncle Teddy had died from the disease. Plus, I knew Magic Johnson of the L.A Lakers was still fighting the HIV virus.

I responded, "I know it's two different stages."

"Well don't get too caught up about having aids. You shouldn't think like that."

"The girl, Chis, left the message, and this is why I'm thinking this."

"Do you know where she's at right now?"

"She live in Winston Salem NC."

"Do you have her number?"

"No."

"The reason I'm asking you this is because, if your test comes back positive, I have to inform all the people you have had sexual contact with.

The doctor went over all the papers with me that I had to sign and then left the room. The nurse entered with several needles in her hand. She introduced herself.

"I'm Nurse Miss Grier. I need you to be very still while I draw this blood."

I did as the nurse ordered. I closed my eyes as the needle went inside my vein. The jazz over the PA system sounded good, and it reminded me when I used to go to the park with Big Mama when I was a kid. I could hear every instrument.

After Miss Grier finished filling three tubes, she spoke, "I think you going to be alright. We have people all the time thinking they got something and they end up having nothing."

Miss Grier was a thick boned woman that looked like she could beat a man in a fight. Her demeanor told me that she cared about people. Here she was, a white woman caring for a black man that could be infected with the HIV virus. She wasn't afraid to touch me like the other nurses had been afraid to touch my Uncle Teddy before he had died.

After I finished up with Miss Grier, I was told by the doctor that my test would take weeks. During this time, I would have to take it easy and just wait.

I left the Health Department more confused and afraid than when I came in.

After I left the health department, I stopped by Family Dollar and purchased me a Five Dollar Diary. Then I headed over to my mother's house. I wanted to pay her a visit before I went through with killing myself. There was a lot I had to do before I could actually take my own life. First, I had to decided how I would take my life and when.

Since I purchased the diary, I thought it would be good that I wrote in it about why I was talking my life. Then this would explain to everyone why I did it. Before I could do this, I had to tell someone about all my transgressions.

While driving, I thought more about how my life could have been better. If I wouldn't have had sex without protection, I wouldn't have landed myself in a bad place in life. I was thinking more about Tiffany and the girl Chis now. Then my thoughts switched to Denise and the kids. I even thought that J-Rock could have given the virus to Denise, but I dismissed this thought after I was interrupted by Denise.

I looked down at my phone. It was her home number. I pushed the button on the phone to send her to my voice mail. Then I pictured her face. I knew she would be mad if she knew that I was sending her to my voicemail, but I didn't care. In my eyes, I was already dead.

CHAPTER 35

QUALUDE

When my mother opened her front door to her house, she was dressed in a worn-out blue dress that covered most of her body. Her hair was wrapped in a black scarf and she had a pair of brand-new slippers.

She spoke, "Boy, I thought you were coming over later."

I responded, as I made my way inside the house, "I was, but I was close by so I stopped over." Then I said, "It's looks good in here."

The house smelled like fresh paint. I gave my mother a hug after she closed the front door.

She spoke, "Where is my money?"

I responded, "What money?"

"The money you promised me for my nails."

"Here."

I handed my mother a hundred-dollar bill.

She said, "Your stepfather just left."

I watched as she put the bill in here pocket. In the past, she hadn't like taking money from me.

I said, "That's not my father."

My mother cracked a smile. She knew how to push my buttons. This is why I decided not to discuss my transgressions with her. She wasn't as understanding like Big Mama.

Then she asked, "Do you want something to eat?"

"No. I have to go over to Big Mama's apartment and talk to her. I don't have no time to take in a whole meal."

"What's wrong?"

I responded, "There isn't nothing wrong with me. I just need to tell Big Mama I love her."

"I can see there is something wrong with you. I can see it in your eyes."

"I just need some rest."

I covered my mouth when I started coughing.

My mother spoke, "And that cough. It sound like you have the flu."

"Really, I'm okay."

"Just let me cook you something."

"No. Thank you."

My mother was really concerned about me. Her demeanor told me this.

"Please, just tell me what's wrong with you."

"Nothing."

As I walked back over to the front door, my mother rushed off to the kitchen and returned a few seconds with a plate of food in her hand.

"Here, Q"

"Didn't I say I didn't want anything to eat?"

"Just take it with you."

I took the plate and walked out the door. My mother watched as I got into the rental car. I didn't even tell my mother goodbye. I didn't want this to be my last goodbye to her, even though I felt like it was. My reckless behavior had me acting like I was dying.

As I drove along the John Belk Freeway, I couldn't hold back my tears. I rode around listening to 2Pac's 'Me Against The World' as I thought about what would happen to me if I had Aids or HIV. I had seen people become outcasts when people found out they were HIV Positive or had Aids. People in the hood were cruel to these people. I didn't want be treated like those people had been treated. I didn't want Big Mama to have to care for me

CRUMBLING TALENT

like she did my Uncle Teddy in his last stages of Aids. I couldn't help but to blame my mother for my bad decisions and choices. I felt like if she hadn't left me with Big mama over the years, then I would have been raised better. In my eyes, my mother was the person that could have prevented me from making a mess out of my life. On the other hand, she didn't because she was so much in love with Butch.

I turned my attention back to reality when I turned into Dalton Village Projects. Everyone and their mothers were standing out enjoying the beautiful day. Even though it was cold, the sun was shining bright. I waved at a couple people I recognized after I stepped out the car. Then I quickly made my way to Big Mama's apartment, because I didn't want to be bothered by the neighborhood junkies who were lurking in the abandoned apartments in the hood.

I used my key to get into the apartment. This was after I had checked my watch for the time. It was close to 3:00 pm. This was the time Big Mama was usually watching her soaps. When I walked in Big Mama was on the couch with a bag of pork skins in her hand. The smell of hot sauce was in the air.

I said, "Hello beautiful woman."

She responded, "What bring you to the neighborhood?"

"Just wanted to check on you."

"Well, I'm fine. Your mother just called. She say you wasn't fine."

"My mother don't know what she talking about."

I made eye contact with Big Mama. It felt like she was looking through my soul.

She said, "You can tell me. I can see it all over your face."

Big Mama was good at reading people

I said, "I don't want to talk about it."

"This must be bad."

"Yes. That's why I don't want to talk about it."

"You have to talk to someone about it. Or it's going to kill you."

"No."

Big Mama pushed on. "Well, I know it isn't girl problems, because Denise would have called me."

"No. It's not girls."

"What is it? You can tell me."

"I went to the doctor."

"For what?"

"A test."

"What kind of test?"

"Aids test and HIV."

"You got me worried now."

"That's why I didn't want to tell you."

"Now, you know I need to know what's going on."

"There is nothing going on"

"That's what Teddy use to tell me."

My grandmother gave me an uncertain look.

I responded, "No. I'm not gay."

"Thank God."

"Why would you think that?"

"You know how everyone thought that Aids came from gay people."

"You need to stop watching the news."

"Maybe I do, but your Uncle's situation taught me not to put nothing past no one. Not even my kids. All the times that Teddy had told me he was using protection with the guys he was sleeping with; he was lying to me."

"What do that have to do with me?"

"I want you to tell me the truth. Now I know what had happened in college with that white girl and you."

I cut Big Mama off. "I don't want to talk no more."

Then I took off toward the kitchen. Big Mama hopped up off the couch and followed me inside.

She spoke, "You know I love you like I had you out my womb."

I interrupted, "I don't want to talk about it."

"You going to have to talk about it, Q."

I waited for a full minute then said "I don't know if I have Aids. I had sex with someone that has aids."

The hurt in my grandmother's eyes told me she was disappointed. She put her hand over her mouth. Her stare tore through my soul.

I spoke, "Don't worry. I'mma be okay."

Big Mama wasn't the type to tell her family business to anyone. I didn't have to worry about her running off and telling the family. Even when my Uncle knew he had Aids; Big Mama still denied the fact to anyone that asked her.

A month later, the doctor called me in. The trip to the Health Department felt like I was going to my death. This didn't stop me from thinking about my kids' future. I wanted them to still be able to remember me if I was to pass away. This is why I set up a trust fund for them, and I did this without telling Denise. I wanted her to be surprised when it was time for our kids to receive the money.

My senses were at a height that they had never been before. I could smell the scent of rain as I stepped out the rental car inside the parking at the Health department. As I walked towards the brick building, I could hear the raindrops. My hands were sweating, so I wiped them on my blue jeans. I could taste the bacon and egg that I had purchased from the coffee shop a block away from the Health Department. This was the same place I had written my last entry inside my diary. This was also where I made the decision to end my life if I had HIV or Aids.

Once inside the lobby of the Heath Department, I took a seat after I let the lady at the front desk know who I was. Then I got lost in my thoughts. My thoughts quickly returned to Denise and the kids. The question that I had been asking myself all morning was, what would Denise think? I really didn't know how she would feel if the test came back that I had Aids. I didn't see her staying along my side like Magic Johnson's wife was doing for him. Then there was the possibility that she could have the virus, because I had had sex with her after I found out that Tiffany was, in fact, infected with Aids.

I decided, if I had Aids, that I would end my life and put my diary where Denise could find it. I had written over fifty entries in my diary explaining how I had caught Aids and how I needed Denise to get closure. Plus, I needed everyone to forgive me for taking my life. This is why I decided it was best to wait until I got home to take my life.

When the Doctor showed up inside the waiting room, he spoke, "Qualude Jones."

I responded, "That would be me."

"Come this way please."

It seemed like every eye in the room was on me. There were about twenty people inside the lobby when I arrived and several more had come in while I was lost in my thoughts. I followed the Doctor to a small room about fifty feet from a lab room in the back area of the building. Once inside the room, the Doctor spoke.

"I know you remember me from your last visit."

I responded, "Yes."

"Do you know why you here today?"

"Yes."

Suddenly, the room felt cold and the Doctor's voice sounded like he was delivering a death sentence. His voice was a deep tone.

He said, "Here are your labs. I usually don't like to give my patients bad news, but I felt like it was my duty to tell you, because you are younger than most people I saw here."

Instantly I knew something was wrong. The words 'bad news' had told me this. Plus, the Doctor's demeanor was distanced when he came in contact with me.

I spoke, "Just tell me. I understand."

The Doc hesitated, before he said, "You are, in fact, infected with the HIV virus."

Instantly, the tears came. The Doc handed me a roll of tissue. It was like he didn't want me to get any fluids on anything in the room. He was still distanced after he had delivered my death sentence.

CHAPTER 36

DENISE

Qualude was starting to act distanced. This all started when he came back from his Doctor's appointment. I found out he had gone to the health department, because had I found a medical slip inside the glovebox of his rental car. The slip didn't say why he had visited the Health department. While looking over the slip, I thought about the time Qualude gave me a disease. Old emotions resurfaced. The mental picture of the day when Qualude had told me that he gave me the STD reappeared right before my eyes. I was heartbroken that day. I was now feeling the same emotions as I put the slip back in his glovebox. I slammed the door to the rental. Then I went back into Qualude's apartment and acted like everything was okay. A week later, I decided to ask him about his visit to the Health Department. This was a big mistake. We got into a lip boxing match and Qualude became more distanced.

❖   ❖   ❖

QUALUDE

Denise wouldn't stop asking about my visit to the Health Department. I felt guilty after she packed her things and went back to her mother's apartment. She took the kids with her and she told me that she was going to take out child support on me. I wanted to tell her that I had the HIV virus, but I didn't want to hurt her more than I had already had. Killing myself was the only way to fix all my problems. There was no other way. After deciding that a gun would do the job, I headed over to the liquor store and purchased a bottle of white gin. Then I returned to my apartment and opened the bottle and drank from it. After about thirty minutes, I was drunk as a Cowboy in a western movie. It took me ten minutes to get to my bedroom.

After I opened the closet door inside my bedroom, I grabbed my diary off the top shelf. I dropped the diary on my bed, right before I picked up the .22 pistol that I had purchased for Denise.

All my emotions hit me like a whirlwind, and tears filled my eyes. I really didn't want to kill myself, but I didn't want to suffer like my Uncle Teddy had suffered right before he passed away from Aids. I just couldn't tolerate my family having to take care of me as the disease would took over my body. Mental pictures of Teddy haunted my mind.

I walked back to the living room of my apartment, after I had loaded the gun with six bullets. I turned on the living room sound system. 2Pac's 'So Many Tears' came flowing from the speakers. There had been so many tears in my lifetime. It was time to end the tears.

DENISE

When I heard Qualude was in the hospital, I was arriving back from the mall. It seemed like everyone and their mothers were standing out in the projects. My mother and my sister were in tears as I had approached them with bags in my hands. I was looking around for my kids to make sure they were safe.

I asked, "What's wrong with y'all?"

My sister answered, "Qualude is in the hospital."

The word hospital sent a shockwave to my heart. I grabbed my chest. My mother and sister rushed over to my side. Before they could tell me what happened to Qualude, I had already formed a mental picture on why he was at the hospital. The only thing I could see was someone coming in his apartment to rob him while he was asleep. I don't know why I thought the worse but I knew the life Qualude was living was going to catch up to him.

After I got the whole story from my sister and mother, I decided to go to Qualude's apartment. This was after the people at the hospital wouldn't let me see him. I still had my key to his apartment.

When I walked inside, I could still smell the strong scent of blood. There was blood on the floor where Qualude had been laying. I could see how it was smeared. Tears formed in my eyes as I looked over the scene.

After ten minutes inside the living room, I made my way to Qualude's bedroom. The first thing I noticed on the bed was a diary. I picked up the diary and opened to the first page. The words were in Qualude's handwriting. The first entry was addressed to me. There was no date or time.

I flipped through several more entries after I had read the first one. Every entry revealed something new to me that I didn't know about Qualude. When I got to the entry about him having HIV, I nearly had a heart attack. Then I read the reason he was going to take his life. My world was crashing fast. I didn't know if I had the virus or not. I didn't even know if my kids had the virus.

I cursed Qualude, and then I threw the diary against the wall. My emotions took over. I cried for hours.

The next day, I went back to the hospital to see Qualude. I was met by his mother.

I spoke, "I'm not here for trouble. I just want to see him."

His mother said. "You are not family. The hospital policy says you have to be family."

"You can get me up there."

"My son is in a coma. He won't be able to hear you."

"I just need to see him."

"I don't think it's a good idea."

"You know how much I love your son."

"It's not about how much you love my son. I just don't think it's the right time for you to see him."

"Is this about last time?"

"Yes. You were very rude."

"I'm sorry."

"Sometime sorry don't get it. I suggest you leave."

"I don't have to."

"Please, Denise don't make a scene."

"I just want to see Qualude."

"Maybe some other time, but not today."

I wanted to lash out at Qualude's mother, but I decided that wouldn't help the situation. I left the hospital feeling helpless. I didn't know if Qualude was going to recover from the gunshot wound, I didn't know if I could live on without him.

EULOGY

QUALUDE

I couldn't believe that the bullet went inside my nose and exited my ear. The doctor said I was lucky, because I didn't even suffer damage to my inner ear. After two weeks in the hospital, I took another Aids test, and it came back negative.

I had cheated death a second time. The doctor at the Health Department made a big mistake with my results. He got my results mixed up with another male's results that had the same last name as mine. The good thing about this was, I got to meet the guy. He didn't even look like he had the virus.

My father showed up at the hospital, alongside Denise. I was happy that they had met and were getting along. This was a new chapter. I learned that the talent that other people see in you; you might not see in yourself.

The talent I didn't see in myself was me touching other people's lives with my writing. Denise told me how much my writing in my diary touched her heart after she read them. I wasn't mad that she read my diary. I was glad she did, because she made me realize that I wasn't A Crumbling Talent. And that talent comes in different forms and fashions. I didn't get to go back to the shelter and donate money, but I went back and hosted an AA meeting with my father. I kept my word.

THE END

QUALO LOWERY

Sneak Peek
Queen City Mafia

QUALO LOWERY

CRUMBLING TALENT

The South
Spring of 1975

The biggest political celebration in the city of Charlotte was tonight! Everyone who was someone in state government was supposed to be in attendance. Even though Elizabeth Johnson wasn't into politics, she had been given an invitation. She received her invite from her boss lady, Irene Tyson, and she had been informed by Irene that she was picked out of thirty women for the job. Her beauty and her Northern accent led to Irene's decision.

Elizabeth was flattered when she got the news that she would be working the political event, and she was also pleased and honored to win the job. As she slipped into her white and black cotton-tailed dress, she thought about what lay ahead; as far as the party. She knew there would be undercover Klansmen, and the thought alone had her nervous, but she knew she couldn't let this stop her from attending the event. Her main goal, as far as for her attending the celebration, was to make a connection so she could get her brother out of prison. She set this goal after her friend Annie Mae told her that Mayor Cherryfield would be at the event.

Mayor Cherryfield was the man that had gotten her brother a ten-year sentence for robbery. She found this out when she first migrated from New York City to the city of Charlotte.

While she was admiring herself in the standard size motel mirror, she was startled by the sound of a car horn. She quickly gathered her thoughts and turned towards the window where the sound had come from. Then she grabbed her six-inch black heels off the floor and raced over to the window like a kid given chase to an ice cream truck. Once at the window, she pulled the curtain back and looked down below at an awaiting Yellow cab.

"Annie Mae is early," She said.

Then she quickly slipped into her heels, grabbed her purse off the nightstand and she headed for the door. Before she locked the room, she checked her purse for her camera and found it at the bottom. After she had locked the motel door, she pulled out her bright red Cover Girl lip stick, and applied it as she made her way downstairs to the cab. She grabbed the silver handle to the cab and swung open the door. As she made eye contact with her friend, the smell of cigarette smoke hit her nose. The driver had been smoking.

She said, "You could had come up to my room."

"We don't have time. We are already running late," Annie Mae responded.

After she pulled the back passenger side door shut, she handed the driver a white piece of paper with the government center's address on it. Then she gave Annie Mae a New York minute stare.

"What is your problem?" Annie Mae asked.

"Irene didn't give me the name of the contact person. She only said that he or she is supposed to meet us at the front entrance," She said.

"That should be the least of your worries," Annie Mae replied.

"Well, it isn't and I can't stop worrying about it. You know I don't like to be made a fool of," She responded.

"Before I let you be made out to be a fool, I'll get in the way of that," Annie Mae said.

"Such a good friend," She said.

She smiled at Annie Mae, pulled out her Kodak camera, and watched Annie Mae as Annie Mae stared at the device like it was something from another plant.

"Why did you bring that thing?" Annie Mae asked.

"I got to make the other girls jealous," She responded.

"Irene doesn't allow cameras when we deal with politicians," Annie Mae said.

"What she doesn't know won't hurt her," She retorted.

CRUMBLING TALENT

The Yellow cab turned into the downtown area, and as it passed West Trade Street, both women looked at the corner of the street. This area was where they both worked during the week. The street was filled with hookers and drug dealers. A dog dotted out in front of the cab as the cab turned off of the street on to Main street.

The driver smashed the horn as he shouted, "God damn wild animal."

As the driver continued the drive, both women looked at each other in a nervous and weird manner. Then Elizabeth asked, "Are you okay Ann?"

Annie Mae spoke, "I'm okay."

Then Elizabeth watched as Annie Mae pulled two small black masks from her cotton-tailed dress pocket.

"Irene gave me these masks. She said we must wear them at the celebration, and she said the theme of the celebration is Phantom of the Opera," Annie Mae said.

"I thought we were on our way to a political event. Not a masquerade party," Elizabeth said.

"Irene lied a little bit. She didn't want you to be nervous about dealing with freaky politicians. They are human beings too, you know," Annie Mae said.

Elizabeth smiled. Then she said, "Very funny."

Twenty minutes later, the cab pulled up in front of the government center. As Elizabeth and Annie Mae exited the cab, they observed the whole scene. Most of the men that were headed to the decorated buildings were dressed in black tuxedos, proving that the event was formal. The women were laced in gowns that were so long that they looked like they were dragging the ground.

As Elizabeth and Annie Mae made their way to the front entrance, Elizabeth pulled out the invitations. She handed Annie Mae one. Then she said, "Attending this event is a blessing. This is the hottest event in town. I'm glad Irene picked us over the other girls.

Annie Mae wasn't as excited as Elizabeth about the event. Annie Mae said, "There's nothing special about this event, It's just a bunch of political racists brats getting together to drink some wine and eat some food."

"Why do you have to always ruin everything? Ever since I've known you, you have spoken negative about our work," She replied.

Annie Mae interrupted, "You call sleeping with dirty old men work, Girl please."

"It pays the bills, Ann," Elizabeth responded.

"Did Irene teach you to look at it like that?"

"I don't want to fight with you tonight Ann. All I want to do is do the job and have some fun," Elizabeth responded.

"I can see that this working girl stuff has changed you. When you first started working for Irene, you told me that you was going to make enough money so you could find your brother, who is in prison, and you said you was going to get out of this life. Well, I know you made well over a thousand dollars and I know you found your brother," Annie Mae stated.

"Thank you for a recap of what I said, but I don't think this is the time to be discussing this," She responded.

"Well, I think it's the perfect time," Annie Mae said.

"Well, I don't want to talk about it now," She replied.

After her response, she swiftly walked to the front entrance area. She was met by a tall, slim white man. He asked," Do you have an invitation?"

She handed the man her invitation and watched as Annie Mae did the same.

The man asked, "Do you two have masks?"

Both women pulled out their masks and put them on. Then they entered the ballroom. The room was decorated in white and black; and The Phantom theme was on full display and mostly everyone in the room had on a mask. Mountains of food filled the silver trays and tables. The band was playing an old jazz tune from the 60's, and couples were dancing to the tune.

Elizabeth surveyed the room while searching for Mayor Cherryfield. In her mind, she was thinking she could convince him to help her brother get early parole. This thought came to her mind after Annie Mae informed her that the mayor had connections to the North Carolina parole board. As she started to mingle, she bumped into a six-foot seven man wearing a pair of black pants with a cotton white shirt. He had on a dark orange and black mask. This was odd to Elizabeth. She said, "Excuse me. I didn't mean to bump you."

She was looking up at the man, and she could see the coldness in his blue eyes.

He responded, "I've been advised to escort you ladies to the upstairs area."

The man gave both ladies an eerie feeling, but they followed him to the stairway that led to the third floor. Annie Mae had grabbed Elizabeth's arm and said, "I don't think this is a good idea."

She asked, "Are you coming or not?"

"Are you sure he's the contact man?" Annie Mae asked.

"Stop asking so many questions," She whispered.

The man interrupted, "The mayor is waiting."

They followed the man to the third floor. When they reached the floor, Elizabeth looked back at Annie Mae and said, "Your dress is nice but your attitude sucks."

The man shouted, "Please ladies, can you two cut out the nonsense?"

Then he pointed to the last door on the large hallway and said, "The mayor is in that room."

Annie Mae asked, "Can you take us there?"

He responded, "No! I got to get back to the party. I got other guest to attend to."

The women watched as he disappeared back downstairs. Then Elizabeth pulled out her camera and begun snapping pictures. The flash caused Annie Mae to cover her yes with both of her hands. Annie Mae asked, "What are you doing?"

I told you I was going to make the other girls jealous, Elizabeth responded. "Why are you taking pictures of pictures?" Annie Mae asked.

"Because I love to make memories," Elizabeth responded.

The hallway was dim lit and it was filled with large framed portraits of most of the ex-presidents of the United States. The backdrop of the wall was grayish brown, and there were ten rooms on the floor.

Five rooms on each side.

Annie Mae said, "I got to use the restroom."

Elizabeth asked, "Right at this moment?"

"Yes, I drank too much liquor at my motel," Annie Mae replied.

Two males' voices interrupted the women. Both voices were deep in tone and the voices had deep Southern accents. Both women turned in the direction of the voices. Up ahead, both women could see the fourth door on the left was cracked open to the point that they could see inside of the room.

They decided to investigate the voices. Both women walked slowly over to the door and looked in. They both could see two Caucasian men, dressed in business suits, in a lip boxing match over a naked black boy. The boy was laying back on the couch.

Annie Mae asked in a whisper, "What do you think they are going to do to the kid?"

Elizabeth responded," I don't know but I got to get some pictures of this."

"What for?" Annie Mae asked. Then she said, "What about the flash?"

"Don't worry about what the pictures are for," Elizabeth said.

Then she covered the flash on the camera with her hand and started taking pictures of the men in the room. When another Caucasian man walked in the room from the bathroom, Elizabeth recognized him instantly.

She said in a whisper," It's Mayor Cherryfield."

Then she clicked a few more pictures of the men touching the boy on his penis.

Annie Mae replied, "We need to get help."

Elizabeth turned her attention to a table by the door inside the room. On the table was a gold watch.

She looked at Annie Mae and said, "We need to get that watch."

Annie Mae responded, "I'll grab it."

Then she tiptoed over to the doorway and swiped the watch off the table.

Then she said, "Go get help. I'll hold the watch and the camera."

"Okay. I'll be right back," Elizabeth said.

Then she headed towards the stairway and as she started down the stairs, the man that escorted them to the third floor was waiting.

He asked, "Where are you going?"

She responded, as she pointed back down the hallway. "The men in the fourth room back there were molesting a little boy. I need your help."

"Where is the camera," the man asked in a serious tone.

Elizabeth could tell that she was in trouble from the tone of the man's voice.

She responded, "I don't have a camera."

"I don't have time for games," He responded.

"I'm serious. I don't have a camera," She said.

"Where is your friend?" He asked.

Before Elizabeth could get another word out her mouth, the man pulled out his hunting knife from his pants pocket and stabbed her in the chest. She stumbled backwards into the wall. Then she fell to the ground. The man walked over to her and pulled the knife out her heart.

While she took her last breath, she turned her head towards Annie Mae and said, "Run!"

QUALO LOWERY

Sneak Peek
Mama's Baby
Daddy's Maybe

QUALO LOWERY

CRUMBLING TALENT

PROLOGUE
Rhonda…

Jay was still unconscious from the car wreck. Inside his hospital room, I could hear the doctor calling his name. Jay was too weak to speak because he had been injured badly. He had received a broken leg and he had suffered a head injury that required a hundred and twenty stitches. His body went through a lot in five hours.

Jay didn't know my oldest daughter Sherie had lost her arm during the crash. My baby girl Kema had suffered a cracked bone in her face and lost so much blood that I had to call Martez over to the hospital. I really didn't want to call him but the doctor told me that he couldn't use my blood or Jay's blood to help Kema. Her blood was type O, like Martez's. This was why I called him. He didn't hesitate to come.

While Martez was on his way, I told the doctor that Kema wasn't Jay's biological daughter and I had asked him if he could keep this between us. He had zipped his lips like he was zipping up a zipper on a jacket and then he threw away the key in the air.

When Martez arrived, he was dressed like he was on his way to the club. He was still fine as ever and I could tell from his demeanor he was upset. He spoke, "Is Kema okay?"

I responded, "She needs your blood."

Martez quickly changed the subject and made the conversation about Jay. He asked, "Do you love Jay?"

I responded, "Yes. But I'm not in love with him."

Martez asked, "Who are you in love with?"

Martez had taught me about love. He was the one that explained to me what the difference types of love was. This was one of the reasons I was still in love with him.

I responded, "I'm in love with someone that's in love with someone, that doesn't love him."

He asked, "Who are you talking about?"

I said, "You know."

I walked over to the lobby area of the hospital after the doctor told us that it would be a few minutes before he could draw blood from Martez.

My mind was racing a hundred miles a second. The accident had made me realize that I needed Jay in my life and I needed to start to appreciate him more. Just because I wasn't in love with him didn't mean that I shouldn't appreciate him.

Martez waited until the time was right to ask me about the accident.

I responded, "Jay lost control of his car."

"What was Kema doing in the car?" Martez asked in a demanding tone.

"He's her father," I responded.

I knew this would spark a fight.

"He's not her father," he replied.

"Yes, he is," I said.

"Then why did you call me?" He asked.

"You know why."

"I just don't like this Rhonda. I don't like the fact you let her ride in the car with him knowing he's blind in one eye," He said.

"It wasn't Jay's fault."

Martez responded, "Da nigga is blind in one eye It had to be his fault."

I didn't understand why Martez wasn't trying to understand me.

I spoke, "You want me to bring you the police report when he gets it?"

Martez responded, "Fuck a police report. I'm thinking about fucking his handicap ass up."

I spoke, "Like I said Martez, it wasn't Jay's fault."

I didn't understand why Martez was acting so concerned now. Over the last three years, I hadn't gotten a letter from him or money. The only way I had found out he was out of prison was because he tried to talk to my hair dresser, Princess. She told my first cousin, Tanya, that Martez was living with his grandmother in the projects. Then Tanya gave me Martez's number in which she had gotten it from Princess, too.

Martez offered to buy me lunch after our conversation.

I said, "No." I still walked to the lunch room with him. I wasn't in the mood for food. I was too worried to eat.

He said, "Well, after I give this blood, I'm going home to Andrell. She's pregnant!"

I asked, "You got that bitch pregnant again? You don't even take care of Kema. What kind of person is you?"

Martez responded, "The kind of person that say fuck you and that nigger."

I wanted to slap Martez so bad but the hospital was too packed.

I didn't want to cause a scene. Plus, Vanessa was due at work at any moment. She had told me she was going to visit her brother.

I watched as Martez paid for his food and then returned to the table.

He spoke, "It's time for me to be getting home to my family."

I said, "I'm finished with you anyway."

He responded," I think I need to go downtown to get me some visitation rights."

I begged, "Please Martez, don't do that."

He spoke, "I don't want to be a deadbeat like Dewayne."

Martez knew how to still get under my skin.

I didn't want Martez to spoil it so I said, "What do I have to do to keep this a secret between us?"

He started smiling. I knew he loved to inflict mental pain. So, when he said, "I'll be in touch with you and I'll tell you want I want then," I knew I was in trouble.

Part Two
Mama's Baby Daddy's Maybe
Chapter 1
Martez...

The whole time I was in prison, I thought about the life I left behind. The cars and the house I was planning to surprise Andrell with was taken by the cops. They even gave me a drugs tax to pay. It was bullshit. I didn't even pay it.

Almost every day I thought about Andrell, Rhonda and Nikki while I was in prison. Most of the time I thought about Andrell because she was my most prized possession. While I was gone, Andrell managed to keep her legs closed. I couldn't say the same about Rhonda and Nikki. In my book, they were more advanced when it came to the streets. They knew how to go get money with their bodies.

When I left, I left all of them with no money or no means to get money. The police took everything, and what they didn't take, it went back to the sole owners. Now, I was back to square one. I was broke, homeless and hungry.

I was happy to be back in the city of Charlotte. A lot had changed in the nine months I was gone. This chick named Keisha Walker, I was fucking before I went off to prison, now had a baby boy and she still had her body. She was all smiles when she saw me. It didn't surprise me when she said, "What's up jailbird?"

I already knew Keisha's mouth was smart and jazzy. Her mouth had been around my penis on many of school nights and inside her vagina too.

I spoke, "I didn't know you was having a baby."

"You mean to say I had our baby," She responded in a ghetto

CRUMBLING TALENT

attitude.

I didn't know what Keisha was trying to insinuate, but I ended our conversation when I said, "I'mma get with'cha after I spend some time with my grandmother."

I could tell she wasn't going to let me off the hook easily. The face expression she gave me told me that she was thinking I was her baby daddy.

My grandmother wasn't at home when I had entered the living room. Her and my other five cousins were at the mall. It was the first of the month in which my grandmother had received a welfare check on behalf of my little cousins so this told me why they were at the mall. My cousin Duke had been left behind to run the family candy business. He was watching TV when I interrupted him.

I asked, "What's up lil cuzo?"

Duke responded, "I was supposed to go get my haircut but Big Mama didn't take me. She gave me the money."

I looked at the seven dollars in his hand. He had more money than me. Here I was dressed in white prison pants, T-shirt and black boots. I was lucky enough to have gotten a haircut before I left prison.

I spoke, "You can go when she gets back."

"It's going to be too late when she gets back," He shouted back.

Duke had an attitude like he had a grudge against the world. He reminded me of myself when I was his age. Even though he was an only child and I wasn't, I could see and feel his pain. I knew he was mad about not having his mother or father at his everyday expense. I knew that feeling because I had grown up without my parents.

I spoke, "I'll take you."

He responded, "You don't have a car."

"We can walk," I suggested.

"The shop is about three miles up the street. You sure Big Mama won't be mad?" He asked.

"Don't worry. I will explain to her if she gets back before we do," I replied.

After this statement, I asked myself, where is the neighborhood barber. The reason Duke wanted his haircut was he had a big game on Saturday. He wanted to be fresh, because he believed, if his hair was neat, he would play well. I knew the feeling. Especially, when I was playing sports for Olympic High School.

Here it was, Friday afternoon, and the hood was booming with crack sells. I didn't have time to take Duke to the barber shop but I was going to do it. My mind was on finding a new connection because Tyron, my first real drug connection, was in Federal prison. Nikki's brother, Sam, wasn't in the business anymore, even though the Feds had dropped his charges. He was now a jack leg preacher with a small church.

I dismissed these thoughts as I went to my old room. I found me a decent outfit from my old clothes that Andrell had brought over after I had received my prison sentence. Then I took a shower and changed as I decided I would go to Princess's shop. I spoke with a few people in the hood before Duke and I made our way on the main sidewalk that led to Princess' shop.

Her shop was on West Boulevard, a mile from Little Rock road. I was shocked that she had picked this side of town, because she was always talking down about the hood. I was introduced to Princess by Rhonda's cousin, Tanya Hoskins, aka "Thick Red," when they were strippers at Club Choppers. Tanya was from Dalton Village Projects, like me, but Princess was from Keyway Projects, which was two miles from her shop.

I had had sex with Tanya when I was sixteen years old, and she had tricked me out of my sixty-five-dollar work check. I had promised her that I wouldn't tell Rhonda, but I had spilled the beans to Rhonda one night after I had caught her fucking one of my childhood friends. Tanya was mad. Her and Rhonda fell out about this.

Duke and I arrived at Princess' shop. It was full like I thought it would be, and there were more women than men in the shop.

When Duke and I walked in, we were met by this young woman name Cathy. She was a big red-bone, with big eyes, big ass and a big demeanor. Everything was big about her. Her big body Benz was big, too.

She introduced herself while I was looking around for Tanya and Princess. Duke made his move to an open chair in the waiting area while I continued my search for the two women of the hour. Finally, Princess recognized me. She was in the middle chair doing this dark-skinned girl's hair. She was looking in my penis area.

She spoke, "Hello Martez! Boy, I didn't know you was out."

It was like Princess was advertising my penis with her eyes, because all the chicks in the shop turned in my direction. One even winked at me as I gave Princess a hug. I had to touch that big butt of hers.

I asked as we broke out embrace, "Where is Tanya?"

Before I could get the whole question out my mouth, I heard the toilet flush. Then Tanya exited the restroom with a paper towel in her hand.

She shouted, "Hey baby. When you get out?" This diva had to put on a show like she had been waiting on me to come home.

I didn't get no money orders, Christmas package, shoes, or a birthday card from her. Now, here she was acting like we were peanut butter and Jelly.

Tanya continued, "Get over here and give me a hug."

Tanya was good at acting. John Singerton should have put her in one of his movies.

After I let Tanya go, she asked, "Do Rhonda know you out?"

I said, "No!"

"I'm about to call her," She shouted, then she made her way to the shop phone. I stopped her in her tracks.

I said, "Rhonda has a boyfriend. I ain't trying to break up their happy home."

My statement caught the crowd's attention. Even Duke had looked up at me. Before I could say another word, Lee Twon, a homosexual I knew from the hood interrupted, "She don't have a happy home if she let you break it up."

I looked over at Lee Twon. He was dressed up like a woman. This clown had on a wig, fake fingernails, eyeliner and the tightest jeans I had ever seen on someone. The jeans were so tight, I thought he was trying to kill the circulation in his penis.

I waited a few minutes before I said, "Like I said Tanya, I don't want to break up no happy home."

Lee Twon responded, "And like I said, if she let you break up her home, then it was never a home."

I laughed at his remark. I was use to battling homosexuals in lip boxing matches. My uncle Teddy, who was a homosexual, used to always pick fights with me. He had a smarter mouth then Lee Twon.

I said, "Lee-Twon, I don't want no trouble with you man. You know I don't go that way so I'm going to clear this up. I don't want you."

"Child... Don't nobody want your ass Martez," He responded with an attitude.

I knew Lee Twon was only hating because I didn't swing that way. Plus, I knew my value.

I spoke, "I'm strictly for the ladies. All I want is someone that's down for me."

All eyes were on me after I had said these magic words. I knew Lee Twon wasn't going to let me live.

He spoke, "You want somebody that's going to let you run over them. Ain't nobody gonna fall for the banana in the tailpipe."

Lee Twon set himself up for my next comment. It was like the crowd was anticipating a comeback from me. Even though I didn't discriminate when it came to making jokes on people, I couldn't let Lee Twon keep antagonizing me.

I responded, "Somebody already dun put a banana in your tail pipe, that's why you are walking bow legged."

The crowd in the shop busted out laughing. Lee Twon shot

back, "And I enjoyed the banana like a monkey, and if you throw yours my way, I will eat it too, baby."

The crowd busted out laughing again. I had to laugh at the joke myself. I had to clear the air so these beautiful women inside the shop wouldn't get me twisted so I asked, "Why do people always want what they can't have?"

Lee Twon spoke, "If I wanted you, I would buy you, because every dick got a price on it. I would put a couple of your childhood friends on blast but I don't want them to cut me off from that thug luv. If you know what I mean."

I said, "What are you saying Lee Twon?"

He responded, "Everybody business ain't everybody business. But, I'mma leave you with something to think about; your buddies like dick too."

Lee Twon gave me information I hadn't known. He won the first round. I left Princess' shop without getting a connection. Duke was cool because he had gotten his haircut. I had given Tanya my grandmother's number after I had called the number she gave me right before I left the shop. I was looking forward to getting another shot at her ass.

ABOUT THE AUTHOR

    Qualo Lowery is a North Carolina native. He will be residing in the city of Charlotte upon his release from federal custody, with his three daughters and son. Qualo started writing after he had received a ninety-year sentence for three federal drug charges. He has written countless poems, short stories, movies, and this is his second novel. If you want to email him, you can do it at: BOP.COM. Go to Corrlinks. His prison number is #20502058. He accepts letters, too.

www.ingramcontent.com/pod-product-compliance
Ingram Content Group UK Ltd.
Pitfield, Milton Keynes, MK11 3LW, UK
UKHW021301180426
11947UKWH00015B/961